THE MARRIA

THE MAN FROM CONTROL

SASHA BUTLER

The MARRIAGE CONTRACT

UNCORRECTED PROOF

S SALT

CROMER

PUBLISHED BY SALT PUBLISHING 2025

2 4 6 8 10 9 7 5 3 1

Copyright © Sasha Butler 2025

Sasha Butler has asserted her right under the Copyright, Designs and
Patents Act 1988 to be identified as the author of this work.

First published in Great Britain in 2025 by
Salt Publishing Ltd
12 Norwich Road, Cromer, Norfolk NR27 0AX, United Kingdom

GPSR representative
Matt Parsons matt.parsons@upi2mbooks.hr
UPI-2M PLUS d.o.o., Medulićeva 20, 10000 Zagreb, Croatia

www.saltpublishing.com

Salt Publishing Limited Reg. No. 5293401

A CIP catalogue record for this book is available from the British Library

ISBN 978 1 78463 360 8 (Paperback edition)
ISBN 978 1 78463 361 5 (Electronic edition)

Typeset in Neacademia by Salt Publishing

Printed and bound in Great Britain by Clays Ltd, Elcograf S.p.A.

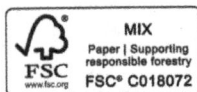

<dedication>

PART I

1577

A TOWN IN WORCESTERSHIRE

CHAPTER 1

H E comes running across the fields in the early light. Eliza would know him anywhere, a smudge against the green through the diamond panes. She is up at once, legs carrying her towards the front door. Francis Marshall rests a hand against the doorframe, swallowing hard, words thick and unsteady: 'It's Arthur again.'

She turns, quick as a hare, feet slipping on stone. The rising sun casts strips of light amongst the shadows as she darts through the house, past the great hall and the parlour, through the kitchen and into the still room, with its smell of rosemary and lavender and thyme. She shouts for Ma, and together they rummage the shelves to the clatter of pottery, searching for the herbs, the tinctures, the something, the anything that could save a child's life.

When they leave, Francis runs ahead. Shirt catching in the wind, hair so dark it is almost black whipping behind him, strong legs pitching him onwards, worn soles of his boots kicking up behind him to greet the sky. It is always him they send: he is the fastest of his siblings, he is the one the family worry about the least. Francis can get himself into trouble, but he will always find his way out again. That's what they say. They follow him through the streets, where the houses become cramped and the lanes narrow. A man with a cartload of cloth swears as they dash past. The Marshall's front door is ajar, and they rush up the stairs to a symphony of creaks and groans, to the room where the brothers sleep.

Arthur is on a pallet. A kind, sickly child, always struck with fevers. This one is ferocious; his thin limbs are slick with sweat, the sheets askew about his feet. Margaret kneels beside him and her hands, as sweaty as her son's, reach for Eliza and Ma.

Ma feels the child's forehead and lists ingredients in a low murmur as Eliza mixes them together. She senses Francis's eyes on her hands as she works, as though she is a conjuror who can pull someone back from the brink. Her breath is shallow and quick, but her hands are steady. They spoon the medicine into the boy's mouth and watch as he grimaces at the inevitable burn in his throat. In times before he had spat it back out, but not today: he swallows it all, eyes half-closed.

Downstairs in the dark kitchen, Eliza mixes more. 'Every few hours he needs to take this,' she says to Francis, her eyes on the phial.

He leans against the kitchen table, his face taut. 'He was up all night.'

'You should've come sooner.'

'We thought it would pass.' There is fear in his voice. 'Do you think he'll . . .'

She knows the question. Children are pulled from their mother's clutches every day; squalling and vibrant one morning, limp and gone the next.

'Arthur is strong. A cat with nine lives.' She tries to smile.

He folds his arms. His sleeves are rolled up to his elbows, forearms corded from daily work. His hands are fists, and she sees a finger worrying at a piece of skin by his thumb. Her gaze lingers upon him a moment too long, and he catches her. He watches her, watching him.

'You did the right thing,' she says.

Ma calls, and Eliza turns to the door. But then she hesitates. Reaches for him, rests her hand on his bare arm, feels the coolness of his skin. He puts his hand over hers. And then she is away, hurrying up the stairs, thoughts tugged back to saving a boy's life.

※

A week passes. Eliza watches Francis finish for the day with the rest of the farm labourers, the sun beginning to fall from the sky. They have been working her father's land, bodies bent low amongst the wheat, the rustle and crack as they cut it from the earth, grime and dust on their skin. The harvest has begun.

She joins Francis in the front yard, just as the men are shouting their goodbyes, spilling off down the lanes towards squat thatched homes and suppers made by their women – wives, mothers, daughters. She checks the contents of her bag again, the clink of the medicines Ma had advised. Ma had advised other things too, as though Eliza had not heard them before, as though she were not a woman grown: don't let your father see you, come straight home afterwards.

She glances back at the house, but it is silent. They walk as though they are strangers – Francis a little in front as she keeps close to the thickets of brambles that soon will be heavy with blackberries – until the lane bends and they lose sight of the house. It is only then that she reaches up and wipes away the smear of clay on Francis's neck with the pad of her thumb and loops her arm through his.

His home is busy tonight; his siblings are barefoot and everywhere, squeezed into the corners of the house, the two rooms upstairs, the two downstairs, the yard out the back where the pig lives and his father's workshop stands. The space is full and round with giggles and squeals, rattling and banging, the sow's soft snorts.

'The mad house,' Francis says, raising an eyebrow.

'I love it,' Eliza says. Francis's younger sisters love her too. They gather about Eliza, admiring her thick hair, the colour of rich soil after it rains, and her soft features, asking her questions: who made her kirtle, can they plait her hair, who will walk her home?

'I'll be walking her home.' Francis manoeuvres himself around his youngest brother, who clutches a wooden doll in his hand. The girls look at each other and giggle. From his stool in the corner of the room Philip, one of the middle brothers, a few years younger than Francis, raises an almost imperceptible eyebrow and continues to adjust the strings of his lute.

Up the stairs and Arthur sits in his bed, propped up by two pillows, his eyes shiny and alert. The fever stutters on but his small fingers cling to life's rough edges. Eliza gently rubs hartshorn and bay salt onto his wrists, suppressing a laugh as he wrinkles his nose at the stink of piss and sweat. 'Sorry,' she says. She pulls out a small mincemeat pie wrapped in linen, watching as Arthur's eyes widen. She places the pie in his palm.

'All for me?' he says, the smell forgotten.

She does laugh then. 'All for you.'

She gives Margaret more medicine for Arthur, and the woman reaches for her purse, pulls out a few scant coins. Eliza shakes her head and closes her hand over the woman's outstretched palm.

'You're an angel,' Margaret smiles.

When they are at the fringes of the town, where the houses peter out and the lane snakes towards the fields, Francis throws an arm about her shoulder. She fits easily, the space familiar, body bumping gently against his torso, her head leant back upon his shoulder. They walk slowly, holding onto the moment like a butterfly caught in a jar.

'Saviour,' he says.

'Don't mock.'

'I'd never mock.'

'Be quiet,' Eliza laughs, but she feels a pleasure, a relief. No lost children under her watch. He squeezes her shoulders all the same.

'I'm sorry about my sisters.'

She flicks her eyes to the lilac sky. 'They're lovely. And they make me feel very important.'

'Vanity isn't attractive.'

'Neither are your boorish ways.'

They grin. If they were younger he might have prodded her in the ribs and burst into a run, and she would've chased him, wheat whipping at their waists, stitches crawling at their sides. But they are older now. He retaliates with a lazy flick of his finger. She flicks him back as her family home spills into view. A sprawl of a building, intricately half-timbered.

She doesn't see him at first. Doesn't think to check, when the air is drunk with summer and life seems miraculous, when Francis's arm still holds her, warming her against the chill of dusk.

They separate at the gatehouse beneath the wooden eaves where the sparrows make their nests. 'Until tomorrow.' He winks, but exhaustion pulls beneath his eyes. The summer is relentless. Winter too.

She doesn't like it when he leaves. But she doesn't say it. Instead she laughs and says, 'Be gone,' and throws her hand out to him as though he may kiss it. But she snatches it away, her attention caught by the shifting of shadows at a window in the house. Francis follows her gaze and steps back, but it is too late.

'Go,' she mutters.

Inside, the scent of lavender and wheat and smoke and dry earth hangs in the air. The kind of smell that lulls you into a false sense of safety. The hall leads to closed doors and the stairs are silent and expectant, waiting for her to take them two at a time and shut herself in her bedchamber. She removes her cloak as quietly as possible, doesn't fumble as she hangs her bag on a crude nail that juts from the wall. Yet still there is a clip of boots on stone. Footsteps coming for her.

Her father finds her in an instant. Like a spark on gunpowder, an explosion ignites.

'What were you doing?'

He closes in behind her as she faces the wall. There is a deep crack in the daub, the bones of the house peeping through. Fear rises within her, as familiar as the cycle of the seasons on her father's land. The door to the kitchen squeals open and Ma rushes into the hall, Thomas's voice drawing her in like a siren.

'She was taking some remedies to Arthur Marshall.' Ma speaks with an authority that has never been hers. One that Thomas can crush as easily as squeezing a beetle between two fingers.

'Is that so, Ruth.' He speaks his wife's name like an insult.

'She is learning skills that will make her, make her most useful as a wife.'

7

'Such as flirting with that labourer on my own land?'

'I wasn't—' Eliza says.

'Don't lie—'

'We're friends—'

His hand closes around the back of her neck and her words stop. His fingers are hot and his nails indent tiny archways across the surface of her skin. She hears the catch of Ma's breath. He pushes her forwards, forcing her neck down and she stumbles, making no sound, her hand reaching up to steady herself, fingertips catching the crack in the wall.

CHAPTER 2

THE candle burns low, the fat rolling down to pool upon the bedside table. Eliza pushes harder upon the paper and the chalk in her hand snaps. She curses under her breath. She chooses the larger half and continues, hunching lower. The lines come with ease, the curve of an eye, the dive of a neck, people real and imagined in her mind's eye. She is a magician, making the transient permanent. It calms her. The control, the focus. A distance grows between her and the man who sits downstairs, his palms still warm from their weight on her neck.

It was her brother who first pilfered a stick of chalk from school and gleefully gave it to her. Henry who taught her how to cut a goose feather, how to make quill and ink work to her will. And so she started drawing in secret, her eyes growing keener for colours and art, her ears for talk of paintings and artists. It surprised her that what she saw in her head could be translated so effortlessly onto her page.

She remembers being a small child, staring into a mesmerising bonfire for so long that she could still see it, silhouetted, when she closed her eyes. That bonfire became the stuff of community legend, the tale brought out to entertain those cradling a cup at the inn, a story intended to be handed down the generations. Once, they said, churches had been filled with paintings of Christ and the Virgin, naves crammed with crucifixes and altars and books. But all of it had been reduced to kindling for the bonfire, rendered into ash. The paintings had contorted, bubbled and shrivelled in the heat. Eliza remembers the way her clothes had smelt afterwards, of warm scorching nights, of pig roasting on a spit, and how Mama had hung them outside to air. That bonfire, they said, along with countless others across the country, was a farewell to the old religion. To Catholicism. And as the fire cackled outside, inside the church's murals were daubed over with the chalk and lime of Protestantism. The religion of Eliza's family, reinstated by the new queen with whom Eliza shares a name.

When they tell this story at the inn, the Protestants can't help but smile, sigh, sink back into their chairs and shout for another cup of beer. Under the old, mad, bloody queen they had known of hundreds of their number bound to stakes and martyred, charred to death, on bonfires more sinister, more deadly than the ones that licked up the relics of the Catholic church. No longer.

Eliza remembers a few years after the bonfire, sitting in church, unhearing of the pastor's ministrations, rubbing her finger on the wall, white chalk softly coming away on the pad of her fingertip, and wondering if beneath lay a frisson of colour, biblical men, the Garden of Eden. She had imagined the artists, moving from church to church, through parishes and hamlets and towns, brushes in hands, painting the walls, standing back to look at their days' work, nodding, pleased with themselves.

The stories, the lost paintings, that initial stub of chalk between her thumb and forefinger birthed a dream within her, planted the first seeds of being an artist. They sprouted roots in her mind and began to grow.

'You've a talent,' Ma says, walking into Eliza's bedchamber. She is always so light on her feet, slipping in and out of rooms like a wraith. She places a cool press on Eliza's neck, easing the bloom of purple finger marks which are as bright and full as plums.

'There's nothing more you could have done,' Eliza says, answering Ma's apologetic eyes. She hides the drawing beneath her pillow and gently kisses the scar that reaches across her mother's cheekbone. A tight, puckered, warning line. 'You've done enough Mama.'

The older woman's mouth moves as though to say something, but the sound of footsteps rises from below, so she merely shakes her head. Silent as a stone, thrown to the will of a raging river.

☙

The shadow of the house falls over her. The thatched roof sags, the wood pigeons coo restlessly in the eaves. She glances out across her father's land. It is a place where Thomas has banished the wild, replacing it with a steady expanse of yellow wheat. But nature creeps and claws its way through the cracks, trying to reclaim what has been stolen from it. She sees it in the foxes that dart through his fields, the forget-me-nots that hem the crops in spring, the starlings that settle like dust on the trees, only to take flight in one joint motion at the sound of a harsh voice. Thomas shouting at a fam labourer.

Eliza prunes the herb garden in quiet anger; the bruises at the base of her skull pulse to the beat of a warning drum. She squats low, stems straining and breaking beneath her fingers, sap oozing green. Her knife moves dangerously, expertly, deadheads coming away. It takes her a moment to register that someone is standing above her, boots amongst the thyme and rosemary.

Francis rocks back and forth on his heels like a boy, a sickle in his hand, the blade hanging by his side like a crescent moon fallen from the sky. He knows immediately. 'What happened?'

'Same as usual.' She lifts her hair from the back of her neck. His eyes are narrow when she turns to look at him.

'Why?'

'He saw us together,' she says, hesitating. It will change them. But she says it because she must, because she has delayed long enough. Because spending time together is a risk, now that her father has set his motive. Because anything she does to obstruct him will come at a cost; Thomas works only in transactions. Refute his will and get a scar on your face like Mama's. Spend time with Francis and receive a cluster of bruises.

What they cannot know, not now, is that the greatest cost will fall to Francis to pay.

'He's arranging my betrothal.'

It was midsummer when Thomas had told her, and the supper in her belly had threatened to heave back out of her. She recalls how his eyes had fixed on her as though daring her to react. How he had said he would make arrangements. She had known about his little network of men, who acquaint themselves with the best people, the best places to trade, who keep their ears to the ground for gossip and news from other towns. Who, even now, as she stands with dirt beneath her fingernails and frustration in her throat, could be casting their nets wide in search of the best catch.

She steadily meets Francis's eyes, and she sees a tightening at his jaw and temple. Clenching.

She could tell him that she doesn't want this, that she's afraid, that she knows, unquestioningly, who she would choose if she were given the choice. All of it would be true. Yet her words dry in her throat like the great drought of years before. Francis's mouth parts slightly as though urging her to speak, and in the midst of this, as something is passing silently between them, Ma calls for Eliza, voice carrying from the washhouse.

Eliza wipes her hands on her apron, the earth smearing. She reaches for him, brushing her hand on his, a whisper of skin on skin. His fingers move to catch the tips of hers.

'I'm sorry,' he says as she walks away.

❧

They say dogs go wild in the heat. So do men.

There are disturbances in the house, when the hot and sweated August days are filled with men in the fields, working all the hours God sends to bring the harvest home. Thomas and Henry argue, rage flickering up to crackle and roar. Sometimes she only hears it, through the walls or the floor. Sometimes she finds her mother lying in bed – eyes squeezed shut, pillow damp – and she will climb in next to her.

One evening, when the midges huff upon the breeze, she sees them in the parlour through the crack of the door. She lingers, catching their fast, jagged words.

'It's your duty.' Thomas has his back to her, but his words are as crisp as if he was saying them into the shell of her ear.

'The world is changing -' Henry starts.

'You'll stay here and you'll inherit.'

'I don't want to work these fields for the rest of my life.'

'You're a spoilt fool who doesn't deserve anything.' Thomas's voice swells, surging into the hall where the stairs sigh and Eliza shifts in the shadows. 'Think of what men would give to be in your position.'

'I would give it to them gladly.'

Faster than the thrum of an archer's bow, Thomas reaches to cuff Henry, but Henry is faster. He holds his father's forearm in his grip. They are surprisingly well matched: Thomas is larger, filling the space, strong beneath a layer of flesh, but Henry, although of slighter build, is younger, smarter, nimbler. He can duck a belt as it comes walloping towards him, has been able to do so since childhood. It was Henry who taught Eliza how.

Thomas prises his son's hand from his arm and pushes him and Henry stumbles, hits his chin upon the mantel. Blood comes instantly, streaming through his neat beard.

Thomas rubs his forearm. 'Get out.'

Eliza slips unseen through the murk of the hall and into the kitchen. She knows of wives in the town who are beaten, has even heard the whispered tales of women, murdered by their husbands, who come back for a haunting, has seen young boys with bruises on the backs of their legs that can only mean one thing. She knows her father is wedded to violence. She grew up thinking all men were.

'You heard us?' Henry asks, the two of them sitting in his bedchamber. Eliza hands him a salve - of yarrow or marigold or comfrey, she isn't sure, it is one of Ma's concoctions - to heal the cuts that regularly nick and cross their bodies.

'I saw.'

Henry shakes his head, 'It doesn't matter.'

She considers her brother, his shoulders hunched slightly. His room is full of papers and a few books, ends of quills litter his desk. An outward display of his sharp mind, head full of calculations, logic, ideas. A memory that forgets nothing. He is not meant for the monotony of the land, the life Thomas is moulding him to.

'Will you stay?'

'If I'd a choice, I'd already be on my way to London,' he says, rubbing the salve onto his chin. He has told her of the city before, he had read about it at school; thousands upon thousands of people, young men arriving to work and make their fortune. Opportunity and goods sailing in from Europe upon the glittering Thames. She knows too, of another reason for his desire for the capital. A longing he cannot quench here.

She had seen it, a few years before. The two of them, her brother and his lover. In a quiet lane, hands on each other's faces, nose touching nose, eyes closed. As though breathing in the scent and feel of each other, imprinting it to memory.

She had wanted to confront Henry as soon as he returned home some hours after, demand he tell her of his private life whilst disguising her hurt that he had kept it from her. Yet as soon as she saw his wretched expression in the gloomy light of the kitchen, her anger had dissipated and she only asked, Brother, what is it? What has happened?

What he had told her then has lodged in her mind, like a precious stone set into metal, never to come out.

Now she squeezes his arm. 'You always have a choice.'

'Do you?'

Eliza snorts. 'Don't be an idiot. Father will guide me and then it'll fall to my husband. And if they both die, which I'm hopeful of,' she smiles wickedly, 'then it'll fall to you.'

Her lightness doesn't catch on. Henry is serious when he says, 'I'll never control you.'

She nods, trusts he will stay true to his word.

⁂

The linen sheet falls slowly, caught on a draught. She pulls it tightly over her parent's mattress, feathers escaping to lie upon the floor as though just plucked from a goose's breast. The dirty sheets are heaped in a pile; later she will scrub them until her hands are sore and cracked. She seldom comes in here, keen to avoid her father's rooms as much as possible. But today there is a freeness to the household, even amongst the labourers, because the master is away. Eliza had watched Thomas leave, wearing his best cloak which he kept smoothing against his chest. He had taken the horse, brushed it so tenderly and carefully that its coat shone like buffed pewter.

But it is still bold, dangerous even, when Francis walks into the chamber, finding Eliza adjusting the coverlet, Ma's delicate embroidery beneath her fingers. A labourer in his master's bedchamber, alone with the master's daughter. It's a scandal at the best of times; a vicious kicking, a cracking of ribs at the worst.

She starts, 'What are you doing?'

'Your father's away.'

His eyes are on the sheets, trailing her hand which still rests upon them, and for a heart-stopping moment she wonders what he is asking. She presses her tongue against the back of her teeth.

He glances up. 'Walk with me later?'

'The men could've seen you.' The other farm labourers, the ones Thomas pays to keep an eye when he's absent. It means he knows things even when he shouldn't, even when you think you won't get caught.

'Nobody did, trust me.' He moves his weight from foot to foot, 'So?'

'Is that all you wanted to ask?'

'Is that a yes?'

They took this path as children, edged with forest on one side and a stream on the other. The sun is unseasonably hot, the September air damp, sweat collecting in the creases of elbows and knees. Eliza paddles in the stream, hose pulled off, skirts hitched up in her hands. Francis follows her, his shadow catching against her body. Shallow water laps their ankles, smooth stones rock beneath toes; their shoes lie forgotten on the bank. He splashes her, water landing in her hair, sprinkling her face and she retaliates, drenching his breeches. The hand he reaches out in a poor attempt to stop her is wet on her waist, and she imagines the water, his touch, seeping through her kirtle, her petticoat, her smock, down to her skin.

They are close to a bend in the stream, where the incessant flow of water has worked away the earth, carved out its place in the land. A sweep of the bank overhangs, held aloft by an ancient knot of root, the tree above grasping for the sky. There the stream deepens, the shingled bed falling away, and the water that swills and collects is deep enough to reach the thigh of a man.

He is looking at the bend, his hand still on her waist, when he says, 'I think I could swim in that.'

'I think it's unlikely you'll drown in its depths.'

He rolls his eyes, grin of mischief painting across his lips. His eyes hold hers for a moment, as if daring her to stop him, and then he is wading towards the bank, his back to her as he unfastens his breeches. She feels a thrill, her body stilled in the shallows of the stream. She glances about them – an innate survival reflex, like a babe crying for its mama's milk – to check they are truly alone.

'If someone comes—' she starts.

'They won't,' he says, gently. As if in agreement, the forest around them sighs, softly. Green light above them, gold shimmering on the water around her calves. 'No one will find us here.'

He bends to ease his breeches past his thighs, knees, shins and steps out of them. His shirt hangs low, so she sees only his legs, a paler strip of skin at the back of his thighs, as he casts his breeches onto the bank.

She looks down at the water, the temperature on her face rising. Nervousness and anticipation and a heightened awareness of her own, clothed body gather within her.

He turns, still smiling, but hesitant. As though he is awaiting her appraisal, standing only in his linen shirt, which he uses to work the fields, to hammer metal in his father's forge, which has been passed from Marshall brother to brother. Only that shirt shields his skin from the world. He looks at her as if to say, this is me, as you find me. She feels it undeniably, a desire to run her hands along that paler skin at the back of his thigh, stand behind him and rest her cheek between his shoulder blades, slide the back of her hands into his palms.

Perhaps it is because they have, for a moment, stopped smiling and have turned completely serious that he abruptly wades into the deeper part of the stream, towards the sweep of bank where the stream swells, and calls over his shoulder to her, 'Well?'

'Well, what?'

'Are you coming?'

'You'll be the death of me, Marshall,' she shouts, moving to the silty edge of the stream, and without pausing to doubt or reconsider, unfastens her kirtle. 'Don't look at me,' she orders, and he snorts with laughter.

'I'm definitely not looking.'

She undresses until she is in only her smock, feeling the breeze and sun on her arms.

Francis is true to his word, some paces ahead, staring at the contorted roots which overhang the twist in the stream. 'Lead the way then,' she laughs, and he bobs his head in assent, mock servant to the yeoman's daughter.

The ground slopes away and stones roll beneath her, scraping at the soles of her feet. She gasps and reaches ahead for Francis, grasping his wrist. 'Steady now,' he says. 'We'll take it slowly.'

She isn't sure when the hand holding his wrist slips into his palm, but she finds their damp fingers interlocked, the pulses at their thumbs overlapping, colliding. They navigate into the deepest part of the water, which laps near her hips. When he looks back at her, his eyes are closed. 'I'm still not looking.'

'Wait a moment,' she says and she bends her knees, plunging herself into the water. The cold reaches up around her, solid and heavy where only the air had been. A transparent cloak bobbing at her shoulders. 'You can look now.'

Their fingers are still threaded together when he opens his eyes. Swift flick of his eyelids. Sunlight on his face. What does he see? She with pearlescent skin, which oscillates around her in the stream's gentle current. The end of her hair darkening in the water. Sea creature, water baby. He bends to her level, shoulders rising slightly as the cool water envelopes him too. His skin beneath the surface tinges green.

Two underwater beings, staring at each other.

He moves his arm and slowly, so slowly, he places his hand on her neck, his thumb resting along the line of her jaw. There is an eruption in her chest, like buds burgeoning in spring. A squeezing of euphoria. She places her hand over his, observing the easy line of his eyebrows which taper away at the far edge, the deeper brown that rims his irises. He recognises her in a way that nobody else does.

They are inches apart. A moment away.

'I thought you wanted to swim?' she murmurs.

He raises his eyebrows as if to say, *we can play this game, if you want*. He moves his hand, and she wants to grasp it, keep it there, but he is already leaning into the water, allowing the stream to hold him. He kicks his legs, beats his arms, splashes pockmarking the surface. He thrashes, working to keep himself afloat, his head held aloft, droplets clinging to his stubbled chin.

She tries not to notice how she can see his back through his shirt, could draw a line with her fingertip along the muscled contours that comprise his shoulders.

'You reckon Thomas is meeting someone about your betrothal?'

He is good at pretending to be casual – sitting languidly beside her on the bank, the stream plashing at their feet as they dry themselves in the evening sun – but his question is too direct. Besides, she'd seen the look on his face when she first told him.

'I suppose.' She crosses her arms over her chest to hide where her smock has turned transparent, places her kirtle across her upper thighs.

'Any idea who?'

'No.' She has heard names but none she recognises. 'I think he prefers it that way, keeping me in the dark.'

'Were your parents the same? Was it arranged?'

She makes a derisive noise in the back of her throat. 'Arranged like counters on a board.' She thinks of her mother, crying into the silence of her bedchamber as her husband and son fight in the room below. What choice was her poor mama given?

'What about yours?'

'Met at a fair. They went to a few dances together before Pa went to Ma's father and asked for her hand.' Eliza can see it; a young man not dissimilar from the one in front of her, shifting from foot to foot, fiddling with his cuffs, wearing his brother's best shirt, waiting for the answer on whether he could marry his girl, whose smiles had shot straight to the heart of him. Francis smiles, 'They make it sound so easy.'

'And that's what you'll have?'

'What?'

'You know.' She tries not to sound childish. 'A love marriage.'

He observes a shoal of fish, each the size of a fingernail, swimming just below the stream's surface. Any higher and they could suffocate themselves. She watches him, noticing summer's story writ across his body, skin bronzing beneath the relentless sun.

'I suppose so.'

'Anyone caught your eye?' She's goading now; she's going right to the place where it hurts her. It is foolish and pointless, but the words are out before she can stop them.

He looks up from the stream and the fish scarper in the jolt of his shadow. 'Stop it, Eli.'

She bites the inside of her lip and rests her head on his shoulder.

※

'Your grandfather worked hard, building this house, establishing the Litton name,' Thomas says.

Her father returned a few days ago, and since then he has been as bullying and provoking as ever. Yet amid this, she has caught him whistling about the house, watched him laugh with one of the labourers. Even overheard him say to Ma, 'You should rest more, you're looking worn out. Perhaps we could hire more men to help.' Something has pleased him and it makes her uneasy.

It is evening, and the four of them sit about the table in the great hall. Thomas is at the end of the table, and Eliza sits furthest from him, facing an empty space. The configuration is unbalanced, but her father would never sit anywhere but at the head.

'I will see my father's work continued,' her father says. 'A great man.'

Ma says Thomas took after his father. Says the latter was a brute, a bully, had outlived two wives, had been an impressive wrestler, taking to the ring at fairs and celebrations, knocking out his opponent's teeth with his bare knuckles. Eliza rubs the back of her hand at the thought of him. He set the standard, the reputation for the next generation of Litton men; his influence has clung to Thomas like pollen, caused a stain that cannot be scrubbed out. She never met her grandfather; he was six feet deep by the time she was born, for which she is glad.

'We all have a duty.' Thomas emphasises the word *all*, so it is full and resonant in his mouth. He speaks as though he has a dukedom or a knighthood, a man with gold enough to crush giants. He puffs his chest, reaching for the pig whose carcass lies in the centre of the table, and spears a slice with his knife. 'Isn't that right Henry?'

Eliza expects rebuttal from her brother, but the gash on his chin is still healing.

'As for you,' Thomas juts his jaw towards her, 'you'll strengthen our position with a match to a gentleman.' He seems almost feverish, like a church minister delivering God's message. A good marriage for Eliza would place Thomas on the map, would garner him recognition from other gentlemen, might even set him on course for claiming such a title for himself. He reeks of ambition, and she despises him even more.

'And what gentleman will take the daughter of a yeoman?' The insult spills from Eliza's mouth. Sometimes she wonders if she says things just to see what is the worst that could happen.

They, yeoman, country people, in their smaller houses, without silver, for centuries working their land, paying labourers to work alongside them. Lower than the gentry, who can afford to gad about on horseback, letting their lands, never laying a finger on their fields, never knowing the pain in their joints after a hard day spent tilling the earth. What gentleman would take a lower born wife?

But she knows the answer: she has watched her father rent and buy more land, watched him hire more men, watched the increased yields wheeling their way to markets. He is one of the richest men in town, and now he wants more. He has grown richer, even, than some of the genteel men he seeks to farm her off to. His money can buy her a place at a gentleman's table. She pinches the skin at her wrist.

'A gentleman who recognises an offer he can't refuse. A good dowry and a woman who is obedient.' Softly now, 'A woman who knows her place.'

A breath.

'Do you know your place, Eliza?'

'Yes, sir.'

'Good.' He picks up his knife and, his eyes never leaving hers, drops it purposefully on the floor. The metal bounces upon the stone, ringing before falling silent. 'Pick it up, woman.'

For a moment, nobody moves. The air is charged, like the gap after lightning before thunder, when you know the growl is coming but you're not sure when, you're not sure how close the storm lies. It is Ma's whispering, please Thomas, please, that makes Eliza stand. If Ma begs too much, she will also be punished.

She looks down at the blade, imagines pressing it under her father's chin, wonders what his reaction would be. The line of blood that would trickle down. She closes her eyes: his violence is contagious. She hesitates then bends low, her fingers finding the handle, the smooth wood fitting easily in her palm. She places it on the table beside him, a clatter.

'Good girl,' he says. 'Now sit down.'

The thunder does not come. Not now. Not this day.

❧

She perches on an upturned bucket and thanks God for the rat. The rat who, a few days prior, had snuck into her father's barn by gnawing its way through a wooden panel, to discover a towering store of grain. Its currant-black eyes would have gleamed with avarice. Anything it didn't eat, it could shit and piss upon, to ensure that no other creature – human nor beast – would be able to eat it or make use of it. This is the sort of nightmare that will wake Thomas in the night, will make him particularly virulent in the morning.

It is not this that pleases Eliza; she has seen grains spoiled and famine claw communities, the poor rendered starving. No, what pleases her is that her father, on discovering the damage, had set Francis to the urgent task of fixing it.

And now she is with Francis, tucked inside the barn, and no one knows she is here – those inside the house think she is in the washhouse, those outside think she is sewing in the kitchen. Only the cat knows they are both here, as he has been granted access to root out any vermin still skulking the store. Eliza checks now; in the strip of sunlight cast through the outhouse's open door, her feline friend lolls indolently on the ground, belly rising and falling.

As yet, no rats have been caught.

Francis saws at a log of wood, shaping it into a panel, his crow-dark hair falling over his eyes which he impatiently brushes away. His body, hunching forward, is partly in profile as she sits in a corner. She imagines drawing him, capturing the shadows on his face, the dark barn encroaching around him. The smock she is supposed to be adjusting lies untouched, a linen ghost on the ground.

'. . . have heard some of the lads say they won't be working here next year,' he continues between breaths over the steady judder of the blade, back and forth, back and forth, carving the wood apart.

'Where'll they go?'

'Rumour is there's another yeoman who's been buying up land on the other side of town.'

'Father won't like that.'

'I don't doubt.'

'What'll you do?'

He lifts his shirt and wipes his forehead with it, momentarily displaying his stomach, a trickle of hair at his belly button.

'I'll go where the money is best and where the master is good. And wherever you are, of course.'

'I would expect nothing less.'

He grins and she sticks out her tongue.

'Don't let your ma catch you doing that. It doesn't befit a gentlewoman.'

'Then thank goodness I'm not one of those.'

Neither of them mention her father's plans for her, although it dances about them in the barn, a shadow that light cannot diminish. With a final push of his saw, a strip of wood cleaves free. He bends to the gnawed gap in the barn wall, covering it with the newly made panel. 'Give me a hand?'

'Am I just a labourer to you?'

'Obviously. Here, hold the panel still.'

She crouches, adjusting the panel so it is flush to the wall. Francis casts about for his hammer. For a moment it seems as though he will rest his hand on the side of her neck and she will lean into his palm. She knows he wants to. Can feel the flow of his thoughts, as though they are tributaries leading into the same river.

Their arms brush as he leans towards his handiwork, hammer poised above a grey-dull nail. She tries not to move, not to breathe. The heat of his body radiates to hers. He strikes the nail once, twice. The space between them is a force, pulling her in. She gives into it, heart's rhythm increasing, resting her cheek against his shoulder. The hammer stills, as though he has forgotten how to strike the nail, and then he remembers, a third strike.

'A few more to go,' he says, voice as soft as a first kiss. But he doesn't reach for another nail; instead, he cups her cheek. Warm against her face. She holds his gaze as she tilts her head, touching her lips to his palm. Smells metal on his hand, sees how his dark eyes darken. It thrills and frightens her, this longing. Everything unspoken between them conveyed via action, by touch, hand, mouth.

There are voices outside. Instinctively they lurch away. He points silently to the corner of the barn, where the walls are patterned with tools, and she scrambles to it, pressing her back to the rough wood, where splinters stick out trying to push through her clothes and catch on her skin.

A man stands in the doorway, identity unmistakable. Her thrill tips along its delicate balance to absolute fear. Fear in her throat, spreading through her body like poison. Why does she do this? Why couldn't she have left Francis to his work and tended to her own?

If Thomas finds her here, the bruises he gifted the back of her neck will be insignificant to those he would gift her now.

'Have you finished?' Thomas asks.

Francis moves deftly to the door to speak to him, innocently standing to one side, blocking where a view of her might be visible if you were to cock your head to the left and seek out the shadowy corner. She can still spy Thomas's boots, a portion of his face, one cruel eye.

'Almost, sir.'

'What is taking you so long?'

Her father surveys the wall of the barn and Eliza realises, sickeningly, that the linen smock meant for sewing still lies on the floor, betraying her.

'Sorry, sir.'

Thomas steps forward and Francis takes a step back, admitting him, but still masking her, as though they are in a dance, and they are, for this is cat and mouse, cat and rat, and Eliza pinches the skin at her wrist so hard it pricks with pain and she closes her eyes and begins to count the moments, before her father will see the linen, and his hands will find her. *One two three four –*

'Hurry up about it, and then after you can chop some more wood and pile it for storing, then set the cat in the other barn for rats,' he pauses and she opens her eyes, panicked, the barn and all its contents blooming back into focus, including the toe of Thomas's boot which hooks roughly beneath the cat and nudges it upright. The cat startles, scampering backwards into the shadows, 'Then you can join the other men.'

'Yes, sir.'

Five six seven.

Thomas looks at the ceiling of the barn. 'The roof in here will need fixing too, at some point.'

His visible eye falls to the ground to something crumpled, luminous, out of place. *Eight nine ten. This is it, this is it,* skin squeezed so tight at her wrist she is sure there will be blood on her fingertips, and he starts towards the smock, and Francis's back is frozen, and she wishes she were in her bedchamber, the door locked, never to come out again, never to face this fear, and the cat hisses and yowls and batters against the wooden wall, causing the whole barn to shake. Her father's step falters. The cat shoots back and forth, swipes a paw, darts in and out of view amongst the shadows, until it stalks into the sunlight, a rat squirming between its jowls.

Thomas says something like, at least the bugger is good for something, but she isn't listening, is too busy thanking God for the rat. Her father makes a gruff word to Francis about working faster, then leaves.

They wait until the sound of his tread is overcome by the breeze swaying the fields and the birds chorusing, and she snatches up her sewing and only then do they look at each other. Francis's hands are at his forehead, pushing his hair upwards. Eliza starts to laugh, exhaling the tension from her lungs with such urgency that it catches; he leans against the side of the barn and laughs too.

'Shit, piss and bull's balls,' he says.

'Shit, shit, shit,' she laughs. And then, 'By God I hate this.'

He stops laughing as abruptly as he started, 'And me.'

CHAPTER 3

THE day before Michaelmas is market day. Two women walk together arm in arm, ready to fill their baskets. Even from afar you'd presume they are related, with their identically pointed chins, their heart shaped faces. And as you draw closer, you'd notice that their hands make the same gestures, and if you heard them speak, you'd hear the same intonation, the same accent, these two who have lived so closely that they've each shaped the other.

The older woman has known greater hardship. Her gentle face is tired, hunted, worn about the mouth. A thin scar scores the side of her face, from cheekbone to chin. Her hands, which know how to soothe a sick boy to sleep, which have clasped other women in the hardest of times, are patched red and dry and tiny cuts have opened across her knuckles, unable to heal. Her eyes are the same as her daughter's - brown like the silt and sand of the earth - except hers are dulled, as though someone plucked out the twinkle and tossed it away to the stars instead.

She birthed three children, buried one in the squelching mud, watched her lucky two grow to adulthood. Someday they will leave her - even her son, she knows with an instinct that is marrow-deep, must leave eventually - and the knowledge is a dull and steady thrum in her head.

Yet she wants them to leave; she wants them to escape to something better. She doesn't mind that her husband is hell-bent on finding a gentleman for their daughter. She clings to the possibility that her daughter will be safer if she is married. That she could be passed into another man's care; protected by a gentleman, a gentle man. And so the older woman works in the margins, talking with other women, discovering the men of marriageable age, ready for the plucking. Don't you see, this is her only way of protecting her daughter, even if she is sent leagues from here?

She'd heard, in this way, of a young man, born from an established line of gentlemen. Protestant, quiet and polite, they say, the private sort. It was she who secretly slipped a coin to one of her husband's cronies, asking him to recommend this young man – although her husband must never know it. Pray God he never does.

Her plan had worked. Her husband visited the young man's father, taking the horse, wearing his best cloak. He made a day of it, journeying to Warwickshire, leaving her and the house and the men working his fields in peace, and returning with uncharacteristic joviality. Evidently he liked what he saw, for he invited the young man and his father to join them for the feast at Michaelmas.

And Michaelmas has come in a blink; the young man will visit tomorrow night.

Her daughter doesn't know yet. Tomorrow night may cast the die for her future. Yes, it will break her daughter's heart; her heart beats, in the way that only young hearts do, for that lad – the farm labourer, the blacksmith's son, the hard-worker, foot-jigger, sweet-smiler. But he won't do. Broken hearts can heal. Split lips, cracked ribs can too. But banged heads? Near strangulations? She's sick of chancing it.

They say you'll do anything for your babies. And so she would – she'd lie to them, betray them, break their hearts into little bloody pieces if it meant protection. If it meant survival. And if you look about you, at the mess of women at the market, all tell of similar stories. Everyone here is doing the best they can to survive.

And then your eye would fall to her daughter. She has the brightness to her that the fates have not yet extinguished. Of course, she has known pain, she has had many bruisings, but she has never truly known loss. Not quite yet. She contains conflicts and battles within her that she hasn't yet realised. Not quite yet.

But you would lose sight of them in the chaos of market day:

there are babes in arms, snot-nosed children, girls whispering and snickering to each other, boys on the cusp of manhood; there are flashes of daggers on hips, youthful anger threatening to transform into drunken brawls at the inn as dusk descends. Men and boys have died at that inn; always have and, the innkeeper reckons, always will. Traders, who have flooded in from neighbouring towns, bellow their wares, whilst townsfolk weave from stall to stall discussing the harvest's bounty or, rather, gossiping about who was absent from church the previous Sunday, avoiding the chickens pecking about the muddied track. If you follow that track for many days, it will lead south to the capital. And beyond that it will lead you to the sea.

⚬⚭⚬

Ma's arm is clasped against Eliza's as they scuffle their way through the market to buy food for tomorrow's feast.

There is a poultry seller with at least two dozen geese waddling around him, honking furiously, yanking on the rope looped about their delicate necks. Ma chooses two geese with feathers white as summer clouds, and shouts above the clamouring wildfowl to haggle the price. They stop at the inn and buy a barrel of sack, and it's Eliza's turn to hassle the cost, winking at the innkeeper when he finally relents. She half carries, half rolls the barrel home, as Ma leads the geese, which waddle merrily beside them, rope still tied around their soon-to-be-broken necks.

When Michaelmas dawns the great hall is scrubbed, the table laid with the best plates for a score of guests. Wreaths of wheat and autumn's first leaves hang precariously above the hearth, threatening to set the whole house – with its thatch, and timber struts, and mice skittering beneath the floorboards – alight. The geese roast in curls of smoke, the smell of fat oozing through the rooms.

Ma has been anxious all day, fussing over small details, organising the cook and the local girls who have come to help. As the sun wanes she looks out across the fields, fiddling with a loose thread at her sleeve. Thomas is shouting instructions at the near-spent men. Henry is out there too, helping with the final push. 'I hope the goose is good,' Ma murmurs.

The farm labourers bring with them the smell of the fields, grain and chaff caught in their clothes, as they crowd the long table in the great hall. Exhaustion and relief makes them raucous. Henry is in the thick of it with Francis and the rest, crude jokes spilling from mouth to mouth, excessive amounts of beer pouring into cups. Nothing binds men more than a long hard summer working the land together.

It's a celebration, but Eliza is on edge, as though the bench beneath her might collapse at any moment. Ma had insisted that Eliza wore her best gown and forced her to tease a comb through her tangled hair; teeth caught on the knots, strands snapped, and Eliza's eyes pricked from the sting. Ma had dabbed excessive amounts of rose water on Eliza's pulse points with fingers that shook slightly, before handing her kohl for her eyes and red ochre for her cheeks.

'Who am I trying to impress?' she had asked, but Ma only tutted and made no answer.

Eliza had known then. Had felt a wash of helplessness, as though her father still had his hands clenching the back of her neck. When Ma left, Eliza had scrubbed the kohl and ochre from her face, smearing black and red down her cheeks, as though black bile and blood were leaking from her pores. Then she wiped it all away.

It is confirmed now, as the wind hurries in with the opening of the front door and two silhouetted figures enter. Her father gives a wide smile, showing his greyed teeth, and pushes back his chair, scraping it across the floor. The strangers fall dimly into focus like players stepping onto the stage for the first time. Yet in this scene of her father's house, the newcomers seem miscast. For if this is a play about new wealth, of her father's rise, buying land, farming, steadily profiting, then these strangers come from a different script. Generations of good decisions, ancestral homes, men who have never worked the land. Men who don't belong in this hall, where labourers drink, living hand to mouth.

Thomas beckons two fingers towards her. 'Eliza, come.'

'Who are they?' she asks Ma.

'Nicholas Cecil is an acquaintance of your father's.'

Thomas bends deferentially towards the men, like a servant desperate for favour. Beside Nicholas stands a younger man, whose hair in the firelight is as bright as the wheat just harvested.

'And the other?'

'His son, Edmund.'

There is no muscle, no bone, no sinew, no inch of skin nor fragment of tooth nor drop of blood within her that desires to greet the strangers and hear from their plush lips why they are here. She doesn't move.

'You need to go to them,' Ma mutters. 'They have come to meet you.'

Her parents exchange a swift conspiring look across the room as Eliza approaches the new arrivals. It is the only time she can ever remember them being in accord. Ma's betrayal is like a bee sting.

Thomas extends his arm to her, his hand finding her shoulder which he squeezes too hard, fingers digging in at the hollow. Eliza glances at Francis over her shoulder and feels the pressure of his gaze on her back long after she has turned away, and knows he watches as Thomas ushers her, the Cecils and Ma into the parlour, the din of the great hall diminishing behind them.

'Edmund, I would like to introduce you to my daughter, Eliza,' her father says.

She is a goose trussed up, put on a plate, handed about for the men to serve themselves.

The golden-haired man nods. He is blue eyed and full lipped in the bob of candlelight. The candles, she realises, had already been lit, the parlour already prepared for their meeting.

'A pleasure to meet you,' Edmund says, voice stilted, his accent different from the men here, consonants catching in his mouth. The stranger holds out his palm. Slowly, unwillingly, she mirrors him, placing hers in his. His is cool and smooth, where hers is sweaty and chapped. She thinks of Francis's hands, fresh earth lining the grooves, their rough warmth. How she is fluent in the language of them. Knows that when he interlocks his fingers beneath his chin he is thoughtful, that his forefinger pointing to the heavens signifies a point to make or a point to prove. Strange what you learn about a person without conscious thought. Their quirks imprinting on you like ink staining skin.

The interloper's lips which touch the back of her hand are brief, dismissive. She thinks of her lips on Francis's palm, and lets go as quickly as she can, twisting her fingers behind her back.

'And you,' she says, the only words she can muster.

The pair regard each other. Is this the man, she thinks, that I am to be made to live and die beside? Is he wondering the same? Does he too want to leave the parlour, alone, and run out into the night? Be away from here. Be forgotten by everyone in this room. Stare out towards the still sky and beg God for a change in fortune?

Their fathers are murmuring now, Thomas is prattling about money and gifts, and an old chest of his father's. Edmund watches them as though he is listening, although she suspects he is not. His mind must be as full as hers.

'I'm sure you will have plenty to talk about,' says Nicholas into the silence that loops around her and Edmund, tying them together.

'Come,' Ma claps her hands together. 'Let us eat, you must be hungry after your journey.'

Eliza sits beside Edmund in the great hall. Up close she can see the finery of his jerkin, the trim of velvet. The soft linen of his shirt. His clean and unblemished skin.

Eliza tastes her own breath, saliva dry in her mouth no matter how much she drinks. The geese are brought out on the best platters and sack is poured into goblets. She holds the sweet thick liquid in her mouth, savouring the taste. She keeps catching Francis's eye, and each time it is harder to look away. After the food, which she eats quickly, trying to fill the settling emptiness in her stomach, there is a rippling about the table as people wipe the grease from their fingers, lean in to talk, swap seats with each other.

Edmund says little, barely acknowledging her.

'Did you travel far?' she asks eventually.

'It took us a few hours to get here.'

'And why are you here?'

With the chorus of noise about the room, echoing from the beams and stone floor, it is strangely intimate. Nobody can hear the words that pass between them. He scratches his bearded cheek with a slender finger and his bright eyes, dark blue in the dark light, assess her.

'They haven't told you?'

She shakes her head, even though she knows. Of course she knows.

'My father wanted to check that Thomas spoke truthfully.'

'About what?'

'About the size of your marriage portion.' He mistakes her silence for incomprehension. 'For our betrothal.'

'So it's not yet decided?'

Her eyes travel across the table to Francis. He's talking to one of the serving girls, Joan, whose tall, slender body leans flirtatiously towards him, but his eyes skim Eliza's. When she turns back to Edmund, he has followed her gaze. He looks at Francis for a moment, who stares evenly back.

'Not yet.'

There is a clatter at the opposite end of the table, as one of the lads upends a jug of beer, and voices raise in a riotous jeer. She observes the chaos, the dirtied lads she has known for years and then Edmund, fish out of water, his starched ruff honeyed in the candlelight. She considers her words, of what her father would do if he knew, but it's a risk she'll take. 'Surely you don't want . . . this.' She waves her hand at the mess, watery hops pooling on the table and dribbling to the floor.

'If I could put a halt to this espousal, I would.'

'Then say you can't bear me. Say you think I'm,' she gestures wildly, 'I'm uneducated, base, an unfit wife. Say I'm ugly or dull or—'

'How easily you berate yourself.' He puts his finger up to a serving girl to refill his cup, 'You're naïve if you think I hold such influence. It's not my decision. And I can't argue with my father, he's suffered enough.'

'You're resigned then?' She squeezes her hands together in her lap.

'I'll do as I'm told.' For a moment he looks vulnerable, seems years older than she. And then it is gone, smoothed away, and he is distant and unreadable. 'Perhaps you should learn to do the same.'

⚜

She paces the path in the kitchen garden, the neat track between her herb beds. The moon is a giant orb, hanging low to light her way. Her father's words have morphed into a man, a distant and apathetic stranger who sits in her family home. She knew it would happen, but she could not imagine it. Now she does not need to.

Ma tried to stop her on the way out, had spoken her name, but Eliza ignored her, pushing her way through the press of hot bodies, heading out into the night.

She runs her hand over the soft heads of the lavender and smells her fingers. Footsteps sound behind her, a careful tread across the earth.

'Who is he?' Francis asks. He has followed her outside, his shirt catching in the night breeze.

'They're still negotiating.'

'Do you think it likely?'

A stranger's hands on her body. A stranger's house as her home. She stays silent.

'Perhaps it won't happen.'

'Of course it will, if not to him then some other man.' Her words are sharp and brittle. She doesn't mean to turn her anger on

Francis; she holds up her hand in apology and he stops, a few paces away.

'You don't have to do what Thomas orders. You've done enough of that.' His voice too is edged with anger, as though it is catching between them like wildfire. He exhales, rubs a hand over his eyes. When he speaks again his voice is softer, and he speaks those heart-breaking words that will reverberate in her memory throughout the years. 'Stay with me.'

They stare at each other for a moment, silver-cast, dream-like.

She steps towards him, can smell the field on him, the rough linen of his shirt, the iron from his father's forge. She runs her hands up his sleeves, feeling the coarse yarn beneath her fingers, and leans her forehead against his shoulder. There is a storm building inside her, a recklessness. When she finally looks up at him, she realises he is waiting for her to say something, to answer his unspoken question. Do you feel the same? Tell me you feel the same.

And she kisses him, then, as though they have done this a thousand times before, as though they have not crossed a boundary from which neither of them knows the journey home. As though their whole history has been leading them to this. Star-written, celestially foretold. His thumb brushes her jaw, her fingertips find the place where his shirt ends and the skin of his neck begins. There is a safety here, with him, that she never wants to leave.

When they pause in the blue dark, she watches him open his eyes. For the first time that evening she feels an easing in her chest, her lungs.

The backdoor creaks and Francis steps back, but still they are too close.

Henry stumbles out, a cup in hand, drunk. He stops when he sees them.

'Good evening. I wasn't expecting to see you both here,' his words slur, loud, ungainly, tripping into each other.

'Hush,' she whispers, trying to supress the nervous urge to laugh. She moves towards him, her brother who will never let her down.

Henry slips his arm through hers and seems to sober slightly, body straightening.

'You do know Father is in there now drinking with those prigs?' He might be drunk, but his eyes miss nothing.

'I know.'

'That man could be your betrothed husband in a matter of months.'

She pulls her arm away from him. 'I know, Henry.'

He doesn't ask what she thinks Thomas will do if he finds out. He doesn't bother warning her that outwitting their father is a fool's game. These things pass between them unspoken, as things can only pass between siblings who have grown up in the same house, with the same fears for over two decades. All he asks, quietly, as he leans into Eliza to keep his balance is: 'Is it worth the risk?'

Francis's palms hang open at his sides, as though he has only just let go of her. She hesitates, thinking of Mama's scarred face, then she gives one, short, certain nod.

Henry appraises Francis with bleared eyes and says, 'I hope you know what you're beginning.'

'I know Thomas,' Francis murmurs.

The moonlight catches on the cut upon Henry's chin, which is almost healed but will leave a permanent white nick through his beard. 'Then do what you must,' he says, unfastening his breeches and pissing on their father's land. 'But by God's blood, don't get caught.'

CHAPTER 4

THERE were stories in her head and she said them aloud, talking to herself as she played outside. She was only a child; she didn't notice that her kirtle was dirty, that it trailed in the dew and collected the mud, that her shoes, which had taken a few attempts to fasten by herself, were damp from the puddles left by the rains.

She didn't see him approach. But her father was there, in front of her, picking her up. There were times when he could be playful. Yet other times it could be a trick, and like a sudden storm his smiles would transform to sharp words and smacks on the back of her legs. She knew, this time, as he dug his fingers into the soft flesh beneath her armpits, that it was a trick. He carried her inside, away from the few men working the fields, and set her down in the kitchen.

'You've disappointed me, Eliza.'

Silence. That feeling of your bowels dropping out of you, insides turning loose.

'Do you know why you've disappointed me?'

She listened for any noise in the house, wondering if Mama or Henry were home and would come running to save her. But the house was still. No one was coming. She would remember later that Mama had taken Henry to his lessons. She bit down on her bottom lip, trying not to think about her father or about her sudden, desperate need for the privy.

'Answer me.'

'I don't know.'

'I told you not to play outside.'

She didn't remember him saying that. But then Father often said things to confuse her, claiming things that hadn't happened, speaking to her in knots, tying her in riddles, forcing her into trouble.

'Look at yourself. Your shoes are ruined and your clothes are filthy.'

He grabbed her face with one hand, pinching her cheeks between his thumb and forefinger. She let out a noise from her throat, halfway between a whimper and squeal. He told her to be quiet, pushing her backwards as he did, knocking her off balance. Perhaps it was an accident; her falling, hitting the floor, the air struck out of her. She gasped, flapping her arms as though it would help her inhale. Panic made her forget that anything other than the present existed, as though she would be trapped on the cold flagstones, staring up at her father, unable to breathe, forever.

'Get upstairs and change.'

She couldn't find another kirtle in the chest in her bedchamber. She wasn't strong enough or big enough to hold the lid open and rummage through the garments at the same time. She crept to the far side of her bed and sat on the floor, putting her head on her knees. If she stayed very small and very still she might be safe. Her cheeks still ached as though squeezed by phantom fingers, her heart still beat as quick as the wings of a dragonfly.

It seemed hours, days, weeks before Mama finally arrived home. Time stretches itself like that, when you're a child, when you're terrified.

'Where are you, dove?' Mama called.

Eliza stayed quiet. She was angry at Mama too, for not being there when she needed her. It was only when Mama's voice was more urgent and she heard the doors to every room being opened, hinges shrieking like distressed animals, that she said, 'Here Mama.'

Mama's eyes were bright with what Eliza would come to recognise as rage, as she squatted down and ran her hands over Eliza's arms and legs and torso, checking for bruises or breakages, before clasping Eliza tightly to her. Mama found some clean clothes, cleared up the puddle on the floor, combed Eliza's hair, tied it neatly beneath her biggin, stroked a cool hand over her cheeks.

'I'm so sorry I wasn't here, dove,' Mama said. 'You're the bravest person I know.'

They walked to market later than usual, after Eliza had heard her parents' voices exploding in the kitchen garden, sound leaking through the cracks in the house to where she had hidden. How can you be so cruel, Mama had shouted, she is your daughter. Does family mean nothing? Does your own blood mean nothing to you? The field had stilled, all action contracting to the centre of the argument. The few farm labourers watched from the corners of their eyes until Father was eventually victorious, yelling Mama into silence.

Eliza calmed with each step away from the house. One of Mama's friends greeted them along the way and walked beside them, but Eliza stayed silent, holding Mama's hand tightly. In the crowded market she glimpsed other children, also brought to the bustle, weaving between the legs of adults. A stray cat sniffed at a cabbage with veined leaves splayed open on the ground, before slinking away, unnoticed. And it occurred to her, for the first time, that she could do the same. She could be a cat. She could escape, quickly, quietly, and no one would notice that she had gone. She would never have to see her father again. She looked up at Mama, engaged in bartering down a haunch of pork, blood dripping to the ground, drop after drop after drop.

Eliza twisted her skirt in her hand as she walked away, nipping behind a big man wheeling the cart of cabbages. She glanced back: Mama was still arguing with the trader, the carcass was still pooling blood. Eliza's legs fell into a run, a steady rhythm beneath her body, and she ducked low between the people, then out of the market square and into the labyrinth of lanes.

She stopped beside a rough stone wall, and leant forwards, placing her hands on her knees as she had seen her brother do after chasing rabbits across the fields. It was only then that she started to cry, at the thought of never seeing Mama or Henry again. She considered going back, but the memory of her father kneeling in front of her, his face big and looming, so close to hers, stayed her. She sank to the ground, and for the second time that morning, tucked her legs up to her chest and rested her head on her knees.

'What're you doing down there?'

Eliza looked up. The boy wore breeches that were too big for him and a shirt streaked with muck. His hair was dark as ravens.

'Hiding,' she mumbled.

'From what?'

'I've run away.'

'From what?'

'Home.'

'Oh.'

He slid down the wall beside her. He seemed a bit older than her, but she wasn't sure. She didn't know many boys, only Henry and his friends, and she wasn't sure how tall boys were supposed to be at different ages. This one seemed quite tall.

'Where are you running to?' he asked, pulling out an apple that had been tucked into his breeches.

Her chest tightened. 'I don't know.' She wiped her face with the back of her hand. 'Do you know anywhere I could go?'

He considered as he bit into his apple. She could smell its sweetness. 'Well, there's Ludlow or Ledbury or Weobley.' Despite her sorrow, she smiled at the funny words, the way the boy's mouth worked to say them. He had a nice voice. 'Or Birmingham, perhaps?' He pointed vaguely with his apple. And then, as though thinking it rude not to have offered asked, 'You want some?'

She took a bite; it was floury, overripe.

'Most girls don't like sharing apples,' he said, impressed.

'Maybe they weren't very hungry when you asked.' She licked the corner of her mouth. 'Do you know the way to Birmingham?'

'We could ask my pa if you like.'

She thought of fathers with big fists and silent, empty houses. 'Is he nice?'

The boy shrugged. 'Sometimes he shouts, but that's only if he's angry. Most of the time he's not angry.'

She had grown cold from sitting on the ground, and the sky suggested rain, clouds grey and dark like the underside of a wild mushroom. When she agreed he extended a long arm and pulled her up.

'What's your name?' she asked as they walked to his house.

He opened a gate leading into a backyard. She saw a wooden workshop, a pig snuffling the ground, a line of washing catching the breeze.

'Francis. You?'

Eliza sat at the kitchen table, legs dangling from the bench, feet not quite reaching the floor, eating a bowl of broth that Francis's ma had given to her. When Mama came to collect her, Eliza was secretly relieved. Mama wasn't angry; she looked lost, as though she was the one who had tried to run away.

Even with the crowding of years in between, Eliza still remembers her mother's arms wrapping about her and hugging her, unspeaking, for a long time.

CHAPTER 5

H E is in the entrance hall. Minutes before he'd let go of her hand, stood outside with the moon above, Henry's piss at his feet, and counted to one hundred; time for her to return to the great hall and act as though something pivotal hadn't occurred between them, before he followed her inside.

He'd thought for so long about kissing her, holding her, and now it has happened, he can't quite fathom it. Imaginary turned reality. *Stay with me.* That was the moment to say it, and he grasped at it like a ripe pear, juice running sweet. Now she knows. Those words, the meaning they hold, have been a steady thrum in his head for – he doesn't know for how long. For years.

The expression on her face when he'd said it. No one has ever looked at him like that; eyes reaching inside him, pulling out everything within him, caught between disbelief and desire. Any longer before she kissed him and he would've confessed it all. Would've searched for words to describe a feeling he knows not how to describe. As though his being is only complete, only settled, when he's with her.

He'd wondered for so long if she felt the same. Now he knows. He could shout and beam for joy – God, she has overcome him, rendered him a silly fool – but a heaviness holds him back. He paces the entrance hall instead, like a man deranged, thinking it over, boots on the stone. Notices a crack in the wall, wattle visible beneath.

A door opens and the noise from the great hall increases, hazy light perforating the entrance hall. A man emerges. Others linger behind him, spewing platitudes and goodbyes in the great hall, and so the two men are, temporarily, alone. They take the measure of each other.

The other is slighter and shorter, less muscular, has likely never worked a day in his life, has hair so gold it could be woven into coin. Francis knows him, has watched him sit beside Eliza throughout the evening, tried not to admire the cut of his clothes, the smoothness of his face. This gentleman, dancing in here like the devil's man, with his high birth and wealth to propel him through an easy life, could so easily snatch away Francis's happiness. What right does he have?

The devil rot you.

There is no consideration in Francis's mind, only a flush of anger. He finds himself doing it instinctively, regardless of consequence. The rich prig dips his head in stilted greeting, and moves past, and as he does, Francis swiftly juts his upper arm forward – firm, muscled arm, strong from months in the fields scything the crops from the land – sharply catching the intruder's shoulder. The rounded shoulder bone yields, forced back, and the golden man fumbles his step, hand steadying himself upon the crack in the wall.

Francis doesn't stop to apologise, doesn't wait to see the stranger's bewildered, hardening stare or the way he rubs his shoulder. Instead he heads into the great hall, all joy forgotten, as though Eliza has already slipped away from him. His victory short-lived, drowned by a wash of shame.

Foolish man, always so impulsive, showing himself up. And for what? The hurt to the man changes nothing. This is Thomas's game.

But he couldn't resist. Couldn't help but want to claw back an inch of power, in a world where fortune is stacked against him. He should accept that he is a smith's son and a labourer, and that he will wed a comely girl from the village and they will have children, and will suffer through the harsh seasons until they are taken by God.

But he can't.

Eliza is across the hall, firelight glancing off her face. She is blazing, her long dark hair turned copper. Their eyes dance, catch and look away, check the coast is clear, catch again, then away. He wants to keep on looking at her. She gives him life. Ignites him. Grounds him. Makes him hope for the future.

⸎

The Cecils leave earlier than the other guests. Edmund gives her a curt nod as a parting gift. Eliza keeps her neck straight, teeth clenched, still feeling Francis's mouth, soft and warm against her own.

She waits until the last of the guests have stumbled into the belly of the night, holding each other up, swaying and stuttering along the lanes beneath a sky painted with stars. Some of them sing the songs of festivals and fairs, voices growing fainter with each step. Eliza lies on her bed fully clothed, boots still laced, staring at the beams streaking the ceiling, waiting for the house to fall asleep. She hears her parents shuffling in their bedchamber, and sometime later discerns Henry's steps making their way unsteadily up the stairs. She thinks of Edmund and his cold goodbye. She thinks of Ma colluding with Thomas to arrange the meeting with Edmund. Ma, always a dependable, peaceable church, offering solace and respite from oncoming storms, is closing the doors, barring the entry. But mostly, she thinks of Francis.

Eventually, when silence descends and light teases the horizon's edges, she creeps away, checking behind her every few yards that the house still dozes, that no one sees her leave, meeting Francis at the curve in the lane, out of sight of the house.

Seeing him is like seeing him anew. She stands before him and they look at each other wordlessly. She is strangely nervous, acutely self-aware, keeps fidgeting with her sleeves. How she feels about him is finally taking shape, forming around them. Something has opened between them and she is at its mercy.

He said he knew a quiet place where they could talk, and so they pick their way through the forest, over claws of roots bursting from the earth. Birds witter above their heads. She slips her hand into his and he doesn't let go. They don't speak much, both in a sleep-deprived daze. Eventually he stops at the site of an abandoned inn, once a place of respite for thirsty travellers. Over the years the forest has reclaimed the inn for her own: ivy creeps along the walls, curling like the tentacles of a sea monster. The windows are gaping holes and the door is rotten on its hinges.

Nothing withstands the steady beat of time.

'I thought I knew all your secret places,' she says.

'Only most of them.'

Inside there are echoes of life; of drunken brawls, of stories told over guttering candles. There are scorch marks on broken wooden tables, places on the floor that have been worn away by the tread of feet. A place of memory, the stuff of folktales.

They don't have long. An hour or two at most, before the house wakes up and finds her absent.

'I meant what I said,' he says.

Stay with me.

She nods. Of course she wants to stay with him, be with him. Have the years in abundance, ripe and sweet as cherries, stretching on before them. Saying yes to him is the easiest decision she has ever made – there are so many things she doubts, but not this, not them. She believes she will always say yes to him.

'But we can't stay here,' she says. Crossing her father always has consequences.

'Then we'll leave.' He says it so simply, as though it will be that easy.

'Where could we go?'

'To another town. Ludlow or Ledbury or Weobley or Birmingham.' He has a way of conjuring words and ideas, of making them sound right. He tells her that living in the middle means they can head out in any direction, go anywhere they want. They could disappear like morning's mist, and Thomas would never find them. Runaways exist, don't they? Vagabonds. Outlaws.

It sounds so heartbreakingly romantic, the two of them, following their feet, creating a new life. She could fall for his words so easily, stifle her doubts, believe it to be possible.

Yet Edmund's words are in her head, calling her naïve. How easily a stranger can take root. And perhaps he is right. How can this be possible; how can they escape their births, their fathers, what God has already decided for them?

Instead she asks: 'What about money?'

'I could labour on farms in the spring and summer, and work for a smith in the winter.'

She bites her thumb. She recalls the bad harvests in the years before, the desperate men her father turned away when he didn't have the work for them. He reads her face, adds, 'I have some coin saved too.'

She loathes the thought that rises unbidden: his idea of money is not hers.

'My father has money,' she says.

'You mean steal?'

'When have you ever cared about stealing?'

Scrumping apples together. Francis pinching vegetables from stalls whilst traders glanced the other way. Loot tucked into his belt or concealed beneath his jerkin.

He cocks his head, concedes. 'This is different.'

'Do you have an alternative?'

A month, they agree. Long enough to prepare, to decide where to go, to fill their purses with coin. A month is soon enough to beat Thomas at his race to trade her to another man. A month means they'll leave when the days are just long enough and the lanes still passable, before winter arrives with its first frosts and barren fields and chafing winds, forcing folk indoors to await the hope and glory of spring. You'd be a fool to run away in winter.

Their words tumble over each other in excitement before finding the word: marriage. To each other. Once we're away, they agree, that's what we'll do. They speak with a glee that makes her feel like a girl again, turns her stomach to an aviary, bird-full, swooping, diving.

Promise me a lifetime of you, they say, and she can't take her eyes off him, and he is drunk on her, and their words bloom to kisses, to holding onto each other as though they are the only people since giants walked the earth, since King Arthur and his knights sat about the round table, to have felt like this.

As they walk back, leaves crackling beneath their feet, he says, 'I never thought you'd be interested in the son of a blacksmith.'

She looks at the profile of his face, pictures his humble home in the thick of town, thinks of him hammering metals into shape. She imagines the life they will build together, and it comes so easily it feels like memory.

'Don't say that.'

Sometimes they are worlds apart, yet right now, as she picks up his hand and kisses his palm, he is in fingertips' reach.

❧

She starts stealing things from Thomas. Small, easy things at first: quill pens, a few sheets of paper, a length of twine, a smattering of coins left loose atop his desk. It gives her a thrill, this beginning of rebellion.

But her mind is a tide, pulling in and out. When the tide pulls in, she succumbs to fear and doubt. Their plan is child's play, foolish. Dangerous. She rehearses the conversation she will have with Francis, where she tells him they need a different scheme. Sometimes she even imagines whispering her most painful worry to him by dim glow of the moon; that she isn't sure there is a plan that will hold them together in the way that they crave. But something always prevents her from saying anything. The thought of a stranger for a husband running his hand up her thigh. The premonition of being jerked awake from a nightmare by a husband she doesn't recognise. The ache of losing Francis. And then the tides within her change, rapidly, rushing out, and desperation gathers at the back of her teeth. This is the only way to be with Francis; he who she would cling to when everything else has sunk into the ground. The thought focuses her. It overwrites her fears, overwrites caution.

It is in the pull of such a tide, in a fit of resistance, that she steals her father's pocketknife.

Thomas suspects something. He watches her in the passageways, asks her where she's going whenever she pulls on her cloak. One morning when the family breaks their fast, when the world outside is a brilliant cresting orange, Thomas questions whether anyone has seen his pocketknife. That damned pocketknife; she imagines its glint, can feel it sitting flush in her palm. She tries not to move too quickly or slowly when he says it, tries to behave like a practiced thief: innocent, guileless. The table – Ma, Henry – is confused, there is a collective shaking of heads, and Eliza joins in.

He doesn't believe it. As soon as they've finished eating he goes to Henry's bedchamber. She hears their shouting through the walls, hears her brother say, 'What use would I have for your pocketknife? When have I ever wanted the things you own?'

Eliza closes her eyes, awaiting the inevitable argument, symphony of slurs, but instead Thomas strides into her bedchamber. Thanks to Henry, her father is riled. Spit collects at the corners of his mouth as he tells her that he always knows where that knife is, his father gave it to him, he wouldn't lose it. She's a girl again as he searches her room, her back flat to the wall. A girl made half of fear, half of anger. But her face is hard, her lips tight together, giving nothing away. He doesn't find it. Her hiding place – an overlarge hole where a ceiling beam meets the wall – holds. Her secrets buried in the walls.

He tips up her mattress in a fury.

And there, beneath the flock, he finds her drawings. Scores of illustrations from over the years. Papers crammed with marks of ink, chalk and charcoal, no blank space spared. It stops him. It momentarily distracts him from his rage. And then he is rifling through them, his greedy hands over her work, chalk smudging on his fingers, beneath his long nails.

'Where did you get these?'

'I drew them.'

He looks from the drawings to her and then back again. Then he laughs. And he keeps laughing. And once the laughter has stopped, he calls her a liar. Says she must have stolen them; where would she have learnt a skill like that. A silly girl like her.

He takes the drawings, and in a blaze of desperation and stupidity she attempts to stop him, and then Henry is at the door, pulling their father away, casting her a warning glance.

After, she sits on her bed, staring at the mattress lying on the floor. She will eventually push herself up, drag the mattress back into place, then find a cloth and salve to ease her split lip. But for now, she can't bear to move. Of all the things her father has done to her, this could be the worst yet. He has stolen away a private part of herself.

Her resolve hardens, like lard left out in the cold. She won't back out of hers and Francis's plan. Someone will have to die first.

CHAPTER 6

O N a cold afternoon, when the trees are thick with autumn's rust and amber leaves tumble from the sky, she walks to Francis's house, the hood of her cloak pulled up around her face.

Thomas left with Henry early that morning, wheat piled high in the cart, taking it to a trader out of town. And Ma had pulled on a thick cloak, on her way out to visit a childhood friend.

'You'll be well on your own?'

The creaks of the house eddied around them as they spoke.

'I might visit Francis,' Eliza said.

Since Michaelmas he has returned to working with his father, heating and hammering metals to shape, honing the blades of daggers for belts and axes for fields, repairing iron wheels for carts which trundle the potholed lanes. She has taken to slipping away, to lean on the wall of the workshop and watch as he works.

'You pair are still so close,' Ma said.

Eliza rarely lies to her mother, but she did then, easily. Had noticed how, since Michaelmas, her mother is angling for Edmund, managing to sneak him into conversation where he has no place. 'It's the same as it's always been, Ma.'

'But now you have met Edmund.'

She felt a rise of frustration, and the walls itched to close in around her. She crossed her hands across her chest, protecting her heart, and couldn't help the defensive turn of her voice. 'What of it?'

Ma's eyes, level with hers, were thoughtful. Her gaze rested upon the cut on Eliza's lip and her mouth lingered over something, but she said nothing. Ma has decades of experience of letting the silence sit, of allowing a fire to diminish before it is started. 'I only want what is best for you. Look after yourself, dove.'

Eliza stands now at the door to the workshop, as father and son work alongside each other, their shirts marked with sweat and soot. She remembers first encountering Francis's father, John Marshall, when she was a frightened child. He was kind to her then, he used to talk to her. Recently he has been hesitant. Some days he is almost cold. Today he barely looks up, mumbling a gruff greeting to the hammer in his hand. Perhaps because what was once acceptable when Eliza and Francis were children – best friends, as close as a stitched linen shirt against your skin – now attracts raised eyebrows and unnecessary attention. She's become a woman, and word in the town is that she's soon to be married to a gentleman with such wealth that he eats only from silver plates and dresses in shirts of whitest cambric. John isn't one for gossip and knows not to believe half of what folk say, but still, perhaps he is wary. Doesn't want his son to get caught up in it. Forget hearts, forget feeling; Thomas Litton is a tyrant. Everyone knows.

Eliza knows best of all.

She leaves them alone, but not before Francis brushes his hand along her wrist, his body positioned so John's view is momentarily blocked. She drifts away to talk to Francis's sisters and watch Arthur race after the cat in the backyard, his eyes alight from the chase and not from fever. When Francis joins Eliza in the house, the cat purring on a chair as she and Arthur stroke its patchy fur, he catches her expression.

'Ignore my pa,' he mutters.

The youngest brother whips past the room, giggling, wooden doll in hand, as Philip – Francis's closest and favourite brother – follows in swift pursuit. They can hear John clearing away in the workshop. They can hear Margaret upstairs chastising one of her daughters. Every room in his house is occupied, noise seeping through the walls, the ceiling, as though the wattle and daub and stone are themselves alive.

Francis says, 'D'you want to go somewhere quiet?'

'My house will be quiet,' she ventures. 'Nobody is home.'

He bends his head slightly to avoid the low beams. It is strange to see him in this room, where he has never had cause to be. Where he shouldn't be. His eyes rove her bed, the chair with her nightgown hastily slung over it, her chest of clothes, the bedstand with a near-spent candle, a bunch of dried lavender, a stub of charcoal. The tiny details of life that give a person away.

Nervousness and excitement seep through her, like blood diffusing into water. For want of something better to do, she sits on the bed, the flock mattress sinking beneath her.

'We'll have a house like this,' he says.

'Not like this,' she says.

'No.' He is apologetic, runs his thumb softly over the healing scab on her lower lip. 'Nothing like this.'

His thumb upon her mouth. The desire to escape, feel, hope, to break unspoken rules not meant for breaking, is strong. Stronger than fear, than consequence. She harbours no doubt that she wants him, only him. Yet still she is afraid. She tries not to think of God, of guilt, of this transgression outside a marital bed, of losing her innocence, of giving something that cannot be reclaimed. But he is with her, holding her tightly, his forehead resting on hers, and her apprehension eases.

There is fumbling, whispered apologies. It takes time, a second, a third attempt. It takes pain and blood. He strokes her face with his hand and she feels the roughness of his palm. It is uncomfortable, the opposite of smooth, it is animal, and he is cautious as he balances above her, until it eases gently, conjuring a rhythm that matches the steady thrum of her heart, as though this is how it is meant to be, this is how it should always have been. She kisses his neck and tastes a hint of salt on her tongue, his shoulder pushes up against her jaw, her fingers leave white marks on his back. A question rises between them, in a moment of joint body, joint consciousness:

why did we leave it so long? You were here, right here, all the time.

They face each other in a tangle of sheets and legs. There's blood on the linen, and a throb within her. She tries not to wince, and he is attentive, stroking her hair. 'I want to know everything about you,' he whispers, sheepish, 'I think I'm going mad.'

She runs a finger along his earlobe. 'I think we both are.'

Their shared memories push through the soft edges of the gathering night. She can see him running ahead, a stitch erupting at her side as she tries to reach him shouting *you win you win* and he turns and he's grinning, his tongue out in glee. She sees him hefting a log across a stream so they could cross, water gushing over stones. Those days when summer bleeds to autumn, picking burgeoning blackberries, juice trailing their fingers.

She tells him, and he adds his own as he lies on his front, head propped against his hand, looking at her as though he is an explorer who has just found a new land.

'Remember the cat we found in a ditch?'

The same cat whose tufty fur Eliza had earlier stroked, feeling it rattle as it purred.

'He was so frail and cold—'

'And when we took him back to my house, Arthur wouldn't let him go—'

'The look on Arthur's little face at the sight of the cat—'

'You know for weeks after he kept telling me that day was the best day of his life . . .'

Their memories are renewed into life, wheeling about them, brightened by nostalgia. They talk of things they've never broached before; remember when we saw a pack of deer leaping across the fields, and we stood watching, transfixed by their grace, and how the back of your hand had grazed mine and we pretended not to notice. Remember when we played in your bedchamber, and Margaret chastised us for lingering too long in there alone. Back before we understood its meaning, and why it was a problem. She had known then, known before we did.

For a while they are silent, their history knotting their bodies together more tightly. His body is warm against hers and they whisper about how their lives will be together, about their hopes and dreams. They talk of their future. She tries to ignore the lingering fear that the lifetime they carve with their words may never be a reality. A fortress made only of air. And she tries not to think about Edmund coldly kissing the back of her hand.

Her chamber feels vacant, her body bereft, after he has gone. She watched him check the track for any signs of her family before he stepped out, and then watched him run back towards her, as though he had forgotten something. He kissed her again, and they both willed for time to stop. Neither of them said how they didn't want to part, but they felt it, clumsily grasping each other, swaying slightly, losing their footing, laughing. Her head resting in the crook of his neck, him holding her, his hand on her back. They kept delaying the goodbye by finding more ways to say it. Delightful nothings, honey sweet. Him: I should be going now. Her: yes you should. Him: before your family come home. Her: yes they'll be back soon. Him: and it's getting late. Her: it is. A pause, her, again: I'm glad you were here, with me. Him: kiss me one more time.

Eventually he strolled home in the early dark, humming a familiar tune, turning back to look at her once, twice. Blink and he's gone.

For want of distraction, she slips down to her father's private parlour in only her smock. She searches for her drawings, rifling through scraps of paper and vellum on his desk, almost upending an inkhorn. She rummages through his coffer until something sharp and cold gouges beneath her nail. She swears, pulling her hand out quickly and sucking the bead of blood. The perpetrator is a silver brooch, tarnished from being stuffed away for too long. She remembers it. And she takes it, stashing it in her bedchamber, in the hole in the wall.

CHAPTER 7

EVEN by the dim light of the candle, which casts the softest of circles about them, Ma notices the fresh sheets. She bends low and pulls out the linen from beneath the bed, which Eliza had planned to wash at daybreak, and unfolds it to reveal the browning stain. Ma knows the pattern of Eliza's monthlies; had seen her daughter carry the stained strips of linen to the washhouse the week before. So this mark, on this sheet? The unmistakeable blot of innocence lost. Eliza watches, pupils wide in the night as Ma stares at it. Ma has never scolded her, not in the shouting scowling way of other mothers, but there is a tension between them, taut as a thread on a loom.

'I told you to look after yourself,' her mother says, the frost in her voice like a December dawn.

'I have been.'

'Your actions will sabotage all that is right for you.'

'How would you know what is right for me? You've never asked me.'

Ma looks as though she will retort, the bloodied sheet still scrunched in her grip. Instead she refolds the linen and slides it back beneath the bed.

She sits beside her daughter on the mattress. 'I need you to understand,' Ma speaks low. 'Before your father . . . there was another.'

Eliza can't hide her surprise. 'What happened?'

'It had to come to an end. Your father and I were married soon after.' Ma has an expression Eliza hasn't seen before; it looks like longing and it looks like sorrow.

'I never knew.'

'It isn't something I could talk about freely. I've spent a long time trying to forget.'

'You miss him.'

'Sometimes I wonder what might have been but it's easy, I think, to idealise. The reality would've probably been quite different.'

Eliza feels a twist in her belly that has nothing to do with her mother's past love.

'Does Father know?'

'You think he is only cruel for the sake of it? Jealousy hounds him, and he will hold a grudge until his final breath.'

'A dangerous combination,' mutters Eliza, tracking the scar on Ma's cheek.

Old lover, stalking the edges of her parents' marriage, stoking the fires of her father's paranoia. The house's timbers groan. The night has turned blustery, making the shutters rattle as though memories are trying to force their way inside.

'Francis is a good man.' Ma takes hold of Eliza's wrist and rubs it with her thumb. 'But it can't continue. I need you to be safe.'

'He makes me feel safe.'

'You think either of you will be safe if your father discovers you? Do you think you will somehow be protected from his bullying, if you spend the rest of your life in this town with the blacksmith's son?'

The words sink, slowly.

'You wanted the Cecils to come, didn't you?' It is the first time they have spoken about it: Michaelmas, the golden-haired stranger arriving in their hall. 'Did you imagine I would give up all I have for a stranger?' Eliza's voice rises unbidden, her chest compressing, as though parasitic mistletoe has bound itself to her lungs, tightening its tendrils about her. 'That I would fall in love with Edmund at first glance?'

'This has nothing to do with love—'

'This has everything to do—'

'Don't throw away your chance on someone who can't protect or provide for you.' Ma looks furious. 'Edmund lives far enough away from here, away from your father.'

'How d'you know Edmund will be any different from your husband?'

'It's a gamble I am willing to take.'

'On my life.'

'For a chance of something better.'

'That hasn't been your experience, being forced to marry Thomas.' Eliza is waspish.

The flame fades from her mother, and she looks exhausted, defeated. 'Which is why I want to do all I can to protect you from him. I know the pain of giving someone up, but a chance of a better life is worth it, dove.'

Eliza forces herself to exhale her anger. She closes her eyes, hating that she understands her mother's reasons, and then opens them, glancing towards the closed door, thinking she hears a noise on the stairs. But it is only the gale, causing the house to sigh and whistle. She squeezes Ma's palm. She doesn't want to fight.

'Do you ever see him?'

Ma knows who she means. 'He married and had his own family. I've seen him on occasion, in the lanes or trading in town, but I've found I don't know what to say.' She kisses Eliza on the forehead and stands holding the candle, causing their shadows to throw themselves across the walls, long and pulsing, as though they are trying to escape. 'Life moves, Eliza. There's nothing left of what came before.'

Eliza thinks of Francis in this bed, only a few hours before. Thinks she can still smell him on her skin. Thinks too that she can smell the smoky, bitter trail of a tallow just blown out.

The room is empty and dark after Ma leaves. Sleep won't come to Eliza, her mind preoccupied, churning over Ma's words. The thought of giving him up is too painful, makes a sickness rise within her. She could escape this place that is gradually flattening her, and go to Francis, pull him from his bed, tell him they must leave this evening. Now or never. She swings her legs from her bed, splashes her face with water from the bowl on the chest. She is going to flee into the night. She will pull on her kirtle, will tie her hair, will wear her thick cloak.

But her eye catches the hiding place in the wall. A month they had agreed, and then they would leave. It is not long now, only a fortnight.

She changes her mind, swift like a punch in the gut. For that is what it will be: a gut-punch. When she realises she should've gone, should've listened to her instinct and taken the chance before it was too late.

Instead, she reaches behind the beam to the gap in the wall, pulls out all the things she has pilfered. Counts the coins and feels better. Absently tests the blade of the pocketknife against the tip of her forefinger. The nick of pain, the streak of blood, makes her drop the knife on the floor. It skids beside the chest filled with her clothes, and she sucks her fingertip, tasting metal.

It is easy to miss things. Easy to be caught in the moment, in the sliding of seconds, to think of the people you love and how they will leave you, to hear your own thoughts, to be lost in your mother's story as she lays bare a part of herself that has always been concealed. A tale that tells of your own destiny. And perhaps that is why neither of them, Eliza nor Ruth, realised the creak of the landing for what it was, nor heard the accompanying slow, steady breathing. The clues that warned of someone standing outside the door, a hastily extinguished candle in hand, head cocked to catch the whispers within.

༖

She scrubs at the blot on her sheets in the washhouse, the dull clay day spilling in through the open door lighting her chapped hands, covered in lye and cold water, as they work. The room dims and she glances up.

Her father's frame fills the doorway. His eyes linger on the sheet, at the rusted water. She inhales; there is no way he could know what secrets the sheets hold. She dips her head in greeting. He doesn't speak. His expression is grim. She stops scrubbing and waits, the water lapping at the bones of her wrists. She waits for his fingers to dig into her skin, for a cuff to caress the side of her face, waits for him to advance so she is forced to stumble against the crude wooden walls. She waits to learn what he will punish her for this time. But he does none of those things. And into his silence and stillness creeps her growing unease.

'I found something.'

He reaches into his cloak and pulls it out, his palm flat to show her. She is aware of the pulse at her throat, how it quickens.

The blade of his pocketknife glints dimly.

The cut on her finger. The knife skidding on the floor, lying forgotten.

She removes her hands from the water. A thought dimly threads her mind that here, out the back of the house in the stark fields, no one will hear their struggle.

Thomas curls his fingers around the handle and raises it high above his head. The vat of water crouches between them, but he could reach her easily with one slashing motion of his arm. She thinks of the minister's prayers, that God is gentle and merciful, and bites down on her lip, hoping He will intervene now and protect her. She can see nothing but the blade, the taunt of it. Her father brings it down, down, so it digs into the wood of the doorframe with a *thunk*. The force is so heavy she hears wood splintering, feels the shake of the washhouse's walls. He lets go of the handle, leaving it protruding at her eyelevel.

He turns to leave and says, 'Your mother's right. There will be nothing left of what came before.' He doesn't bother to look back and witness her reaction, and thank God he does not, for the smack of shock and realisation stings across her face. How much did he hear of her and Ma's conversation? What does he know? And most importantly, what will he do?

After that, it becomes harder for Eliza to be alone with Francis.

Her father's threats have her checking over her shoulder whenever she is alone, have her jumping at the sound of doors shutting, at the sounds of swift footsteps. But this, alone, is not enough to stop her. She was raised with her father's threats; they are feral wolves she grew up with that she has now tamed, found a caution and determination that allows her to live alongside them.

Instead, surprisingly, it's Ma who presents more obstacles. Ma is constantly finding her new tasks about the house; more laundry, more cleaning, cooking, darning, mending, bottling, preserving for winter. It is incessant, as though the house's needs have multiplied overnight.

Any task that provides a reason to leave the house Ma undertakes herself or assigns to Henry, diminishing Eliza's chances of slipping away. Ma's actions are, of course, purposeful. This is for Eliza's own good, her own protection. *For a chance of something better.* Ma, trying to keep her daughter housebound until a betrothal is confirmed. It infuriates Eliza, causes ruptures in the mother-daughter relations that have, for so long – for always – been harmonious, sacred.

Instead Eliza, quick-minded and witted, firm-hearted and goddamn stubborn in her mother's eyes, turns to Henry for support. And he, having confided in her about things she will carry to her grave, obliges. Siblings thick as thieves. As an alibi, Henry lies on her behalf, says she is places when she is not. Yes, he will say, she is in washhouse, where else would she be; yes she is still in her bedchamber changing the sheets; yes I'll run this errand but I'll need Eliza with me to help with the medicines as I know nothing of it. Yes, of course my sister has been with me this whole time. Perhaps Ma knows she is duped – after all, they are her children, are they not made of the same stealth and resolve as she? – but to confront the lies would only confirm that she cannot chain Eliza to her, Ruth's, own will.

Under the protection of Henry's lies, the brief snatches of time Eliza garners with Francis feel more urgent, more compulsive, as though they cannot be together long enough, or say enough, or hold each other enough in the time they have. They gorge upon it and yet are never satisfied. Their parting always feels as though Eliza has left a piece of herself behind. As though she is an apple de-cored. Each meeting brings them closer to their escape. She feels the tingling, an itching to be away. For life to commence anew.

One evening, on the bend in the lane just out of sight of her father's house, Francis takes her hand, and they stare up at the stars that are starting to amass above. Henry gives a whistle, a warning that their time is up.

'This will all be over soon. We'll be through all of this and laugh,' Francis mutters into her hair.

She looks up at him and has to fight the welling in her throat.

CHAPTER 8

A few years earlier, the Marshalls celebrated the birth of their first grandchild; Francis's eldest brother had become a father. Fifteen of them squeezed around the kitchen table on benches – including the babe, who slept in the crook of his mama's arm – elbows knocking, spoons dropping to the floor. The younger children kept glancing at the delicate whorl of hair on the slumbering newcomer's head and whispered to each other with suggestions of where babies were made. Eliza heard the words 'quack doctor' and 'belly button' before Margaret told them to hush.

After the trenchers had been scraped clean and cleared away, and John had refilled the jugs of beer on the table, Philip fetched his lute. He was a humble boy, and took a lot of cajoling to start playing, but when he did, he transformed into someone else. His fingers found their rhythm, taking on a confidence of their own, dancing along the frets. The room fell silent. Even the baby, who had by this point been bawling, paused in surprise at the sound.

Margaret started clapping along to the familiar song. Francis lifted Arthur – his then youngest brother – into the air and laughed at the boy's squeals of joy. The eldest sister twirled another sister around the room. The younger children needed no further encouragement; they were up, hurling each other about, narrowly missing the furniture. The table and benches were pushed to one side, the floor opened for the stepping, pounding, stamping of feet. Philip continued playing, his face flushing with happiness.

Eliza hugged the walls, an observer. In social situations she enjoyed the chatter and clatter of life around her. In conversation, she could match another with ideas of her own, could meet a quip with a quick retort. But the thought of dancing, of freeing her body, made her fearfully self-conscious. She'd danced at fairs before, learnt a few basic steps from Ma, but never like this. Never danced from pure exaltation, moving arms and legs and hips and neck to the lilt of the lute and the clap of palms.

Francis found her and held out his hands. 'You'll like this,' he grinned.

'I'm a terrible dancer,' she said.

'I don't believe you.'

He pulled her gently from the wall. Even the new mother stood swaying from side to side, shushing the babe to sleep. One of the sisters sang – her voice as pure as spring-water – and Eliza held Francis's hands tightly and took a few steps. And then more, more. The tension in her shoulders ebbed away. Her skirts swished against the floor, sweat gathered at the nape of her neck, and she put her head back, feeling the gentle crackling release of her bones. And he was doing the same, body moving, feet tapping, confident, talented. She laughed from the pleasure, the release of the dance.

Later she would say it was at that moment – when he looked at her, eyes sparkling from fire and exhilaration, hands warm in hers – that she realised she loved him.

The songs finished, and the room applauded and gasped for breath, and the dancers let out sighs of happiness and reached for their drinks to soften dry throats and sat heavily, gracelessly on the benches, and the back door was thrown open to let in the cool summer evening.

They were still holding hands when he said, 'Not so terrible.'

She looked at him, wondering if he had felt the same. His eyes were bright like shooting stars on hot August nights. 'Perhaps not.'

She goes back to that room often. Back to its smokiness thrown up by the fire, to the honeyed tones of the lute, to the stamping of feet on the floor. To that first feeling for Francis. The room, the memory, holds a kind of wonder, a rich joy. A safehouse in a long, darkening night.

CHAPTER 9

S OMETIMES things change, unravel. Moments, happenings, can lead to a thread of events, that slip and spin out of your control, that stitch and scar across the years.

He comes to her late afternoon. Darkness has already fallen, stars speckle the sky. He pounds on the door, and when her father answers it, Eliza squeezes her wrist tightly. What could have called Francis here so blatantly, so urgently? She knows it before he says it. Arthur.

With sickness in their midst, with a child's life once more in the balance, Ma's qualms about Eliza being with Francis seem to dissipate. She hardly notices the way her daughter and the blacksmith's son share a look of understanding; panic and longing combined. Thomas says nothing as Ruth and Eliza rush to leave, idly scratching his chin with his thumb and forefinger, as the women of his house take on the burden of life and death.

They run together, the three of them. Francis stays near to them this time; the dark is dangerous, a dagger glints at his belt. As the lane narrows, turning into the thick of town and Ma takes a step ahead, Francis silently, momentarily, fits his hand to Eliza's.

The house is cramped and oppressive, the family squeezed into the room where the sons usually sleep. The fever rages through Arthur, tossing him from overheating to shivering, his skin damp to the touch. Ma kneels beside him, forcing medicine into his mouth, but it dribbles out the corners, the boy too weak to swallow. The cat sits in the room, mewling beside its fevered master.

The younger children are put to bed in the other room by their older sisters, their eyes moon-wide, blinking with tiredness and confusion and fear. Eliza crushes and grinds herbs on the kitchen table, following Ma's instructions, glad to be useful, glad to be out of the bedchamber where the walls seem to be shrinking.

'We need the physician,' Ma says when the draught fails to ease the fever.

Arthur's parents exchange a look; John leans against the wall as though it is holding him up and Margaret whispers, 'Where are the coins—'

Ma waves her away. 'I'll sort it.'

Francis is gone before they can ask, sprinting towards the physician's home. When the boys used to race on the green, Francis would always win. Even barefoot, even when a thorn caught in his heel, he kept going and won. Eliza prays he wins this time.

They wait. And wait. Minutes are hours.

Arthur breathes slowly, his body cold to touch, the sheets piled upon him, his forehead burning beneath the fingertips that reach for him. The cat falls asleep. They hear the youngest child crying in the next room, the soothing shush of his sister.

When Francis finally arrives back, Eliza sees at once that he is angry; there is an energy to him that cannot be contained. 'He wouldn't come.'

'Why?' John grasps Francis's shoulder, holding him up and holding him back.

'He wanted the pissing money up front.' The meaning is clear: the physician didn't believe the Marshalls could pay.

'God damn him,' Ma curses, her hand a fist that beats on the wall. She stands from her stool beside the pallet, skirts flicking across the woven reeds on the floor. 'Let's go together,' she says to Francis.

If it is the longest and worst wait of Eliza's life, then she cannot imagine how it is for Margaret and John. The night is still velvet black but the clouds have come in, snuffing out the stars and the moon by the time the physician arrives.

Still, he is too late. Arthur's hand has gone limp in his mother's. The unsteady rise and fall of his chest has ceased.

Ma holds a furious conversation with the physician downstairs, whilst upstairs the younger children are woken by the noise, and start asking for Arthur, and the older sisters, with tear-stained faces, usher them away from his chamber. Eliza knows she should vacate the chamber and allow the family a private grief, but she cannot peel her eyes from the boy, who looks as though he could be sleeping, cannot stop seeing his milk-teethed smile when, weeks before, she had given him a pie to eat all for himself. She cannot believe nor comprehend his stillness.

Francis hangs his head as though his neck has given up, and Eliza wants to wrap her arms about him. In the face of death and the reminder of life's transience, she is made bold. She moves to him, cups his cheek, feels the coarseness of the hair at his chin, and he leans into her palm, his eyes great chasms, and if anyone were to look at them, they would have seen that they were lovers, in that his pain is hers, his family hers, his love hers. But no one does look over, for Arthur is dead, and there are people crying and Margaret and John are on their knees by their son, a vigil he will never know they held for him, his spirit already ascending to heavenly heights.

CHAPTER 10

YOU would presume the house is empty. You would look at the dull, vacant windows, and then you would tramp around to the back of the house, through the thick mud of autumn which would stick and clump to the soles of your boots, where you would see the shutters – a sign that the Littons are not quite moneyed enough to have glass at every window – and you would feel the quiet. And then you would continue your jurney, past the kitchen garden now withered in the morning frosts, and turn the corner until you had almost made a full circle of the house. And there, through a window, you would see candles lit, a fire jangling in a grate.

And if you dared, you could go up to the window, shield your eyes against it, watch the intricate panes fog beneath your own breath, and you would see Thomas in his parlour, and you would realise that he is waiting for something, or someone. You would see how he fiddles with a callous on his palm before stopping abruptly. You would see how he stands then sits then stands again. Cruel, unflappable Thomas, you would realise, is on edge.

Of course he is on edge. He is waiting for a man to arrive. But the man is late, having taken a wrong turn some miles north of here, being unfamiliar with the lie of the land, with the slight undulating hills, the woodlands and rivers of Warwickshire and Worcestershire. The man has journeyed through Birmingham, past the black smoke from its forges and the stink of decaying flesh from its tanners, and out again into the clean country air.

Thomas opens his door, listening for movement. The house is quiet. Everyone is out, he made sure of it. Ruth is tending to an ailing woman in town – there is always someone who is sick, his wife's work is never done – and he sent Henry on an errand to Stourbridge, to look at a new horse. It should take his son the best part of the day, journeying there and back, and with any luck the seller will be a garrulous man who keeps Henry even longer. If Thomas wasn't so anxious, he might've laughed at the thought. And since the death of the Marshall boy, his daughter has left each day, making her way to that labourer's house. Thomas has watched her leave and has bitten back the words on his tongue. Bitten down so hard his teeth have ground together. He has realised, for the first time, that his threats will not stay her. He doesn't hold her in his palm anymore. Somewhere on her path to womanhood he lost her, if he ever truly had her at all. But he doesn't need to say anything else; he can unclench his jaw. Because retribution – her retribution – is coming.

It comes now, finally, in the form of a dishevelled man, who carries the stink of ale and something else, something rancid, on his clothes. You can almost smell him through the windows. Thomas doesn't offer him a seat. The man stands before the desk holding his mud flecked hat and rotating it between his fingers, his gaze roving unashamedly about the room.

''Tis the man.' Thomas drops a folded slip of paper on the table, so the other has to pick it up. He is relieved when the man opens it and his eyes move from left to right across the note – at least he can read. In it there are details: of hair, eye colour, height, age, name. All the things that, when combined into a whole, mark out one man from another.

The man nods. 'Where will we find him?'

We. It is the first time Thomas considers there will be more than one of them. 'The Phoenix, about a mile away. And if he's not there, plenty there'll know.' He gestures in the direction of the inn and the man follows the line of his finger as though he can see it from here.

Thomas reaches for the coffer behind his desk, which you wouldn't have noticed before, shrouded in the dark of the room. He pulls out a handful of coins and begins to count, dropping each one on the table with a clink. One, two, three. The stranger's eyes are transfixed on the battered moons of metal. Seven, eight, nine.

Thomas pushes them towards the man. 'Payment for now.'

'What of the other half?'

The man seems sharper than Thomas had first anticipated. He understands now why this man came recommended. 'Once you have completed what I asked. Only then.'

The man fiddles with the coins in the bag hung at his belt as he leaves, and a smile of satisfaction graces Thomas's lips.

You would step back from the window, rubbing your hands together, skin numbed with cold. You would wonder what storm is gathering like a mass of black ravens on the horizon. At least, you would've done, had you been there. But of course, you weren't. No one else was there – Thomas's schemes, his secrets, are safe.

CHAPTER 11

I T is a cloud-heavied morning when Philip, pale and jittery, arrives at the Litton household. He tells Eliza that Frank is in a bad way, and please, please, will she go to him. Eliza looks to Ruth, waiting for her to deny her visit, waiting for her to give her another futile task. But she should never have doubted her ma, who is kind and empathetic, who feels the loss of this child more acutely than Eliza knows. Ma tells Eliza to go, to be with him.

Philip doesn't lead her to the Marshall's home, but instead takes her to the abandoned inn. A safe harbour in the forest, concealed from the world. He is solemn, shaking his head, says that he has never known his brother like this. He peels away some yards from the inn, leaving Eliza to enter alone.

Grief is writ in different ways. And in Francis, on that meeting, just the two of them, the first time they have been alone since Arthur's death, it is writ like a breaking. In all their years she has never seen him cry. But he sobs now, his body concave, bent forwards. His sentences are almost incoherent. He feels responsible for Arthur's death; he, Francis, failed to protect his younger brother. He recalls him entering the world, and now has seen him depart it. She can feel his pain, it is palpable, a figure sitting beside them in the inn, and it makes her clench her eyes shut to stop her own tears. She cradles him, sinks to her knees with him, rubs his back to ease his erratic breathing. She has always believed there were words for everything. But no, there are no words for this. Only touch and time.

After, when his mouth is so dry she wishes she'd brought a skin of ale, and his face so swollen she sees the boy he once was, he says,

'What would I do without you, Eli.'

'You'll never have to be without me.' Silently she sends a prayer to God, begging Him that what she says will always be true.

❧

She sits with Francis in the workshop, the two of them huddled by the low fire, faces burning, backs freezing. Since the funeral there has been a stream of people trickling in and out of the Marshall's house, crowding the rooms. There's no space inside for them to be alone or to speak privately, so they retreat to John's workshop, which stands dormant, tools left as they were the night before Arthur's passing.

They haven't spoken about their plans to leave since Arthur, even though Michaelmas was over a month ago. They should be on the road by now. They haven't talked about them, about *us* at all. Eliza doesn't expect it of him, but it simmers between them, unspoken. Time skips away, a thief in the night, and winter has begun to clench the land in its cruel grip, and Thomas writes letters late into the evening and rides away at first light. Eliza doesn't know where he goes, or what he does. Since the washhouse, the rusted water, the blood on the sheets, her father hasn't touched her. Her body is bruise free. Something is shifting. The things she has stolen, the brooch, the coins, collect dust in their hiding place.

Francis rubs the heel of his palms into his eyes. His grief is heavy and it swings from rage to guilt to despair.

'There's nothing more you could've done,' she says. Still he blames himself, his inability to persuade the physician to come sooner.

'The way that ass spoke to me. Came to his door with a knife in his hand as though I was a criminal, and even when I spoke to him, he didn't lower it. He wouldn't believe me at first, kept eyeing me, and when he finally believed he didn't trust me to pay. If only I'd taken some coin with me.'

She reaches for his shoulder, but he shakes her off, caught in the web of his thoughts.

'When Ruth arrived with me, he was instantly apologetic, slipped his knife away as if it'd never been on his mind.' They have been through this before, rung circles around it like kites wheeling the sky. He hunches on a low stool, clutching a cup of ale. Bitten fingernails, grime in the grooves of his hands. 'You know folk are saying we were too poor to save Arthur.'

'What do they know?' she says. 'Besides, Ma said the physician couldn't have saved him, even if he'd come earlier.' They had talked it over, Eliza and Ma, on the morning of Arthur's death, gone through the night as though it were a cloth of gold, observed every single stitch. Recounted the tinctures they made, all the ingredients, all the measures and quantities. Ma had eventually concluded, with that blunted clarity that exhausted people sometimes possess, that there was nothing more they could have done. God had needed him, Ma said, He had decided that Arthur belonged with Him. Eliza doesn't say this now, doesn't imagine it will bring Francis any comfort. 'Money would've made no difference.'

He observes the thick wool of her cloak, the kidskin gloves on her hands. 'You don't know what it's like.' For the first time, she feels his judgement. There's an edge to him that is unfamiliar: he is angling for a fight. 'It's easy for people like you.'

'I didn't mean—'

He stands, knocking the stool over with the back of his knees. 'You know the lads laugh at me for chasing a girl whose father has ten times the wealth of my own?'

She feels the workshop around her, the leaking roof, the battered tools, holes at the base of the wall where the mice sneak in.

'You know I don't care about what money you have—'

'You seemed interested when we talked about leaving together – '

'Out of pragmatism – '

'Even my own father is telling me to be wary. Says it'll never happen.'

A beat. Ice slipping down her throat. It is grief speaking she knows; it is frustration and hopelessness, and it spills out at her because there is nowhere else for it to spill. But his words are designed to maim her, and they do. The doubts and fears she has tussled with, has buried deep within her, he speaks aloud. He makes them undeniable.

'I wanted to run away with you, and it could've happened if we'd left when we agreed.' Once the words are out, she wishes they'd stayed within her mouth.

'What does that mean?'

'We can't leave now, not now the season is changing. It'll be too dangerous. We'll have to wait until the spring.' She doesn't say, and by then, it'll be too late. But they both hear it, and they catch eyes and have to look away.

'We couldn't have left before. It isn't my fault my brother died.'

'I'm not saying – '

'Maybe they were right after all.'

'Right about what?'

'That I'm wasting my time with you.'

The air holds its breath between them.

'Is that how you feel?'

'How I *feel* changes nothing. Look at the difference between us. I'm a blacksmith. You're soon to be married to a goddamned gentleman.' He aims a kick at a bucket filled with wood ready for the fire. It topples over, cut logs tumbling onto the floor. 'Your father's money buys you a safety I don't have.'

She wonders, briefly, if they have ever understood each other. His words ignite a bright, brilliant anger within her. She has always known anger. Raised with it, born of it.

'Safety?' Life with her father, like balancing on the edge of a sharpened blade. She thinks of Ma's words. *I need you to be safe.* She thinks of Thomas's latest threat. *Nothing left.* 'Money which buys me a betrothal to a man I don't know? Is that the sort of safety you crave?' She is shouting now. 'Or perhaps you envy me the safety of living with my father?'

'Don't twist my words. You love to be the victim. Perhaps you dislike that someone else is suffering more than you.'

He strikes something deep within her. She doesn't want his apology, doesn't care for any more of his words. Can't bear, even, to look at him. She stands, stepping over the chaos of logs, ducks beneath the doorframe, walks through the yard, unlatches the back gate and strides out, out, into the street. The gate claps shut behind her. If he wanted to apologise, he could come after her. But he doesn't, and she doesn't turn back. The town thins, falling away behind her as she approaches home. Her eyes brim and she wipes at them furiously.

Autumn, its golden brightness, is ending.

She slumps on her bed, pulls a blanket around her shoulders which scratches against her neck. She lies there a long time, listening to the unsettling screeches of a barn owl. There is an uneasiness in her stomach, a sickness at the back of her throat. Sleep is slow to arrive, but when it finally does, it is full, dreamless, smothering.

CHAPTER 12

DAMN him for losing his temper. He should have followed her, run his hand up her slender, pale arms, where the veins run blue rivers beneath her skin and apologised, told her he meant none of it. But she will be home by now, and her father will be there, and he, Francis, is exhausted, from everything. He does not have the stamina tonight to grovel and pick over his words and remind himself of Arthur lying cold on his pallet, eyes closed, never to open. No, tonight he wants to forget.

It is this. This decision that will alter the course of his life. Will change him as a man, will confirm both of their fortunes.

The Phoenix, when he arrives, is crowded. The usual faces, the familiar smell of old beer and rushes and sweat. Some of his friends are there, labourers from the fields, who greet him, push out a bench for him to sit. A few cups of beer relax the muscles in his shoulders, make the corners of his mouth feel pleasantly slack.

The inn empties gradually and his friends drift away, a nod here, an affectionate clap on the back there, a murmured 'don't stay out too late Frank', as they go home to their women. It makes him wonder, in his light stupor, whether he still has a woman after all. He orders another cup – the last one before home and bed where he'll sleep off this regretful melancholy, and in the morning he'll go to her and apologise and all with be well. He drinks it down, and as he tips his head back, he spies two travellers he hadn't noticed before. Yet from the way they are positioned, it seems they have noticed him. Been watching him.

They raise their cups, sidle over.

'Mind if we join you,' says the bigger of the two, and they sit beside him before he has a chance to answer. They look the rougher sort; teeth blackened and shirts frayed and the bigger reeks so badly that Francis, despite his beer-slowed senses, has to lean away.

The bigger, rancid-smelling man asks him questions, name, age, work. Francis's occupation has almost escaped his tongue, which feels full and loose in his mouth, when he stops and says, 'Who's asking?'

The stinker grins, motioning to the innkeeper for three more cups. 'Just tryin' to talk to you lad. No harm meant.'

And perhaps because his senses are blunted and he feels grief and loss at the periphery of everything, always there in the shadows, and perhaps because he unknowingly seeks connection, he talks easily to the strangers, lets them buy him another drink, another drink. Answers their questions about his work; how his father is the blacksmith, how he himself works there all seasons apart from the summer when he works for Thomas, how Thomas is a brutish, unpleasant man. Another drink.

'Doesn't sound like the kind of man you'd want to do business with.'

'But if he has the work and is willing to pay, what can a man do?' Francis says.

'Perhaps it pays to be wary of him all the same,' says the rancid man, absently pulling out a short blade to pick at the underside of his dirty nails.

'And women?' the smaller man asks.

Francis gives a non-committal reply and the smaller man chuckles. 'Aha! I know that look. So you've found the one that you want.'

And all he can do is nod and wish, not for the first time that evening, that he'd gone straight to her and held her face in his hands and apologised and tried to find the words to tell her that his life is so loud, so full of unrelenting labour, so empty of privacy, and that she is his respite, his quieting from it all.

He leaves not long after, turning down the men's offer of a final drink. Outside the air is cold, causing him to blink his heavy eyes, feel an unsteadying rush. He stumbles slightly, foggily considers how dark it is, how fast the seasons have sped onwards, pulling the early nights and shorter days down upon them.

He wishes he had run away with her whilst there was still time.

He is only a street away from his home, from his bed, from his siblings who he adores, when a heavy footfall sounds behind him. He knows these streets as though they are etched into his mind, yet it takes only a noise to transform the places that shaped him. The familiar turned unfamiliar, untrustworthy and ugly in an instant.

The newcomers corner him against a rough stone wall. He feels them before he sees them; hands clawing his shoulder, rank breath on his face. He tries to shrug away, but his body is loose and ungainly after drink. His mind, however, sharpens. Like a bottle tipped over, then righted on a table. What do they want? His eyes dart from man to man. They are colourless in the dark. Grey beasts hemming him in. The rancid one catches Francis on his mouth, and the soft inside of his lip jams into his teeth. He tastes the bloom of blood, like iron, like his father's workshop.

'What the fuck are you doing?' he shouts, holding his lip. 'What do you want with—'

The smaller man rams him in the stomach, and Francis buckles. He half-rights himself, tries to strike them, but the bigger, rancid one, twists Francis's arm behind his back, until it feels as though it will snap from his body.

'You've got the wrong man,' he shudders, and when they make no response, he struggles harder. There is no time for fear, only ragged determination to free himself. He can get himself into trouble, but he'll always find his way out again, that's what they say.

He thrashes, catching the smaller man on his cheek with the knuckles of his free hand. Another punch for that. The ground rises up to meet him, and the arm behind his back is released so he crashes down, grazing his chin. Spits blood. Skin stings. Why have these men come for him? For this was premeditated, he is sure of it; the steady flow of beer at the inn, the inquisition that was disguised as conversation—

The smaller man is on him, straddling him, weighing down upon his chest. Francis tries to squirm away, thinks of Arthur's cat, contorting beneath fences and climbing up walls. Arthur, who is dead.

Something cold presses against his throat. 'Gently, son,' the voice croons. Rancid holds a knife. Terror comes now. Oh fuck, oh Lord save me. Francis stills, gasps like an injured animal.

It is easy then.

With the blade to his neck the men are his masters. They steer him down the lane, away from the home he has always known. No one opens their shutters or runs into the street. The whole world has gone quiet, turned its back. Their only witnesses are a black cat, which flees across their path into the night, and a faint tease of the stars. The strangers force him onto a cart, their eyes acclimatised to the uncaring dark. Francis climbs on, shaking. He feels a sharp pain at the back of his head and then, even the stars go out.

When he wakes, he has no pissing idea where he is. He is face down in the back of a cart, a foul taste in his mouth, whole body aching, head throbbing. Wheels trundle over stones and uneven lanes beneath him, rocking him into unease. He swallows, dry-mouthed, echo of blood. Turns his head to see the land and sky slipping by sideways. And then he remembers: the rancid man who had held a knife to his throat.

'He's awake.' The smaller man speaks, riding behind the cart. 'Don't give us no trouble lad.'

He doesn't know how long he's been unconscious, body exposed to the November air. But it is light; bright sky meets grey thoughts. He feels a chafing at his wrists. They are bound with thick rope knotted and knotted again, pinching the skin raw. A glance down: ankles too.

'Where're you taking me?' His voice is groggy. He tries gracelessly to shift himself to sitting. The cart stops, and Rancid, riding ahead, jumps from his horse.

'Pleasant sleep?' A ghost of a smirk lingers at his coarse mouth.

'Tell me where.'

'You'll see soon enough.'

'Why me?'

The man leans against the cart. 'In our chat at The Phoenix, we talked about being wary of a certain Thomas Litton.' He says *Litton* with emphasis on the t, as though he wants to spit. 'Little too late for you. I agree with you though, unpleasant man, yet you said it yourself, a man can't turn down paid labour.'

The taste of iron in Francis's mouth intensifies. 'What has he asked you to do?'

'Be rid of you.'

CHAPTER 13

I F there is a day for news to travel fast, it is either Sunday, when the whole town has attended church and listened through yawns and watery eyes to the minister's sermons, or market day, when the townsfolk surge out, ready to peruse, trade, eat, talk. Today is the latter, and such a fine day as this – a perfect November day, with sky angel-blue and frosted ground sparkling like glass – brings even more people flocking out of doors, so the news travels faster still, carried upon wagging tongues, gossip as contagious as the plague.

But Eliza does not hear it.

The late morning sun rims the shutters when she finally wakes, her eyes thick with sleep. It disorientates her, the weak sun so far risen. It is the first time she can remember Ma leaving without her, and it is too late to follow; most of the day's trading will be over. Yesterday's argument seeps back to her, making her feel heavy. She remains at home, washing her father's shirts, wringing them tightly between her hands. No one is home. The fields are empty. It is unpleasantly quiet, making her thoughts unpleasantly loud.

Early afternoon snags past as Eliza darns stockings in the dimming light. Ma arrives home late, her skin the colour of sun-bleached bone, despite the cold that should've pinched her cheeks pink. Ma fusses with the contents of her basket, filled with market's spoils, and the stockings piled on the table and refuses to meet Eliza's gaze. Something is wrong.

Eliza stands. Her blanket slips from her knees to the floor, but she doesn't pause to pick it up, instead pulling the basket and the stockings from Ma's grasp, guiding her into a chair. 'What is it? What's happened?'

'You should sit dove.'

'What is it?' She stays standing.

Ma presses her lips together before she speaks.

'Francis didn't come home last night.'

It is strange that her first reaction is laughter. It bubbles from her in disbelief, in a moment of misunderstanding. She imagines him with a whore, another woman's hands across his body, breasts pressing into his chest. The image repulses her, flickering and taunting before extinguishing. Her mind is playing tricks, giving her blessed, precious moments, before she must confront Ma's words.

'Didn't come home?' she says, when her laugh has hardened like a walnut stuck in the throat.

Ma's lips seem almost bloodless. 'He is missing.'

She feels the urge to laugh again. Grown men, strong, tall, reapers of the fields, don't go missing. Men might die, might get killed in brawls in the swipe of a dagger; but then there are corpses which need to be carried by five men, the fifth supporting the limp head. Children go missing, as she almost did. Women go missing. But not Francis. There's been a mistake. Ma must be confused, she looks exhausted. She, Eliza, must take more care of her.

Eliza shakes her head. Ma says nothing and Eliza keeps shaking her head, and the words start falling from her, like pebbles dropped into a stream. 'He can't be missing. What do you mean, missing? How can he be missing? He can't be.'

'He left The Phoenix last night and hasn't been seen since.'

She pinches her wrist, feeling the skin between her thumb and forefinger. Her disbelief gradually turns to a sickening feeling, as though the ground has turned unsteady beneath her, as though a nightmare has escaped through sleep's cracks and encroached upon her waking. Her stomach churns as though she might retch. She is shaking, and she bends low to ease the weakness in her legs, shock taking her body as its own.

Ma is there, hands beneath her elbows, and she's saying things that

Eliza doesn't really hear. But one thing does get through: 'They're out there now, looking for him.'

⌘

Where the land ends, giving itself over and rolling away, there is a great expanse of grey which reaches to the horizon. Mist hangs low above it, waiting to smother the men on the shore. The line where the grey expanse meets the sky is faint, blurred, and it reminds Francis of her, smudging charcoal with her fingertips. Not that she is ever far from his mind. But thinking of her, so far away - further apart than they have ever been - wondering how she learnt he was gone, makes him want to thrash against the ropes that still bind him, for the blood to come from his wrists, throw himself from the horse he sits astride, spit in the small man's face and punch the other in the stomach. He wants the fear he cannot shake from his chest to morph to brute strength, and yet he can't seem to tear his eyes away from the great, flat grey. He has never seen something so vast.

Salt in his lungs, salt on his tongue.

'Ever seen the sea before, lad?' Rancid asks, riding beside him, watching.

He shakes his head dully.

'You'll be well acquainted with her in no time.'

Rancid raises his eyebrows maliciously, and Francis learns the answer to the question that has been churning his mind the whole journey: what will happen to him?

He understands, now, what Rancid had meant about being *rid* of him. They have not journeyed all this way to leave him at the bay. They mean for him to sail into it, beyond the horizon, to never come back. Not quite a murder, not quite a death, but near enough.

⌘

Eliza asks all the neighbours. She goes to Francis's friends, the

83

labourers, and asks what they know, but all their answers lead to the same dead ends: they left the inn long before Frank did. The innkeeper shrugs, says nothing unusual happened, that he served a couple of strangers. No trouble there, though. Newcomers pass through all the time. And when Francis eventually left for home, he left alone.

His family are out searching – John and Margaret, the small army of Francis's siblings – in their boots and thickest cloaks. Henry does the rounds to the nearest villages, have you seen a man, about this high, looks like this, have you seen him, have you seen him? The townsfolk are out too, looking for one of their own. A midland boy, a good lad, an honest man people say, as they try to piece together what happened. They search every wood, every nook, every hiding place.

The rain starts on the first full day of the search and doesn't stop, creating bogs of the fields which freeze over at night and thaw to mulch in the morning. Eliza's skirts are dragged down by the mud, making each step harder. She goes alone to the abandoned inn, memory pressing upon her like another body. She shouts his name in the streets, to the forests, the fields, but only the crows caw a response, their wings thrashing. She says his name so often it begins to sound other, foreign, in her mouth. She steps over streams, observes ditches which have filled with stagnant, murky water, searching for a body face down, praying she never finds it. She speaks to strangers as though she is a madwoman, stopping them in their tracks, her face close to theirs. She prays in the church, begging for help, until her knees are red from the cold flagstones, and the local church minister makes an announcement on Sunday service, his deep voice resonating throughout the nave, asking for anyone who knows anything to come forward.

Margaret keeps saying that Francis can get himself into trouble, but he'll always find his way out again. She says it so much it begins to sound like an incantation, as though words alone have the power to bring him back to her. Other people start saying it too. Sometimes Eliza murmurs it under her breath. But as the days seep onwards, like mildew creeping along the walls, and still Francis does not reappear, the incantation begins to sound more like a wish, a plea.

In the absence of answers, folk start making up their own. He must've left for a job far away, he was lured by a bewitching woman by the ink of night, his father kicked him out after a grief-stricken brawl. There are rumours that a stranger who stank of something indefinable came asking for Francis at the inn, although where that man is now, no one can tell. There are musings that the spatter of blood on the ground in the market square is of a man, rather than a pig, and whisperings that he was carried off in the great, comforting arms of a green-eyed giant. Their scraps of lies and incoherent clues only cloud the search.

One week of him missing. Two weeks.

She is frantic, her mind like a fever, rabid and unstoppable. She finds her father in his parlour, where he sits behind his desk, a cup of something half-drunk beside his hand, his eyes idly skimming a paper in his other hand. She strides in.

'Do you know anything?' If she sounds desperate it's because she is.

He looks up at her over the paper. The room smells of old leather, skin, dust. 'What are you talking about?'

'Do you know what happened to Francis?'

A frown graces Thomas's forehead. He leans back slightly in his chair, 'Why do you think I would know anything?'

Heat rises from deep within her before she speaks. 'You saw us coming home together when Arthur was ill. You overheard Ma and me talking, and you threatened me in the washhouse, after you found your pocketknife.'

'How does that relate to the lad's disappearance?'

'He threatened your control of my future. I've grown up with your rage, it's perhaps the one thing I have learnt from you. You've hurt Ma, Henry, me, time and again,' the breath catches in her throat, and she is raging and crying, the words coming without care for consequence, 'and I don't think you would stop at our family if you felt threatened.' He watches her as though he is a scarecrow, permitted only to stare, and her words as inconsequential as blackbirds skittering across the fields. 'You want us to fear you, perhaps because you fear so much yourself. Well I will give in to fear, I will obey, I will do whatever I must but please, Father, please if you know where Francis is or what happened to him, you must say.'

She finds that her nails are digging into the fragile part of the skin beneath her eyes, her body crumpling inwards. She had known it all along; theirs was a dream that would never come true. Thomas stands and before she can retreat, he takes hold of her wrists, steadying her, and almost gently prises her hands from her face.

'Don't do that,' he says quietly, as footsteps sound in the passageway. 'You've got a pretty face. You'll need it.'

※

Rancid and Second sleep beside the barn door. The place stinks of shit and animal and hay and men who haven't washed in weeks. Francis can smell himself as he lies in a corner. He has lain still for at least an hour, feigning sleep, despite the hard press of the ground at his ribs, the itch of his groin that he has fought not to scratch. He has kept his eyes open, vision befriending the dark. He can see shapes, can spy snatches of indigo sky through the thatch. One of the men lets out a snore. That is his signal. Now or never. Now or die trying.

Stealthy as a grass snake, wrists and ankles still bound, he slides towards the sleeping men, who are reduced to great lumpen creatures in the dark. His shirt rides up against the ground, grit and sharp hay finding his stomach. Second is on his back, a knife tucked into his belt. It is graspable if Francis lies beside him, like a lover. He reaches across him, as smoothly as slipping his hand up a woman's skirts, and finds the handle. Gently, gently, increment by increment, he eases the knife free.

Behind him, Rancid opens his eyes, shifts his head to watch.

Wink of the blade in Francis's hand. Its touch is a change of fortune, but it is clumsy, slow work, trying to cut the rope from his wrists, the knife blunted from use.

You know from the condition of a man's knife the sort of man he is. Second isn't a man who routinely uses it as a weapon – he leaves that to Rancid – nor is he an innately violent man. It's just that violence often comes with the jobs Rancid asks of him. If Francis had taken Rancid's blade, the rope would've cleaved in one swift motion. Instead, the rope weakens gradually. He strains his wrists apart, pulling the twine taut, causing burns on his skin. Strand by strand, the rope is cut. The eventual freedom of his arms, their ability to move independently of the other, is a relief. He circles his wrists, feeling the bones crack, and rubs at the places which he knows by daylight would be red as uncooked meat.

He reaches for the ropes at his ankles, unseeing the motion behind him. It is taking too long and then Rancid is behind him, his forearm pressed against Francis's throat, squeezing his windpipe. Francis drives his arm backwards, aiming a stab at the man and the knife pierces cloth, spears something firmer, skimming a shin, and for a moment Rancid might release him to clutch at his leg. But Rancid steps backwards, hauling Francis to his feet which, still bound, are unsteady, immovable, whilst Second, fumbling from sleep, shouts about getting his pissing knife back, and the quiet of moments before is ruptured with scuffles and grunts and Second's swearing. Rough hands rip the blade him Francis's grip, pressing his fingers so they squeeze in pain.

Finally Rancid releases him, and Francis falls backwards, the ground knocking the breath from him. There is an altercation above him: Rancid shouts at Second, 'You thickheaded idiot, what did I tell you about keeping your knife safe?' and then he looms above Francis, who sees bursts of white in the dark.

'As for you, you shit, you cock, I've had enough.' He kicks him in the stomach, and the pain is so great that Francis thinks he might be sick.

'Try that again lad and I'll kill you. Understood?'

They reach a town, bigger than the home he has unwillingly left behind. The horses are left at a stable – the cart having been abandoned a few days previously – and Francis's captors shoulder their way through the melee of people, Second gripping Francis's elbow. He could try to run but Rancid has a knife up his sleeve, and Francis is sure one of his ribs is broken from the other night. It hurts to breathe. Although that could easily be because of the ache in his heart.

It's raining, a fine mist that slowly soaks to the skin, makes your clothes stick and slick to you, and Francis has nothing but the clothes on his back. They pass by churches, oyster sellers, fishmongers, wending through the twist of lanes which abruptly spill them onto the port. Boats bob in the water which slurps greedily at the harbour. The bracing air reeks of fish and seaweed, and the sound of men calling to each other is whipped away on the breath of the wind.

'Welcome to Plymouth, lad,' Rancid says, face screwed up to the rain.

They corner a labourer on the harbour, who explains he is repairing a ship which sailed straight into a gale some weeks back. 'It'll sail again, as part of the fleet, once they're all mended,' the labourer says. They learn that some sailors had jumped ship – the voyage, the seasickness, the God-awful storms, not for them – once the damaged fleet returned to the trusty harbour. Rancid's eyebrows raise slightly at this news. One man's escape is another's shackles.

'Where're they heading?' Rancid asks.

'To the Mediterranean, so I heard. Led by a fellow you might've heard of, called Francis Drake.'

In another life, he might have been impressed by his captors. They might be rough, lawless, jack-of-all-trades, but they know how to talk, manipulating knowledge to their advantage. For later, in a dingy alehouse – where sailors congregate, staring at women who loiter in the shadows, who will give them what they want for a fee – they find a master of one of the ships in Drake's fleet and ply him with ale. How many times have they done this, Francis thinks bitterly.

The master eyes Francis, takes in his black eye. 'An unfortunate evening at the inn,' says Rancid, 'but an excellent seaman.' He waxes lyrical about the strength of Francis's arms and the build of his shoulders, attributing it to a history of seafaring. 'Get him on your ship and you won't regret it, my friend.' Rancid winks and slides some coins across the stained table. The master wets his lips, takes a long sip from his filthy cup.

He could run now. He should. But his chest aches, his eye streams. He is exhausted; he has spent days fearing for his life, experiencing a wrenching whenever he thinks of her and their parting words, keeps thinking of Arthur on his pallet. His belly is empty and bruised from Rancid's kick, his clothes are only just beginning to dry by the smoking fire. He has no money, no weapon. He is a week's ride from home, and if he returns there, Thomas will surely kill him.

Not if you kill him first.

He wants nothing more than to stay in the warm and allow his eyes to falter shut.

The master of the ship gives a curt nod, 'I'll see to it.'

Rancid dips his head, a modest bow, confirming their agreement and the master drops the coins into his purse. It is done. Fate sealed.

There is frost on the deck when, for the first time in his life, he climbs aboard a ship. Rancid and Second leer from the harbour. Their parting words linger like a siren's call: 'Best to not come back, lad.'

He spies the fleet's captain, Francis Drake, climbing aboard the largest vessel, named the Pelican. Drake is red-haired and cock-sure, the kind of man who is somebody and will become somebody, with a clear intelligence and a tenacity that suggests he is destined for greatness. Observing Drake he can't help but feel like a lesser Francis.

And then they are navigating their way out of the harbour, and he is being told to do things that he doesn't understand, so he surreptitiously copies the man beside him. Sweet fecund England slips gently from view, and his legs feel weak as he thinks about Eliza, how she has slipped away from him.

※

Three weeks missing. December comes in a freezing fury. Four. Eliza returns home from church, soaked through, her smock sticking to her skin. She had sought solace in the church's barren walls but found none. She sits heavily on the stairs, listening to the rain pattering upon the thatch, threatening to drown them all. Henry sits beside her. Places an arm around her sopping cloak. 'Any luck?'

She isn't sure whether he means with God or with Francis. Either way, she shakes her head, then rests it, damply, on her brother's shoulder. She feels like a cloth, wrung out. Limp and numb. They sit on the stairs until she starts shivering and, as though she is a child, Henry fetches Ma, and they fill her a bath, heating the water in pots above the fire. She slumps alone in the tub beside the kitchen fire, staying in the water until it turns cold and her fingers wrinkle like a plum on the turn.

It is only as she climbs out, wrapping herself in a sheet and glancing outside at the assembling dusk, that she realises the rain has stopped. And she realises that her frantic searching, her frenzy, is at an end. He is gone, and no amount of searching can bring him back. In the stillness her feelings come back to her, forcing through the thick layer of shock, like shoots rupturing sodden earth. This is her awakening, her rending. All feelings before pale by comparison. He is gone, and how, how is she to survive without him? The devastation shocks through her whole being; mouth, knees, thighs, waist, settling on her chest. She releases a raw cry that doesn't sound like it should come from her body. Banshee in the dark. It's as though she has run and run and only now has stopped to realise that she is breathless, lungs emptied, gasping for air.

PART II

CHAPTER 14

LATE December: silver frost on the windows, silver breath on the air. Layer upon layer of skirts. Shivering at night. The fields are churned and brown, the ground made sludge and marsh. The mornings collect mist in their pockets, shrinking the corners of the world. The town is quiet; people keep to the dark indoors where dim fires barely abate the chill. The winter days are slow, dark and quiet; the season is always hard, but this one is the worst.

Grief lies with her at night, stroking her hair, whispering to her until she curls in on herself between sheets that feel so cold they could be damp. Sometimes she thinks she will go mad with it; trapped inside this body and mind, spirals of complete disbelief. The grief feels infinite. A knife in her side that she cannot pull out, a spot she cannot scrub clean. It makes her head ache, it makes her feel like the broken shell of an egg, all the golden yolk and goodness scraped away. She does not know a life without him. Does not know herself without him. She finds the mornings, the slow opening of her eyes, the hardest act of the day.

His body has not been found. All grieving is hard, but perhaps this is the worst kind, not knowing exactly what it is she grieves. Does she grieve a death or only a temporary absence? Could he be walking across the front yard now, hand reaching to knock upon her door? Every moment is steeped in the possibility of his return, creating a grief laced with painful hope.

The kitchen fire is hot on her knees. Henry sits with her, but they don't speak. She doesn't have the words today. Hasn't had the words for the past fortnight. He fills her cup with small beer, pushes a plate of bread and cheese towards her. She's found that no food can touch her, her belly a constant hollow however much she eats.

'If he's alive,' Henry says, firelight bronzing his eyes, 'he'll come back to you.' His words conjure the life that runs parallel right now: Ludlow or Ledbury or Weobley, marriage in a small church, myrtle in her hair, Francis's fingers looping through hers.

'Don't, brother,' she says.

She'd told Henry of their last argument. Had even voiced the thought that traversed her mind, like an insomniac that cannot sleep, that perhaps Francis had chosen to leave her. Henry had looked at her in surprise and said, 'I saw him every day over the summer, the way he waited for you. I saw him on Michaelmas, the way he looked at you. You don't give up on a love like that.'

Everyone has a history. A person their mind trails to in the deepest part of the night. Her brother is no different – his hands have reached for someone who should never have been his. His being has yearned for another. Still yearns. She has seen Henry cast his eyes about the market square and about the churchly congregation, searching vainly for a particular pair of eyes to meet his own.

His response had caused her to cry those kinds of tears that wrench out of you, her hand gripping his. She knew, once the taunting voice within her had bedded down for the night, that Henry was right. Francis was a constant feature. They were, are, built into each other's foundations. He wouldn't have left her.

She has tried to fill in the gaps, to understand what could've happened that night – when, where, how. Her mind has settled on ideas, frantic birds, which swiftly burst towards another thought, wings flapping within her skull. It is overwhelming, making up fiction to compensate the facts, and increasingly she finds trying to find the reason, whatever it may be, futile. Either way he is gone, leaving no mark, disappeared like a ghost.

Ma slept beside her for a few nights after he had gone. The nights were better when Mama was beside her, their bodies curled into each other. Ruth fought Thomas for the right to comfort her brokenhearted daughter. Let me be with my own daughter, Thomas. Grant me that. He capitulated for a few nights, and then he changed his mind and forbade it: Eliza is a woman, not a babe at the breast dependent on her mother.

So when Ma comes tonight, sliding her bony body in beside her daughter, Eliza knows something is amiss. They lie facing each other, the sheet pulled up beneath their chins. The candle is almost burnt out.

'What is it?'

'I should have told you before,' Ma whispers. 'There are visitors coming tomorrow.'

'Who?' But she knows the answer before Ma opens her mouth to say it.

'Edmund Cecil and his father.'

Eliza feels the weight of her body pressing down into the flock mattress. Ma takes Eliza's hands in her own, cold beneath the counterpane. 'Your father wouldn't let me tell you. He was concerned about what you'd do if you knew.'

She remembers gouging her cheeks with her fingernails in her father's parlour. *You've got a pretty face. You'll need it.* Perhaps it had concerned him, the lengths to which her sadness and desperation might stretch.

Ma watches her, eyes brown and round. 'I'm sorry dove.'

※

Two men emerge, dark flecks against the wide grey sky. It is the last few days before Christmastide, when the country will cease to work for twelve days, and the town waits will sing carols and children will hide from each other amongst the streets in a game of by-your-leave, and labourers will rest their wearied bones to feast and drink. She smells Ma's wassail drifting through the passageways, a mixture of apples, cider and spices. All of it leaves Eliza feeling hollow. She watches the men grow larger, until hooves sound on the hardened earth and she cannot watch any longer. They want this done now, she thinks, before the festivities, before any more time can trickle away.

The visitors morph to full-bodied, full-blooded men, standing in her father's great hall. She nods at them, but words will not come. Nicholas Cecil smiles encouragingly, says something like, it's good to see you again, and for a strange moment, she wishes it was him that had come for her. The older man, older than her own father, with white hair at his temples, lines scoring his neck, hand leaning on a cane for support, seems kind. His son beside him is flinted, body rigid and upright; as though he is a sentinel, not a man about to chain a wife.

Thomas leads the meeting, his words running easy as water from a spring. In another life he could've been a lawyer or perhaps a player. Weaving tales and threading lies so easily. He talks of a happy union, of his own pride, his joy, and his hand flings out towards Eliza. She moves towards him, as her mind drifts to another man and the life they had dreamed.

Francis stands opposite her clasping her hands, the grip so familiar, before kneeling at her feet, for a moment her servant. Giving himself to her before God. Blink and he's gone.

Edmund stands before her, weakly holding her hand in his. She feels the heat of his palm beneath her fingers and resists the urge to pull away. They are the same height, eye to eye, chin to chin. His eyes are the colour of the sky reflected in water, a smooth, easy shape that she would enjoy drawing. She stares back, bites the inside of her cheek. He looks away first and it feels like a victory.

With a nod from Nicholas, another from Thomas, Edmund says quietly: 'I shall take thee to my wife.'

A promise, a contract that he will meet her in the church on their wedding day.

She is strangely calm, as though it is happening to someone else. As though she is drifting beneath the surface of a lake, looking at a scene of everyone else, dry, on the bank. The silence lingers, and the room is jittery as it awaits her answering oath. Edmund's hand still loosely rests in hers. Henry shifts against the wall behind her. Thomas impatiently scratches his jaw. She thinks of Ma's words, as she helped Eliza step into the wide hoop of a farthingale this morning: 'You will get through this. You have to.'

How has she become this helpless? Anger pulls her from the lake of her thoughts, causes her to tighten her grip on the stranger's hand, pinching the meat of his palm. His face is an unknowable mask, but she catches the blink of surprise, the movement of pale eyelashes as she digs her nails into his skin. It grounds her, a momentary act of defiance.

'I shall take thee to my husband,' she says, swearing it to he who is lost, him in the sheets, arm warm beneath her neck.

But he doesn't hear her.

It is Edmund who hears her promise. It is he who nods in response.

Edmund finds her in the parlour, where she leans against the window, her breath collecting and evaporating against the glass.

She could not bear to stay in the great hall after Edmund released her hand, their promises hanging in the air, feeling like a sentence. Could not bear to listen to Thomas's gleeful conversation or force her face to match the relieved smiles of Ma and Nicholas, or observe her brother's apologetic expression. So she excused herself, and even her father had let her go; she'd done her duty for the day.

And now promised to each other, on the boundary before churchly union, they are alone for the first time. They could lie with each other this very hour, bodies pressed up against the whitewash, steadily heaving together, and be forgiven by God. She waits for the thought to pass, keeping her back to him, watching as two geese fly past the window in a low arc.

He doesn't speak, even though he came to find her.

She sighs. 'So it is decided after all.'

'Yes.' He sits, tapping a ringed finger against the arm of the chair. 'Were you trying to hurt me?'

She turns as he holds up his hand where her fingernails have left a faint red mark.

'Forgive me. I wanted to feel some control.' How easily the truth appears before this man.

'Are you out of control?'

Some nights she feels it, the slip and tilt of the earth as she tries to keep her balance. 'Perhaps.'

He stretches his neck back to look at the ceiling. 'Aren't we all.' He says it lightly as though he is joking, but there is no amusement in his eyes. The pupils are wide and dulled.

She runs her hand over the window casement. This is only home she has ever known. Four weeks – a fleeting stitch of time – and she will have a different home, a different name.

'Where will we live?' she asks.

'Thomas didn't say? Cecil Hall, my family home in Warwickshire. My father has his own separate apartments.'

'What of your mother?'

'She died.'

He doesn't invite sympathy or comment, so she murmurs her apology before his silence has her turning back to the window. She wants to be alone. Perhaps he senses it, perhaps he feels the same, for she hears the rub and movement of fabric as he stands, hears him take a couple of paces towards the door. Then he asks: 'Who was he?'

She watches their transparent reflections overlap in the windowpanes.

'Who?'

'The lad at Michaelmas who followed you outside?'

And here, she learns her first things about Edmund: he notices. He is perceptive, curious, calm. She observes his glassy reflection, seeking an edge, a danger. But Edmund is inscrutable. Is this the face of a man who could beat her? Is he the sort who, when they are alone, will bar the door and not let her leave? Will he tell her lies, catch her in double binds with his words, so whatever she does will always be wrong? These are the questions you ask of men when you have grown up as she has. These are the fears you carry, that stick to you like flock caught on a thistle.

She hesitates, not knowing if her words will come back to haunt her. 'He is gone. He won't be coming back.'

CHAPTER 15

THOMAS has been crying the banns; declaring the marriage in church on three consecutive Sundays, his shoulders thrown back like a gambler who bet all his earnings on bear-baiting and won. Eliza prays for someone to object, prays that for once in Thomas's life, things will not turn out as he predicted. But she is wishing on a fate that has long been etched in stone. The banns is how the whole town – the whole of Worcestershire, as Thomas likes to boast – learns of the Littons' rise.

Folk on the road far from here, who have never met her, discuss it. The wealthy son betrothed to a yeoman's daughter, to be married in January, winter's bitter heart. Not waiting even for the marrying season, of late spring and summer. Some speculate that she's carrying already, that this must be a fleet marriage. Others land closer to the mark; the father wants the deal done, wants his status risen, wants the marriage portion paid before anything can upset the spoken agreement.

The townsfolk want to know every detail. They accost Eliza in the streets, stopping her, congratulating her. Some are in awe – they've heard of the Cecils and their great family home – some want all the details to weave into a good story to tell at the inn over a small beer. She tries to smile, to take their well-wishes, but the muscles about her mouth are rigid. These are the same people who, only two months before, had whispered about Francis, poured poison onto his memory, traded in lies, and who seem now to have forgotten him.

When they ask her what her betrothed is like, all she can think of are his eyelashes, the way they had fluttered as she dug her nails into his hand. They are the sort of eyelashes that, when caught in direct sunlight, would become invisible, drowned out by the bright light. There isn't much else she can tell them. She doesn't know him, nor what it'll be like to be his wife. But can you imagine it? the townsfolk ask. What will it be like living with a *gentleman*? Their voices go soft and dripping around that word, as though it is sacred.

Joan, the serving girl, who had leant low towards Francis at Michaelmas, breasts pushing up towards him, a vision which Eliza recalls with surprising clarity, finds her at market one morning and asks about the Cecil's wealth. Eliza shakes her head vaguely, realising she doesn't know. Joan snipes, 'I suppose you don't worry about things like that.' Like what she asks, and the girl grins, veering on spite. 'Money and jewels and things. When you're as rich as your family, it means nothing.' The words catch Eliza like a pinch on her arm, reminding her of the last argument with Francis.

He is with her each day, always just out of arm's reach. She feels his absence like an ailment. She is tired even after a long night's sleep. She is heavy-limbed, as though something is holding onto her wrists, trying to drag her back to hell. She loses focus in conversations, when women from the town arrive to help prepare for the wedding, when the local tailor visits to alter her best gown, smartening it for the occasion, tightening it at the waist where the weight has fallen away. Eliza's mind is with him, no longer in the sharp shock of his absence, but grappling with sadness, rage, guilt. With the emptiness, the space that he has left behind.

She notices that Thomas does not linger in a room alone with her, will not hold her gaze, seems only to look at her when he thinks she will not notice. Perhaps he is reflecting on how distressed she was after Francis disappeared – how he got a madwoman for a daughter. Perhaps in some deep, unknowable place he is reckoning with himself. Or most likely he needs nothing more to do with her, having finally gotten his wish.

Once at supper, she reaches across the table, her sleeve pulling back to reveal the thinness of her wrists, the rounded bone protruding like a pea, and he says, 'You need to eat more.'

His concern irritates her, after a lifetime of his bruisings. She observes how the scar on Ma's face has reddened, even though it was dealt years ago and has long since healed.

'You mustn't worry, I'll be Edmund's concern soon enough.' She doesn't say, you'll have no control over me then, but the words crackle in the room as she defiantly holds his stare. That is her one comfort, and she knows it gives her mother great solace: she, Eliza, will escape Thomas. What else can he do to her? He needs her healthy and pretty, perfectly parcelled for matrimony if he is to climb his spindly status ladder. She hopes he finds it rotten, that it crumbles and snaps beneath his feet.

He takes a sip of his wine and when he takes the cup away, there are purple marks at the edges of his mouth. 'Eat your damned food.'

The house is quiet the evening before the wedding. Thomas has gone out. The smell of a slow cooked stew, already eaten, licked clean from their fingers - chunks of pork and slices of onions and skirret - loiters in the air. Ma, Henry and Eliza play cards by candlelight, their plates forgotten on the table, their shadows stretched across the walls. They don't speak much. Eliza doesn't want the evening to end; tomorrow causes dread to swirl within her like rising mist. Yet she can't quite grasp that her life will change so irrevocably in only a day. When she thinks about her marriage for too long, she feels renewed grief for Francis. Knife through the heart.

She loses the final round against Henry, and despite his smile, she knows his victory is bittersweet. She tells him she will even miss losing against him at cards. Her words make Henry blink rapidly, as though something small has found its way into his eye and cannot get out again.

☙

Women crowd her. They are family friends and distant cousins; they are local girls drafted in to help with the feast afterwards; they are the innkeeper, the butcher, the bakers' wives, preparing food in the kitchen. Ma's voice is soothing beneath the women's exuberant conversations and frenetic activity. The day is strung through with anticipation. Everyone, except Eliza, seems excited.

She washes in the kitchen before the fire with a freezing wet cloth and scrubs herself with lye until her skin is pink and sore, as women come in and out, ignoring her naked body and the way she tries to cover herself as they prepare the food for the feast, mincing meat, kneading dough, seasoning chickens. She steps out of the tub, wet footprints on the floor, wrapping the sheet around herself as a brash woman, one of Thomas's sisters, thrusts Eliza a bottle of rose water to dab upon her damp pulse points. 'And below,' the aunt says, eyes dropping euphemistically between Eliza's legs.

She takes the stairs two at a time, shutting herself in her bedchamber, pulling her smock roughly over her head, hands frantic. Breath beats in and out of her chest; one moment it seems measured, the next it is as though she has sprinted through town, and the next it is out of control, uncatchable, clawing at her windpipe. Instinctively she crouches low, hands on the floor in front of her, grounding her. Ma finds her, the newly altered gown slung over her arm.

She says, between gasps, 'Mama, I can't do this.'

This is the last time, she realises, that she can call on Ma for help. After today, she'll be sent to live leagues away. A few hours' ride on the back of a man's saddle, and a lifetime in a place she doesn't know. The thought makes her breath come faster, and the edges of her vision spot and fade to darkness.

Ma squats beside her, strokes her hair as though Eliza is a child, makes noises that are soft and kindly. But Eliza can't stop. Air won't stay put within her lungs. Nothing Ma says will calm her, will remove the furore of fear.

Today is her wedding day. And Francis is gone. Eliza's hands strain for her face, fingertips pushing into her hairline. She feels as though she is crawling up the walls.

He is gone. He is gone.

And what will become of her?

And now Ma is talking to her more sternly, words underscored with panic, 'Eliza, Eliza listen to me, you need to stop this, dove. Stop this now.' And Henry is there too, although he shouldn't be here, he should be with the men, but he came back having forgotten his purse – it's as though he knew, a connection the siblings share – and he helps Eliza to her feet, his grip steadying, as Ma fetches a wet cloth to wipe Eliza's face.

The women downstairs, directly beneath the boards where Henry holds Eliza, have fallen silent. This will be a story to tell late in the evening. The melancholia of the yeoman's daughter. The gentleman who married the lunatic bride, who took on more than he bargained.

The cloth is cold, ice-like. It shocks her out of herself. The women downstairs have long resumed their activities by the time Eliza's breathing returns to normal, to unthinking simplicity.

She is exhausted and her mind can reach only for the sensory. The crisp petticoat on her skin, the touch of the supple blue gown, the warm squeeze of Henry's hand before he leaves, the wall beneath her fingers which stays firm and unyielding as Ma tightens the laces of the bodice, the slight tremble of Ma's lip as she arranges the ruffs about her daughter's wrists, the prickle of Eliza's scalp as she combs her dark hair so it falls down her back, the smell of the garland of rosemary, hellebore and winter berries, tied about the crown of her head.

People are gathering outside to make the walk from the house to the church. Thomas is amongst them, a smile of triumph on his face, shaking many hands, laughing with townsfolk who are keen to know a man on the rise. It is his glory after all. He barely looks at Eliza when she steps out, feeling the cold January through her skirts. Henry is there, and he steps towards Eliza, as though he can protect her from the vulture-eyes of the crowd who've came to see the bride. He tells her how lovely she looks, but she knows her eyes are swollen and rimmed with indigo tiredness. She lowers her gaze to the mud on the ground, to the little pools of water that have collected in the track.

Margaret and John skirt the edge of the throng. She weaves through the crowd towards them, trying to be subtle. But all eyes that aren't sycophantic for her father, travel to her. The bride-to-be in blue. Margaret holds Eliza's hand, bows her head. 'Always knew what a beautiful bride you'd make.' They embrace and Margaret whispers into Eliza's hair, 'Francis always said so.'

'Has there been any news?'

She feels Margaret shake her head against her shoulder.

The procession is slow. People trip up the lanes towards the centre of the town, drinking from leather sacks. Her father has hired some musicians who walk alongside the horde, playing joyful melodies and songs of romance. Eliza requested he hire Philip, the lutist, but he'd ignored her, favouring more expensive, less talented players. Younger, prettier girls come out and dance in the streets to the music, clapping their hands, showing off. More folk join as they draw closer to the church, flocking to the revels. Eliza concentrates on her breathing, willing it not to bound out of control like a horse bolting at a sudden scare. She doesn't let go of Ma's hand. Every now and then Henry brushes against her shoulder, mouth clenched, dagger strapped to his hip, as though he is a guard and she a prize.

Perhaps he is thinking about his own marriage, what it would be to wed a woman he didn't love. The one he loves, far away. His life could follow the same path as his sister's, if the unlucky stars aligned. Perhaps that is why he stays so close to her, because he understands her pain.

Their progress almost stops completely as people ahead slow, chatting to neighbours, and she hears Thomas's voice, jovial but hard-edged, shouting at them to keep going, saying something like, we don't want to miss this, I'm not sure who else will take her, which is met with laughter that sounds like crows cawing.

She wants it all to be over whilst never wanting it to arrive. The church grows in the distance, a blot, a tumour, threatening her future.

Guests with the sour tang of beer on their breath congratulate her, laying their hands on her as though one touch will cure them of their sins. Edmund sits beside her in Thomas's great hall. She doesn't look at him, her husband, but he is there, pervading her periphery. He barely speaks or eats, despite the feast pooling out before them, but he drinks a lot. Serving girls fill his cup, trying to tempt his eye. This wealthy, mysterious man, with golden hair reaching down his neck, his emerald clothes softer than anything they will ever wear, a ruff feathering his shoulders. Other women would, no doubt, tell Eliza to count her blessings that her father selected such a fair-faced man. He is a catch, and the serving girls want him for their nets. It's as though they have forgotten that he is just married, that this is his wedding feast. They have forgotten the wife who sits beside him.

There is movement outside before daylight makes its early exit – Thomas has paid men to load her possessions and the few physical goods that make up her marriage portion onto the back of a cart. Some fine sheets, a cask of wine, a great wooden chest that belonged to her grandfather. The players have come inside, singing and strumming songs about first love and damsels and princes and dragons, and some of the guests are on their feet. Soles on the floor. Fists thumping tables, missing the beat of the music.

'We should dance,' Edmund says.

It is the first thing he has said to her since the ceremony, when the crowd had stood in knots beneath the church's cavernous roof, leaning forward to listen as they had vowed to each other, for better, for worse, for richer, for poorer. She promised to obey him, her husband, and the words were rope, looping and tightening about her, forever binding. The candlelight had caught in the pearls of Edmund's eyes, cast his hair to a golden halo, and she might have thought him attractive, if it wasn't for the rise of bile in her throat. The ring he slid onto her finger had felt too large, looked too garish on the hand that had only ever known fields, earth and chalk.

She obeys him now, standing beside him as others eagerly join them, forming a circle. The dance is popular amongst the common-folk, and she wonders how Edmund feels, dancing their steps. She saw the look on some of his party's faces when she arrived at the church, the slight curls of smirks, the nudging of elbows. They wore cloaks trimmed with fur, breeches made from velvet, linens fine and starched. Another breed compared to the group that accompanied her, hardworking people, in their best clothes of cheap canvas linen and itchy serge. The townsfolk's revelry had faltered briefly when they saw the groom's party, before they hitched their spines a little straighter and continued more spiritedly.

The hall watches as the circle joins hands and the dance begins. His grip is surprisingly firm. If she closes her eyes, it's Francis's hand in hers, dancing at his parents' house. Sweat on her back, euphoria pounding within her, feeling the heat of Francis's body near hers. But she doesn't close them. The memories are taunting, they could rip the air from her again if she spends too long in their company. She pulls her body as far away from Edmund's as she can, and he must sense it, for the hand in hers slackens.

They turn to face each other following the easy steps of the dance, and she watches a gentle flush creep in a bright line across his cheeks, and recognises that he is just a man, once a boy, suffering through the day just as much as she. In another lifetime, his vulnerability would have caused in her a rush of feeling. Empathy and sweet sorrow. In this other lifetime they would be confidantes, rallying together, their future decided by a throw of the same weighted die.

But this man is the wrong man. And for that she can't forgive him.

❧

The guests have gone, leaving only the smell of beer and sweat. The cart with her possessions has already departed, along with the few smirking guests who had arrived with Edmund. Thomas waits outside with the Cecils in the grey daylight. They must be away, they must ride hard to get to Cecil Hall before the pitch of night.

Eliza stands awkwardly in the hall, the grief of goodbye like a mantle about her shoulders. Henry gives her a present in a cloth bag; sheaves of paper, chunks of chalk and charcoal. She hasn't drawn anything since Francis, which is a loss in itself, and her brother has noticed. She swallows the rise in her throat. Ma embraces Eliza and Henry, and they stand in a circle of arms and bodies for a long moment. The smell of them, of fields and lavender and beer after the feast, fills Eliza's lungs. Her family say kind, sweet things that she wants to write down so she can read them, verbatim, over and over again. But all she can do is nod, keep nodding, her words too painful, catching like thorns in her chest.

When will she see them again? These people who are her safety.

Ma kisses her cheek a final time, squeezes her fingers, a final gesture of reassurance, *you can do this*, and then Eliza is walking away, legs carrying her forward, stepping up into the saddle behind her husband, bullying herself not to cry. She doesn't look at her father. The house recedes behind her, and Henry and Ma grow grainy in the distance as they stand outside, waving her off.

CHAPTER 16

S H E holds Edmund's waist as they ride, feeling the movement of his muscles, the jolt of his body beneath his clothes as the horse passes over uneven ground. She tries not to think about him, her husband, nor what they will do when they arrive at his house. She thinks of Francis, how they've both left the place they once shared, the only place they'd ever known each other. She thinks of her mother and brother, waving goodbye.

It is the first time, she realises, since she climbed out of bed this morning – back when she was an unmarried woman – that she has been unobserved. No one watches her now. Easily she drops pretence and slow tears leak from her, chilling her cheeks, blurring the landscape. They follow lanes which skirt fields and cut through forests, cross a bridge which straddles a river inking the landscape, pass the invisible line that marks the end of Worcestershire and the beginning of Warwickshire, and all of it is unfocused, the colours smearing, the edges losing their focus. She wipes her eye with a gloved hand, and Edmund must feel it, or else the shuddering of her body, for he slows the horse, says over his shoulder, 'Do you want us to stop?'

'Please keep going,' she says, swallowing the thickness in her throat. It's a lie, of course. She wants to say stop, please, take me back. Let me find Francis. Take me back to a life that never existed. Instead, she replaces her arm around him, and they continue, following Nicholas' steadily bobbing figure.

In the last hour of the ride night falls and gradually drains the world of colour, casting it to blue and grey. Eventually a darker shadow emerges against the dark sky at the end of a track. They stop and Edmund climbs down, rubs his hand along the horse's neck. They say men who are kind to animals are usually kind, yet she has known men who treat animals with a respect they never learnt for women. She jumps from the saddle, not waiting for his hand, her legs stiff, cold-rigid. A stableboy runs out, exchanging a lit torch for the reins of the horse in Edmund's grip.

The torch light jumps and jeers as they walk, Edmund a few paces ahead of her. He doesn't look back, but he is aware of her, walking slowly so she can keep up in all her skirts, the dim circle of light reaching just ahead of her shoes. The path falls away and is replaced by a bridge, which they cross, the moat-water beneath reflecting the black night. They continue through an arched gateway that temporarily blots the sky, then out into a courtyard, filled with a barren-January kitchen garden. The true size of the house unfurls itself to her, wrapping around the courtyard on three sides, the fourth side occupied by the moat which surrounds the whole house, as though they are on their own island, cut off from everyone else. At the entrance – a heavy wooden door set into light grey stone, made visible in the lick of firelight – Edmund twists the iron handle, and the door creaks open, the interior of the house revealing itself in increments.

Nicholas stands in the entrance hall beside a fire surging in the grate, warming his hands. It takes time for her eyes to adjust, blinking like an animal waking from hibernation. Dark wooden panels line the walls, the high ceiling is threaded with beams. A carved bench stands alongside a wall and she wonders how many people have sat upon it, weary from their travels, unfastening their boots and cloaks, dusting themselves off. She senses the echo of previous lives lived here; a house passed through generations, Cecil fathers to Cecil sons.

Her father-in-law says tritely, but genuinely, that he hopes she'll be comfortable here, in her new home, then with a nod to his son, excuses himself. They listen as his footsteps and the tap of his cane fade to silence.

Edmund fiddles with the skin at his neck, watching the fire. 'I'll show you upstairs,' he says.

She squeezes her hands together tightly, feeling her bones crush into each other. The stairs at the back of the entrance hall are built in a square, so that when they reach the top of them, they are almost back where they started, albeit a floor above. The night air exhales through the house, sneaking through cracks in the windows and between floorboards. In some ways, Cecil Hall is similar to her father's house; cold and silent and alone at the edge of the world. She always wanted a house like Francis's, crammed with people, their voices filling the spaces.

They reach a door along the passageway and Edmund hesitates before pushing it open, whilst Eliza holds her cloak in her hands as though she is only visiting, will be on her way in a moment. Inside, two chairs stand beside the fireplace, a tapestry hangs on the wall, a heavy curtain frames the window. Everything is a gentle sage green, tinged orange in the hearth light. In different circumstances, she would've run her hands over the sumptuous fabrics, laughed at the richness of the bedchamber compared to the one she has left behind. But it hardly registers. Her eyes are on the bed in the centre; its great wooden posts reaching up to the ceiling, its ornate coverlid embroidered with leaves, pulled tight across the feathered mattress.

In this bed that she will lie, staring skyward, the seed of a stranger sliding down her thighs, hoping it will lead to a full belly, a son for the family. The bed will be a site of contemplation in the grey dark, a place to think about everything that went before, and everything lost. Her hand travels instinctively to her mouth, wondering if she's going to be sick. She's barely eaten; whatever comes up will be bile from her stomach, a part of her, expelling itself, trying to escape.

Edmund pretends not to notice. 'I believe all of your things have been unpacked already.'

She hasn't the clarity of mind to ask how or who. She only clutches her cloak in one sweated hand, Henry's gift in the other.

He crosses the chamber and she steps clumsily out of his way, her foot rolling over, her ankle bending painfully as he pulls the curtain across the window, muffling out the sky. The door, she sees, has clicked shut.

He pauses. This is it. Brace yourself.

She thinks of all the women who have come before her and been in this same situation. Women younger than her, virginal women with much older men. Women who would've been much more frightened. Women who had more to lose if they didn't do this. It is a hideous comfort to know that through time, through ages and epochs, she is not alone.

She raises her head slightly, jaw bone slicing the air. Edmund steps towards her, and she waits, eyes on the fire. Only when he is directly before her does she look up, their eyes at the same level. It unnerves her; she has always been used to looking up at men, and for a moment it's as though they are equals. He squints slightly, his mouth tightening. He has a beauty spot on the soft pink of his upper lip. She observes him as she does when she wants to draw something, appraising every detail, a furious calm settling within her. If he's going to take her, fuck her, then she will endure it, rigidly, unceremoniously, forced into it, like everything else.

But he does something she does not expect. He moves past her and rests his hand against the door. Those clean, slender hands that have never had to scrub a pot, never had to delve into the rich earth, never, she believes, known hardship. 'Goodnight, then.'

'You have another room?'

He assents and something within her releases, like warm honey spreading through milk. Relief.

When he has gone, she slowly removes the gown that Ma had so carefully dressed her in this morning. How much can transform in a day. She pulls the garland from her head, stems catching in her hair. The sprigs of rosemary – herb for remembrance and for constancy – shed their needle leaves upon the floor.

It takes her a moment to remember where she is, sleep-heavy eyes focusing on the room. Then memory reaches her like the cuff of a hand across her face. Morning light creeps about the seams of the sage curtain. The tapestry, which she'd given only a cursory glance the night before, stretches across a wall. She has never seen one so large – she could wrap herself in this. She has missed noticing and observing beauty and beautiful things; had forgotten how to, in the fog of the past weeks. She climbs out of bed, and squats low before it, running her fingers over the yarn and all the shades of green: grass and juniper, jade and fern. Has never seen such workmanship. She wonders how many women cricked their necks bending over the work, squinting in the low light as their skilled fingers looped thread after thread.

It is a detailed scene of men hunting, their spears sharpened and poised for a kill, dogs sniffing the ground for the boar which hides in the foreground behind ancient oak trees, helpless and frightened. At face value, it's an England of the wealthy – the truly wealthy – one she isn't familiar with. But she recognises it as a depiction of England's hunters and hunted, superiors and submissives, of which she is all too familiar.

She places her forehead against the arras, and isn't sure when the tears start, but once they come, she fears they may never stop. She stays with her head against the needlework, kneeling as though in prayer. Except her hands aren't clasped together for God. No, her palms are limp against the wall, opened out and upwards, a forced surrender.

CHAPTER 17

SHE stands above a carved window seat in the long gallery, watching through the window as guests glide across the court-yard below. They are splashes of azure, indigo, plum, vermillion, expensive gowns and cloaks swirling in the glow of the torches bracketing Cecil Hall's main entrance.

Her husband's voice carries from downstairs, deep and melodi-ous, along with Nicholas's polite chuckles and the tread of guests, climbing the stairs from the entrance hall to the great chamber, with its stone carved fireplace and oak panelled walls, and a long table which lies waiting, festooned with goblets and plates. She knows she should be there, greeting these strangers, filling her cup, faking her laughter, celebrating her marriage. But it means enduring their judgements: so what do you think of the new bride? Chosen by Nicholas for his only son – oh, let's hope she's fertile – and imported from a town which I'd be damned if I claimed I'd ever heard of it, certainly never visited, have you?

The new wife: an exotic fruit that could repel or delight.

'Eliza?' A voice pulls Eliza from her musings. It's Dorothy, her kind grey eyes wrinkling at the corners. 'Edmund is looking for you.'

It was Dorothy who found Eliza that first morning, her head pressed into the tapestry, sobbing like a child. Dorothy who so diligently unpacked Eliza's possessions before her arrival. All the gowns and kirtles that comprise Eliza's different guises – girl, woman, daughter, sister, friend, lover, wife. The clothes are now threaded with memories, tales from home; the stockings Ma had darned, a spare needle held firmly between her lips. A pair of kid gloves Henry had bought her, softer than puppies. The gown she pulled on each Sunday before walking to church, marking the passage of another week on God's green earth. The smock that she had pulled shyly over her head before she forgot the whole world, that first time with Francis. It was Dorothy who washed Eliza's old kirtles, the ones with stained hems from working in the garden, from tramping through mud-caked fields. Dorothy who introduced Eliza to a tailor, who took her measurements and made her a dress to wear for this evening, three weeks into her marriage.

Eliza wears it now; a great farthingale pushing out a skirt the colour of forget-me-nots, body laced tightly at the front, sleeves attached, slashed through to cream beneath. It is more expensive than the gown she wore for her wedding. It makes her move differently – feet straighter, spine locked, gestures measured – as though any wrong motion could peel away the façade and expose the lonely, sad woman beneath. How, she sometimes catches herself wondering, how has it come to this? How has life changed so irrevocably in a few, short weeks? Weeks albeit, that have felt like a lifetime. An earth-shaking shift.

Eliza cocks her head to the visitors below. 'What are they like?'

'Mostly harmless.' Dorothy smiles, assessing her, as though searching for traces of someone else. She has served the Cecils for decades, knows all their acquaintances. 'But I imagine you'll be very capable of handling them, if you don't mind me saying so.'

Eliza wonders whether Edmund has spoken about his wife. Does he conjure her as a sullen, base woman, who pinched his hand and spoke too directly? But more likely, he hasn't spoken of her at all. He has barely acknowledged her presence at Cecil Hall. They have not touched each other at all – and why would they? They are only husband and wife. Perfunctory, contractual. Not lovers. Days pass without her seeing him, the house large enough to absorb its occupants, for bodies to come and go and not cross each other. And she finds that when they are together, she can think of little to say, and he, distant and impenetrable, holds the silence. Words were once so easy for her to find, that sometimes, if she forgot herself in Thomas's presence, he would reprimand her for being too interested or too eager or too bloody quick for a good woman. Perhaps grief and displacement and loneliness suit her, mould her into the woman she was always expected to be. Her father should be proud.

She exhales, gives Dorothy a small smile and gathers her whispering skirts.

She stays close to the great chamber's walls, not wanting to draw attention, forgetting that with her wide skirts, her unfamiliar face with eyes that dart the room, she is as inconspicuous as a butterfly landing on a white linen sheet. A few people watch her from the corners of their vision; others lean towards their neighbours and whisper, that is she, over there, look, the new wife. Eliza recognises a few of the men, who came to the wedding with their furs and their smirks.

Nicholas has his back to her, absorbed in conversation. His hand clasps his cane tightly, knuckles protruding. In the few months since she first met him, his back seems more stooped, his movements slower. Edmund is at the opposite end of the chamber, talking to a man and a woman in a tight, exclusive circle, heads inclined towards each other. The woman draws Eliza's eye like the needle of a compass drawn north. She is petite, shorter than Eliza and perhaps a few years older, with a glimpse of chestnut hair parted at her forehead before it is lost beneath her French hood. She has a vibrancy, a hum and pull of life about her. Closer to, beneath the polite conversation of the room, Eliza discerns the woman's thick and husky voice, and hears a sharpness in her tone. The other man, lounging casually against the mantlepiece, who Eliza realises is also someone she could gaze at, unashamedly, for a long time – cropped hair, smooth chin, wearing his clothes with such ease it seems as though he was born in them – glances up at her. He stares as though she is the one worth looking at, then graciously dips his head.

It's this which causes Edmund to see her, blue eyes on blue

gown. He breaks away from the group, slipping through the guests towards Eliza.

'Where've you been?'

He doesn't wait for her reply, doesn't give her any time or warning before he turns to the room which, after much hushing and whispering, like thrashing rains upon trees on a stormy night, grows quiet. 'I'd like you all to meet my wife, Eliza Cecil.'

Her name hums on the air like lazy wasps in late summer. The inevitable assessment follows, oval faces staring at her. There is no pretence now: they stuff themselves on the sight of her. Inevitable questions form in their minds – judgements Eliza had been dreading – waiting to be unleashed in late-night conversations once the party has disbanded, once the candles at Cecil Hall have been blown out. Who is she, and how did her family secure such a match? And they will speculate, fashioning tales to entertain themselves, gossip to keep their tongues loose and their minds sane. And if Eliza were a fly on each of their walls, she would learn one thing: that people, regardless of birth, wealth, finery, graces or lack, are all the same.

The room drinks to the health of the couple and a few people clap enthusiastically. Eliza stands before them, without a cup, her mouth dry. She thinks of her clothes stored in the chest in her bedchamber. All her different skins. She feels this new skin become her. Wife, outsider, woman with a new name.

His hand is on the small of her back, and he guides her towards the guests, introducing her, as though he'd already told her how the feast would be, as though she understands who these people are. As though they are the sort of couple that lay together on the first night after their wedding and have been lying together ever since, easily intimate, utterly inseparable.

It surprises her: Edmund is a better actor than she. Why does he pretend to adore his wife, for all to see? Everybody here will know it was an arrangement. Does he care what folk will think? Or does he have something to prove, this gentleman masquerading as a player?

When the babble of the room has resumed and backs have been turned, when the guests have drunk their fill of the new wife and need their goblets to be replenished with wine, Edmund removes his hand from her back. She is surprised at how unsupported she is without it, and she wants to ask him to wait, to stay with her this evening, because she doesn't know anyone here and has forgotten how to make idle talk, because she is lonely and sad and maybe he could help her, because it has been weeks since anyone touched or embraced her. But he is already moving away into the press of guests, as though already forgotten that he has a wife.

She takes her place beside him at the table. The magnetic woman sits opposite, watching Edmund as he speaks with the guests about the table, spearing food with blade of her knife, ringed fingers clinking occasionally against her pewter cup. Eliza feels strangely drawn to her, as though she is a riddle waiting to be solved.

'How do you know Edmund?' Eliza asks.

'Our history is complicated,' the woman replies, drinking from her cup, her lips leaving a red mark on the rim. 'I'd rather hear how you met.'

'Our fathers arranged it.'

'You must have had a first meeting.'

'Briefly.' She leaves out other words that rise; cold, uncomfortable, taut. The memory of Michaelmas, sitting beside her future husband as Francis watched from across the table. Meeting Edmund again for their espousal, when Eliza had been out wading, deep in other griefs.

'Surely it was love?' There is the softest tang to the woman's words. Milk on the turn.

'We didn't know each other.'

'You must've grown close—'

'Annabel—' Edmund says. Eliza wasn't aware he'd been listening. 'What is it, Eddie? You don't want me speaking to your wife?' A slight shake of his head. 'You didn't have to come.'

'You invited me.'

'It seemed the right thing to do.'

'I don't require your pity.'

Eliza sits, lost.

'Perhaps you should explain to your wife,' Annabel says.

'Leave her out of this—'

'That'll be difficult now that you're married.' The other woman looks away, and Eliza observes the side of her face, her nose, the neat edge of her eyebrow.

The clamour of the chamber rises up to fill the silence that follows: irritating laughter, the scrape of knives across plates. Edmund's hand moves instinctively to his neck, where he tugs at the skin. When the other woman looks back, her face is sunken. The ceruse on her face is cracking about the corners of her eyes, as though she is an eggshell on the verge of breaking.

'Perhaps that haven't yet realised your duty as a husband,' Annabel says, quietly.

'I don't require lessons from you about duty.'

Eliza feels a disconnection. The more that these people bicker across her – hackles raised, urging for a fight – the more she begins to drift. She left behind one tangle of problems, to arrive at a labyrinth of jibes and histories and secrets. She traces the smooth wood of the table beneath her fingertips, absently running along a deeper grain of the wood, thinking of the Marshall's pockmarked kitchen table, before realising that Annabel and Edmund have stopped talking, and that her husband is watching her. Maybe it is her unconcern, or because she is an outsider still, or because she has asked nothing of him, not yet, that causes him for the first time, to give her a small, apologetic smile. A soft, humbled curve of the mouth, which she, slowly and uncertainly, returns.

Annabel pushes her plate away and stands, leaving the table without a word.

She scrubbed the pots and plates, sleeves rolled up to her elbows after the guests had left. Most of the servants who came to help had also gone home; only Dorothy, who lives at Cecil Hall, in the small chamber further along the passageway from Eliza's, remained. Dorothy had protested, said it was Eliza's wedding feast, that she shouldn't be clearing it away. But Dorothy had looked worn out, like crumpled paper shoved beneath a mattress, and Eliza told her to go to bed. She finished cleaning alone, cold water settling between her fingers, making the creases sore.

She had realised that she was this woman's mistress, that the older woman was under her instruction, but also her care. It was an unpleasant feeling, knowing she could ask Dorothy to do anything, and the servant, whose livelihood depended on it, would have to oblige. Such power is uncomfortable when you've seen authority manifest in the worst ways.

That was the first time she sensed him. As she scoured, she felt someone watching her at the edges of her vision. He disappeared when she turned her head to look. But she knew it was him – he who has vanished, he who she waits for, he who never could stand still – knew he leant against the table, sleeves pulled back to his elbows, arms crossed over his chest. He laughed and said, *leave that now, come to bed*. She exhaled through her teeth, rubbed her eyes with the wet heel of her hand.

It is a surprise when she does eventually go to bed, back-weary, sleep-ready, to find Edmund waiting in her bedchamber. It's the first time she's seen him in his nightshirt – he looks smaller, stripped of his clothes, only a thin layer covering him. She won't allow herself think about his bare skin beneath. She pauses in the doorway.

'Can I?' he says.

She isn't sure what he is asking. Join her, sleep beside her, lie with her, bed her. The euphemisms pool in her head. What else can she say except yes, the back of her neck growing warm. She changes slowly, delaying the moment when she will be in nothing but her smock, then nothing at all, before she slips into her nightgown. He clears his throat and looks away. She tugs her night-gown on roughly, clumsily over her head, pulling out her hair as she does.

He sits on the bed and slowly raises his eyes to look at her. She feels exposed, the flesh of her thighs pressing together as she stands.

They climb into the bed, bare feet sliding over the sheets, careful not to touch each other, careful not to look at each other more than necessary. The coverlid pulled up over them, they stare upwards to the bed's carved canopy. She lies rigidly on her back, waiting for him to reach for her. He doesn't. The gap between them is a wall which stays firm, solid. She feels herself relax slightly, release of shoulders and neck, softening into the goose feathers of the mattress.

'How did you like the feast?' she asks eventually, when she realises that he isn't going to speak first.

'Yes, good.'

Silence lapses. He behaves as though he's never been with a woman, although she knows from the way women look at him, that he must've been. She won't believe that he's nearing thirty years and never touched nor been touched.

'Who is she?' she asks. Ma always remarked that her blunted talking would get her into trouble. She knows he understands who she means by the way he shifts slightly beneath the sheets. He is quiet for a while, and she steals a glance at him. His face is closer than she expected. His profile: the dip where his upper and lower lip meet, those sunlight eyelashes.

'A family friend. Her family, the Sackvilles have known the Cecils for generations.'

'It didn't seem particularly friendly.'

He moves onto his elbows and blows out the candle beside the bed. The room plunges to darkness, except for the amber embers in the grate.

'She has her reasons.'

She waits for him to elaborate. But he doesn't. She turns away, facing the window and the tapestry, although she can't see it for the dark.

'Goodnight, Eddie,' she murmurs, just loud enough for him to hear. He takes a breath but says nothing, words lost on an exhalation.

CHAPTER 18

H E sleeps in her bed every night after that. And every night is the same; the short, terse conversations that give away nothing, but start to say everything. She learns things about him without meaning to. How he doesn't talk for the sake of talking. How he is a naturally early riser, unlike her who drags herself from the warmth of the bed in the morning. How he doesn't snore when he sleeps, but how sometimes, just as he is crossing the boundary between consciousness, he mumbles sad, incoherent words. How he often falls asleep before her, his body growing limp and heavy in a few heartbeats, while she lies awake, fidgeting, memories crowding in. Once she wakes in the night to find his arm thrown over her, the dead weight pressing against her ribs, and she considers, fleetingly, whether his display of affection and unity towards her at their wedding feast wasn't as much a pretence as she'd first thought. She imagines that it is Francis's arm, that his dark hair splays across the pillow behind her, that the steady rise and fall is the beat of his heart, the rhythm of his lungs. Then she carefully moves his arm from her, breaks the spell.

Spring, the first buds, start to push through. The days develop their own monotony. She heaps and stokes the fire, pumps the bellows, pays a lad to sweep the blackened chimneys. In Dorothy's company, she learns the lanes that wend to the village and the church and beyond to the nearest town, where on market day she barters down handfuls of chestnuts and sacks of salt for preserving meat and flour for baking in Dorothy's clay oven, and haggles over braces of rabbits, strings of onions, clutches of eggs. She mends clothes in the fading light when nothing else can be done, tired feet stretched out in front of her. All the things Mama trained her for, she does here.

She plants and prunes her own garden in the courtyard. Thyme, rosemary, sage, lavender – the same earthly concoction she grew with Ma. But Edmund has a habit of leaving extra coins at the end of the kitchen table for the household, and Dorothy persuades Eliza to buy different seeds and take new cuttings, to grow things that she would never have been able to in Ma's herb garden, not when Thomas routinely asked the cost of everything, or else questioned its usefulness. So now she plants honeysuckle and mint, camomile, sweet williams and fennel, and when she comes into the entrance hall, the clinging smell of sweetness and the sharpness of anise follow.

She starts drawing again in quiet reverence, using the paper Henry gave her; rediscovering her creativity is like finding a way back to part of herself. She is more careful than ever not to be discovered. Regardless of all the herbs and flowers she is allowed to grow, she knows there are limits to the freedoms men will give women. And hasn't secrecy always been intrinsic to her work; concealing it beneath her bed, Henry admiring her drawings before their father came in from the fields? Hiding her work and talent is second nature.

When she draws, she thinks of Francis. Whether he is dead or whether he dreams of her too. Her chalk is no longer able to calm or distract her; her mind, given a moment to itself, is pulled inexorably to him. Her work is changing, her hand mirroring thought. There is more shade and darker, harsher lines. Her drawings are growing up with her, hardening.

She hunches over beside the fire in her bedchamber, the paper on her lap, chalk smudging her fingers. April's mid-morning sunlight casts shafts of light over her wrists. She hears footsteps downstairs, snatches of voices. A woman's voice. Eliza moves to the door, carefully stowing her drawings in the chest at the foot of the bed. The conversation dilutes as the speakers move away, their words uncatchable.

Eliza doesn't know what impels her to step quietly from the room.

She spent her childhood, girlhood and early womanhood hiding behind doors which had been left ajar, fearing her father, listening to volatile conversations, seeing things she could never unsee. It is a perverse force ingrained within her, to uncover things, even if it hurts her; because it hurts her.

Her pantofles muffle her steps as she descends the stairs, like a fox slinking the streets.

'You didn't seem particularly keen to see me when you were last here,' Edmund says. Eliza can't see him from where she stands, tucked into the corner of the stairs leading to the entrance hall, her back to the wall.

'I need your help.' The woman's voice is clearer now; low and husky, cracking under the strain of something. 'Please.'

The house waits. Eliza can't imagine Edmund turning a woman away, but then he is still an enigma. She has seen the streak of his unkindness, when he is a cold, impenetrable veneer. But he must have accepted because the two sets of footsteps fall away from Eliza. She follows along the passageway, which wraps itself around the central courtyard and leads towards her husband's parlour, keeping to the corners and crevices. Draughts climb her ankles. His parlour door clicks shut.

She hears only the sibilance of words, which, short of pressing her body flat to the door, she can't decipher. But then there is a moan, guttural and low. Her mind jumps to something sordid, the twists and turns of infidelity rioting her imagination. It makes little sense; they had seemed hostile towards each other, arguing at the wedding feast. But people are strange in attraction, or love, or whatever this could be.

The moan comes again, this time more of a howl. It is not the sound of lovers. This is someone in pain, heaving up sorrows, retching out sadness. Edmund's voice rises above it, trying to quieten the sobs. 'Annabel, what is it?' He sounds concerned; Eliza imagines him cupping the other woman's face, wiping away her tears with his thumb.

She can't hear Annabel's reply, incoherent amongst her cries, but Edmund's voice, when it eventually comes again, says, 'Are you certain?' and then, speaking as though to a sweetheart, 'I'll make arrangements. Please, trust me.'

She doesn't expect it. The door swings open to reveal her husband, his hand on Annabel's back, framed in the doorway looking like a painting of reconciliatory lovers after a fight. Annabel looks different without her painted face: less domineering, eyes red-rimmed. Her posture has changed since their first meeting, as though she carries the weight of a great bird, its wings splayed across her shoulder blades, pulling her down. There are wet patches on Edmund's shirt beneath his shoulder.

Eliza takes it all in. She can't imagine her own expression, how she must look in her old kirtle, coif askew upon her head, pantofles padding her feet, chalk on her fingertips. But she doesn't wait to read it on their faces. She heads out into the courtyard, ignoring Edmund's calls for her to come back.

He watches her go.

No, not his wife. The other woman. The smaller woman, who wipes her streaming eyes as she walks. Not like his wife, who can stand at his level and meet his gaze unflinchingly.

He runs a hand through his golden hair, strands catching about his fingers, exhales, a low whistle. He turns over the other woman's words, hovers above them like a hawk coasting the air.

He is not the same man now she has uttered them.

He closes the front door, the click of the latch, and leaves his hand there, door pressing back beneath his palm.

You must understand. He isn't a bad man. He contains shades, of light and dark. He made a mistake. Only a few months ago, he reached for something he never should've reached for. Suffered a loss of judgement. Back before the woman with the dark hair and her hidden drawings had bound herself to him, and he to her, in the buttered glow of the whitewashed church beneath the scrutiny of God.

He had found his wife's drawings, rifling through a chest for an old shirt of his father's. There, beneath her neatly folded stockings and petticoats and kirtles, nestled a few sheets of paper. He hadn't been able to stop looking at them: dark drawings of faces and people and babies, cats sniffing at cabbages and children playing amongst lines of laundry. He'd heard voices, his wife and the servant's, drifting in from outside, and quickly, carefully, returned the papers to their hiding place.

Before all of that.

A rush of shame and sorrow rises in his throat.

If he were a crying man, this might've been the moment when everything leaked out of him. As a child he had cried a lot - when his mother died, when he'd been ill, teetering on death's boundary, like a boy walking along a narrow wall. But since last year, the tears have not come. Perhaps, after the shock, he has no more saltwater left to give. His body a shoreless island.

He moves through the entrance hall, pacing back and forth, disturbing the dust that dances in the light. It's a place that has seen generations of men, such as himself, pace and pace and make poor decisions.

He will not tell his wife. His own shame forbids it. Pride can be a cursed thing. And a few words - arbitrary sounds, formless things - can ruin a marriage, fracture relations with the woman to whom you are God-bound to spend the rest of your days.

His wife. The way she looks when she sleeps in the mornings, she the night owl, he the morning lark. If things had been different, he might've fallen for her quick tongue and the way she strides out of the house when she's in a decisive mood and her smile of perfectly aligned teeth, except for one incisor which sticks forward, a little out of line, giving her a devil-may-care grin. The way she smiled at him at their wedding feast at Cecil Hall. In one look she had seemed an escape from the tangle of his past.

In other circumstances, he might've loved her instantly, furiously, fully. Perhaps one day he will.

He pulls his cloak from the hook in the hall and wraps it about himself, wondering what is happening now for the other woman, telling the truth beneath her parents' roof. Then he steps out into the early spring to find his wife, to spin her a tale to protect them both.

⁂

She has always needed air. Out in the fields, slipping out the back as a child, boots sinking into soft earth. Finding ladybirds, letting them crawl across her fingernails. The immensity, the detail, the fragility of the outside, has always helped her find a distance from what was happening inside. She needs it now. She crosses the courtyard, passing her new garden. Cool wind on her face, the smell of damp earth after spring rains. Blossoms on the crab-apple tree.

She walks over the moat, and out. Out along the winding lane, heading to the fields and forests. She tells herself that she doesn't care about Edmund's feelings for this other woman – Eliza will always be moored to another man. She tells herself that she doesn't yearn for someone to put their hand on her back, to hold her up. Yet it does bother her that the man who lies beside her each night, with whom she shares a name, to whom she is bound beneath God's ever watchful eye, makes private promises to another woman. That he can take her pride, and compress it like clay between his palms.

She walks in a loop, remembering her vow *to obey*. Whatever his choices, she is sworn to bend to him, like a sapling bowing sidewards beneath the force of a gale. She walks and walks, and eventually sits at the base of an old tree, bark rigid against her back, cloak pulled tightly around her. The cold ground seeps upwards through her body, but she doesn't move, resting her head against the oak's bole, looking up at the branches splaying out against the pale sky.

As a child she would sometimes fall into rages, monstrous things that would tear through her and not let her go. Mama would be there, rubbing her back, voice gentle in her ear, reminding her to breathe. Wherever you go, she would say, you always have your breath. Remember it.

She remembers it now, in and out. A life married to Francis instead. In and out. Where could he be now? In and out. Him returning to find her gone. In and out.

There is a fleck across the field, which eventually takes the shape of Edmund, walking towards her, hands behind his back. She hadn't expected him to come searching.

His usually enigmatic face betrays a worry, and the blue of his eyes have faded to dull grey, like cloud-smothered skies. He looks down at her. 'I've been searching for you.'

'And now you've found me.'

'You shouldn't disappear.'

He moves his hands in front of him, right hand tightly grasping his left wrist.

'What did you hear?' he asks.

To confess that she heard very little reduces her power, reduces even the validity of her anger. His eyes dart across her face as she tells him, leaving out how she imagined their bodies close together, his immaculate hands moving a strand of hair from Annabel's cheek. Her own hands are tinged green around the nails from where she has been absently pulling at the ground, clumps of grass snapping beneath the tug of her fingers.

'What was she upset about?'

Edmund's forehead creases before smoothing out. Perhaps it's her directness that shocks him, or perhaps he's shocked that his own wife, the woman who owes everything to him, his inferior, is interrogating him. He hesitates, but when once her questions would have garnered a jewel of a bruise across her cheek, they now procure her an answer.

'Annabel is . . . how to put it. Struggling. She was recently widowed.'

Eliza's recollection reshuffles, adapting to this new fact. *I don't need your pity*, the other woman had said, her painted face cracking at its vulnerable edges.

Edmund sits beside her, his shoulder inches from hers so she can't see his face. 'I think, seeing me, us, married is difficult for her. It reminds her of what she had not so long ago.' His hand twists about his wrist. 'Her father wants her to remarry, but, well, how can you move on from something like that?'

There is a man at the edges of Eliza's vision, in the shadow of the forest, a sprite following her, moving his weight from foot to foot, hair raven-dark, beckoning to her. She blinks him away.

'You can't,' she says softly. 'Annabel came to you for help?'

'She asked me to speak to her father, to try and dissuade him. Or failing that, whether I knew anyone, a kind man, who she could marry.'

'She trusts you.'

'As I said before, she's a friend of the family, we've known each other for years . . . She was married to my brother, Samuel. He died not long after Midsummer last year.'

This revelation is a shock. She takes it all in: the grief he must have carried when she first met him at Michaelmas, mere weeks after his death. The cold indifference she interpreted in him, instead a façade for a cavernous sadness and a mind that was far, far away.

'Edmund I'm so sorry.' Instinctively she reaches for his hand, grasps it in her own. She cannot imagine losing her own brother. He shakes his head and stares at her palm in his, an intensity settling across his face, the downwards pull of his mouth.

'I struggle to talk about it,' he mutters not unkindly, and she understands that he is saying, please, can we not discuss it. He runs his thumb gently across the back of her hand. It feels strange, their first moment of intimacy.

There are starlings havocking above them in the branches, wings beating to a blur. They both pause to watch. The simplicity of the birds' lives. Edmund stands and helps Eliza up. He keeps hold of her hand for a moment once she has stood. They don't speak again as they walk back to the house, falling in step together, but she feels him glancing occasionally at her.

CHAPTER 19

THE saltwater stings his hands as he scrubs, settling in the cuts on his fingers. His knees rest against the deck which rocks slyly beneath him. Filth and grit stain the cloth which he rubs across the planks, before he plunges the rag back into the bucket's already browning water. His stomach churns from hunger and his tongue worries at a tooth that has started to come loose. He glances up and gazes out to the sea, the lull and bob of it, glinting in the sunlight. He can just make out the land they skirt. South America. The men had cheered, clapped each other on the back when they first sighted it after months of sailing across open, unblotted waters. Even their captain, John Wynter, had permitted a rare, mischievous smile.

The labourer at Plymouth's dock had been wrong: the fleet had not headed for the Mediterranean, as had been the chatter along the harbour, rumours spread purposefully from Whitehall. Instead, they had headed much further in the opposite direction. Across the Atlantic, towards the Pacific.

At first this had meant nothing to Francis, places and names unfamiliar, their direction and distance an enigma until Anthony befriended him. A sailor since boyhood, all muscle and sinew, descended from a line of sea-loving, sea-fishing, sea-faring folk, Anthony drew transparent lands and seas in the air before Francis's eyes. He explained how their route would allow them to pillage the Spanish and discover new lands along the way. 'Drake's mission is backed, if whispers are to be believed, by the Queen herself. We'll be lucky if we're back in a year,' he explained, rubbing the bridge of his nose, 'if we make it back at all.'

Francis had been unable to speak, thinking of her, of whether

Thomas had gotten his way and married her to that preening golden stranger.

He clenches the rag in his hand, staring absently at the waters. Green lad turned sailor, green with jealousy. God, he misses her. She lives in his mind like a plague, incurable, unpredictable. Will he return to their town, a place intrinsically bound to his memory of her, and find her gone?

A hand clips him around the back of his head. The master of the ship, the coin from Rancid still in his purse, says, 'Stop idling Marshall,' before continuing his walk along the deck. Francis places a wet hand at the nape of his neck, rubbing the smart, and sends up a silent prayer: *please God, may he drown.*

CHAPTER 20

SHE walks through the courtyard, beneath the gatehouse, over the bridge where the stone is speckled with moss and lichen and the moat where the ducklings' spindly legs beat beneath the surface, heading for the brewhouse built in the gardens. A low wooden building with barrels enough to feed a village stacked inside, full of fermenting hops.

Eliza lifts a lid of the nearest barrel, dipping two cups into the murky surface. Beer swills in greedily, the slightest haze of bubbles rising to greet her. She sips one as she walks back towards the house, spilling some on her hand, turning it sticky and sour.

She recalls Francis's hand cupping his drink. His face close to hers, his hand resting on the back of her neck. Everything is a gateway to a memory of him. She stops in the doorway of the brewhouse observing Cecil Hall's reflection in the moat, allowing the past to roil within her. It is painful, and yet she can't stop, can't drag herself from the thought of him.

She takes a cup to Edmund, shouldering his parlour door open. He sits behind his desk, letters and sheets of paper and parchment in neat piles about him. Ink on his fingers. A goose quill set down on the table. He glances at the wedding band on her finger as she places down his cup and gives a nod of thanks. It has been easier between them since he found her beneath the oak.

He turns back to the paper in his hand, a crease forming between his eyes.

'What is it?' she asks.

'An agreement from a new tenant, but it would be helpful if I could read his reply.' She stands behind his shoulder, sees the tangle of letters straddling the page, crossed out, amended above sentences. A chaotic mind expressed in ink. She bends to take a better look, aware of her proximity to Edmund, close enough that she can smell him; she'd noticed before the smell of hay and horses, from days spent riding, visiting tenants to collect rents and solve disputes, occasionally journeying out with close friends. But recently he has been away less, retreating to his parlour, emerging smelling of vellum and leather. And today there is a thicker, unpleasant smell, like old sweat and hartshorn. She has noticed too, as you do when you sleep beside someone every night, when you unthinkingly observe and learn another's habits, and when they break them, that he has been sleeping longer and later. The exhaustion about his eyes never diminishing. Sometimes she wakes and he's still out dreaming, his eyes shut, sleeping so heavily that she can lean over him and see the delicate veins running over his eyelids.

Her eyes run across the page, slower than she would like, her mouth moving about the words, murmuring to herself, sentences leaking from her.

'You can read?'

'I'm not some farmer's wife.' She gives him a small smile, their faces inches apart.

She remembers Henry teaching her, patiently correcting her, laughing when she made the same repeated errors and cursed beneath her breath. She remembers the evenings afterwards spent with Francis, showing off all she'd learnt, trying to impress him – not realising her impact until years later, when he told her how he'd begged his father to teach him his letters so he could impress her too.

'Did you think I wasn't clever enough?' she asks.

'I didn't doubt your intelligence.' A subtle curve of his mouth, 'I just didn't know.'

'Well now you know to keep your private letters safe.'

His eyes glaze slightly as she speaks. A gleam of sweat sits on his forehead despite the springtime chill.

'Are you well?' she asks.

'Just tired. I've not been sleeping well.' They both know it's a lie, that he's been sleeping like a dead man every night, but she says nothing.

∞

She wakes to sodden sheets. It's the deepest pit of night and she can make out nothing. The bedchamber is cold, the fire having burnt itself out hours before. For a moment she panics that she has pissed in her sleep, but as she reaches down beneath the cover, she realises the damp is coming from Edmund's side. She lights a candle, the tinderbox taking a long time to catch, by which time she is completely awake. In the solitary candlelight, she sees the bedsheet is tangled about his feet. His arms are heavy upon the coverlid.

'Edmund.' She rocks his shoulder gently, feeling a dampness through his nightshirt. He doesn't answer, so she rocks harder, the material sticking now to her fingers. 'Edmund,' her voice louder. His eyes flutter open. 'You're burning hot.'

He is disorientated, his hair slick about his temples, eyes clogged with sleep. He moves his head. 'It's so hot,' he murmurs as though she'd said nothing.

She touches his forehead. His skin afire. A fever.

'Your hands are cool,' he says, closing his eyes.

Her knuckles beat upon Dorothy's door. Eliza's words are gabbled, remembering last autumn, a boy with a fever, the weakness in Arthur's body, how the household had stilled and wept when he died. It rushes to her, clawing her throat. Dorothy gently takes her hands, asks her to speak plainly.

They return to Edmund, who has shifted from hot to cold in an instant. He has pulled the sheet up hastily, and it hangs awkwardly, half of it rumpled on the floor. He doesn't seem to notice their presence, shivering between the edges of listless dreams and feverish wakefulness. He says he urgently needs to piss, and he goes in

138

the chamber pot, Eliza behind him, a steadying hand on his back, looking away.

It smells bad. Sharp. Rancid. He groans in pain, rubbing his side with his hand. Dorothy has already left the room, running to the kitchen to fetch salves and ointments.

The women work together. They open the windows so night's breath flows into the bedchamber, soothing the man within, who has returned to scorching heat. Dorothy cooks a chicken broth and instructs Eliza to make a draught. It feels dreamlike, the two of them up at the late hour, the hour for witching, the low crescent moon slinking at the windows. Eliza uses all the knowledge she absorbed from Ma, sage for headaches, wormwood for sickness. Recalls crushing herbs from the garden, rubbing pastes across young children's sickly chests and wrists.

She spoons some broth into Edmund's mouth, supporting his shoulder as he sits, his breathing heavy. She changes his nightshirt for a fresh one, thankful that the dim light shrouds her view of his chest, the contours of his upper arms. She catches his torso with the inside of her wrist as she pulls the nightshirt down.

Later, when he is a little more lucid, when the dawn has risen and turned the house pink, he'll say to her, please stay with me, and her panic will reduce, the uncomfortable thrill in her stomach easing. But for now, they keep going, keep checking on him as he sleeps and wakes.

It's more difficult manoeuvring an adult body to apply a poultice to his aching side than it was with Arthur's small frame. Edmund growls when they move him. Pain makes feral beasts of men; it makes them swear and shout and scream things that wouldn't usually come out of their mouths. In his delirium he calls for his dead mother and his dead brother.

Once he's eventually settled, the women pause, taking a moment out in the passageway. Eliza can see the whites of Dorothy's eyes.

'I couldn't have done any of this without you,' Eliza says. She reaches for the serving woman's hand, and it's a comfort to have this connection with another woman. 'Please rest. I'll tell Nicholas what you have done.'

'I will check on him in the morning, but I fear it may be like before.'

Eliza frowns.

'He's suffered stones in his bladder ever since he was a boy. He has periods of being well, but they always seem to come back.'

Dorothy squeezes her mistress's wrist goodnight, and Eliza watches the older woman make her way carefully through the dark towards her chamber. She stays there even after Dorothy has gone inside, shut the door, has likely climbed gratefully into bed. Eliza feels the gnawing of worry for the man sleeping just inside the bedchamber. She pauses, as though waiting for someone to come and scoop her up. She wishes that Francis was here to whisper in her hair that everything will be well – and then she reflects how impossible, how painful, that would be for them both.

⁂

She's right, Dorothy. This sickness isn't finished.

The physician arrives late in the morning, checks Edmund's pulse and spends a few moments observing Edmund's piss from the night before, holding the chamber pot to the light, grimacing and nodding to himself. He speaks quietly to Nicholas, excluding Eliza from his medical words as though afraid she'll steal his ideas. There are murmurings about the possibility of Edmund's sickness continuing even after the stones have passed, which could see the whole summer swallowed up to bedridden fevering. None of them question whether he will survive, but the thought is there, unspoken, a hooded figure skulking behind them. Nicholas looks pinched and paled, a hand clasping one of the bed posts, and Eliza wonders if his son's sickness is bringing to the surface previous sicknesses and deaths.

She has never asked Edmund for the details of his mother's

death, but Dorothy had elaborated as they sat at the kitchen table one spring evening, shortly before Edmund took to his bed. The same table where, one night almost three decades before, a fist had leant as waters broke. The waters that birthed Edmund.

'What happened to her?' Eliza asked.

'To Rose?'

Eliza imagined Edmund's mother to be a woman filled with colour, the kind of woman she would draw in motion, never stopping.

'Consumption. Those were dark days, when Edmund was only young, ten perhaps.' Eliza can see it in Edmund's silences, in the way he collapses in on himself: a child left without a mother.

One evening when the sun has left all but an orange streak on the horizon, when the physician has visited for the fourth or fifth time – Eliza has lost count – and Edmund experiences a brief reprieve from day upon day of shaking and vomiting and pissing red, Dorothy brings Eliza some mead. Its honey is sweet on her tongue, smooth in her throat. She leans her head on the doorframe of the bedchamber, blinking with fatigue. Edmund sleeps exhaustedly within.

Dorothy says, quietly, 'Some things are sent to test us. But you learn things about a person when you experience the worst with them. It binds you.'

'You speak from experience?'

'I nursed my husband, God rest his soul.'

After, when Eliza sits beside her husband's supine form, he wakes and reaches for her hand, his clutch sweaty and weak. 'This is bad,' he sighs, and she tells him he'll be fine, this will pass, banishing the image of Arthur playing with the cat. She helps him drink some weak ale, wipes the liquid that trickles out the corner of his mouth. It is strange how necessity has made their intimacy so easy.

The hand in hers grows soft and limp with sleep. She remains at his bedside until all the light outside has slunk away, worrying about him, wondering at all he has lost, mulling over Dorothy's words and wondering if his illness, and her caring, and these long hours spent together – not their vows spoken in the bare church before God – is the true beginning of their binding.

☙

Strength returns to him slowly. It's a good day when he eats his first full supper, pigeon pie and sweetmeats, which Eliza brings to their bedchamber for him to have in bed. Summer presses in at the windows, the days gloriously long, teasing them to come outside. She adjusts the curtain so more light gushes into the room, and her mind catches a memory of last summer. Francis walking her home, his body bumping against hers.

When she turns, she sees he has been watching her.

'Do you need anything else?' she asks.

He shakes his head and she bends to pick up his plate.

'Wait,' he says.

She straightens.

'I owe you thanks.'

'For what?'

'Your care . . .' He gestures wordlessly at his body.

'When I'm on my deathbed I'll expect you to feed me some broth.' She smiles, daring herself. 'What sort of wife would I be otherwise?'

'You're a very good one.'

'Your flattery tells me you want something.' She is teasing, but the eyes that meet hers are so sincere that she stops.

'I want to give you something, as thanks for all you've done,' a pause, 'for me.'

She waves her hand in dismissal, surprised to feel a flush of emotion rising upwards through her.

'Name it. Tell me what you want, and I'll give it you,' he presses.

She considers the sea of his eyes, tinged gold.

'I'd like to see my ma and Henry.' She takes no pleasure at the thought of seeing Thomas again, but it is necessary. She needs to go home, to satiate the question that circles her mind. Is Francis there? And yet, she knows, if he is there, he will find her changed. She has become someone else. Wife of a gentleman, a gentlewoman, a Cecil. And what of him? Will he have changed too?

There is a hideous picture that keeps intruding her thoughts, of a body, face down, features lost to the earth, a tangle of unmistakable dark hair crowning the head, a woollen shirt, askew and dirtied. She recognises the arms, that once would have reaped the fields. Hands that once would have cupped her face, frozen by frost, the skin rendered a bloodless blue.

As the months have beat by, another thought has haunted her, pursued her half to madness. If the worst *has* happened and he is dead, at least it explains his gaping absence. Yet how to explain it if he still lives? Does he choose to stay away, or is he forced to?

Over half a year of silence. She must go home, seek her answers, seek her peace, or both, if such a pair can exist.

'Done,' Edmund says, reeling her back to the room, the bright light, the smell of pastry on the air. 'Perhaps we could make a trip of it. Go to London on the way.' She doesn't question his idea of on the way; it is completely out of the way. But he has been bedridden and bored, a man in his should-be prime. 'Meet my cousin Walter there. Show you some of the city.'

CHAPTER 21

THE officer, Doughty, kneels. Francis has spoken only a few scant words to him, for they have always sailed on different ships, but still he feels for the man, wants this whole business over, wants a drink.

Doughty stares towards the heavens, clasping his hands together. What final earthly words he says to God, murmured softly through lips that barely move, none of the sailors will ever know. Francis squeezes his hands together behind his back, wintry cold tearing through him as he, the crew, the officers stand at the harbour of Port St Julian. A wide, quiet sandy curve, the land dissolving away into the gentle hush of sea, blue grey waters punctuated by their ships, whose masts are fingers pointing skywards.

He is still becoming accustomed to the feel of land beneath his boots. To not being awoken by the sickening lurch and drop of the hull. They are moored here for the worst of the winter, and whilst he is glad to be away from the ship and the stink of the other men, packed in so closely that sometimes he felt he would suffocate, he can't help feeling that every moment spent on this land is time wasted, when he could be getting back to England, and her, and piece together the strands of his old life.

Doughty glances at Drake, the red-haired captain, leader of the fleet and the whole damned expedition. It is a final look between old friends turned rivals, where trust has disintegrated to paranoia, where accusations of mutiny and betrayal have been allowed to fester. The sea, great stretch of hardship, can do that to a man. Can change a man.

Drake nods slightly, *rest my friend*, before Doughty places his head on the block.

The executioner raises the sword, and it cuts through the air. Whistling gives way to *thunk*, to cleaving, to a gush and rush of blood which stains the sand beneath.

Francis will not look away even though he feels like retching his guts upon the silt. They have already had to throw dead men overboard, who wasted and died from sickness. With each death something is chiselled out of him; the joy he used to feel, the light he could emanate, the energy he carried. Now his body is still, but Doughty's is stiller.

How easily men carry out their own judgements on others. The things men do to each other. What wrong, Francis thinks for the hundredth, thousandth time, did he commit to set him here, to have him watch a man executed on a wintry port, on a land unfathomably far from home? Because he loved – loves – a woman and wanted a life for them both. Wanted to tether himself to her, wake up beside her every morning as the sun crested the land. Where is the wrong in that?

They are moving the limp, headless body, will bury it in the bowels of this foreign land. He imagines Thomas Litton's body, limp beneath his hands. Repayment for the wrongs Thomas has inflicted on him. The thought does not shock him. He has seen enough dead men now, seen enough life worthlessly spent.

He spits. Kicks the sand with his boot. Realises that most of the sailors and officers have dispersed, moving away from the scene. Anthony nudges him on the elbow. 'Come, let's walk.'

CHAPTER 22

A fortnight before they are due to leave for London, the air thick with crops soon to be harvested as the season slips from summer to autumn, Edmund rides away. He doesn't tell her that he's leaving. She wakes to find him gone, sheets pulled tight on his side of the bed. The day still in half-light, barely risen.

It is the first day in months that they've been apart, the first day she hasn't crept into their chamber as he napped, checking he was only tired and not fevered. It's a listless day without him. She tries to draw but gives up, walking instead through her kitchen garden, her mind distracted. What if he never returns? It has happened before, why not again?

Without him, she is surprised to find a loss of balance, as though she is standing on a floorboard that tips as she moves.

He returns home as the day dims, when the candles have been lit, the fires banked, the supper prepared, and she is relieved. There are puddles of exhaustion beneath his eyes, and he holds the sheepish expression of a man who has made a journey he shouldn't have, who should've stayed near his bed and hearth. They face each other in the entrance hall. He holds up his hands, a sign of peace. An apology on his lips: he should've told her before. An explanation in his mouth: he needed to visit Annabel's father, which in his illness, he'd neglected to do all summer. The father seemed placated and agreed to wait a while longer before pursuing a match for his widowed daughter.

Edmund hangs up his travelling cloak. It slides off, falling to the floor in a heap and he picks it up, hangs it again.

Dust circles the space between them. He opens his arms. She moves into them easily, head on his shoulder, his thumb resting against her spine.

CHAPTER 23

THEY ride, stop in taverns along the highway, kip in the inns, swap horses halfway along the journey, agree to pick up their two squat palfreys on their return. By afternoon on the third day, the lanes begin to widen and they pass more folk on the road, young men riding confidently to fulfil their errands. The city slowly unravels itself, a great grey spool of thread reaching out towards them.

They had heard from journeymen on the highways that the capital was in the clutches of the plague. But weathered traders had shrugged saying, d'you remember the outbreak before, must'a been over fifteen years ago? It's nothing compared to that. Eliza does not remember: fifteen years ago she was only a child, growing up in a forgotten middle town. Yet her husband seemed eager, fervent almost, to go, and Eliza had felt the same. She has heard murmurings about the city her whole life, listened to Henry's colourful stories, but never seen it, never felt it.

Until now.

London. It is an assault. Town houses are squeezed against each other, homes jostling for space, upper floors jettying overhead, crowding out the daylight. There is more of everything: more churches, more markets, more vendors, more strays, more graveyards. More shouts from windows, more screams of children, more clatter of hoof and shoe and bare feet and wagon wheel on the uneven streets. Tongues wag in different dialects and languages; she catches the lilt of French, and remembers her brother reciting his verbs to her after a day spent at school. But there are others she doesn't recognize at all, spoken by men with skin much darker than hers, darker than Francis's when he'd spent all summer beneath the sun.

They leave their horses and walk the final lanes to the inn, picking their way over the shit in the lanes, the smell rising and catching in her throat, past stacks of firewood leaning against the front of houses, the interiors already too cramped to accommodate it. They pass a crowd of people jostling for position, bodies crushing against each other. Someone knocks into Eliza and she feels Edmund's warm hand on the small of her back, hears his short sharp words to the careless offender.

'What is it?' She shouts over the din.

He grins. 'A cockfight.'

A mess of feathers and bone and blood.

'I didn't know you enjoyed suffering.'

'I don't go for that sport.'

'You gamble?'

He is next to her now, the crowd falling away behind them.

'I may have bet on a good cock a few times in my life.'

She swallows her laugh. 'You've been here before?'

'Several times.'

The inn, when they arrive, is small and dingy, the low ceilings soot stained. The landlord unlocks the door to their room with a rusted iron key and removes a cup as he leaves, remnants of the person who had been there the night before. Edmund wrinkles his nose and absently smooths the front of his jerkin before throwing open a shutter. The noise from the street below is with them once more. He looks out, then beckons to her. They stand cheek-to-cheek at the window, and he points, and tells her to lean just there and look past the thatch rooves and ashy chimneys, and there, just there, do you see it? She nods. Yes, she sees it. A slither of the Thames. Ships and boats of all sizes balance on its murky brown surface; masts propping up the heavens and men clambering over decks and oarsmen heaving their arms to their chests, carving their way across the river. Salt on her tongue, she watches the river dance to the beat and bustle of the city.

'Your father is a farmer then?' Lettice asks.

'A yeoman.'

A smirk. 'How quaint.'

Edmund had described his cousin's wife as *difficult* as they rode together to Walter's house, Eliza behind him, catching the words over his shoulder. She'd decided to reserve judgement – most women with a tongue or thought in their head can be described as difficult – but now Eliza flicks her gaze to her husband and suppresses a smile. There is a draught in the hall despite the fire in the grate, and the chill catches about Eliza's knees, shivering up her thighs as she sits on a hard wooden chair.

'He isn't particularly.'

Lettice ignores her and turns to Edmund. 'You must be very happy with your new wife.'

Edmund gives a tight smile. Eliza recognises his annoyance in the straightness of his back, in his reluctance to answer. 'Not so new, but yes.'

'My husband told me you were unwell?'

Edmund bobs his head. Eliza had seen her husband dispatch letters filled with his looping script to messenger boys, to take on the long journey to London. There had been replies too, multiple letters from Walter.

'Such a shame. Your brother was never ill.'

'It didn't help him in the end, Lettice.' Edmund's tone is clipped, and Eliza wants to go to him, squeeze his hand, glower at this cruel woman.

'He was such an impressive man. Such a tragedy.'

The sound of the street pours in for a moment before it is shut out again, a door closed, a soft groan, the hurrying of heavy footsteps. A man with flushed cheeks and a waistcoat straining about his belly appears.

'Walter,' Edmund takes his cousin's hand, a genuine smile pushing at the corners of his mouth. The newcomer begins apologising for his lateness, the familiar golden hair inherent within the Cecil line bouncing slightly as he describes how a cart in the road had simply blocked the whole of London. Lettice softens slightly at the sight of her husband, who wipes his face with a linen cloth and greets Eliza. The men are away then, discussing rent prices and wool prices and Walter starts on about his hawking, 'Magnificent creature, such a delight . . .' and they leave the room, heads close together.

Eliza doesn't question why the men must talk alone, leaving her with this bitter woman. Her father did it all the time, long conversations with male friends, leaving his wife excluded in the hall. Ma always practised such restraint.

'I suppose you'll be having children.' Lettice studies her nails, something caught in her voice.

'I suppose.'

'Edmund doesn't seem ready for fatherhood. There's so much to adjust to since Samuel's death.'

Eliza fixes her gaze on the woman, trying to decipher her game. Lettice doesn't look up.

'It isn't something we've discussed.'

'But you will.'

'What is there to discuss? As wives, isn't it our primary purpose?' She pushes her hands against her stomach, feels the answer of flesh and muscle beneath her gown and can't imagine something living beneath. It wouldn't be possible, anyhow: the absence of intimacy in her marriage grows more noticeable each day. And what is that, which seems to have crept stealthily upon Eliza, that she refuses to look in the face? Longing.

'Not all wives.'

A wife unable to carry, or unable to produce a child that lives. A nightmare festering its way into daily life. The impatience of a husband waiting for his wife to do her God-given duty, blaming her when she cannot.

'I'm sorry.'

'I don't need your pity. I have Walter.' Lettice is defensive, a mask for tragedy. 'It's you who should be pitied.'

Lettice excuses herself when the men return. Walter takes them to the long gallery, the jewel of his house which although more modest than Cecil Hall, is still impressive. There are a few tapestries, a painted map of London. But the prize of Walter's collection is a miniature, a painted face that sits in the palm of his hand.

Eliza stares, gorges upon it. Amidst the rich background of brilliant blue is a woman. A ruff cups her pointed chin, and extending across her body is a fur-lined doublet of black velvet, embroidered with golden leaves. The painting, its detail, how the artist must've peered along a brush as delicate as a single strand of hair, holds Eliza spellbound. The men talk of the subject; Walter explains how she is a Countess of some neighbouring county, starts gossiping about her family. All the while the Countess, a woman Eliza will never know and never meet, stares back unblinking, as though listening, her face recorded for eternity in the most intricate of brushstrokes.

'It's beautiful,' she murmurs.

'The seller assured me it's a Teerlinc,' Walter beams, handing her the miniature. 'Can't be too careful though, plenty of counterfeits circulating.'

She mulls the foreign name in her mind. Teerlinc. That there are men who exist to paint such beauties, or perhaps that paint to exist – to make a permanence in a world that is too quick to forget – makes her prickle with excitement, with possibility.

'Does he have other works?' she asks.

'Oh yes. *She* painted for the Queen herself. Levina Teerlinc is known for her miniatures.'

Eliza stares from the circle in her palm to Walter, and back. A woman.

'An extraordinary woman, if you ask me,' Walter says. 'A rare breed. The weaker sex aren't known for their creativity.' Eliza grips the miniature in her palm and wonders if she preferred Lettice's company after all.

'I didn't know you liked paintings,' Edmund murmurs, and the way he looks at her, searchingly, taking her in, his mouth close to her ear, placates her.

'I've never seen one before, at least, not like this.' Perhaps she really is quaint. A silly country girl, daughter of an overreaching yeoman.

'But you're skilled at drawing.'

Her face widens in surprise. He who misses nothing, who is watchful but never interfering.

'Forgive me. I accidentally found some of your drawings.'

'It's no matter. They're silly really – '

'Would you like to paint?' Edmund says, ignoring Walter who is ahead, pointing at another wall hanging.

Eliza glances at the stranger still nestled in the cup of her hand, and finds she longs to create something as intricate and perfect as this. She looks at Edmund, eye to eye, mouth to mouth, remembering the drawings she used to stash beneath her mattress and, hardly believing they are having such a discussion, nods.

∞

'That Teerlinc is definitely a fake,' Edmund laughs, as they ride steadily back to their lodgings, the horse swaying beneath them. 'Poor Walter's been duped. There's no way the family would have sold such a piece.'

'Mm.'

Counterfeit or nay, she doesn't care. She'd held a piece of art. Gloried in its colours. Learnt that women have existed, do exist, who paint and create, who have been paid for it, who have been appointed by royalty.

'What is it?' he asks over his shoulder.

The city heaves and sprawls about them. The early evening lures a different kind of people: those rushing to get home, pulling children in their wake before dusk gives in to the night; gentlemen heading outside the city's walls to sordid establishments; link boys, their torches held aloft to guide folk from one place to another.

'I'm not sure Lettice and I will be friends,' she says.

'I did warn you. She's always hated me.'

'Why?'

'She's resentful. She doesn't think I'm a capable heir of Cecil Hall. I'd wager she thinks Walter would be a much better owner.'

'She was awful to you, what she said about Samuel.'

He pulls hard on the reins stopping their horse just short of a man who staggers in front of them. A waft of beer chases the air, marking a local tavern.

'He was always the favourite,' he says, so quietly she nearly misses it beneath the thrum of the street. 'Did she say anything else to you?'

'That she pitied me.'

Edmund urges the horse onwards, and the beast obediently lurches into a trot beneath them. 'I wouldn't listen to her. She's a sour woman, trying to bring people down into her own misery.'

'Tell me about Samuel.'

She says it so plainly that Edmund rubs his hand over his mouth, unable to avoid the question. The other tables are empty; dark has descended outside, pressing in through the gaps in the shutters. They have eaten the bread and cheese brought by the innkeeper, and Edmund sips his second cup of beer. She is still on her first, not wanting the fuzziness at her edges when she wants to talk, to understand. 'You asked for him when you were sick.'

He clasps his cup tightly, knuckles pale and protruding. 'Sam fell from his horse during a hunt.'

It takes her a moment to understand the violence of this death. A man falling from his stallion, hitting the ground. The breaking of bones in his neck, down his spine. The hush of the green forest about him. The men rushing their horses towards the broken body. Had they watched him fall, the sight impressed upon their eyes for years to come? A body in unstoppable motion before irreversible change. For how long after the fall had he lived? Was he already dead when the others got to him, an instant of pain for an eternity of bliss? Or did he live through the agony, waiting for death?

She doesn't ask which ending he was given.

'That's terrible.'

He shakes his head, eyes fixed on something just over her shoulder. She reaches for his hand resting on the table, taking his palm gently in her own.

'What was he like?'

'Lettice spoke the truth when she called him impressive, Father had stepped back and Sam was already running Cecil Hall. He was a natural, made for the life of riches and feasts, the hunts and games. He had such life about him, an easiness around others, and he loved the attention. We were very different.' There is admiration, but also a bitterness, sharp like sour fruit lurking beneath. 'I was often ill, whereas Sam seemed invincible. His death upset the order that everyone had come to expect, even though he was older. Yet one afternoon he was gone and everything he had . . . his life, Cecil Hall, it all fell to me.'

He stops, ghosts pressing in. Takes a long drink, emptying his cup. Sets it down. Their hands break apart, and she feels awkward, not knowing where to put it before settling it in her lap.

'How else were you different?' She wonders, fleetingly, if the brothers had looked the same.

'Sam wasn't so good with money. God love him, he was a skilled gambler.'

'Cockfighting?'

'Yes,' he says, and Eliza recalls the crush of people they had passed when they arrived. Once there were two more in that crowd, two inseparable golden brothers, purses at the ready, eyes wide for the blood sport. 'But he enjoyed dice and cards too. It preoccupied him, probably consumed him, although he never spoke about it to me. When the ledgers finally came to me, there were rents he hadn't collected, and gaps where money had come in, yet no clue to where it had been spent. I fixed his debts, to my detriment. I'm not half as popular with our tenants after collecting in the rents he'd let slip.' He raises an eyebrow. 'Yet Father still worried. He wanted some extra coffers, to feel secure.'

She remembers the heft of her marriage portion, the cart of goods that trundled along the lanes from her father's house to Cecil Hall. 'You needed a marriage contract.'

He looks embarrassed, whether for the fact that their union had been so blatantly transactional or that his family had once struggled financially, she isn't sure. Likely both. 'Exactly.'

'No doubt, Nicholas wanted an heir for Cecil Hall as well. Unless Sam had – '

'He didn't.' For the second time in a day, Eliza balls a fist into her stomach. 'If Sam were still alive, we wouldn't have met,' he says, voice forcibly lighter.

'Then you really must resent him,' she says mildly, realising as it falls from her mouth that she wants him to contradict her. When was it that she started wanting things from Edmund?

The innkeeper brings two more cups, and she notices a small midge in her drink, struggling to heave its way out of the liquid. She lifts it out with her finger and places its sodden body on the table, so she doesn't see his expression when he says, 'I don't resent him.'

She glances up at him. Candlelight bounces off his face, where a streaking line of a blush creeps below his cheekbone. They are leaning in, as though their bodies have magnetised to each other of their own accord. She could reach for him, could run the back of her fingers down his cheek.

A squeal of wood across the floor, as a tall, broad-backed man with dark hair pushes out a bench and stands from another table, drawing her eye.

A breath.

He has come back to her, to make true the promises they made

156

in the crumbling inn in the deserted forest, a place meant only for them. The man turns.

It is not him, not Francis. She cannot trace the features she knew so well onto this stranger. Her rush of anticipation leaks away, and Edmund leans back, changes the subject, muses what they should do tomorrow, his expression guarded. She could kick herself. The moment they had shared, as bright and rare as Halley's passing comet, moved on, leaving only a fast-fading silvery track.

CHAPTER 24

'WHERE are we going?' she asks as they weave through the people on the street, the city awake since dawn, fires already lit, errands already run. They have been walking, cutting through lanes, darting through alleys, and sweat gathers at Eliza's back.

'You'll see,' he smiles, a rare playfulness to him. She wants to capture that playfulness, stopper it in a phial, keep it with her.

Eventually Edmund leads her inside a dim shop, the faded wood absorbing the sunlight. The cramped room is filled with heaps of fine powders, spices, great bottles of oil lined upon shelves and barrels stacked in a corner. One of them is open and from it oozes a thick clear liquid, with a honey-like consistency and smelling of forests.

The grocer emerges down the stairs in a corner, wood groaning beneath his heavy tread. Eliza stands back, allows the men to do the talking, voices vying for space in the treasure-filled room.

'Pigments?' the shopkeeper asks, looking Edmund up then down as though assessing his wealth and how obsequious to behave. The man points to the piles of powder. There is rich indigo the colour of hot summer nights, white lead brighter than the petals of a daisy, yellow the colour of a whore's ruff. 'I have others too,' the grocer says with a bow of his head, evidently deciding from the cut of Edmund's doublet that he has a bulging purse, and disappears back up the stairs.

Edmund turns to her. 'What would you like?'

She stares.

'So you can paint,' he says, misunderstanding her silence as incomprehension, rather than disbelief.

'Are you sure?' she asks. Teerlinc's miniature in the palm of her hand.

'What do you mean?'

'It wouldn't . . . anger you if I painted?'

He frowns, bemused. 'Why would it?'

She realises she doesn't know why. It just is. Women create quietly, at the edges, leaving the flourishes, the preening, the swaggering to men.

'Choose any colours you want,' he says.

The shopkeeper reappears, a cluster of small jars in his hands. He unstoppers one and tilts it towards her. Inside is a rich red powder, deep like earth, thick like blood. Another is bluer than lupines, which he calls azurite.

'Your wife has good taste,' the grocer says as Eliza's eyes linger on the boldest colours.

'She does,' Edmund murmurs.

She keeps telling Edmund that it's fine, really it's fine, but he says, 'We won't get these at home.'

He buys paper, chalk, resin to bind the powder together, two fine paintbrushes made from wiry hairs plucked from the back of a hog. She likes the way he reaches for his purse, his casual, self-deprecating movements as he hands over the coins, likes that he doesn't clink the silver loudly, isn't intent on displaying his wealth for the shopkeepers to marvel at. Of course, the shopkeeper does marvel; any man who behaves with such ease around money must be accustomed to its abundance. But the shopkeeper prides himself in being professional, keeping his face plain, although his eyes give him away, lingering too long at Edmund's purse after he has fastened it at his belt.

It is only once they are back at the inn, the purchases laid on the counterpane in the room, Edmund's purse notably lighter than before that she says, 'Why would you spend so much on . . . this?' *On me.*

He narrows his eyes playfully, 'Don't tell me now that you don't want it. The shopkeeper would be devastated to have to give back the coin I gave him.'

'Of course I want it, it's not that,' she says quietly, moved and embarrassed by his generosity. Before him, she had never had anything bought for her. Not like this. Not something so superfluous, so unnecessary. Ma allowed her sometimes to choose fruits at market, or they might have gone to the draper's stall to pick out a yard of fabric to be made into something, choosing cloth that would last, that would be easy to work a needle through. And Eliza was one of the luckiest in town, growing up in a large house, a bedchamber of her own, glass in their front windows.

Perhaps Edmund is learning that her father's dowry did not represent the wealth she was used to; perhaps he is realising what it was like for her, living with Thomas; perhaps he remembers how they once thought there could be no happiness in their marriage. Whatever the reason, he moves towards her and kisses her cheek, and says, so simply, 'Because I wanted to.'

⁂

They lie in their rented bed, the quiet punctuated by sounds of the sleepy city; the cry of a baby in the dark, the echo of voices in adjacent rooms, the distant song of a fiddle drifting in with the moonlight through the cracks around the shutters. Eliza has always slept surrounded by fields, unbroken by people, with only the creaks of the trees and shrieks of fowl for night company. The sound of other lives is a comfort.

She tells him this in the dark and feels him shift onto his side, towards her. 'I like the noise too.'

Eliza hesitates, then mirrors him, turning her body to face him. Only his outline is visible, becoming firmer and clearer as she blinks. He moves his arm, and rests his palm on that soft place where her neck meets her shoulder. She finds his other hand in the darkness and feels the bump of his knuckles, laces her fingers through his.

It is strange to find yourself in the arms of someone else, someone you swore was the wrong man. To find yourself in the arms that aren't those of the person you love most.

And yet Eliza finds herself full of contradictions, capable of feelings she previously thought could never exist. So much of what she thought she knew about herself has changed. She has outgrown parts of herself, shedding her skin like a grass snake, leaving trails of herself behind to wither in the dark.

He sits in bed, removing off his nightshirt. She watches the light and shadow fall around the tight muscles on his back; watches him fold the shirt, lie it on the floor; watches him pause a moment before turning to her. They haven't spoken; the room is quiet, waiting for the first words of the morning, unaware they have already been said with a look, which passed between wife and husband when they woke.

She had awoken thinking of Edmund. They'd fallen asleep with their hands still interlocked, a fist the size of a heart. She watched him open his eyes, the flick of his long fair eyelashes, and realised that he'd already been awake, waiting for her to join him at the surface. His eyes had darted between her own, left to right, as though reading what was written there. Slowly, he moved his hand to her waist, and he leant in, putting his mouth on hers. It had made her shiver, made her press herself closer to him, skin separated by only the thin fabric of their night clothes. It made her want in a way that she hadn't wanted in a long time.

She has never seen him properly before. When he was ill, she looked away, her mind firmly on helping an invalid. But now she looks. Sees he is slender, thinly muscled beneath the surface, poised and firm from years of hunting, riding, hawking, archery. She runs her fingers up his torso and down his back. She remembers another body, which was sun-browned and thickened from labouring the fields.

The blackbirds are outside playing in the dawn as his body is hot above hers. Her nightgown is lost in the sheets. The bones of his hip push into the softness of her thigh. His golden hair falls low over his eyes as he props himself above her, one hand against the wall, the other holding her. There is the dimple on his chin that she has always wanted to rest her little finger in, and she does it now, and he smiles and she shrugs. She feels relief, that it could be like this. It is not the thing she had dreaded in the wintry first months of their marriage. She wants this. She had reached for him as he was reaching for her.

She closes her eyes and Francis is there. She forces her eyes open, looks into these blue, blue eyes.

It is easy, not like before, so smooth he makes her breath hitch at the back of her throat, gasp in a way she never has – and she sees how he takes joy in her pleasure – and she wonders, briefly, how often he has done this. Everything feels different – not just in body, the way their bodies slip and fit so surprisingly well together, but in mind too. This time, with this man, there is a different kind of weight; not the weight of keeping secrets and the threat of danger and the thrill of first love, but instead the weight of consummation, of husband and wife, the physical binding of their marriage.

And the snaking, deepening weight of betrayal.

It frightens her: to be so vulnerable, so exposed to a man she is still learning. And it frightens her too, that she could be so split in half; devoted to one man and yet, now, so desirous, so willing, to lie with another.

She stares at the dark patches of soot on the ceiling which mark the room's edges, Edmund's legs entangled about hers. She feels grief and joy. In consummating one vow, she has broken her promise to a man who might still be alive, who might be thinking of her and what happened to them; and yet she is forging another bond, full of promise, that causes in her a rush of elation.

She wonders if she can hold the tides of feeling for them both. If it is possible to be true to them both. *Stay with me.* She sighs, and her breath through her teeth sounds like the Thames as it rushes over its pebbled banks.

'What is it?' he says.

She kisses his neck, and he wraps his arms around her, preventing her temporarily from climbing out of bed. Part of her wants to stay, nestled into him, whilst the other part feels guilt that needs a greater distraction. She breaks from his arms, forcing herself out of bed, bare feet on the floor, and dresses herself. As she pulls on her smock, eyes on the cracks of light breaking through the shutters, she realises that there will come a time when Edmund knows her body better than Francis ever did.

CHAPTER 25

THE dawn hasn't reached Francis yet; it hesitates, a timid servant on the horizon. From his vantage point, he can make out the edge of the world, the line where the sea kisses the sky, and ahead he sees the pinprick of the other ships' lanterns. A trio in convoy, a constellation floating across a rippling sky. At the front is the flagship, the Pelican, which Drake had renamed the Golden Hind before they left the shores of Port St Julian. The port where they left behind the body of the executed man. Sometimes Francis dreams about dead men. He dreams about finding a corpse on a deserted shore, only to realise that he had been the killer.

They had set sail again, through the Straits and out into the Pacific. Francis watches it; the ocean, great dark vastness, stretching before him like a sentence. He shivers, glancing at the sand in the half hourglass, which has barely begun to fall. It will be a long time before he can sleep. His tongue plays at the tooth in his mouth which rocks back and forth, then quite abruptly, comes away completely. Iron and salt flood his tongue. He spits blood and tooth overboard, a piece of him lost to the watery depths.

He can't seem to shake her from his mind this night: her tooth near the front of her mouth that juts out slightly, an irresistible taunt whenever she smiles. The oval birthmark on her neck. Her determination that could cow kings. He remembers her forehead touching his, the sweat on her skin. How his body had curled around hers like a shell.

But those aren't, really, the things you remember about a person. You start to lose the individual brushstrokes that comprise them, that comprised who you were when you were with them. Memory, an adulterer to truth. Instead you remember their physical impact on your body; how they made you feel.

He remembers the warmth in the base of his stomach when he was with her, his unwavering belief in their future. The ache at the back of his teeth after their last argument, which even now makes him clench his jaw at the memory. He should've followed her. The feeling of his knees giving way when he learnt that he couldn't get back to her. The tightness in his chest when he realised that he loved her, how the idea of losing her would've been the end of him. And how that proved true: the old him, that lad back home with steady earth beneath his boots, is lost to memory.

He feels it still, that tightness in his chest. But it is harder, coarser, will take no prisoners. When he returns home, he plans to pay what is owed and take what is his.

And what of her? Will she wait for him to return from the edges of the earth?

The sail above flaps and snaps and his hand tightens about the thick rope that reaches above him. The night is beginning to lighten. But he can see a gathering, a quickening of skies ahead. Charcoal on the horizon. A violent storm, a blinding fog, coming for them.

CHAPTER 26

THERE'S a boy on the street below when she opens the shutters. He appears to be waiting for someone, lounging against the wall of an opposite building, eyes snagging people as they pass. Then as though remembering himself, he stands upright, itches his scalp, rechecks his bag.

It is only when Eliza and Edmund have emerged from their room, that the innkeeper says, 'There's a boy for you. He says he has a letter for Edmund Cecil and he won't give it to no one else.'

Outside is noisy, the morning bringing tides of people trying to survive another day. Edmund's hand brushing Eliza's wrist as they cross the street, passing a trader carrying baskets of oysters to whom local women flock, and thread through the bustling of feet, hoof, paw, claw. As soon as the lad is in earshot Edmund introduces himself, asks, 'What news?'

The messenger, who can only be about twelve with barely a hair on his chin, reaches into his bag and produces a folded sheet of paper. Edmund hesitates before cracking the seal with his thumb and unfolding the letter. His eyes work frantically across the page before turning it over, looking for more words and finding none. A short, urgent note.

'What is it?' Eliza asks. Behind them a woman has begun to to argue with the oyster-seller, accusing him of cheating her out of change. Edmund's expression tells a story Eliza doesn't understand; he seems startled, his mouth filling with air for a sigh that doesn't arrive. He tucks the note away in the purse hanging at his belt. The lad shuffles impatiently, his job done, eager to earn his reward. Edmund pays him, the silver coin disappearing into his fist as he slips behind the heckling gaggle amassing around the oyster-seller.

The messenger will never know the significance of the news he has just delivered, nor how its contents will ripple across the years.

'Well?' she asks.

'Father is sick. I must go to him.'

'It is serious?'

The oyster man is swearing now, fingers pointing in anger, and Edmund guides Eliza by the arm into a side street where the gables overhang, blocking the overcast day. They are alone except for a stray pissing on a doorstep. 'I don't know,' he murmurs, words quick, colliding with the other. It occurs to her that his hold of her arm is steadying him. 'We'll travel to your family today and then I'll leave for—'

'I can come with you—'

'No, please . . . you must see your family.' There is no chance for further discussion; he guides her by the arm, sidestepping the seemingly disgraced oyster-seller – the argument in the street grown so loud and attracted such a crowd that Eliza's protests ('really, my family can wait, I'd prefer to be with you if your father is unwell') are lost – and hurries to the inn to settle the bill and ready the horses.

He rides ahead, cloak whipping behind him, setting the pace. London falls away behind them, its stench retreating to be replaced with the familiar damp scent of fields, earth and leaves mulched beneath hooves. He is silent, withdrawing into himself, and Eliza understands: the thought of losing the family who made you, shaped you, would diminish any man's words. After Nicholas is buried deep in the earth, she and Walter will be Edmund's only remaining kin. Edmund and she: oath-takers, bonded thick as blood.

On the second morning they are reunited with their palfreys they left at the inn on their way south, and on the third they reach the edge of her father's land, Worcestershire darkening beneath an assembling storm. They climb from their horses and stand beneath the gatehouse.

'Ride safely,' she says, thinking of the route they took after their wedding, a few hours ride north and east, out of Worcestershire and into Warwickshire. 'Send Nicholas my love.'

Edmund closes his eyes for a moment and his hands come up to his mouth as though he is praying.

'All will be well,' she comforts, 'I'm sure.'

His thumb strokes her jaw and then he is mounting his horse, spurring the beast onwards. The rain comes, rounded droplets spattering outwards, creating dark spots on her travelling cloak. Her palfrey whickers softly; the animal needs rest and water, and Eliza leads her towards the stable, a wet hand stroking the horse's muzzle. So she doesn't see Edmund pause at the turn in the lane, hesitating, pinching the skin at his neck, before racing away into the smothering rain.

⁂

They sit around the table in the great hall, just as they used to, her father saying a prayer of thanks for the meat at the table, the fowls of the air, the beasts of the field. It's strange to be back in this house that holds so many memories. The smell of the place hits the back of her throat, dried wheat and woodsmoke. Ma's bunches of lavender and wild clary hang over doorways, their crisp, dead petals decorating the floor. Nothing has altered – the beams across the ceiling, the deep hearth, the worn oak table – yet everything seems smaller than before. She's still wary of her father, but less fearful, safer under his roof than ever before. Now she belongs to another man, what can Thomas do to her?

The four of them eat from pewter plates, with knives, spoons, hands. Ma sits beside her and keeps glancing at Eliza as though she's a phantom returned from the dead. Before this, before the wedding, before anything notable ever happened, they'd never spent more than a night apart. Henry is opposite, the candlelight casting the bruises about his eyes into violent relief. The wheel of time has brought the harvest again, and her brother is out each day with his scythe, or in the barns tying the wheat, or working with his father negotiating sales. It burns a man out, and Henry, a man not made for working the fields, is burning out swiftly.

Now, Henry takes a long slow sip from his cup, and Eliza tries and fails to catch his eye. He hasn't smiled once since she arrived, despite the long, hard embrace he'd given her as greeting.

Thomas eyes Eliza's new gown and the matching moss green sleeves which drape upon the table. She saw him touch her travelling cloak when he thought no one was watching, rubbing the quality of the kersey between his fingers and thumb. Is it jealousy? Does he see how her fortunes have altered, just as he planned, and yet his have remained the same? Eliza works to conceal her triumph, but perhaps he senses it regardless.

'What business did Edmund have in London?' Thomas asks.

'He wanted to visit his cousin and show me the city,' Eliza says.

'All that way just for a visit?'

'I came all this way to visit you.'

He snorts. 'You're an overly sentimental woman.' Beneath the table Ma squeezes Eliza's hand. 'He wouldn't journey all that way for a mere visit. He couldn't even stay to sup with his in-laws. A man with things to do, I'd warrant.'

Thomas's words release a flurry of unwanted thoughts in her mind, as though he has removed the roof of a dovecote and caused the birds within, their pearlescent wings, to beat and thrash and take flight. Had Walter and Edmund shared private words when they left her with Lettice's spite?

'Nicholas is unwell and Edmund needed to go to him,' she says.

'Poor man,' Ma mutters.

Thomas ignores all reference to Nicholas's ailing, his eyes fastened on Eliza, head cocked to one side. 'You don't like that do you? Not knowing your husband's business. You thought you knew everything when you lived here.'

The storm beats on outside, the rain unrelenting since Eliza arrived, pouring out its heart. Henry moves his slice of mutton with his knife, trailing rings of blood on his plate. She smells the uneasy rise of metal.

'You need to tell her,' Henry says, looking up for the first time.

'Remember your place,' Thomas says.

'I will if you don't.'

'Shut your mouth.'

'Or what? What will you threaten me with this time, Thomas?'

She's never heard Henry call their father by his name.

'Get out.' Her father's words a familiar song.

Two strides and Henry is around the table, knife in his hand, the blade pointing at his father's neck. Eliza catches her brother's eyes and there's a wildness she doesn't recognise.

'Tell her,' Henry snarls, voice guttural.

'Tell me what?'

Thomas doesn't speak. Henry closes the gap, so the blade rests against their father's throat, where the skin pales under the pressure.

'Francis,' her brother says.

His name aloud, like a body dragged from a riverbed.

A moment: time expands before it speeds up.

'What about him?' Eliza asks, her every sinew, nerve and muscle taut.

Thomas slowly picks up his cup and sips it, as though his son isn't holding a blade to his neck. He seems so calm, so uncaring, but his hand betrays him, slipping slightly, causing beer to escape the side of his mouth, trickling down his chin. Eliza wants to grab his face and squeeze the words out of him, wants to scream for him to answer. But she can't. She is transfixed on him, waiting. They are all at Thomas's mercy and he doesn't miss the irony. He puts down the cup, intertwines his fingers together in his lap.

He looks at his only daughter and says, 'You were making a whore of yourself. Who would've had you if you'd carried on? Where would you be if I hadn't intervened?'

His words are stones in water, the ripples bursting out from the epicentre, affecting the lives of all that it touches. She doesn't recall standing, but she stumbles back, bench hitting the backs of her knees, Ma's hand at her elbow, steadying her.

'What do you mean?'

'I was protecting this family.'

'What did you do to him?' Her voice rises like a flood.

'I paid a man to take care of it.'

'Thomas!' Ma gasps, 'What have you done . . .'

'Is he dead?' Eliza chokes out, spit and sound coming from deep within her. The picture comes back to her. Clear like a memory. Vivid like a nightmare. A cadaver face down in a body of water.

Henry glances at Eliza, and in his lapse of attentions, Thomas grabs hold of the blade, ripping it out of his son's hand and skidding it across the table, where it collides with a plate, sending both scattering to the floor. Henry draws back as Thomas stands. Eliza takes another step towards her father, head tilting upwards to face him, hardly feeling Ma's fingers upon her arm, nor hearing Ma's words of Thomas, please, Eliza, please dove –

'Tell me.'

He holds up his hands, as though to placate her, as though he is a just and innocent man. 'No blood on my hands, daughter. I asked them not to kill him.'

She hates him. She wants to watch him suffer. Wants to see him hurt in the way she has hurt, all those countless times. 'Is that to appease your conscience? Does that allow you to sleep like a babe at night?'

She reaches for all he has taught her – for violence, for anger. It is easier than grief or hurt or shock. She wants to upturn the table, watch it crash upon the floor. She wants to set the house alight, watch everything Thomas owns transform to flame. Instead she shoves Thomas, the flat of her palm thudding against his chest. She balls her fist to beat against him, but he catches her wrist in his hand and squeezes, sending a spear of pain up her arm.

'Where in God's blood did they take him?'

Her attack, her blasphemy, temporarily stills the family. There is only the sound of breathing, of rain, of the fire hissing in the hearth.

She twists and wrenches her wrist free as Thomas's hand raises, but she meets it, positioning her arm to cover her cheek. She pushes against his hand, and her defence, momentarily, holds. She who is no longer his to harm. But Thomas overpowers her, his other hand swinging across to meet her face. The roaring sting on her skin, the crunch of her teeth coming together. Ringing in her ears, like metal being hammered into shape. That faint, soothing melody.

She staggers, as she has done so many times before, hating herself for being so weak. Ruth lets out a shriek, reaches for her daughter, is shouting at Thomas, how, how could he do this. How could he live with himself beneath God? Henry bends down to pick up the knife, has it in his hand, is shouting if he touches Eliza again, Thomas'll have it, he'll be in for it.

'I don't know where they took him, I didn't ask,' Thomas says eventually. She expects to hear victory, the sound of trumpets and bugles in his voice, but he is agitated, breathing ragged. The open rebellion of his family. 'You brought this on yourself.'

CHAPTER 27

I T is late. Eliza lies on the bed in her childhood bedchamber, her body leaden. It smells of a room left vacant, of mould, straw and unwashed hair. She never noticed how shabby the room was, with its bare yellowing walls, shuttered draughty windows, the skittering of mice or wrens in the thatch above. Henry lies at the other end, his feet next to her cheek which bruises steadily. It's what they did as children, when her brother would sneak through to her room and tell her stories – about giants who first walked the land, sirens who swam the ocean depths, harpies who soared the skies – when she couldn't sleep or when one of them had had a belt to the back of their legs.

Her anger has cooled, and Father's words are heavy on her, as though a great rock has been placed upon her chest, pinning her down. She cannot imagine moving her body ever again. The weight of Thomas's truth unleashes a chasm of memories. When she learnt Francis was missing. Waking up to remember that he was still gone. Their final argument. Her father finding her scrubbing her bloodstained sheet. Her thoughts are feathers falling from the sky, chaotic, uncatchable.

'He's alive, at least,' Henry says.

'Surely he would've returned by now?' she asks.

The loss is closer here, in her old bedchamber. He'd been in this room, lain beside her in this bed. Sadness expands like a lung inside her, an empty space that can't be filled. Almost a year, a full cycle of the seasons in his absence. She is exhausted and glad Henry can't see her face when she rubs her eyes, saltwater hot.

'He could be trapped somewhere, unable to get away. He mightn't have the money to get home.' He doesn't say what flits across both their minds; that perhaps Francis doesn't want to come home, that perhaps he has found a better life elsewhere.

Eliza brings her hands to her face, blocking out the chamber. 'I keep thinking this wouldn't have happened if Francis and I had never . . .'

Never what? Never met, never been two children playing in the yard, never grown up, never followed the inevitable line where things had ended, to first loves and first lovers, groping in the dark for something more than themselves. Never been.

'Thomas wants to burden you with the guilt, so he never has to.' Henry swings his feet to the floor, sitting upright. 'Your marriage to Edmund would've separated you and Francis.'

'But it wouldn't have been enough,' she says. Thomas must have felt his control slipping, like fingers doused in butter, when he'd learnt that she'd been secretly carrying on with Francis, had perhaps given her maidenhead to him, had stolen the pocketknife. He realised that his threats and bruisings amounted to little. Such unwomanly defiance needed punishment. A loveless marriage to a stranger wasn't enough; after he'd finished, she would feel pain like she'd never known. She'd grieve as though Francis had died. And Thomas, puppet-master, would once again hold all the strings in his palm.

'No,' Henry agrees. The amber candlelight tosses his shadow on the wall behind him, as though a restless giant sits with them, watching.

'How did you find out?'

'I'd been out with a friend and came in through the back, and overheard Thomas talking to someone. Usually I don't care what he has to say, but I caught your name. See, Liza, I'm sorry, but I'd barely heard him speak of you, so hearing him talk about you to a man I didn't know made me stop and listen.' She can see it; Henry unlocking the backdoor into the kitchen, his ears tipped pink from the fresh air outside as he waited in the hall. Truth-catcher, secrets-smuggler. 'He explained how he'd paid a man to kidnap Francis, didn't care where they took him, that he didn't want to know. The less he knew, the better.'

Kidnap. The word like a farce, spun into tales to frighten children.

Her brother hesitates, the words reshuffling in his mouth, as he omits the parts she doesn't need to hear. 'He was bragging. Kept saying how he was rising.' A rasping laugh rips from Henry's throat. 'He called himself a gentleman.'

'What did you do?'

'Confronted him.'

'Hen—'

'I had to say something. How dare he, scum of a man. My loyalty has always been to you, and anyway, what had I to lose?'

'Henry.' She could cry for him, too.

'I told him he had to tell you, that you deserve the truth and should hear it from him. If not, I would tell you myself.'

'When did it get so dangerous?' she asks, eyeing the shadow, thinking of the wildness in her brother's eyes, the blade pressed to her father's throat.

'It's been worse since you left.'

'I don't want you to get hurt.'

'I'm not sure how much more I can take.' His suffocation rolls off him like a smell of something rotten. His mind, skills, dreams, wasted in this house.

'You've outgrown this place.'

'You could say that.'

'Couldn't you marry?' Her, the hypothetical wife, bringing a marriage portion of opportunity. A union could bring him freedom.

His eyes track across the beams of the ceiling until they slowly, slowly, fall on her face. 'You know a wife wouldn't suit me. I don't think I'd suit her either.' She thinks of Henry sidling into the house through the backdoor, and wonders who he was with.

'Careful, brother.'

After Henry leaves, after he has kissed her cheek goodnight and she has blown out her candle and the chamber smells of burnt fat and smoke, she thinks of Francis. Thoughts of him are like a pulse within her, beating in time to her own heart. She wonders if he is lying awake somewhere too, his mind tossed about like rabid seas. If he is somewhere now, trying to get home to her.

❦

Henry rides beside her, eyes scanning the lanes for trouble, dagger glinting at his hip as they make the journey to Cecil Hall. It takes longer in the rain which still falls, catching on eyelashes. Mud churns beneath the horses' hooves. They pass a cart, its wheels sunk into the squelch, the driver cursing. The ground seems thick enough to catch and drag her under.

They skirt the edges of Birmingham to the clank and clang of metalwork, the cutlers, the nailers, the smiths. She tries not to think about her own blacksmith, how Birmingham could've been their safe harbour. But each peal of metal on metal brings him back to her: leaning against the wall of his father's workshop, the smudge of clay on his neck, his voice whispering in her ear. The man, she thinks, her thumb twisting her wedding band, who is not hers at all.

When they arrive at Cecil Hall, Henry pisses round the back of the stables, swaps his horse, kisses her cheek, and rides for home, racing against the descent of darkness. Eliza stands in the stable, her hand on the palfrey's neck, waiting until the sound of Henry's ride, hoof on soft ground, has retreated to silence. Only then does she notice that one of the stalls is empty, a horse missing.

She knocks the front door as though she is a stranger seeking refuge, not a wife returning home. Dorothy greets her, and the warmth Eliza feels towards her makes her want to cry. The older woman's eyes linger at Eliza's cheek where Thomas left his mark.

Eliza listens for Edmund as she removes her boots and her safeguard, the hem slick with the road's mulch. She waits for his hand to brush her arm. But the only sound is her and Dorothy's tread climbing the stairs to her chamber, and the only hand that touches hers is the kindly servant's. Eliza removes her coif as they walk, hair tumbling loose, runs her hand across her scalp, smells the lankness of her hair.

'How is Nicholas?'

Dorothy busies herself with folding Eliza's safeguard in her arms to take to the washhouse, explains how he is much better, how he had a fever of sorts.

The fire in the bedchamber is ashen and grey, as though it has not been lit in days.

'Where's Edmund?'

Dorothy frowns a moment. 'Once it was clear that Nicholas was improving, he had to leave.'

In the days that pass she kneads dough to make bread, the mixture sticking to her fingers, and scrubs off her skin in the washhouse, washing coverlets and hanging them to dry in the courtyard where the moat reflects them like pale sails. She picks herbs from the garden and strings them from the beams in the kitchen to dry out in the autumn air that whips through the house. The activity, the commonplace, the safety in daily action, doesn't calm her. The comprehension of what her father did to her, to Francis, is steady, like water leaking through a ceiling, dripping until the floors of her mind are full, drowned.

Edmund's absence lingers in the walls and the halls of the house, making her feel uneasy. He left no note, no explanation. At night, after evening prayers, when she asks God for sleep and finds He still won't grant it, when she feels like she is a beetle crawling up the sides of her mind, she reaches for the paper Henry gave her on her wedding day, and starts to draw, great insects with shiny bodies and veined wings.

She visits her father-in-law's private quarters, expecting to find him in bed, but instead he sits beside the window in a pool of morning sun, looking out at the roll of the land below. An arras hangs on one wall, a woman on her knees in supplication, a gathering of men standing before her, as though determining her fate.

'Are you well?' she asks.

'Quite, thank you. Just old, Eliza,' he smiles. 'You'll feel it too, someday.'

The lines of his face look deeper than she remembers, carving their way about his eyes, from too much smiling, and his forehead, from too much frowning. His hair is pearly at his temples, as though transformed by an alchemist from the gold that traces through his family. She thinks of how Nicholas has survived the loss of his wife and son. Aging and slowing in the face of grief.

'Edmund returned as soon as he heard you were ill.'

'I'm sorry to have interrupted your trip.'

'Where is he now?'

The old man steeples his fingers beneath his chin. 'There was a dispute between some tenants that he had to attend, but nothing to worry yourself with.' Nicholas looks back out of the window. 'He won't be gone much longer, I'm sure. He'll be missing you.'

CHAPTER 28

S H E is out blackberrying, her fingers scarlet and sticky, her basket full. Sweet juice trickles steadily through the weave of wood. Something pulls at her to return home, but nature keeps giving, revealing new brambled bushes abundant with berries. It isn't until late afternoon that she returns, hunching over the kitchen table to sort through the basket, picking out the flies and earwigs which live within the berries, eyes squinting in the vanishing light.

There is a sound on the step down to the kitchen. The rustle of a body leaning against a wall. The shadow from the wall masks half of his face, and when he steps into the low sun seeping through the window, she sees how neglected he looks; shirt creased, yellowed with sweat about the neck, eyes tired and bloodshot. She is relieved to see him and also annoyed. They have been adrift since London, a distance welling between them.

'I didn't know you'd returned,' she says, consonants sharp as a whip.

'I only arrived earlier this afternoon. I'm sorry I wasn't here when you returned from Worcestershire.'

'I heard you've been busy – '

'Disputing tenants, one arguing that the other is encroaching on his land, and before that Father being unwell – '

'He seems much better now,' she says, and they both pause, taking the measure of the other. Edmund's lips part, but for a moment he is quiet.

'A relief,' he says, absently rubbing his wrist with his hand.

'Indeed.'

She deftly picks out a bruised blackberry from her hoard. He exhales, the sound of a man who has been awake all night and needs his bed, and sits opposite her. 'The berries look good.' He is quiet, then: 'What's that on your face?'

He reaches across the table for her bruised cheek, tilting her chin gently in his hand. She lets him, giving in to him.

'Who did this?' he asks.

'Thomas.'

His eyes grow flinted, 'I should never have left you there.'

'You needed to be with your father.'

She thinks of Thomas's truths that burgeoned to the surface, precipitating the bruise on her cheek. If Edmund had been there, neither Henry nor Thomas would've spoken a word. It is better this way, to know part of the truth – however incomplete it may be – than to grapple in the dark. These past days she has swung from hopefulness that Francis may still live, delighting in the same sky as she, may easily stroll back into being and resume his place in her life as though he never left. Although this, of course, is a folly. And then she has swung to hopelessness. Even if he came back, it changes nothing of her circumstances. All the gaps have been filled, leaving no space for him.

Her husband looks concerned, his hand still on her chin. She cares for him, has missed him, has wanted his body beside hers at night. But the ache she feels for Francis has its claws in her and will not release.

'I made the choice I thought was right at the time.' Edmund moves his hand so his fingertips drift along her neck, her arm, before finding her palm. The berry juice sticks their skin together, and she wonders, faintly, whether he is trying to convince himself. Whether there is something else he is trying to tell her.

⁂

She lies awake. The night, only just begun, stretches ahead. Edmund's breath beside her tells her he too is awake. She wonders what he is thinking and knows that if she reached out to touch him, his body would give way beneath her, would respond to the trail of her fingers.

A shout shatters the quiet. Then silence.

'Did you hear that?' she whispers.

She strains to hear if it will come again. It does. Another shout. Then a beating, ferocious and urgent, sounds on the door. Her hands find the bedside, fumbling for the candle, the tinder box. She knocks it on the floor, cursing. The banging grows louder. She scrambles to the floor, cursing again, the cold air fierce, gooseflesh rippling across her.

When the flame flares, casting the room in a jaundiced glow, Edmund is already out of bed pulling his doublet over his nightshirt. He reaches for his dagger, pale hand about the hilt. The shouting at the door has intensified, but the words are muffled, travelling through wood and stone. She lights another tallow, hands it to her husband.

'Stay here,' he says, slipping out of the door.

Tavern brawls, shouts fracturing the night, men with punctured sides, the burble of blood. The dull thud of her father's fists. She doesn't recall deciding, but her body moves in Edmund's wake, as though a string connects them both. The candle in her hand jostles with fear.

It's only when she reaches the midpoint of the staircase, where it turns, a perfect square corner along the wall, that she makes out the shout above the thunder of hands upon wood.

'Eliza!'

For a moment her mind is consumed by worry and wonder: could it be him? Has he returned to her? She twists her lip in her fingers. Again it comes. 'Eliza, Eliza!'

This time, she recognises the voice. It puts fear in her belly. She takes the stairs two at a time, her feet sliding on the wood, and Edmund, his hand on the latch, looks at her, incredulous, admiring. She bumps against his shoulder as she removes the bolt on the door, the thick metal rasping, and the door swings open.

He shakes in his chair, even though Eliza has lit the parlour's fire, ash smeared across the knees of her nightgown. His hand quakes so badly that she takes the cup from him.

'What happened, brother?' she asks.

Henry's eyes, eyes the spit of hers, look back at her. He'd arrived with that same wildness in them that she'd seen once before, when a knife had found a home in his hand as he wielded it at their father's neck. His eyes had softened as she held him tightly in the entrance hall. He was mud-spattered, wind-beaten, rain-drenched. The rains, he said, had barely stopped since she left, turning the lanes about their childhood home to quagmire. She thought about the danger of the road – how his horse could have fallen, gone lame, how he could have been ambushed by bandits, how he could have drifted to chilling sleep in the saddle, and fallen to the ground with a cracking of bone – and gripped him tighter, until her nightgown was soaked as though she too had taken the night journey, and Dorothy had fetched dry clothes for them both.

Edmund rests his elbow on the mantelpiece, looking towards the thick blue curtain which drowns out the night outside, face in flickering profile. She senses her brother's discomfort at his presence; his hands keep finding his face, keep rubbing at his beard. But she can't ask Edmund to leave; not when it's his home, not when Henry has arrived in such a state and dragged them from their beds.

Eliza's unanswered question hangs in the air until eventually Edmund takes it up and says, 'Whatever it is, it will not leave this room.'

Henry nods his head, the reassurance he needed from the man of the house – always, always they must defer to the man of the house – and explains.

He'd been out late, not wanting to come home. He returned to find Thomas waiting for him, emerging from his parlour like a hangman walking towards the sentenced. Henry skims the details of their argument, his eyes flicking to Edmund, describing only the lilies floating on the pond's surface, and not the groping, reedy depths beneath. Words had turned to deeds, to blows and cuffs, to a candle knocked to the floor and sputtering out, so the two men, bound by blood and hate, fought in the gloom of the hall. After, when Thomas was split-lipped blue-black-eyed, the armpit of his shirt ripped, leaning against the wall, glugging the air, Henry had stood back, unscathed, a man who had finally learnt to outmatch his father. Thomas knew it. Perhaps their father been afraid, knowing that he couldn't win anymore. Thomas had shouted for his son to get out, to not come back.

Edmund sits in the chair opposite Henry. 'Why did you argue?'

'I've been careless, Liza,' Henry says.

'Brother,' she says, warningly. She knows what is coming. All things must come up for air, must reach for the light.

'Thomas accused me of sodomy.'

Spoken aloud it still shocks her, that blunted, cruel word. A man can be hanged for sodomy. She has heard the minister talk of the city of Sodom in church. A place the Lord destroyed, raining brimstone and fire upon its plains. Turning livelihoods to smoke and desolation. Punishing the city for its wickedness.

But her brother is not wicked. He is a pillar, strong enough to support churches and cathedrals, who has held her across the years. Without him, who would she be? Where would she be? Not shrewd enough to survive Thomas nor creative enough to realise her art, her skill, without him.

There is a flicker on Edmund's face, the severity of the argument warping and hardening before him. Henry reaches for his drink, partly masking his face with his cup. Eliza places two fingers on Edmund's wrist as if to say, please help him, please.

Edmund could throw Henry out into the night. Where would her brother go, and what could she do about it? She would beg, on her knees, for Edmund to change his mind and let her brother stay at least until morning. Her husband places his hand over her fingers, and she is reminded, again, that he is not the kind of man who enjoys a fight or throws people from his home. She has never heard him raise his voice.

'So you need a new home and occupation.'

Relief on her brother's face mirrors that in her chest. Sweet like honey, like spring.

'I plan to head for London and become a merchant.'

'Either become an apprentice, or pay your way to becoming a freeman, so you can trade within the city walls with whoever you please.' Her husband turns business-like with ease; he is the man who cleared his brother's debts, who collects tenants' rents and placates their disputes, who turns a deaf ear to others' gossip. He doesn't ask whether Thomas's accusation is true. 'From what Liza has told me, I'd say you're too old and too clever for an apprenticeship. Better and quicker to buy your way in.'

'I haven't enough.'

Henry presses the heel of a palm against his eye. He worked for Thomas all his life and the money he made was syphoned back into their father's coffer.

'How much do you need?' Edmund pours himself some small beer and offers the jug to Eliza, not looking at Henry. It's tactical; a way of making people feel at ease, so they can say what they really mean, as he pretends to be distracted. But his expression tells her that he is as alert as a hart who has smelt a pack on its trail.

'Four pounds.'

In a different room filled with different people, there would have been a stillness or a joint intake of breath. If Francis were here, he would've laughed - or spat - in disbelief, would've counted on his fingers how many meals that would've fed his family.

But Edmund only nods and says, 'You'll have it.'

Henry says he'll repay him, of course, his hand on his heart, his body stooped in gratitude, but Edmund says something like, only when you've made your fortune, we're family, we look out for each other, and although his eyes are on Henry, she knows his words are meant for her. Her brother's face is like a child's, giddy with relief and exhaustion. They talk, the three of them, until the dawn arrives and the sky is grey like a bird's feather.

She stands, so tired she is almost stuporous, folding her arms across her chest to keep in the warmth that is fast leaving her. Edmund leads her upstairs, his fingers woven through hers. In the green of their bedchamber, before they fall into bed, each craving the warmth of the other's body between the sheets, she reaches for Edmund's face. Whispers, 'Thank you.'

Any distance between them dissolves. He rests his forehead against hers, murmurs, 'Anything for you, my love.'

꿍

Edmund covers her eyes with a strip of cloth, tying it gently at the back of her head, and laughs as she demands to know what he is hiding from her. He guides her along the passageway, his arm slipped around her waist. She hears him reach for a door, feels a draught of answering air as he pushes it open, and then slowly, his fingers fumbling at the back of her head, removes her blindfold.

She stands on the threshold of a disused chamber. Before she had only given the room a cursory glance, finding nothing of interest, it being punctuated with a singular chair and dust on the window casements. Now she sees how the room has been cleaned, the dust wiped away, the fireplace refilled with fresh timber. Furniture has been added, a polished table and three chairs, and a faint scent of beeswax lingers on the air, the residue of Dorothy's never-idle hands.

The chamber, set upstairs into the corner of the house with the moat glinting below, has two windows, one overlooking undulating lands, fields and woodlands, the other revealing the lane weaving towards the village. You could sit here and imagine yourself a queen, overseer of everything, scanning your land, watching folk approach. The light crosses itself, meets on the floorboards beneath her feet, a glorious blue-orange autumn day.

For the first time she notices how the walls are veined with thick wooden beams and in between, in some of the square gaps, the daub is painted with bursts of colour – flowers, curling stems and pomegranates. Eliza reaches for one of the pomegranates, running her finger over it.

'This was my mother's parlour, she had it decorated. It hasn't really been used since she . . .' He falters. Over the years, the men have barely come in here, as though it is a sepulchre where the spirits are too loud. He gestures to the table which waits beneath a windows. 'I thought this could be your chamber, if you wanted. Somewhere for you to paint.'

A room of her own, bright and humming, where she can retreat, shut out the world and be lost to charcoal and pigment. It is a beautiful gift. But the greatest gift is Edmund's permission, his seal of freedom. The memories of stuffing her work beneath her mattress, of stilling her hand to listen to footsteps on the stairs, of her father taking all her work, are only that. Only memories. A wisp of smoke dissipating on the breeze.

Joy propels her towards him; in two strides she is across the room, throwing her arms around him, resting her chin on his shoulder. 'It's perfect,' she breathes, her mouth against his cheek. 'Thank you, thank you.'

She retreats here when Edmund and Henry go riding together, sometimes with a group of her husband's friends, who, once smug and sneering at her wedding, are now accepting and greet her with boisterous exuberance. Sometimes she rides with them and observes the flush of Henry's cheeks and how he throws back his head laughing, succumbing to the life of a gentleman. She grins to herself; it'll be a shock when this is over, when he leaves for London.

Other days the two men sit and talk, of trade and politics, of the markets, of Antwerp, Venice, Naples. There will be the sound of a palm being hit flatly upon a table in agreement, of Henry's enthusiastic voice – 'exactly, exactly!' – carrying to where she sits in her painted chamber. The years of clandestine whisperings when she and Henry were children – about London, heretical ideas that there must be more than harvesting grain from the unforgiving land – are over. He can speak freely, mind and tongue unyoked. Sometimes she joins them in their discussions, leaning against the doorframe of the parlour, watching as her brother's capable mind expands like a river after the rains, smiling into her cup as he makes notes with a scratch of his quill.

Today the house is quiet, the men out riding. She watched them leave from the two windows, a pack of dark blots receding into the bronzing landscape. She has been practicing drawing her own fractured window reflection, to see if she can recreate its likeness. It is strange to look at herself for so long, to notice details of a face she has spent a lifetime with but barely seen. In the distortion of the panes, the lead breaking through her features, so her nose is lost and one of her umber eyes is split in two, she recognises her father, the jut of his chin, the slope of his forehead. But more of Ma surfaces across Eliza's features: face heart shaped, cheekbones pronounced, eyebrows curved, eyes earthen.

Poor Mama, left alone in the house with that man. No one to protect her, no one to hear Thomas's wrath through the walls in those isolated fields. Sometimes at night, when she and Edmund wake, and the worries are huge and looming, worse in the dark, she whispers them to him, and he reaches out his hand and places it gently on her cheek. Your ma survived before you were born, when your father was younger, stronger, more volatile, more belligerent, he reassures her. She'll survive again now.

Eliza paints herself in vibrant hues. Bursts of colour, indigo and azurite and verditer, nestle in the pearly hollows of her mussel shells. The paintbrush's hog bristles slide over the paper between her chalked lines. How easy it is to reinvent herself on the page, or present a particular version. Paint can smooth away unhappiness, grief, age – anything, if you let it. She recalls Teerlinc's miniature and wonders how truthful the depiction of her subject really was; how many lies have been told by a paintbrush, to flatter or seduce? Wonders if truth can ever, really, be captured.

She accidentally drops a spot of vermillion on her fingertip, brilliant red like the heart of a fire, like lust, like blood. And he comes to her then: Francis dead, a red ribbon trickling down his neck. She shakes her head, reds reshuffling. Instead, she sees sweet williams, the inner crimson centres of their petals, growing in a front garden. His front garden. A small cottage, where he lives with his faceless wife, a babe swelling in her belly.

Still she craves him, feels forlorn at the thought of him with another. Yet time, week after week, is widening the space between them. Sometimes she struggles to remember his exact expressions, has found it difficult to replicate the cadence of his voice in her head. She wipes her finger on a cloth. Focuses on the bristles of her brush, how the paint clings to each hair. Remembers to breathe. Thinks of Edmund's arm around her waist, pulling her body into his.

Henry bowls in later, a brace of coneys in hand, the blood dribbling to the floor. She smells a trip to the inn on his skin, the whiff of beer. Edmund is behind him, smelling the same, although his eyes are more focused. She and Dorothy skin the rabbits, tear the fur from flesh, cook them on the iron pot over the fire, the scent of smoke and meat rising about them. And later still, after they have eaten, when she feels heavy with drink and a good meal, and has bundled Henry to bed, his tongue thick, his words slurring over how much he loves her, she slips back to the great chamber, to find the golden-haired man standing by the window, waiting for her.

'I want to show you something,' she says.

She leads him along the passageway, his hand in hers. Their skin is the same temperature, making it is hard to tell where he ends and she begins. In the painted chamber she holds a tallow above the unfinished portrait of herself. Her hair in a coif, the neck slipping down to shoulders dressed in a gown. He bends closer and she observes his eyelashes moving as he looks at the wealth of her painted clothes, the eyes that have never known violence, the mouth that has never spoken vulgarity, the chin smoothed so it bears no resemblance to her father.

He puts his fingertip lightly on the cheek of the painting before turning and tracing his finger along the real Eliza's cheek. She is holding her breath. Yearning for his approval. For how long has she craved his admiration?

He is silent still.

'I mean, it's no Teerlinc,' she says, attempting flippancy but sounding imploring.

He shakes his head, and in the wake of her concerned expression, a smile ambles across his face. 'I think Walter will be jealous.'

She frowns.

'That I'm to have a collection that will rival his.'

'Don't mock me,' she says, but she her shoulders relax.

'How did I find such a wife? It's brilliant, truly.'

'Did you doubt?'

'No.'

'Good.'

'Although . . .'

'What?'

He glances back at the painting, flickering in the candlelight.

'I think the real thing is better.'

And he steps towards her, easily, and presses his mouth to hers, and she can't help but feel a soaring, tumbling joy.

CHAPTER 29

'**B**E careful,' Eliza says, shivering in her cloak. They'd risen at first light, Henry eager to be away, to take the three-day ride south and east to London. The smell of the horses is strong about them in the stables, and his ride whickers softly beside him.

'When am I ever not?'

'Where would you like me to begin?'

He smiles and softens, 'You worry too much Liza.'

'With good reason.'

She will miss him. She has grown used to his presence these past weeks, recognising his tread on the stairs, hearing his voice in the halls. But today, their goodbye is different. She feels a hope for him; there is a crackling possibility that he could become the man he has always wanted to be, who he is meant to be. When he arrives in the capital, he will travel to the lodgings Edmund has arranged, and will work for a merchant, which Edmund too has arranged, running errands, keeping ledgers, surveying stock as it bumps into London's harbours. He will learn the markets, watch as wool and cloth are stashed into the bowels of ships headed to Antwerp, or perhaps to the watery arteries of Amsterdam, to be traded, metamorphosised into spices and wines, silks and alum, brought back in the bowels of the same ships.

And when he is ready, Henry will pay his way and become a freeman.

They step out of the stables, horse in tow, and the weak lemon sun falls across her brother's face, casting his eyes to twinkly excitement. The grey stones of Cecil Hall are bright, the still moat reflecting buttercup heavens.

'You've done well,' Henry says, nodding. They stare at the Hall, the beauty of the place, the thick gatehouse offering a glimpse of the courtyard beyond.

'Mm. Pinch me.'

Henry obliges, quickly, gloved fingers nipping the skin of her arm before she can smack him away. 'Little sister,' he grins.

'It feels like home.'

'And you've never looked so well.'

She hasn't considered it. But she supposes her skin is free of bruises, her belly full of good food, her mind bursting with ideas. The seams, the limits of her are expanding, alert to brightness and beauty. Her first small portrait, herself in full colour, is finished. She completed it a few nights before and had shown it to her brother, and the past had risen around them. That first stick of chalk he pilfered for her, all those years ago, when they were children, when they had expected nothing more for themselves than what they had in front of them.

'You look better yourself,' she smiles.

The Henry who arrived had been lean and bony, shoulders hunching, violet smudges beneath his wild eyes. The man leaving seems collected, has a certainty to his gait, is a more confident steersman passing through murky shallows and out into wide, open sea.

'What do you plan to do once you're settled?' she asks.

He looks at her shrewdly, knows what she's angling at. His close friend, his lover, who he told her about years before, when she had confronted him in their parents' kitchen. Brother, what is it, she had said. What has happened?

'I've been a fool,' he'd explained. 'He is bound for London with his wife and I'm bound here, to this God forsaken land. I'm not sure how I can cope without him. You must understand . . .' Trail of voice, like trail of fingers on skin. Love wasn't a word his lips could bear to form, 'I care for him. Please understand . . .' His voice was justifying, beseeching.

He confirmed what she had already witnessed: a shadowed lane, two men, forehead to forehead, nose to nose. Whispering: close your eyes and wish you can hold this moment infinitely. Close your eyes and swear to me we'll find each other again.

'You were saying goodbye?'

He dipped his head in affirmation, and her mind whipped with fear – for his safety, his future, how such plain truth would affect them, these two siblings. She hadn't known there was a wife. But she wanted, more than anything, to comfort him. She'd never seen him so vulnerable, opened like the spiked green casing of a conker, revealing the shined seed within.

'If it's what you want, then I think you'll see him again. And you'll cope without him in the meantime, you've made it this far, Hen. Besides,' and here she'd wriggled close to him, tucking herself beneath his arm, 'you'll always have me.'

She needn't have worried about how it would affect them. After their discussion, where he laid his soul bare, something seemed to lift in Henry; more than ever, he was unequivocally himself around her. He trusted her in a way made her feel tethered, purposeful, carried her through the hardest parts of living with Thomas and losing Francis. And she reciprocated.

After that, they had understood each other as completely as one person can understand another.

Now, the Henry before her, wiser, older and hungrier than ever for life to unspool before him, says, 'I might find him, if that's what you mean.'

'Might? You once told me *you don't give up on a love like that*.' After Francis had gone. She can't bring herself to say his name, but luckily her brother, the person she will know longest, thicker than thieves, understands and smiles. 'So you do listen to me.'

'Occasionally you utter something of interest.'

He pinches her again, smiling. Concedes, 'I know where he is, I'll go to him.'

'And his wife?'

'Their marriage will remain unchanged.'

She considers her brother's staunch heart. Those who have come in between have been a distraction for Henry, filling the void. Slipping in through the kitchen door with the smell of another sticking to him. Strangers' skin to mask a yearning. Is this wife the same? Just a distraction – or a tragedy? A casualty? – for a man waiting for life to begin again, anew, with Henry's arrival.

'I hope London is all you dream it to be,' Eliza says. She means it: she wants him to find contentment, a peace, that he has, for so long, been searching. And isn't she seeking the same thing?

'It can't be worse than what we've left behind.'

Francis in the fields, Francis in the sheets.

'Edmund is a good man,' Henry says, gently.

Eliza nods; she knows. By God she knows.

'I'm in his debt.' Henry takes a breath to continue, then doesn't.

'What are you thinking?'

'He couldn't have given you this, Liza.'

He catches her off guard, and she tears her eyes from the façade of the Hall to glance at her brother. And then she understands.

'I know that, brother.' She is careful to keep her voice even.

'I just don't want you to be hurting.'

'I'm not,' she lies.

He squeezes her shoulder. 'I'll write you.'

After he has left only horseshoe imprints in the mud, the recognisable shape of a farrier, she makes an impulsive decision. She heads back to the Hall to fetch a parcel, before taking the meandering lane into the village. People know her now, are deferential, nod to her, the not-so-new wife at Cecil Hall, whilst others purse their lips in jealousy, pretend not to see her, the once one-of-us women turned gentlewoman. She finds the scrawny messenger lad who Edmund sometimes uses, gives him payment upfront.

'Deliver this and I'll pay you double when you return.'

The lad nods, tucking the parcel under his arm, slipping the coins into his threadbare purse.

Inside is her portrait which he will take to Ruth. A painting that says, look at what I can do Mama, look at what I'm allowed to do, look at how your love, your protection turned out. Please know you are not forgotten.

✿

They walk together, towards the woodlands that lie just within sight of Cecil Hall, if you stand at the right window on a clear day. Cloaks atop jerkins and doublets to shield them from the chill. But despite the cold, the sun persists, a swansong before the thick of winter.

Eliza had needed to get out, having spent days with Dorothy building and lighting fires in hearths, and putting them out again, scraping and brushing ash from the floors, making jams from soft berries that dyed the grooves of her palms maroon in a bid to preserve autumn's fruits until the following year, picking pears and storing them in the hoard house. And when that was over, Eliza had shut herself away, drawing and drawing, painting and painting, passion turned obsession.

The forest is an old place. When they enter its entanglement they are greeted by ancient, gnarled trees, moss snaking up their damp trunks, their roots protruding through the ground amongst scattered leaves.

'My mother used to bring us here,' Edmund says.

Us. Two brothers, reduced to one.

'What was she like?' Eliza asks. He barely speaks of her. She wants to coax his memories without frightening them away, like a red deer, spry legged and russet coloured, always on the verge of escaping.

'Shorter than you. I was as tall as her by the time I was ten,' he says, a wisp of a smile on his face, 'but she had presence. She loved dances and feasts, and in my memory she always had visitors. We had more servants then, which gave her more time to entertain.'

Eliza can see it: Cecil Hall restored to its fullest grandeur, the bustle of people rushing to ready it in the final moments before the guests arrived. The chest squeeze of excitement before the beginning of something.

'Mother had her own ethos. If it wasn't beautiful, she wasn't interested.'

'Do you agree?'

Edmund removes his glove and places his bare hand on the bole of an elm, glancing upwards at the branches which clutch for the sky.

'I appreciate her sentiments, but I wish I'd asked her more. I could've learnt so much from her.'

'You were only a boy.'

'I grew up after that.'

The wind stirs around them like a sleeping child waking up, bringing with it the smell of mushrooms which push through the earth. She brings her hand to her head to prevent her coif from being carried away.

'What happened to the servants?'

'Father tried to dismiss them all after she died, but Sam stopped him. He was so similar to her. Of course, after her, it wasn't the same. Sam's feasts and gatherings often felt as though she, the epicentre of it all, was missing. After Sam, Father dismissed all the servants except Dorothy. I didn't have the will to stop him.'

She thinks of the rooms left empty, doors closed, dust settling. Two men left behind, rattling about like pins in a tin box, living amongst the relics of a life passed by.

'Everything changed, it became a different house, really. So quiet. Then you arrived.'

'You must have been lonely.'

'I can't begin to describe,' he murmurs, words almost lost to the creaking of the branches above. He swallows, the bob of the cherry at his throat, and she knows that he has given her all he can today. Has offered her his heart and now must have it back. The light through the branches cuts across his face, and he is temporarily cast in an ethereal glow, the sun turning his hair almost white. If she could, she would capture it, hair bone-gold, inky cloak pulled high to his neck, eyes dry in grief. She hooks her arm through his.

'I'd like to paint you.' It is on impulse that the words drop from her mouth, but she finds that once she has said them, watched them settle, she desires them even more.

'She'd have liked you.'

'Why?'

'You say exactly what you want.'

'Are you saying yes?'

He kicks the leaves at his feet, mouth settling into a secret smile. 'If you like.'

'You know I've never drawn or painted anyone else before. Not properly.'

'Am I to be your first muse?'

Behind him, through the tangle of oaks and hornbeams she senses a figure. A tall man, hair so dark it is almost black, watching them. Blink and he's gone, blink and he's there. Haunting her. His edges just out of focus. He leans against a trunk, his arms crossed. First muse? he says. I thought I was your first. She tries to ignore him, to observe the golden-haired man who stands before her, whose arm is strong beneath hers, whose eyes appraise her. Their faces are close, their cheekbones almost touch. At this proximity, it could be the other man's cheekbone. It could be the other man beside her. The two merge, overlap in her mind.

Blink and he's gone. Dark hair transforms to ravens, which take flight, croaking through the trees. She waits for the present to crystallise, for the past to slowly ebb back to where it belongs, locked away in time irretrievable.

'You're my first,' she says. And then, because Edmund's face is hopeful, because he has suffered, because she recalls her brother's parting description of him as a *good man*, because of the kindness Edmund has shown her and because she doesn't know how she can ever thank him, and because she wants to stay rooted in what's real and is realising that how she feels about him is diving, whirling down into something deeper, she says, 'And only.'

CHAPTER 30

T H E winds which precede the storm are icy, ripping against his face, making rivers of his eyes, turning his hands to frozen agony. But he and the rest of the crew keep working. No man is asleep below deck, it is all hands; they have felt the swell of the waves, have heard Wynter, their captain, shouting. The men hasten to secure anything loose, checking the guns are tied up, making futile attempts to protect their dwindling food supplies from rot and ruin.

As evening falls, the storm arrives. It throws waves higher than the mainmast before the ocean plummets down onto the deck, transforming the boards to white-foamed water. The lanterns go out. The crew try not to panic, but you can see it in the depth of their pupils, in the prayers that are on their lips as they work. The rats and cats that have found a home on board run havoc about their feet. Sailors are sent to lower the sails, and Francis sends a prayer of thanks to God that it isn't him up there; small fragile bodies clinging onto the masts high above.

The ship is forced upwards, bucking over the waves before dropping downwards. The men lurch, stagger, grab onto anything they can, cast about like a toy in a child's careless hand. The motion makes Francis sick, but it is washed away instantly, as seawater spumes up the body of the galleon. He slips on the gush of water. Face forward. Cheek upon the deck. His hair, longer than it has ever been, slicks to his face. He is so exhausted he could stay here, allow the ocean to do whatever it wants to him. Swallow him up. It has been so hard, for so long. This is it. He closes his eyes, and thinks of her.

A hand finds his arm, grip firm about the flesh that has reduced to wasting muscle. Anthony is hauling him to his feet, slapping him on the shoulder, trying to yell above the crash of the storm, although what he is saying, Francis doesn't know.

⚘

Quiet.

The water, lapping gently at the hull, is flat and grey like the iron in his father's forge. The world has shrunk to the size of deck, as though everything else has slipped over the edge of a flat world. Only a thick white surrounds them. A dense, unyielding fog, lasting for a turn and yet another turn of the hourglass.

Francis goes below to sleep on the damp floor which earlier he and others of the crew had bailed out with buckets. His clothes will not dry, and the rough linen chafes his skin, gives him sores about his neck and groin. He drunk his fill of beer and it has bloated his empty stomach, making him lethargic and light. There are men and men and men around him, either already slumped on the floor or else picking their way through exhausted bodies, trying to find somewhere to rest.

Anthony lies not far away and mutters, 'I don't think we'll find them again Frank, not after this.'

'Do you think they survived?' he mumbles from the borders of uneasy sleep.

'If they did, they're on their own, just as we are.'

As he drifts, he imagines the other two ships, gone, lost in the gaping, unrelenting maws of the Pacific. The constellation they had made across the ocean, disbanded.

⚘

He feels the pulse of collective anger as he stands amongst the crew, shoulder bumping shoulder, as they gather on deck, surrounding Wynter.

198

'I'm not fucking doing it anymore,' one of them, says raising his voice above the wind that whips their bones, rattles the sails.

'Neither am I,' says another.

'Where is our promised gold and glory?'

Others weigh in, so their voices are a cacophony of complaints: how the last of the food supplies are wet and rotting, how they're running out of drink, how they've had month on month of shitty sleep. The officers, who would usually beat a man for speaking so, hang back. They are haggard, weary. Their clothes are disgusting, their bodies smell. The sea has levelled them all the same.

'How can we even discuss this?' Francis hears himself say. 'How can anyone here think we'll find the other ships? Have you seen the ocean? The size of the Pacific?' His arm flies out, takes in their surroundings.

Anthony grunts in agreement, and some of the others join in. Even the master of the ship – whose own weakness for a bribe is the reason Francis found a place aboard this damned deck, for whom Francis has a hatred that will never abate – makes a noise in the back of his throat.

Wynter scratches his windburned face, then raises his hand in the air. Francis breathes in sharply, wondering if he'll be punished, realising he doesn't care. Silence falls, like the fog that has gradually dissipated, leaving them alone in the ocean. A tiny wooden vessel atop endless blue. Despite the anger amongst the men, they still respect their captain; they aren't yet at the point of mutiny, if he can give them what they want.

'We have two options. We either continue on the route Drake set for us, and see if we can bring back the gold and glory we were promised.' One of the men tries to speak but Wynter silences him with a look. 'But that is only achievable with a willing crew, which it seems I no longer have. I can't do it without my men. So we must look to our other option. To get home, alive and lose no more of our number. To tell our women that we sailed all the way to the Pacific Ocean and have them look at us in wonder when they don't know where on earth that is. At least this way, we will see our women again.'

Wynter drops his hand to his side, and the whole ship waits. 'Let's go home, lads,' he says, and the men crowd in, relief in every line on their exhausted faces.

Home.

To his family – his anchoring parents, raucous siblings, baby nephew. To her. Eliza on his tongue, in his throat, in his brain, his arms, his soul.

CHAPTER 31

THE dairy is freezing. Eliza's sleeves are rolled up to her elbows, the stink of mould and curds catching in her clothes. She beats at the churn, dull thud of the paddle against the wood, like a woman possessed, arms aching, waiting for the cream to transform to butter. Through the kitchen, then the passageway and into the entrance hall, she hears Dorothy greeting a visitor. Eliza keeps churning until Dorothy returns, carrying an expression that Eliza cannot decipher.

'Who was that?'

The older woman busies herself with wiping up the cream Eliza has dribbled. 'Annabel.'

Eliza passes the paddle to Dorothy and wipes her hands on her apron before tossing it onto the table. Curiosity grows inside her as she walks towards the hum of voices.

'I didn't expect you to visit,' Edmund is saying to Annabel, who is hardly within the entrance hall, standing close to the door, whilst he commands its centre. The distance between them is marked, the stone floor an impassable sea between them. The feist and allure of the woman who had sat at Edmund and Eliza's wedding feast with frosted words, fiery tongue and magnetic quality, has disappeared. Even with tears slicking her face in Edmund's parlour, she had more vivacity. Now Annabel looks sunken and moves as though she has forgotten exactly how to manoeuvre her own body.

'My family are organising a feast for Twelfth Night, and they wanted to invite you,' Annabel says, acknowledging Eliza. Her husky voice is quieter, cracking at the ends of words. 'Both of you.'

Eliza waits for Edmund to speak, and when he does not, she stiltedly accepts the invitation.

'I've not been out much lately,' Annabel says, seeking Edmund's gaze which is bound to the floor.

'Oh?' Eliza says.

'I've not been well.'

Eliza wants to ask what ails her, is there anything she, Eliza, can do. She has herbs, tinctures. Ma's voice in her head, the questions she would ask. But Edmund speaks first, an edge of concern: 'You should be resting at home.'

He moves to usher Annabel out, asking if she wants someone to accompany her home, which she declines. Yet she lingers, the corner of her mouth pulling down, a sadness about her that makes Eliza want to ask her to stay. Briefly, so briefly you would think you'd imagined it, Edmund moves his hand so it hovers above the other woman's arm, as though he is going to touch her, console her. But he changes his mind, instead opening the door, letting in a gust of winter.

Eliza doesn't miss the hurt on Annabel's face. Crestfallen. She dips her head towards Eliza and leaves without another word, body braced against the chill, pulling her hood over her head.

Edmund shuts the door, rasps the bolt into its place.

'What was that?' she asks.

Once, in a time that now feels like eons and epochs ago, a serving girl, Joan, had pressed herself close to Francis during the celebrations at Michaelmas. She experiences now a similar rise of jealousy, its steely fingers reaching for her lungs and squeezing. The feelings she had, has, for Francis she now holds for Edmund; both men compete for the scope of her emotions, wider than the horizon.

He is close to her, and when he frowns she can see the etch of lines deepen on his forehead. 'She shouldn't have come when she's been so sick. A note would've served.'

She wants to understand her husband's harshness and the way he had reached for Annabel's arm, to unpick the exchange and undercurrents she has witnessed, as though she is an anatomist, carefully observing the intricacies of a body and discovering its impulses, its connections, whether everything leads back to the beat of its heart.

Instead she says, 'I didn't know she'd been ill.'

He shakes his head, then reaches the tips of his fingers for her hairline. 'You have cream in your hair.'

⌘

He sits for her. She faces him from her table, chalk in hand, drawing him on paper from different angles, trying to imitate his likeness. The first few times had felt strange, almost awkward, their silence strung with laughter about things they wouldn't usually find amusing.

But now Edmund recasts himself easily into the same position, his muscles remembering. Now, when he sits, they talk and talk; of the past, of his family, of hers.

She tells him things she has never spoken of before. How Ma earned the scar on her cheek, when the harvest had been poor in the years before, and every week the townsfolk had recited the litany in church, humbling beseeching God to *send us such weather, whereby we may receive the fruits of the earth in due season.* Thomas had held some grain back illegally, and only when other traders had sold out did he start selling his own grain, at cripplingly high prices. Folk couldn't afford to eat, folk starved those years, and yet Thomas profited still. And with his extra coin, he bought Ruth a brooch. His dear wife, who he'd tormented for half a lifetime, deserved something pretty. But she wouldn't take it, wouldn't wear the stain of blood, the waste of life on her bosom. Instead, Thomas ensured that the sharp edge of the brooch had met with her cheek, and Ruth had worn the scar instead. A scar that is but one bloody sentence in a book of abuses.

She does not mention where the brooch is now. Hidden in the wall of her childhood bedchamber, when she'd planned to run away with another man. He resurfaces in her mind. He is an association to so many things. Dark haired man, Francis. Hiding place in the wall, Francis. Childhood, Francis. Brooch, Francis. All rivers lead back to him.

When she finishes her tale, Edmund stands and works his fingers into the knots and tensions of her shoulders, kisses the hollow beneath her chin and suggests they have an early supper.

They talk of the future, what they once imagined it to be, what it could be. Of their future. She talks of everything except Francis, omitting the places where he would've been. Sometimes she is so engrossed in their conversations, she loses her concentration, curses when she makes a mistake, and Edmund, who has never known her like this, pushing herself harder and harder to unobtainable perfection, will stifle a laugh.

'Once I've completed the drawings of your face and hands, and started painting, I won't need you to sit again,' she says, arching her spine, rolling her shoulders back after being hunched over her paper for so long, documenting the contours and shadows of his left hand, his nails, knuckles, half-moon cuticles.

'Then I'll return to being banished from your chamber?' His joviality fails to mask his disappointment.

She smiles. It is true. When she's not drawing him, she draws or paints alone. Cannot have distractions to pull her away. And as the months have unravelled from autumn to winter, Edmund has become more of a distraction: where his body is in relation to hers when they are in a room together, whether he is watching her when she is pretending not to watch him. They have gone to bed together more than before, their rhythms falling in time with each other, waking in the night to kiss and open the curtains so their bodies are lit by the chalked, silvery moon. That is how it goes; their love characterised by observation, paint, skin, touch, moonlight.

Sometimes she thinks of Francis and feels sick with her own betrayal. Sometimes she thinks that he is gone, he is gone, either alive and not coming back for her, for a myriad of reasons that she doesn't know, or that he is dead, his spirit now with God. In either case, he cannot comfort her, hold her, reach for her. Surely, then, her betrayal is understandable. Is forgivable.

And sometimes, all she sees is Edmund, and she doesn't think of him – the other him – at all.

Edmund watches her, as the last of the December day's light filters in. Her eyes dart from page to flesh, the interpreted to the reality, learning every part of his skin, every blemish and beauty spot. He is the map and she the cartographer, making new discoveries, inking in his edges.

'Never banished,' she murmurs. 'What could you ever do that would make me want to banish you?'

She casts around for her charcoal, unaware of how the playfulness in her husband's eyes fades slightly, how his hands tighten in his lap, preventing him from pinching the skin at his neck.

CHAPTER 32

THE Sackvilles' home is smaller than the Cecils' but it's a trove of richly carved chests, tapestried walls, wainscoting reaching up to beamed ceilings, high stone-chiselled fireplaces. A house that hasn't known loss like Cecil Hall. Death has not caused decline. Ivy is strung about the stairs and holly festooned with red berries hangs above doorways. Annabel's parents embrace Edmund as though he is a man returned from war, as if he is their kin, and sweep him away towards other guests, leaving Eliza alone in the entrance hall. No one is interested in Edmund's wife. She loses her identity, existing only as an extension of him, as though the edges of herself have been blurred away as an artist blends her chalk.

If only Nicholas was here, then there would be another familiar face. But her father-in-law had shaken his head when Edmund told him of the invitation, had said that no good could come of it. And when Edmund had mentioned maintaining appearances, Nicholas had shrugged, named it a young man's game.

Eliza crosses the entrance hall, towards the stairs where noise carries from above. She glances up, once again a child, back in her father's house, peering around doors, seeing if it is safe to enter. And being well practised at such observations, she notices a figure standing on the stairs, obscured in shadow, a ringed hand against the wall.

'Annabel?'

The other woman takes a moment to realise who addresses her, then makes a noise, like a hum of satisfaction, and steps gingerly towards Eliza, her loose gown trailing, skirts wide about her legs, hair tied up in a coif that glints with coloured glass and pearls. Close to, Eliza smells the woman's breath as she greets her, the spices of the wassail, clove and ginger and cinnamon. The scent of a person who has been drinking all day, with eyes glazed to match. Yet despite the revels, she seems vacant, forlorn, as though she has been trampled by giants.

'Is Edmund here?' Annabel asks.

Eliza nods, experiencing that familiar, unpleasant squeeze in her chest, expecting the other woman to ask where, or else pick her way through the glinting chambers in search of him. But Annabel makes no comment. Instead she offers Eliza the cup in her hand, half-drunk, the amber liquid tilting dangerously – mead, strong and honeyed – and unexpectedly encircles Eliza's wrist with a damp palm, and leads her up the stairs. Light and sound, hum and vibration of people already drunk, despite the earliness of the afternoon, spill from the great chamber. When Eliza motions towards them, Annabel's clutch on her arm tightens.

'It's so crowded in there,' she says. A tremor in her voice causes Eliza to hesitate. 'Perhaps we could sit somewhere else?'

They enter a smaller parlour further along the passageway. The hearth is unlit, the room cold. It is dark, the corners extending out of themselves, oak panels swallowing the light. Candle stubs litter the room, as though someone has sat in here for a long time, into the night, until the wax had all but burnt out. Annabel seems to relax as she closes the door on the din of the guests.

There is a table with a piece of linen laid flat, a partially completed embroidery of songbirds and swans. Eliza runs her fingers over it, feeling the intricate patterning of the threads, the hours of attentive skill.

'You know swans mate for life?' Annabel says.

'I did not.'

'Most faithful.' Annabel's face is in shadow as she looks down, smoothing her skirts. 'It's a shame no such man exists. Not anymore.'

Widowed before she was thirty. Eliza has heard it before: husbands are always dying, women are always frantically searching for a replacement, to support and protect them. A life can be filled with three or four marriages and countless children. It strikes her as odd that there are none here.

'I'm sorry to hear about your husband. From what Edmund has said, he was an impressive man.' She skims over the part about Samuel's excessive gambling and debts.

'We lived at Cecil Hall, all of us,' Annabel says, leaning on the back of a chair, sounding drunk and wistful and older than her years. She tells her of the numerous celebrations she and Sam had thrown at Cecil Hall; of their gambling, the thrills and the lows; of drinking so much they could barely walk to their bedchamber; of dancing in the great chamber with Sam's dog, Bo, yapping at their heels.

And all the while Eliza listens, thinking of her husband. Where had he been whilst all of this was unfurling? Had he been drinking with them, losing his coin to a game of primero? Had he danced with all the women who came for the celebrations, his cheeks tinged pink like an early morning sunrise? Or had he been upstairs, trying to sleep, feeble from another spell of the stones, always the younger, overshadowed brother?

Annabel answers her unspoken questions, 'For a time, when Edmund was well, the three of us were inseparable.'

Eliza sits upon a wooden chest pushed beneath the window, observing the other woman, the blinding paleness of her face, chestnut hair smooth and parted above the curve of her forehead.

'How long did you all live together?'

'The whole of our marriage, so nine years.'

Edmund has never mentioned how closely he lived with Annabel. It'd seemed inevitable that they may have lived together – the eldest son and his wife, slowly taking over his father's estate, and the sickly younger brother, back and forth to his bed – but he'd never alluded to the bond they shared, which now appears to be in fragments. The omissions make it seem like a secret, as though Edmund is a gatekeeper, locking her out of some truths. She recalls too her husband's coldness towards his once sister-by-law; her kind, thoughtful husband, with a mean streak that she doesn't care for.

His nebulous, thorny relationship with Annabel makes Eliza shift upon the chest, fiddling with the skin at her wrist.

'Nine years, all gone now. So many things we were never able to do,' Annabel sits heavily beside her, as though they are girls, sent to a separate chamber whilst the adults feast. Maybe the drink has made it easier for her to talk. Maybe she is lonely, wants to open herself to somebody new. Maybe she senses that Eliza has that rare quality, being someone who can truly listen. Regardless, Annabel makes a confession: 'Sam always wanted a child. We both did.'

Eliza has an apology in her mouth, but Annabel waves her hand.

'You would never remarry?' Eliza asks, gentle.

'How can anyone love again, after that?'

Eliza has asked herself the same thing. Once she would have described herself as staunch, stubborn. Perhaps she is not.

'Even if I could, I don't want to lose someone again,' Annabel says.

'That might not happen.'

'It's easy to say if you haven't experienced it,' Annabel smiles, trying to make light of a matter so heavy. When Eliza makes no answer, Annabel's mouth comes to a thoughtful pout. 'Or have you?'

Eliza hasn't spoken about him to anyone – not here, not in this life. His name has not crossed her lips since Thomas's confession. Her wedding band glints. For the first time in weeks, she wants to weep for Francis. Wants his arms around her.

'No,' she forces herself to say, and changes the subject.

❧

It happens gradually, the two women meeting for a drink or a game of cards or a walk to the village. Annabel teaches Eliza primero and relentlessly beats her at it – 'you're a terrible bluffer Liza' – but Eliza improves with the passing of each wintry hour, and by the time the Lent Lilies of spring are pushing their way through the damp soil she is, albeit inconsistently, a match for Annabel. They fall easily into habit, fall easily into friendship.

She hadn't realised how much she had been craving female companionship, her life so often governed and surrounded by men. With Annabel there is no obligation; no need to play the role of obedient daughter or gentle wife. And over time Annabel seems increasingly contented, laughing more, settling back into her own body.

Yet on a cool March morning, Eliza discovers how Annabel's mask can slip. A servant admits Eliza to the Sackville's house, and on asking about Annabel, the girl's eyes dart like a cat wriggled loose from its owner's grip, 'She's not left her bedchamber all morning and she said she didn't want anyone disturbing her.'

'Is she unwell?'

The girl sticks her tongue to the corner of her mouth, calculating her response, whether the woman before her can be trusted. Eliza apparently passes all scrutiny, for the servant says, 'She shuts herself away sometimes and won't leave her chamber for days. Her family don't know what to do about her. They pretend . . .'

'Pretend what?'

'They pretend she isn't in the house. It's as if they don't have a daughter.'

The door to Annabel's bedchamber is unlocked. As though, contrary to what the servant said, she wants someone to find her, scoop her up and take care of her. Annabel sits at the end of her bed, beneath the richly carved canopy, wearing only her smock, her bare toes skimming the floor. The curtains are closed and the room hasn't been aired; it smells of someone who has slept sweated and awoken in the mugginess of their own making. A cup of wine, red and gleaming like the devil's smile, rests in her hand, half-drunk. Her body is small yet softer than Eliza had imagined and her neck droops towards her chest.

Only when Eliza moves into the murk, does Annabel raise her head, jerkily, as though awoken from a night terror. And isn't this terror enough? Her mouth is stained burgundy, flicking up at the corners like a smile. But she is not smiling. She looks pitiably sad.

Eyes glazed and puffy, hair at all angles about her face, jaw slack.

'What's happened?' Eliza starts as Annabel, head bobbing back to her chest moans, 'You shouldn't be here . . . Why've you come . . . Please leave, they all do . . .' She stammers to crying silence. Eliza gently removes Lucifer's cup from her grip, and the way Annabel's hand falls to her lap, and the way she crouches forward as though there is a ceaseless pain in her belly, reminds Eliza of how Mama used to sit and cry, when Eliza was a girl, for the child that was robbed from her, the one Henry and Eliza never knew, the one laid to rest in the earth.

She has nursed enough people with Ma and seen enough people in enough states to be unphased, but it does catch her. Like a hook in the mouth. To see this woman – who is beaming bright – brought so low.

'I'm not leaving you.'

She calls for the servant to fetch some small beer and a damp cloth, and to light the fire. The girl and her catlike eyes scuttle about, trying not to gawk at the mistress, whose ability to perform even the simplest of tasks has leaked away.

Eliza wipes Annabel's face, the dampness at her neck, then helps her back to bed. Sleep off the stupor, wake with a clearer head. Wake to after-drink blur and regret. Annabel slurs incoherent gratitude, blinking heavily a few times, until they shut for good.

Later when Eliza asks her friend about it, Annabel will laugh it off. Will say she was ridiculous for drinking so much. And Eliza will puzzle over it, like a navigator will the seas.

They never mention the incident again. But sometimes when they go for walks together, the air crisp and smelling of grass and bluebells, Annabel will take Eliza's hand and press it between both of hers. And sometimes, when Annabel arrives late or doesn't show at all, and later will make excuses – an issue with a servant, a disaster with a gown – Eliza knows the true reason. Knows that Annabel was in the cavernous dark, where Eliza could not reach her.

CHAPTER 33

SHE adjusts the panel upon which she has started to transfer Edmund's likeness, confident of her sketches of him on paper. The mussel shells, pearlescent halves, lie open before her on the table, each holding a bright paint, which she had mixed earlier, smoothing and smoothing powdered pigment into linseed oil to make a fine paste. She asked him to sit again for her, a final time, so she could experiment with colours, match his skin and doublet to her paints.

She limns his likeness to the wood, and as the hours pass, he slowly appears stroke by stroke, inch by inch. She paints along the outline of his chin, brushes over the curve and swell of his wrist opening to his palm.

She moves closer towards him, observing the details of his irises, the light and shade, the brown star that stands in a sea of blue, feathered by those long, fair eyelashes. He watches her intently and raises his hand, which had been so still, and rests it on her neck.

Eventually, pigment on her thumb, fire burned low, she nods. She has enough of him recorded without needing him to sit again. It will take weeks, perhaps months. She doesn't know; she has never created art like this before. She is learning herself as much as she is learning him.

He stands, stretches his arms behind his head and she hears the crackle of his bones in his back. She apologises, smiling. Tells him his patience is a positive trait.

He looks at her, then, eyebrows raised.

The floor has warmed in front of the fire, and her back presses into it, in the pleasure of it, and he is all around her, within and without, and she can taste his skin, the vellum of his study, the lye from his clothes, the hay from the stables, the sandalwood from across the seas. The setting sun gashes the walls in fire. It catches his hair, burning the gold of his head to copper. He is a shape shifter, a form changer; the man she thought he once was, cold and desolate and unreadable has faded, and as she leans onto him, the soft hairs of his chest tickling her, she realises she has found him, the true him, after all.

Perhaps he is thinking the same. There is a creaking of the stairs and they both sigh with relief that they locked the door, then shake with silent laughter. Eventually, when the laughter has quieted and the footsteps on the stairs have passed, he stokes her bottom lip with his thumb and he whispers, 'You know I love you.'

She does know. She understands. She is falling, spinning, repeating it to him, journeying to the words that she has never spoken before. The words ancient, passed from mouth to mouth for millennia; the feeling boundless and ubiquitous, engulfing her, woven to sinew and soul. I love you, I love you.

CHAPTER 34

THERE is a cry. One of the young lads has his arm extended, pointing ahead. Francis looks up, feeling the rest of the crew do the same. He holds the banister, knuckles scored with white scars. When he sees it, he releases a laugh, a rasping sound like salt drawn across wood. After the long, unending months journeying to reach it, it is a miracle.

It. A smudge on the horizon. A smudge that looks like home.

When the ship reaches the harbour and there is a groan of wood against wood as the vessel stills, the men on board take a simultaneous breath, of relief, of disbelief.

The voyage is over.

The gangplank is slid out and the crew flock towards it. Then it's his turn: he walks across the plank, sees the tease of the water below. Then his foot is on the harbour, the ground solid and firm. He manages a few paces before the land reaches for him like a lover, pulling him to her, and his knees meet the summer-hardened ground, the smell of earth familiar yet so long missed, filling his lungs.

He hasn't cried since Arthur. Almost two years. But tears come now, gasping and shuddering their way out of him. Salt from his body washing away the sea's own salt, an ocean armour that has encrusted his skin.

He sees it again as he shuts his eyes: the fog pressing in on all sides. Imagines a score or more of men, swollen, drowned in the uncaring depths. He opens his eyes: now another journey. Navigating his way home and what remains of his place there. Finding his way back to her.

A friendly hand touches his shoulder, the squeeze of fingers into the hollow above his collarbone. Anthony, the friend he should never have met and may never meet again. 'Easy,' he says. 'Let's find an inn.'

Francis understands his meaning. A full meal, cups filled to the brim, a warm bed with a good woman. He can see it in the glint of the man's eyes, the carnal desire for what they've been deprived for so long.

He grimaces, shakes his head. There's money in the purse that hangs from his belt – more than enough to get him back to Worcestershire – but a meagre payment for the amount he gave, and lost, at sea.

'You need a wash, my friend. A shave, a good meal and a good sleep. I won't let you go for less.'

Anthony, who had shown Francis the ropes, explained where the Pacific was in relation to the Atlantic, who had walked with him, calmed him, after they had witnessed Doughty's execution – when Francis had seen blood, seen red, realised with clarity the vengeance he would pay once he returned home. He had trusted his friend then; he should trust him now. He rubs the wetness from his face with his sleeve, and realises how much it stinks. 'Maybe some fresh clothes.'

His friend slaps his back. 'Definitely.'

'But I'll leave tomorrow.'

'Home?'

Francis stares back at the sea. Her peaceful lap against the harbour, as though she has always been this innocent and calm. He tries to fathom the journey they have made, but it will take years for comprehension to seep into his bones. The magnitude of it, too great now to grasp.

He exhales slowly, salt out, earth in. 'Home.'

CHAPTER 35

ELIZA'S eyes are rimmed with kohl, like a woman from the ancient era, places murmured about in learned circles, Egypt, Rome, Greece. Annabel's fingers slide the grease over Eliza's cheek, releasing a clinging, sulphurous scent of egg. Eliza watches her reflection in the window as her face transforms to a shined paleness, as though dipped in moonlight.

'It smells hideous,' she says, trying not to move her mouth.

Annabel tells her to hush.

An acquaintance had invited them to a feast, and most of the previous day had been spent with Annabel pounding her fist into her open palm, counting the steps of the Almain dance, laughing as Eliza misstepped and misstepped again, cursed and slumped in a chair in surrender.

'Up,' her friend ordered. 'Do it again.'

Eliza had thought of all Ma had taught her; to grind herbs, to make a poultice, to read the ingredients from her housewife's book, to keep a secret. But never how to dance with a gentleman. She has only ever known the sweaty fast-paced kind, grabbing her brother's hands and dancing until her legs ached. Or another time, dancing in a hall, the furniture pushed against the walls, Francis's pulse beating to her own. Years ago. But never these dances that have trickled from court, bursting along the estuaries of wealth to gentlemen's circles. She'd felt, for the first time in months, out of her depth; a stranger in an unfamiliar world that should've never been hers.

After the dancing and her poor mastery of the steps, Eliza led Annabel to the painted chamber. She pulled off the linen cloth from the wooden board and Edmund's incomplete likeness stared back at them.

Annabel took a step towards the panel, her eyes fixed on the face before her, then shook her head. 'You don't like it?' Eliza asked.

'He . . . looks like my Sam,' her friend whispered.

Something in Eliza twisted.

'Did they look the same?'

Annabel paused, clasping her small hands beneath her neck. 'There were differences, of course. Sam was taller and broader, being a keener hunter and rider.' Eliza recalled Edmund's words, how Sam had *seemed invincible*, leaving a great, hulking gap for Edmund to fill. 'But their faces were similar, and they had the same gold-spun hair.'

They were brothers, blood-sharers, kin, it was expected they would share similarities, yet Annabel's words had dripped with a longing and lingering that caused Eliza to twitch the sheet in her fingers, keen to recover the panel.

'It's as though you've brought him back.'

She reconsiders their conversation as Annabel dabs red to Eliza's lips with her fingertips. They have not mentioned the portrait since, but Eliza has watched her friend pause in the passageway outside the painted chamber.

Eliza reaches for the gown from her chest, a modest piece.

'You do know tonight's host is one of the most influential men in the middle of England?' Annabel's eyes glint, and for a moment she looks hungered. She sips her cup of wine, her lips trailing the rim as though she is a master seductress.

Eliza raises an eyebrow, forgetting not to move her face too much, feeling the paste solidifying about the creases in her skin. 'How rich?'

Her friend leans forward in mock collusion. 'Like nothing you've ever seen, country girl.'

Eliza swats at her, laughing. Annabel rifles through the chest, pulling out the finest gown Eliza owns, one she had embellished herself with a thread of silk, with a cluster of glass gems across the bodice.

'This.'

The ruff kisses her neck as she and Annabel wait in the entrance hall, cloaks about their shoulders. Edmund approaches, looking at her as though she is a flower just bloomed. She gives a small smile, this time remembering her painted face, feeling strangely powerful. She holds out her arm and enjoys how he ignores it, instead slipping his hand about her waist, and the three of them, Annabel in front, head out into the afternoon.

When they arrive, they are greeted by the manor, a great stone edifice that demands their admiration. Outside in the mild summer's afternoon men juggle torches of fire, heads bent back towards the bowl of the sky, flames arcing above them like comets controlled by the hands of men. The front door is open, and as they climb from their horses, Eliza hears the fury of musicians; the beat of drums, a hum of a lute, an ecstasy of bagpipes.

Annabel grabs Eliza's hand, her eyes bright, already drunk on wine and drunker still on the spectacle, Edmund following behind.

There are forgotten goblets set down on tables as almost thirty pairs of feet fall upon the flagstones in the great hall. Bodies are lifted into the air. She watches Annabel taking turns with a partner, leaning in close to hear his words. The heaviness Eliza has witnessed her friend carrying seems forgotten as she flirts and dances. Edmund talks with a group of men at the other end of the hall, a hand resting idly on his hip, occasionally catching Eliza's eye. She sips her wine, feeling it rake the back of her throat.

At the end of the dance Annabel finds Eliza, and her breath is sweet and quick as she says, 'Come, let's have a look around.'

They head away from the noise of the hall, taking the dark wooden stairs, and Eliza, already feeling the effects of wine, bends her head to smell the wood. Wax and honey.

'A potential suitor?' Eliza whispers, thinking of Annabel's dance partner, the way her friend had held his gaze after the music had finished.

Annabel laughs, a catch in her throat. 'Don't be silly. No one will have me.'

She pulls them towards a door which is ajar at the top of the stairs, a slither of light dancing on the landing. Inside is a great chamber. More lavish than the hall below, where wealthy, drunk people with their arrogance and carelessness are allowed, can wreck the place if they want. Up here, it is private. A curated collection of beauty and objects, shown only to a select few. Windows, intricately latticed, line the walls, looking out across the estate where the evening beats on. A chandelier studded with candles hangs low from the ceiling, making their shadows shrink and grow as they cross the room. An arras hangs from ceiling to floor, every stitch, every inch, covered in flowers and plants, some the size of her thumbnail, others the size of a man's fist, ancient ochre and night-sky blues and fern greens. Crouching in the foliage are animals, partridges and pheasants and, drawing her eye, a luminous unicorn, pale like moonshine.

Ma told her, years ago, when Eliza was a child lying in bed fighting sleep, how a unicorn's horn, if used in the right way, crushed with the right herbs, could save a man dying from poison. Eliza being precocious, growing up fast, learning to question things even if it got her into trouble, had asked if unicorns really existed, and crossed her fingers beneath the sheet, already imagining walking the forests, searching for mushrooms, and finding a silvery beast plucked from myth, staring at her through black onyx eyes. Ma had pinched her nose and whispered, 'If you know where to find them.'

A pang. She misses her mama. Wonders what she is doing right now.

'An impressive piece isn't it?'

The voice pulls her back to the chamber. A man leans in the doorframe, his doublet trimmed in velvet, slightly open at the neck to reveal a tease of his chest beneath. Hair cropped short, a smooth beardless chin. Something about him seems modern, unconventional, as though expectations are an old cloak that he hung up long ago and forgot about.

'I don't believe we were properly introduced at your wedding feast,' he says.

She realises then: he was the third, elusive member of the group when she first saw Annabel talking to Edmund.

'I'm Leonard Hatton.'

The owner of the house; the wealthiest man she has ever met.

'You forgot the Sir,' Annabel chimes from a chair by the hearth.

Eliza dips her head in greeting. 'How do you know each other?'

'Leonard was a great friend of Sam's,' Annabel says, and in a moment of intimacy, Hatton gives her a warm wink.

Annabel holds up her cup, tapping it with her forefinger so it makes a dull clink. Leonard reaches for a jug and fills Annabel's cup and two others, handing one to Eliza.

'To Samuel,' Leonard says. 'He truly was the best of us.'

Annabel does not meet Eliza's eyes as they drink. The ghost of a man settles into the silence.

'Eliza is an extraordinary painter,' Annabel says. 'You should see her painting of Edmund. It looks just like my Sam . . .'

'I'd be keen to see it, I'm interested in art,' Leonard says.

'Anna exaggerates—'

'Don't be coy, Liza,' Annabel says.

'Where did you learn?' Leonard asks.

'I didn't, really. I drew things as a child.' And then, because she feels like she needs to explain herself, 'My father is a yeoman. My family are not like the people here.'

'Yet look how gentility becomes you,' says Annabel, raising her cup again.

Eliza drinks, and catches herself in the twinkle of glass panes and wonders who it is that stares back at her. Pale faced, richly adorned. Her gown sweeping about her, pushed wide by the farthin-gale beneath, the jewels on her torso crawling across her breasts, the taste of grapes, pressed in verdant foreign vineyards, pooling in her mouth. The table where she places her cup is inlaid with pearls.

Would Eliza of the past recognise her? Where is that girl, who smelt of wheat and field, with dirt smeared on her shins, hair free-flowing and matted by winds, the same pair of boots beating down the earth? When, exactly, was she lost?

For the first time Eliza, here, now, understands her father's desires – his ambition to meet with strangers, to barter his daughter to secure his own ascension. To secure a life like this. She fingers the inlaid pearls. If she'd known it could be like this, would she have craved it, would she have done the same? Can she conjure an inch of empathy for her father? Although, of course, Thomas didn't know what he'd gifted her; an unanticipated consequence of his own ambition was a life of freedom, pleasure, safety, and creativity for his daughter. But Ma did. It was a gamble she was willing to take. The unicorn glints on the wall.

Eliza recalls fists on her face. Breath knocked out of her lungs. Failed harvests. Desperate farm labourers. Cold damp rooms. Thomas's greyed teeth.

'I couldn't go back to that life now,' she murmurs. She is a creature metamorphosising into something else. Emerging slowly from its chrysalis.

'Why would you ever need to?' Leonard muses.

Clearer now, right at the corner of her eye she sees him. So close that if he were real, she could extend her arm and touch him. He sits beside her on the tabletop, hands blackened from the forge. He smears the inlaid pearls with soot in a defamatory way. He gazes at her as though he doesn't recognise her. A deep crease forms between the eyes she once knew so well, and he shakes his head, dark hair caressing his neck.

A portly, older man asks for a dance and, unable to refuse, Eliza is led to join the rest of the dancers, where limbs have grown looser from drink, and the air is humid with the slick skin and scent of sweat. Her partner is surprisingly exuberant and competent, guiding her when her newly learnt steps falter, nodding with encouragement. The musicians are more ferocious, stamping their feet, the tune increasingly improvised. The more she dances, the more she realises that she is drunk and that she enjoys the movement of her body amongst the press of other guests. The steps Annabel taught her come easier now that her inhibitions have been drowned in wine.

It is only by chance, when her partner spins her outwards, with a practised arc of his arm, that she looks outside of the flail of bodies, and glimpses her husband and Annabel.

He is holding her wrist, preventing the other woman from walking away. On another, less gentle man, it might have seemed threatening. And yet. And yet, despite the image of tension, of argument, there is an intimacy, their bodies close together, Edmund's words spoken into Annabel's ear as though his mouth has been there before, as though his breath has previously kissed that same neck. Edmund releases his grip and Annabel faces him over her shoulder and her lips are a whisper, a wing of a moth, a thumb's width away from his.

A figure blocks Eliza's view. The dance is ending. Her partner is talking to her, thanking her, leading her back to her cup which a servant has refilled, and she nods at him, feels the cold metal in her hands, the taste of wine sour on her tongue, and when she looks again through the tangle of bodies dispersing across the room, Annabel has disappeared and Edmund stands near the doorway, face set to cut glass, fingers flexing as though missing the wrist they had just held.

CHAPTER 36

I T is dark inside Cecil Hall, the last embers of the fire caressing the floor, as the three of them take off their cloaks in the entrance hall. Soon it will be light. Early summer dawn. Annabel is to stay the night, sleeping in her old bedchamber, where she slept when she was Samuel's wife, which lies across the hall from Eliza and Edmund's. Only a few steps between the thresholds.

Things are reshuffling in Eliza's mind. Their bodies and faces close. His hands about her wrist. It makes her feel sick, like water rising in her throat. She watches Annabel and Edmund navigate the space in the hall, avoiding each other's gaze. The silence is tight like a string about to snap, and she can bear it no longer. Wine has made her tongue loose and easy, but she is in control. The ride home whipped her senses back to her.

'What were you arguing about?' she asks.

For a moment she thinks Edmund will deny it. Instead he says, 'It was nothing,' pinching the skin of his neck. 'I told Annabel to stop drinking so much.'

'Which is no concern of yours,' Annabel says, voice brittle.

Edmund holds up a hand in apology.

Eliza could leave it there. She could. But she doesn't. Because Edmund is still pinching his neck. Because Annabel is rapidly blinking her usually stable doe eyes. Because the two people Eliza has grown closest to, who she has rarely seen interact these past months, had held a private, intimate conversation whilst she was distracted in the same hall. Because the question slithers into her mind of what could have, would have, might have happened between the two of them in quiet, unseeing chambers. Because Mama always told her to trust her instincts.

'What has happened?'

'What do you mean?' Edmund is swift to respond, hackles undeniably raised.

'You lived together for nine years and you know each other well. Yet you barely speak. When Anna visits, you make yourself scarce, and when my back is turned you argue in private.'

She doesn't say, you held her wrist in a way that was so intimate, so furious, it told of an unspoken history. Two people she has never seen touch.

The other man, the other woman silently negotiate as Eliza forces down the welling of anxiety that gathers at the back of her teeth, swallows saliva in her dry throat.

Edmund looks carefully at Eliza. 'You know I love you.'

He waits, but she says nothing, pulse yammering at her neck.

'I had a baby.' Annabel speaks so simply, so abruptly, that for a moment the whole world stills. Eliza tries to grapple with the fact, to meld it into her understanding of the woman before her.

'You told me you and Sam didn't—'

Annabel's eyes fill. 'No, we didn't.'

There is a sinking, down, down to the depths of Eliza's stomach. Down to her womb that is yet to grow. The knowledge of something she doesn't want to face. There is a rush in her head. She looks at Edmund. 'Tell me it is not.'

His hands are clasped tightly in front of him, skin taut about his knuckles. He looks at her, then has the decency to skim his eyes to the floor.

'How long? How long have you been lying together?' Something is building within her, something is breaking. There it is, her old friend: anger, gathering at the shores of her mind. She tries to steady her breathing, to calm this ugly side of herself that she has so often supressed. 'How long have you been fucking behind my back?'

'Liza, it's not like that,' says Annabel.

'It was finished before we were married,' Edmund says, raising a hand to his hair, pulling it back tightly against his scalp. 'Last December.'

She recalls that December: those first few weeks without Francis. Trying to learn a life without him. Her memory of that period is foggy, blanked by grief. Near the end of that month, two men had appeared in her father's hall, and she and Edmund had spoken their first vows, a mere four weeks before their wedding. She remembers too the time that had followed: the crying of the banns; Mama sleeping in her bed; the pain of Francis's absence; the agonising December which bled to a cold January morning when she and Edmund married; and now, this new knowledge. A babe had started to quicken in Annabel's womb.

'You were promised to me and yet you lay with her anyway?' She is daring him to contradict it. She is incredulous, sickened, hating the sight of her husband but unable to take her eyes off him. 'You lay with your brother's wife?'

His silence is confirmation.

She bangs her fist against the wainscoting and the sound echoes in the hall. Her husband tries to hold her beating palm, but she wrenches it free, catching him hard on the chin. His hand flies to his jaw and he inhales sharply, but he doesn't step away. He keeps his eyes on her, those deep blue eyes which, of late, she has grown to want to languish in.

'After our betrothal, all I could think of was Sam's death. How if he were still here, everything would've been different. The whole goddamn thing.' Edmund sounds like a desperate man, justifications leaking from his mouth. 'I didn't want to marry you, and you didn't want me either, you can't deny that. Annabel was still living here and she understood, we'd both loved Sam – '

'It was a mistake . . .' Annabel whispers, 'I just wanted my Sam back.'

The question Eliza hadn't thought to ask at first shivers its way through her, 'Where is the child now?'

'Walter agreed to take Blythe in.' Tears drip from Annabel's chin, splotch on the floor. The name makes the child real, like a punch to the gut. 'My family wouldn't allow her to stay with me. They've forbidden me to speak of her.'

A perfect little bastard, forged in grief, rendered to only a whispering thought, a secret, kept for Edmund's pride – for what man takes his brother's wife? – and Annabel's reputation – for what man would have such a harlot?

'She was the reason you wanted to go to London,' Eliza says, looking at Edmund. The private words between Edmund and Walter, which Eliza had convinced herself were nothing more than men's talk, were women's talk. 'I thought you wanted to show me the city.'

'I wanted to—' Edmund shifts towards her, but Eliza moves away.

'I told Edmund as soon as I knew I was with child . . . You overheard us. He arranged everything. Then my father wrote to Edmund whilst you were away in London. Our daughter had been born, but it was a terrible birthing. We thought I might not . . .' Annabel covers her mouth, stifling her sobs.

With this information, the past unfurls anew for Eliza: that spring afternoon when Annabel arrived, crying; the clandestine meeting in Edmund's parlour. After, when Edmund had found Eliza beneath the oak tree, sitting in the field beneath the splay of branches, and lied that Annabel was being pressured into remarrying. Then following his illness – after months of her care – when he rode away for a day without a word to his wife, to visit Annabel's father and relay his plans for London, where the babe would be sent after the birth. And then the news that arrived the morning after Eliza had first lain with Edmund, in their rented bed to the thrum and beat of the city. The messenger boy with a note he'd hand to none but Edmund; the words within too delicate, too private to share with another. Edmund's urgent departure, riding away in the rain. She realises that Nicholas had never been unwell, that Cecil Hall hadn't been her husband's destination. Instead, a tiny babe took its first breaths as Annabel was in peril.

'You lied to me, Edmund. You lied so easily.' Eliza's voice is hollow. It's not an accusation; it's just the hard-won truth.

'How could I tell you? I thought it would ruin us, whatever we might be. We'd sworn to a lifetime together.'

'And you don't think that this is our ruining?'

'Don't say that.'

'How can I trust you? If you'd told me, I could've forgiven you. We all have histories.' And there is hers, just there, a tall man with raven hair, darting in the shadows at the edge of her vision.

'I was trying to protect you.'

'I never needed your protection.' Her tongue is forked, her words vipers. 'You were right when you said we would never have chosen this. I would never have chosen you.'

His face turns carefully blank as he retreats, deep within his fortress. The space between them is an empty battlefield after conflict. Annabel sits on a stool, crying silently.

Anger and violence are catching, rearing. A flame when it first finds kindling. It's in her making, in her bones. She could crush men now; she could eat a heart whole. Is this how Thomas feels? Is it?

Francis is with her, two paces ahead, and she follows him, up the stairs, longing to reach for his hand. They walk along the passageway and into the painted chamber, which is lit by the moon. She feels a clarity settling about her, such energy at her centre, such controlled fury. Years and years of it, now untethered.

She bolts the door, crossing the room in three paces. She lifts the corner of the table, the heavy wood against her palms, and hauls it over so it crashes upon the floor, a leg splintering, paper and charcoal, powder and brushes and shells falling, spilling, bouncing, pattering, powders clouding. The noise resounds about the chamber, the house a drum, magnifying sound, shaking its timbers. She hears shoes on the stairs, but she doesn't care.

Through the gloom she realises that her companion has gone, and she is alone. Her breath comes now in sharp, ragged sobs.

For so long she has sought safety and peace, had thought that she was finally grappling with it, falling in love, falling into trusting. She grabs her drawings of Edmund and rips them. The careful sculpturing of his hands with her chalk, disintegrating to pieces. She thinks of her father who beat and betrayed her, of Francis and what happened to him. Francis, who she lost, swapped for this. Her hands reach for the painting, the interchangeable image of Edmund and Samuel, who shared blood. Shared a woman. She thinks of her husband, who she gave herself to, who she allowed in like a nut cracked open, who peppered their marriage with lies to mask one, great damning secret.

Somewhere a man lies with another man. Somewhere a wife waits for her husband to come home. Somewhere a man takes his revenge. Somewhere a woman destroys all she created.

Edmund is banging against the door, and Annabel is calling her name. Eliza brings the wooden panel down on the upturned table, bashing it again and again. It splinters down the middle. Deep fissures form through her painting, through hours of work, mind and soul in paint. Down and down.

Finally, finally, as sweat collects at the nape of her neck, it snaps in two.

CHAPTER 37

SOMEWHERE, leagues away, a woman stares absently out of a window.

She looks out towards the dark, to the front yard and rickety gatehouse where the sparrows nest. She has watched the summer evening turn from violet to navy, watched the stars begin to speckle the sky, and wondered where her husband is and why he hasn't come home.

Not that it makes a change, he is often out late: ever since the fight between him and their son, a mass of swearing and shouting and reaching and cuffing and ducking and punching and shoving. Ever since she tried to separate them, her coif askew as though she were a madwoman, hands and nails scrabbling at their arms and necks. Since their son left, taking the horse, spitting on the ground that her husband had spent his life tilling. Since then, her husband has withdrawn into himself, drinking more, squandering his coin at the inn.

She has wondered, vaguely, if everything he has done is starting to catch up with him. But she has little empathy. Why should she? He hasn't wasted any on her in near thirty years.

Now, as she looks out of the window, her fingers playing absently with a strand of hair that has come loose from her coif, a twine of dark brown spun with silver, she thinks of her daughter, dearest dove, with the same dark hair, of her neck bent low as she squats to tend the herb garden, of the blemish that sits on her neck, small and round like a child's thumbprint.

She received a letter from the daughter some months before, had almost torn it in two in her hurry to take it from the messenger's hand. Inside, the folded paper contained a small portrait, of face caught by sunlight, of eyes staring straight out, determined, unyielding, of body dressed in a gown richer than anything the mother has ever owned.

Her daughter seems happy. You can forgive the woman for thinking so; she does not yet know what has happened this night, leagues away, in another man's hall.

It is late, very late, by the time the husband arrives home. She dozed off on top of the coverlet, a cool breeze dancing on her face through the ajar casement window, but she is shuddered awake by a slam of the door below, the staggering of steps. Her eyes flutter open in the dark. The candle must have blown out whilst she slept. She waits and listens. Silence falls like dust. And it holds. And holds.

She swings her feet from the bed and calls, tentatively to her husband. She is cautious, always she is cautious around him, but especially when he has been in his cups. He is volatile, unpredictable. And she is aware ever since her son left, of how alone she is.

The husband doesn't answer. She calls again, louder.

Nothing.

She lights her candle, using the embers in the grate and the breath in her lungs. Out of the chamber and across to the top of the stairs, flame held high. She sees a mass slouched on the bottom step, head lulled against the wall.

'Husband,' she says, rushing down the stairs. The reek of him hits her first, swells into her nostrils, stink of beer and cheap ale clinging to him like an ague, before she sees him properly. Before she realises what has happened. She stoops, grasps his chin with her spare hand, feeling the cold of it and the rough of his beard beneath her fingers. Blearily he half opens his eyes. A groan in the back of his throat.

There is something sticky beneath her hand resting on his face. In the single, bouncing light of the candle, her eyes travel upwards over his cheek which is wrinkling with age, pouches forming beneath his eyes, over the jut of his brow, to his forehead, where, just below his hairline, sits a great bulging bruise amid multiple ruptures of the skin. He is baptised by blood. Across his forehead, between his eyebrows, slicking his left cheek.

A gasp catches in her mouth and she instinctively removes her hand, blood on her palm.

He lets out another groan and his eyelids close. Something has impacted his forehead – a rough edge, perhaps a door or wall or the butt of blade, again and again.

What happened, she asks, not waiting for his answer, bloody handprint on his shoulder, shaking him, telling him to stay awake, and then she is rushing though the kitchen into the still room, rummaging through her life's work for the treatments for deep cuts and deeper bruises. She rummages in the dark and finds torn strips of linen, and a pail of water, which she heaves back to the slumped man on the staircase.

She dips a cloth into the bucket and mops at the stickiness of his face. He winces, screws up his eyes against whatever dulled pain he can feel in his stupor. His exhalation on her face. By God he stinks.

Again she tells him to stay awake, stay with her, and again she asks, what happened, and it's only on the third attempt when she says, 'In God's name, what happened to you?' that his eyes open slightly, like the low slip of the moon on a clouded evening, and she has to watch the shape of his lips to understand what he is saying.

'Came . . . came out of The Phoenix . . . round the corner. Someone . . . came up behind me . . . wasn't . . . fair fight . . .'

She could smack him. A fair fight. As though that matters. As though coming home in this state after a *fair fight* would've been preferable. As though a version of events could ever exist where he held up his hands and said, yes I was nearly beaten to death, but at least it was an honest beating.

But when, sly whispering in her mind, has Thomas ever played fair?

'Who did this?' she asks.

He shakes his head. The blood is still guggling thickly from his forehead, cuts deeper than she first thought. She uses nearly all her cloths cleaning and bandaging his head.

How she manages to get him up the stairs she will never be able to recall. She will remember only her pulse at her temple, the weight of his arm across her shoulders, the laboured thump of his feet upon each step.

Onto the bed. This bed where they conceived their three, now two, children, where sometimes she has lain at night, crying silent, shaking tears about this, all of this. How it all turned out. He slumps backwards, eyes drooping as she eases off his boots, noticing blood spattered on the toe, caught in the twine. Is she bitter that she'll have to scrub them later? She awkwardly manoeuvres him, so he is propped upright on the bed and removes the jerkin from his broad back.

She is calm now. The shock of the blood has faded and the world is quiet. He must not sleep, must not close his eyes, lest he never open them again. He shivers and she closes the window, shuts out the night, and sits by his feet. She keeps nudging him awake.

She begins to talk. Of her day, of the people she saw at the market, of the gossip she hadn't dared tell him before, that the rival yeoman on the other side of town has just taken lease of more land, and that folk are saying openly that more lads will work with him this harvest, that they don't want to work for Thomas, with his menial wages and volatile manner.

Her husband grunts, slinking between waking and unconsciousness. She shakes his shoulder and adjusts his head and forces him to drink some small beer.

But her tongue is unleashed. She tells him of their daughter, of the painting that she has kept hidden, of what a talent she is, of how she is outshining her father; her father who always wished for another son. She tells him how their son is thriving, finally free, that all the teaching at the local school has equipped him to set out on a path without his father. Oh, the irony, that the father gave the son the tools to do it, like a whip for his own back.

And then the years are spilling from her, all the things she never said, all the things she should have. She talks of the man she loved before, who showed her a kindness that she has craved across the years, a craving Thomas never satiated. She tells him how she has never forgiven him, and never will. Not for the way he treated their children. Not for the scar on her cheek. Not for what he did to that poor labourer, that sweet-smiler, foot-jigger who held their daughter's heart in his hand, for a time.

It is the mention of the lad that gets through to Thomas. He opens his eyes, shiny and squinty in delirium. 'Be quiet woman.' It is an effort for him to speak; the pain in his head must be throbbing, must be like birds attacking his skull. It would've been easier for him to say nothing.

She falls still and silent, like a woman cast from stone.

'Leave me,' he adds, words breathy, like a curtain caught in a gust of wind.

She wavers, on the cusp of saying no, he shouldn't be left alone. But then she changes her mind; she should've left him long ago. 'As you wish.'

She reaches for the candle to light her way, the house a dark tunnel about her. She goes to her daughter's bedchamber, where she climbs into the cold sheets, imagining she can smell her, that she is with her in the chamber, a little girl giggling and asking Mama Mama, why are you in my bed?

Her heart squeezes.

She thinks she won't sleep. But she does: it settles about her like the first snow of winter, muffling, comforting, covering all the shit in its pale glow.

When she wakes, the sun is rising, the first men already outside. No one has knocked to see if their master is about, to ask what needs to be done for the day. It is a comfort to know the men are at their work, life continuing as usual. She opens the shutters and watches them share a loaf of bread together, talking and laughing, an easiness beneath the scarlet-streaked sky.

There is no movement from the bedchamber across the landing, no creaking of the floorboards, no sighing of the bed, no swearing under the breath as a man, bleared from sleep and too much beer, tries to find his jerkin.

When the red of the sky has faded, and the labourers have finished their breakfast and are picking their way through the crops, she goes to her husband's bedchamber.

The place that has witnessed so much, now witnesses something new. He lies on his back, his head turned towards the window, as though watching the light. He doesn't answer when she speaks his name. She walks tentatively around the bed and looks at his face. Eyes closed, peaceful. An arm at an angle, overhanging the mattress.

When she touches him, he does not wake. When she places her cheek beneath his nose, there is no gentle exhalation of air. When she whispers his name, *Thomas*, she receives no reply. When she holds her fingers to his wrist where his pulse should beat, she is met with a stillness, like a great empty sky.

CHAPTER 38

E LIZA swings from shock to that marrow-deep feeling that she had an inkling all along. Secrets running blood deep. Edmund has a daughter.

She sleeps alone and badly, waking each night, feeling the cold in the chamber. At the first glint of dawn, she goes to the window seat in the gallery, unable to lie awake any longer. The place where she stood months and months before, watching guests arrive for her wedding feast, becomes a vigil for her sadness and rage. She rests her cheek against the glass, one leg propped up on the seat, the other skimming down to the floor.

It has been like this for over a week. Seeing in the morning like this. The first morning had been the hardest, and yet it was the most beautiful. Dramatic red slashed the sky like a wound.

She had wanted to leave. After she had desecrated the painted chamber, destroyed everything she had created, and her voice had grown sore from the pain that comes when a lump grows in your throat, and her palms were red and searing, she had wanted to be away. But where could she go? Not to her brother, who is still living in a small room in the belly of London. Not to her father's home, where she had not the strength to face his questions and abuse. If she had known where he was, or whether he was alive, she would've gone to Francis.

Her mind has slipped to where it always slips when things get too much. To Francis. The comfort of him. The home of him.

Now, she sees a cloaked figure enter beneath the gatehouse, cross the courtyard, his face concealed by a hat. There are sounds from below, doors and voices. She doesn't get up to listen, her head resting against the glass. There is movement behind her. Edmund stands in the passageway, his shirt untucked. He looks as though his night was as sleepless as hers. The morning light catches in his eyes which today look watery and weak.

They stare at each other. After the portrait had splintered and broken, she had slumped in the painted chamber amidst the artist's rubble, pigment smeared on her cheek, skirts spread and flattened about her like a wilted rose, and stared out at the moonlight which filtered across her face. When he eventually managed to open the door, he offered his hand to help her up, but she wouldn't take it. They have barely spoken since.

'Your brother is downstairs,' he says.

She is on her feet, her old kirtle rumpling around her knees, curiosity coursing immediately, where moments before she'd felt only lethargy. 'What is it?'

When Henry tells her, standing in the hall in his new boots, running the rim of his hat through his deft fingers, Eliza feels a surge. A great weight, which she has carried for as long as she can remember, lifting.

'He is gone.'

There is a before and an after. They live now in the after.

Her brother embraces her and tears spring to her eyes. Not grief, but exhaustion, overwhelm. Relief.

The horses are readied, Henry mounted by the time she emerges, a bag packed, Dorothy squeezing her hand in farewell. Edmund tries to help her into the saddle, but Eliza shakes her head. I can manage.

Her husband offered to come, but she had looked at him with tired brown eyes and he nodded, sorrow across his face, and said, 'Come back to me, when this is all over.'

❦

It's as though her life since her marriage has been defined by travelling from one place to another, the pillars between which the rest of her life settles. Rain lashes them as they ride. The earth throws up its scent of mud and stagnant pools as it is disturbed by water from the heavens. They could stop at an inn, dry off beside a hearth, but they don't. They cannot arrive soon enough.

As the siblings wait, side by side, impatient, for a farmer to cross the lane, herding bleating sheep across the track, Henry explains how he'd received word from Ma, and left London the same day. That he gave his lover a swift kiss goodbye to before he left the city – the one he loved all those years before, the one with the wife who does not know of the affair, the one who has been warming Henry's bed each night – is another tale. A story within a story. One he will tell his sister another time, when change isn't upon them, when she looks less bone tired. Instead, he explains that he journeyed three days to fetch her, keen to share the news with her as soon as he could, and for them to return home.

He pulls out a leather sack from inside his doublet and hands it to her. The double beer within is strong, burns her throat, but she takes another swig, observings her brother's profile. Chin up, eyes watching the last of the sheep falter past.

'You're free,' she says, throwing the sack back to him which he catches with one hand. 'Freer now than you've ever been.'

'We all are. Let's hope he burns in the purgatory the Catholics whisper about.'

His words would once have shocked her. She once swore in the name of God in front of her father, and felt the weight of his hand at her cheek.

'God knows, he deserves it.'

'All hardened now to blasphemy?' Henry grins.

She doesn't smile, hands gripping tighter to the rain-slick reins. 'Something like that.'

The house appears on the lane before them. The outside is the same, giving no clue of the changes within: the front yard, the gatehouse, the glimpse of the blooming kitchen garden stretching around the back. The half timber is darkened by the rain. For a moment, Eliza wonders if her brother had misunderstood. Perhaps Thomas still lives, and this is a trap to lure his children home. She senses Henry's uneasiness, as though their thoughts are connected by a string.

In the stable, their fingers scrabble with ties and buckles, they sling their bags in their hands. Eliza's skirts whip her ankles as they run to Ma who waits for them at the front door. One look at her face, and they know it is true. Their mother steps out into the downpour, and the three of them hold each other beneath the deep clay sky.

※

They missed the funeral. By the time Henry had received word in London, their father had already found solace in the ground's soft embrace. Thomas couldn't stay festering in the house any longer. Not with the summer heat, the close air eddying into the halls. Two days was enough. After the washing of the body, the shrouding in a linen sheet, the sawing and hammering of the local carpenter to conjure a crude coffin, Ruth had taken the final walk with her husband, along the lanes to the church's graveyard.

The church bell had rung with a clang, metal on metal, holy blacksmith's forge, calling the folk to witness the coffin as it was lowered into the ground. And folk had come, the death of the yeoman cause enough for an outing, with rosemary pinned to their clothes which emanated a pure, comforting scent, so at odds with the man they buried. The minister spoke of Thomas's salvation and Ruth had wondered, unashamedly, whether her dead husband had done enough in life to save him in death. Folk turned to her, clasped their hands about hers, gave her conspiratorial nods, as if to say, you survived, you're free.

She had dressed in mourning, but it looked like her rebirthing. Her eyes were dry as the bones that lay beneath their feet.

After, the grave diggers had moved in, shovels in hand, eager to get the job done so they could go home, rest their weary legs. Their work, never-ending. The soil had thudded gently atop the wood, and with each thud, Ruth felt as though she was coming home to herself.

⁂

The three of them sit at the end of the table in the great hall, beside the hearth. They drink thick, aged wine that wound its way to them by ship and cart, passed from hand to hand, which Thomas had been saving for best. They drink to his good choice in wine. They eat cuts of salted beef with their fingers, enjoying that there is no one watching them, no one to answer to, salt dissolving on their tongues.

They talk, without fear or hesitation. Ruth tells them every detail of his death, her eyes flicking from daughter to son, son to daughter, imploring them to understand, to forgive her. Eliza places her head on Ma's shoulder, Henry stands and kisses his mother on the cheek. You gave him everything, they say. The night he met his maker you had nothing more to give. You followed his wishes. You allowed nature and God's will to run their course.

That night Eliza dreams of her father's burial. She peers into the trench dug to admit her father and sees, with a jolt that turns her insides to water, that the body lying there is not Thomas, but Edmund. His eyes are huge and unseeing, cast skyward, golden hair spread across the mud. She steps back, a shriek rising in her throat and there, at the edges of her vision, is a man. Raven-dark hair, longer than before, reaching to his shoulders. He has blood dripping from his hands.

She wakes, mind uneasy. Ma's tale of Thomas's death is fresh on her mind, like a grave, newly dug. The house still sleeps, first light purpling the sky when she opens the shutters and feels a rush of cool air christen her lungs. The rain has stopped.

She goes to her father's parlour. It's smaller than she remembers, the furniture shabby and cheaply made. His desk plain and worn.

The dead man's travelling cloak still hangs from a nail in the wall. She never had much chance to linger here whilst he lived. But now as she opens the coffer in the corner, she takes her time to observe its contents: bags of coin, trade contracts for the harvest that he never lived to see fulfilled, notes in his scrawled hand, quills, a spare inkhorn, a scattering of wheat kernels in the corners. And there, as her hands rifle through, not knowing what they are searching for, she finds a wad of papers, neatly stacked together, tied with string. Papers marked and smudged with chalk.

Her drawings. The ones he took, shortly before he took Francis from her too. An archive of her childhood, a record of every time she felt her anger and frustration about to spill over, and had turned to her chalk and charcoal, ink and paper, letting it flood onto the page.

The papers are worn, the edges battered as though someone has thumbed through them, again and again, before returning them to a neat pile, hidden in the chest. She always presumed that he had burned them, that he had no sentimentality within him, that he cared nothing for her.

She will never know.

How to live with her father's cruelties. How to process the wake of violence, the marks he left. How to reconcile it. She closes the heavy lid of the coffer and sits upon it, lingering with her father's ghost.

CHAPTER 39

NEWS travels like a flood, swirling into homes, washing through whole towns. But in the debris of the mourning period – trying to understand and grapple with change, and experiencing a grief that is strange, that makes you feel relief yet makes you yearn for something that never was – some news can be lost. Some news fails to reach the dead yeoman's house at the edge of town, the last before the stretch of forests and fields.

The days have a calmness to them, a delicacy that never existed when Thomas lived. Eliza easily resumes life at home helping Ma – cleaning, washing, cooking, cultivating herbs and cures out in the garden in the June heat. It gives Eliza space to mull over Edmund and Annabel's revelation, flickering between frustration, hurt and sorrow.

For a few days, the two women don't leave the house, preferring the solace of home. It's Henry who comes and goes, settling his father unfinished business: paying labourers, delivering grain, repaying the innkeeper for numerous cups of beer, settling Thomas's will. The threads of a life, bound up.

Eliza rarely sees her brother run. Henry always was a quick and nimble runner, had learnt the need for it growing up, but as an adult, especially since his success in London, he is more measured, walking with purpose, as though he has always been the master of his own time. So when she looks up from the herbs of the kitchen garden to see him sprinting towards her, his new jerkin hastily undone beneath the glare of the sun, the words are out of her mouth before he has reached her. 'What's happened?'

He picks his way along the neat path between the beds. 'I heard news at the inn.'

She wipes away the sweat on her forehead with the inside of her wrist. Smells lavender and soil on her fingertips. 'Oh?'

'Francis.'

'What of him?'

'Sister,' he stops, watches her, 'he is back.'

A flap of a wing. A blink. A heartbeat. A finger snap. Just like that.

Her mind is flight. She holds Henry tightly, laughing into his shoulder, her legs growing weak, disbelief alchemising to euphoria, settling eventually on relief, her heart releasing in a way that it has not in almost two long years.

He lives. He is returned. Almost two years he has been lost, and now it takes only a breath, only three words, to bring him back to her.

PART III

CHAPTER 40

THE route is as familiar as a forgotten folksong, the words coming back without conscious thought. She pauses at the edges of her father's fields, which once would have been alive with men, their sweat mingling with the earth. It is quiet now, the day still.

The lanes take more shape as she heads into town, rows of houses casting shadowy reprieve from the sun. Women sit on the front steps, darning and sewing in the shade. The heat has turned the rubbish rancid; the smell of rotten food, and worse, lingers. She turns the corner onto his street, hearing the cries of children from the houses. Closer, she hears the clink of metal, the blacksmith's workshop round the back. Her heart is tight, like someone is crushing it in the palm of their hand. She keeps twisting her wedding band with her thumb, feeling a frantic, nervous energy caught within her.

The front door, when she reaches it, is worn, weather-stained, sun-warped. She hesitates at the point where she will overwrite all her imaginings and expectations of this moment. When reality will form, fix and etch itself in time.

Then she knocks.

A man answers. There is shock thick in her throat at the sight of him. It is Arthur, full grown, the boy who she had seen limp on his pallet, who died when the physician refused to come. And then her throat releases. The man's nose is slightly broader than Arthur's, his chin has a crease in its centre. And he is older than Arthur will ever be. It is Philip, his brother, the lutist.

He stands awkwardly, assessing the woman he once knew, who

was in and about their house since he was a small boy. They swap pleasantries. Eliza's mouth is dry. He cuts her off before she can finish her sentence: 'I've come to see—'

'He's out back. I'll fetch him.' He recedes into the house, shouting, 'Frank, Frank!' Then, quiet.

A figure comes into view in the gloom of the passageway, wiping his hands on a cloth. His step falters. Her belly swoops and dives like starlings. She twists and twists her wedding band. All the questions she has, everything she wants to know, leave her.

They face each other across the threshold.

He is like someone from a dream; someone she recognises but does not know. His once longer, dark hair is cut short, close to his head. His face has thinned, the bones sharper beneath the skin. Stubble shadows his cheeks. A scar streaks through his eyebrow. His eyes, however, are deep brown like she remembers. They drink each other in. Time slows. The cloth hangs limp in his hand, forgotten.

'You're here,' he says hoarsely.

She doesn't trust her words. She has a primal urge to reach for him, to wrap her arms tightly about his now angular body, to feel his bones against her own. Breathe him in. To run the pads of her thumbs along his jaw line, along his cheekbones. Perhaps he does too, because his hand jerks involuntarily towards her before it stills at his side.

Whatever they both want, they quash it. She doesn't know what he wants or expects, nor where he's been, nor who he's loved. And she is a wife now, claimed.

'D'you want to come in?'

She moves her tongue in her too dry mouth, wishing she had a small beer to wet her throat. She feels the size of her skirts, bright green like a jewel in a dark room, compared to his thin shirt, which is gaping, misshapen, blackened from the forge. She has misjudged. She is a fool. She should not have come. She is panicking and fearful and everything, everything – how awful it was losing him, how she lost a part of herself in his absence – floods back to her.

246

'You're busy, I shouldn't have come uninvited,' she gabbles, her body moving away without her conscious decision. 'I'm sorry, silly of me, you're working . . .'

'Come in,' he says.

There's a steadiness to him. An easy simplicity to his words. It calms her. It reminds her of the safety she felt with him. It reminds her of that night in the kitchen garden beneath the moon. *Stay with me.*

He stands back to let her pass, their bodies close for a moment in the doorway. He takes up less space than she remembers.

The kitchen, with its hearth, and pockmarked table, and benches upon which the family squeeze, where the food is cooked and the washing is done when the winter grows too cold, is a part of her history. Dancing with Francis. Grinding herbs to save Arthur. The last time she visited, in the days following Francis's disappearance, she had sat at the table, her mind full of vacant horror. The nightmare of it, the way Margaret's hands shook, the way the currents within Eliza pulled her to drowning, when she thought she would never be able to swim to the surface. How many experiences and memories a room can hold.

Francis observes her, and she wants to pinch him, poke him, grasp him, discover the miracle of him being alive, and here. But she doesn't.

'Do you want a drink?' he asks.

'If you're having one.'

He fills two cups. There are nicks on the back of his head, bright white scars where the hair will not grow. She doesn't know all the marks across his body anymore. His skin holds a map to a life she can never know.

'How have you been?' he asks.

How to answer such a deep, sprawling question.

'Well enough. And you?'

He shrugs as he passes her a cup. There are grazes across his knuckles, cuts scabbing over. Vulnerable, battered hands that once she would've held to her lips. Their fingers touch for the briefest moment and they both look away.

'Henry told me yesterday that you were here,' she says into the loitering silence. The question she has asked these past two years, finally reaching for its answer. 'Where've you been?'

'Thomas never told you?'

'He told me he sent you away, but he didn't know where.'

'He didn't know where they took me?' He laughs in disbelief, devoid of colour. 'Of course, your father wouldn't get his hands dirty like that.' *Your father.* As though she is of the same stock. A twist deep within her; perhaps she is.

'A coward,' she agrees.

There is a look on his face that she doesn't remember. Grim, jaw set. A danger to him that the Francis she once knew hadn't possessed. And she thinks she understands it, being pushed to your limits. Thinks of her mother, leaving Thomas to die.

'I went to The Phoenix,' he begins, cocking his head towards the inn, the safe harbour for a cheap drink, town gossip, bloody brawls and grimy whores. He doesn't say when; he doesn't need to. They both remember that night – after their argument, their splintering, when grief and death had choked the air.

He tells her his tale, the kind spun by players to entertain crowds. Except, he is not a player, only a man whose life veered dramatically off course, and she is not a crowd, only a woman who would've followed him anywhere. He tells her how he drank too much and how two strangers cornered him almost within sight of his home and forced him onto a cart bound for God knew where.

When he speaks of Plymouth, she shakes her head. She doesn't know the lie of the land or where Plymouth is; has been as far as London, and that was far enough. He raises his eyebrows at this, and Eliza sees the questions on the end of his tongue, but she waves him on, anxious to know his story.

He recalls his first steps aboard the ship. 'Jesus, I was terrified.'

She has been clutching her fingers together so hard that their tips are pale and bloodless. 'A sailor,' she says, surprised. His words echo her thoughts: 'Of all the things I thought I'd be, that wasn't one of them. What use is a man from the middle, who knows only about land and hammering metal, at sea?' His tone is bitter, like cloves sharp on the tongue.

'Did they find out?'

'Of course. A space that small and nowhere to escape? The officers tried to make an example of me, said I was deadwood slowing the voyage down. Luckily, I made a friend who taught me what I needed, and I found something to be grateful to Thomas for after all. All those summers working on his damned land had given me strength and stamina. Eventually, the officers grew tired and let me be. All the same, I've had enough of gentlemen.'

'Yeomen too, I expect.'

He holds her gaze, 'Yes.'

She, wife of a gentleman, daughter of a yeoman.

'When did you return?'

'Less than a month ago, Eli.' He softens as her name catches in his mouth. His expression is strangely defiant. Yes, I know you still. I remember.

'That whole time at sea . . . I didn't know if you were alive.'

'You thought of me then?' A flicker of his old familiarity.

Once she would have swatted him away across the table, her hand padding against his shirt. She twists the wedding band on her finger, feeling it snag and wrinkle her skin. He observes her, still as a robin that knows it is being watched, so unlike the constant jig of energy he once possessed, shifting his weight from one foot to the other. Perhaps he lost it somewhere in the ocean.

'I am so sorry for . . .' She realises she can't name one thing. There are too many. Sorry for her father's cruelty. Sorry that he, Francis, is an emaciated man. Sorry he was robbed nearly two years of his life. Sorry that they sit like familiar strangers in his family home.

'You don't owe me anything. It's Thomas who should've apologised.'

'You heard he is dead then?'

There is a commotion on the stairs, the creak of floorboards, and a child runs into the room, his small feet heavy on the floor. 'Frankie, Frankie,' he is saying, holding out his hand, imploring Francis to look at what he'd found.

Behind the boy comes Margaret, arms filled with laundry. She gasps when she sees Eliza.

'I didn't know you were back,' Francis's mother says, dropping the sheets, drawing Eliza into a tight embrace. The last time they met was Eliza's wedding day, and for the first time that afternoon, Eliza feels like crying. 'You look beautiful,' Margaret continues, holding Eliza away from her. Francis seems not to hear, crouching beside the child to examine the ladybird crawling over his palm.

'Who is he?'

'My eldest grandson.' The babe in arms at the dance all those years before. Time waiting for no one.

Margaret regathers the linens, unlocks the door to the yard, calls for her grandson to come, leave his uncle in peace, but the child is pulling at Francis's fingers, begging him to play outside.

Eliza should leave, but she can't bring herself to. There's so much more she wants to know. And she wants him to reassure her, with words that drip from his lips, that when she does eventually turn her back, he won't disappear like smoke on the wind. She observes him, his spent body, the jut of his cheekbone, his shirt sleeves falling away to reveal the stark ball of his wrist as he lifts the child onto his hip. She wants to hold that wrist in her hand, run her thumb over the shape of him. You have missed all of this, she thinks, as the child giggles. You have endured so much. Because of us.

She is almost out the front door, heat rising behind her eyes, when two calloused fingers briefly, gently brush the back of her neck.

'Tomorrow?' he asks.

CHAPTER 41

SHE reaches for the hiding place in the bedchamber wall and removes the contents. Twine, quills, coins. The evil, tarnished gleam of the brooch that her father had bought with the currency of other people's suffering, which had scored Ruth's cheek.

She shows it to Ma, brooch resting in open palm.

'I stole it from him, years ago,' she says.

'What for?' Ma asks.

'I wanted to sell it and use the money.'

Her mother's eyes are a question Eliza cannot avoid.

'I planned to leave . . . with Francis.'

Ma reaches a hand to Eliza's cheek, shakes her head. 'Oh, my dove. "For God hath not given to us the spirit of fear, but of power and of love and of a sound mind." You would've done anything, wouldn't you? To be with him.'

Eliza bites the inside of her cheek to keep her face still. Would she now? Would she?

'It's a shame you didn't sell it,' Ma says, staring at the brooch. A rare expression arranges across her features. Of hatred, anger, pain.

'What should we do with it?' Eliza asks.

The older woman picks it up, runs her finger along its sharp edges. 'I would say bury it, let it be lost to the fields, but it would be a waste.' She rolls back her shoulders, stands tall, magnificent. A fighter. 'Get Henry to sell it. Let us honour Thomas by turning everything he had into coin. Wasn't that all he was? Just a cruel man chasing more, cold coin.'

They walk through the fields of their childhood. It's easier this way, a distraction from looking at each other for too long, from holding eye contact and losing the route of their sentences. She moves more freely, has left her best gown at home, and instead found an old kirtle, the kind she used to wear when she was the girl he used to know.

She listens enraptured as he tells her about the voyage – Drake's mission, the journey across the Atlantic, the men who never returned home. He describes setting anchor beside a bay of white sand, and she tries to imagine it, she who has never even been to the coast. Never felt the whip of sea breeze. She tries to hold it all, to understand; he has been so inconceivably far away. To the edge of the map. She wishes she could've been there with him through the perils, shared vistas and memories, known all that he has known. Once they were so familiar, she could see what he described as though she'd been there, as though she was with him everywhere. Their own collective memory. But not now. His memories, his experiences, are too far out of her grasp.

Above them a murmuration of starlings mist across the clouds, the birds packed tightly together as though they will never leave each other's side.

He talks about the ships by their names – the Pelican renamed the Golden Hind, the Marigold, the Benedict – as though they are people, great sacred bodies holding lives inside. But those bodies gave way to dead men whose corpses disappeared into the great swell. He shakes his head, some memories too painful to speak of.

'What was the final storm like?' she asks.

'Hell. I thought we were lost.' He rubs the back of his neck with his grazed hands, 'Out there, you saw every single detail of a man. I saw men sleep, eat, shit, beg, die. I threw dead friends overboard.' He tilts his head away so she can't see his expression. Roughly rubs the bridge of his nose. 'You learn things about yourself, about your limits, out there.'

The questions she has feel too intimate to ask.

'But I had hope, most of the time, that I'd make it home,' he says.

'Testament to your strength of spirit.'

He shakes his head. 'The ship had a name.'

'Oh?'

He stops walking and light catches his shorn head, revealing it to be flecked with white hairs at his temples. The strain of the sea. When she saw him last, she'd believed him a man. But now, wading through recollection, she sees that they'd just been children, playing at adults. He is a man now. He has seen things that others go whole lifetimes without witnessing.

'The Elizabeth, but we called her Eliza. I knew she'd carry me home.'

When they arrive back, Henry's cloak hangs in the hall, Ma moves in the kitchen. They stand near the entrance, the damson-hued evening hanging at the windows, glancing off their faces as they pretend not to have a heightened awareness of each other. Francis takes off his doublet, spending a long time folding it in the crook of his elbow. 'How long are you staying?' he says.

'As long as I need.'

Their heads are bowed close to each other.

'Won't your husband be asking for you?'

It is the first time he has uttered that word. Husband. His expression betrays him; this isn't the first time he has thought of this other man or her married life. It has stalked the borders of their conversations. They have barely talked about her; her tale contains too many painful truths.

'I doubt it.'

A lie, for her own sake as much as his. If she thinks too long about Edmund, waiting for her, planning his atonement, she will have to step outside into the dusk and shake herself back to her senses. She will have to remind herself that wives have endured much worse, and that her place is beside him. She will have to walk away from Francis. She pushes the thought down, like a relic buried in the earth.

'I wanted to find you. As soon as I arrived home I asked where you were. I'd hoped—' He stops.

'Hoped what?'

He is so still and so close; she could lean in and kiss him. He glances at her wedding band.

'You know I didn't have a choice,' she says.

'I know.'

'You were gone a long time.'

He moves his hand very slowly to her face, lightly tracing her cheek. His expression holds a sadness that will haunt her.

'And I will always regret it.'

The abandoned inn pulls into view. It has changed, engulfed by the forest. Ferns sprout waist-high in the doorway. A tree pushes its branches through the roof, creating a hole that lets in the sunlight, a bright round beam, the edge of the light against the dark a stark line. The furniture that remains is crumbling or rotten.

Before he left the previous night, he'd suggested they come back here. She had felt the imprint of his fingers on her cheek, and wanted it again, wanted to put her hand on the back of his neck, press her forehead to his. And so she agreed, even though they are reaching for each other in a darkness that cannot last, even though things are shifting between them too quickly. After, they stood in the front doorway, as the sky slid from plum to indigo, talking about nothings, sentences lingering on, not wanting to part.

But once she was alone, she had thought of her vows to Edmund. *Forsaking all others.* She had thought of how slowly, slowly he had tried to let her in, in his own way. The painted chamber, the gifted pigments. The quality of his voice when he said he loved her.

'What will you do now?' she asks Francis, walking further inside the inn and testing a table with her weight before leaning against it. He bites into an apple that he scrumped on their walk – she thinks, fleetingly, that they are too old for stealing – and leans beside her.

'I'll stay for now. Pa has asked me to help at the forge. The children have grown so much.' His younger siblings nearly full grown, his nieces and nephews tottering on newfound feet. 'Save some money, keep my boots on the land. It's not a bad life, what my parents have made.'

'I would've given anything to grow up in your home.'

'I know. I was cruel the last time I saw you.'

Their argument before he disappeared. She has returned to his words hundreds of times: *your father's money buys you a safety I don't have*, church bells peeling through the years.

'It's past now,' she murmurs.

He looks up through the hole in the roof to the blue pool of the sky, glorious summer day, and takes her hand. Skin on skin. A quiver through her body.

'It's a miracle it's still standing,' she speaks low, as though any louder and she might disturb the spectres in the place.

'I suppose some things are meant to last.'

She isn't sure who leans first, but they find each other's mouths, and it is familiar yet different, starker, hungrier, wolfish. Hands grasping for anything they can find.

There is a rippling shock at the sight of his body. He is emaciated, the muscles present but smaller, tighter, the excess cut away, leaving only the barest meat. She could run her fingers over his ribs, could feel the space in between them, the gap at his belly where bone falls away. The reduced outline of where his flesh once was. There are cuts, marks of sea and salt relentlessly chafing his skin for month upon month.

She looks away, her chest splitting, and he misunderstands, tells her, we don't have to do this. But she shakes her head, might drown all over again from the sadness of it all, the time lost, fates parted. She wonders if he feels the same as he holds her hands tighter; any tighter and they would bruise, they would leave their permanent mark, and she wouldn't mind, having a part of him brandished on her skin forever.

The grit and leaves on the wooden floor push up to meet her toes. She stands before him in her smock, stepping into the golden beam from the ceiling, sun warming her arms. Her body is unblemished by comparison to his, filled out since he last saw it, from better food, a better life.

Their bodies spell out their difference in fortune, the distance that gapes between them.

There's a final moment when she could pull away and say, this is a mistake. She pauses and remembers Edmund's hands on Annabel's wrist, the lies he spun beneath the oak tree and in London's filthy streets. Her body is charged and her hurt, her fury – at Edmund, at Thomas – is giant and untameable. Her sadness is unwieldy. And her desire, to be held and loved by Francis, to be told over and over that what they had can be recovered, is loudest of all.

She doesn't pull away; she leans into him. His hands skimming down her back, the short crop of his hair beneath her fingers. She smells the sea on him, tastes the salt on his skin. His teeth find the birthmark on her neck. Her legs lock around him as though they'll never release, thigh touching stomach. Carnal fury, insatiable desire. Two people holding onto something they know is sinking. She wants to feel the pain of it, to shriek out, to hold this moment so it lasts and lasts. But it's like trying to stop something blissfully sweet from dissolving on your tongue.

There's a spell about the inn. They remain on the ground, surrounded by the forest, bodies woven together. She feels at peace and knows it cannot last. Soon the inn will collapse around them. She imagines she can hear the warping expansion of the wood in the heat.

They talk quietly, and she watches his mouth move around words. He shifts, propping himself onto his elbow. His hand plays with a strand of her hair, which lies upon the floor, like the curl of a question mark, and untangles a leaf caught at her temple.

'I used to think about you when I was away,' he says.

'What about me?'

'Sometimes I'd try to imagine what you were doing. I'd wonder if you were at home or in the fields or heading into market. It was a comfort to think that your life was the same.' Unspoken words: that you'd still be here, waiting for me.

'You know I thought about you too.' She explains how he has haunted her, the man at the corner of her eye.

He lies down, his folded arm beneath her head, and they gaze at the sky through the gash in the ceiling, like survivors waiting for rain. She hears him struggling to find the words, can hear the breath inhale then release in a sigh.

And then, 'Do you love him?'

Edmund pulling at her thoughts. She tried not to think of him, but even as she'd lain with Francis, she'd felt the thread connecting her to her husband, hook on her guilt, tug it to the surface. She should be on her knees now, before God, begging His deliverance *from fornication and all other deadly sin and from all other deceits of the world, the flesh and the devil.* Is that what she has become? A dancer, a flirter with the devil?

Edmund with those bright crystal eyes and even gaze, the same height as hers. Edmund with the gentle curve of his mouth, his joy at seeing her happy. His words, *my love.* Edmund absorbing, observing and revelling every detail of her paintings. Edmund leaning against the mantelpiece, thoughtful in firelight. Edmund with sorrow on his face the morning she rode away. *My love.* How he promised himself to her then fucked another woman, and secretly had a child by her. How he lied so many times. She glances at Francis's naked body. Is this how favours are repaid? Is this what the Bible meant by an eye for an eye?

Francis waits for her answer, and she desperately wants not to lie to him, and not to break his heart. 'I didn't want to marry him,' she says.

'I knew that already.' Francis says, voice soft, a catch in his throat.

257

She takes his hand in her own and feels the rise and fall of his scars, raised lines scoring his skin. 'Why are you asking?'

'I need to know. I've waited a long time to know.'

'I didn't know if I'd ever see you again.' She doesn't mean for it to come out like a justification, but it does. It gives her away. She digs her nails into her thigh.

He slides his arm out from under her and sits. She could count the notches of his spine. He raises his hands to his face and presses his fingers against his eyes.

'I never told you,' he says, voice cracking like a dead branch underfoot. 'We never said it.'

She puts her hand on his lower back, feels it rise.

'I knew,' she says. 'I know.'

When there seems to be nothing left inside him, he looks at her, eyelashes clumped together from saltwater, like a sailor drowning in the Pacific, and she asks if he can forgive her and he wipes his eyes and places the back of his hand against her cheek.

After he walks her home and they are quiet, as though there are so many things left to say but no sounds, no shape of words by which to say them. Uncertainties gather about them, a conspiracy of ravens. Long shadows stitch to their feet as they walk. His arm bumps against hers, and she remembers a time when he was the only thing she ever wanted.

Her wants, her desires have grown more complex, twisted and knotted like ancient roots.

They stand together beneath the gatehouse, as they have done countless times before. Their past selves, their own echoes, watch them. Some of them weep.

She kisses him, his mouth warm against hers.

'You're lovely. I hope he tells you that.'

Ma hears things from Margaret. That Francis has been sleeping badly. That he wakes in the night, shouting, frightening his brothers. That he has gotten into tavern brawls. That he drinks more than before.

She tells Eliza as they stand in the washhouse, scrubbing smocks and kirtles, jerkins and stockings, lye irritating the movable skin of their knuckles.

Eliza is unsurprised but not undaunted. 'He's had a difficult time.'

They have been in and out of each other's lives for almost a fortnight, Francis visiting the house, bringing with him the smell of salt, of sea, that he can't seem to dispel. They have spent long hours with each other, as though they are butterflies with only a few days left alive. They have fallen into a routine of small things, holding hands when no one is watching, eating with each other's families, laughing at things that only they understand, a private language.

Yet amongst this, other things have crept, bothering her, making her absently chew the inside of her mouth. Like how he said, pointedly, that he preferred her dressed like this, in her old clothes, scraggy hems, scuffed boots. Like how he keeps wanting to lie with her, keeps making hints, keeps watching her keenly from the corners of his eyes, in an almost furious way. Like a man starved. A man wanting to take back what was once his. And she keeps refusing him, thinking of Annabel and her illegitimate child. Thinking of Edmund's earnest face, eyes big enough to drown in. Feeling the weight of guilt and God's judgement. Like how, at supper with Francis's family, one of his younger brothers had started arguing about who had the larger portion, saying another brother was favoured by their mother – usual sibling tattle – and Francis had raised his voice in a way that shocked Eliza. Abruptly and without justification. One look at the brother and she could see he too was startled, unused to this erratic, gaunt man who sleeps in his room and paces the house. Francis had stood, swung his legs over the bench, and walked out into the backyard and Margaret had muttered, 'Leave him.' When Eliza found him later, leaning against the pigsty pulling apart a leaf, leaving only the fragile veins behind, she had hugged him and he sagged against her. Like how Henry told her that Francis had been drinking more often at the Phoenix. Had gotten into a fight with one of the lads over something minor, and Henry had to drag Francis away, who cursed at him, and later begged Henry not to tell Eliza.

Their conversations often grow bleak. Francis talks about drowning men, keeps imagining that he will die soon. Death, a fascination. He questions how he survived the journey, when so many did not. Whether he is worthy of survival. And then he will look at her and pretend that he is joking even though she could spend a thousand years raking through his words and find nothing amusing within them. When they talk of the living, they become fractious. She treads a careful path, skirting subjects such as Cecil Hall, Edmund, gentlemen, and what their future, separate, collective, holds.

'I've no doubt it's been difficult for him,' Ma says now, flicking a fly as it lands on a washed stocking. 'But it's not for you to save him. You have a husband who cares and provides for you. I hate to sound like your father, dove, but your duty lies there.'

Eliza stares at the dirty film of the water. Sometimes she yearns for her painted chamber, her pigments, the courtyard at Cecil Hall, the spacious canopied bed. Yearns for a place to shut out the world. Yearns for home. She misses the intent look Edmund sometimes gives her, when he thinks she isn't watching him. The arm he throws over her in his sleep. She feels watery, untethered, sick in her stomach.

'I don't know what I want anymore,' she says.

'Just remember the vow you took beneath God.'

As if she could forget. Eliza bows her head, as Ma glances to the heavens, as though checking that He is still there.

CHAPTER 42

T H E cards are sticky beneath her fingers, grained with dirt, the corners creased from too much play. She lays her final card and Henry swears, slides another coin across the table towards her, saying, 'One more.'

She laughs, her pile of silver growing. Henry is selling Thomas's possessions, slowly removing evidence of the man who had lived here, and the great hall echoes in emptiness, magnifying the sounds of their hands shuffling over the table, the clink of metal on wood. The windows are open, the sun on its track down, heat beating on.

Francis arrives midway through the game, letting himself in, the door on the latch. She barely looks up, set on the game, chasing the win.

'Did Annabel teach you?' Henry asks after she wins another round.

She nods.

'I'm still awaiting an introduction,' he says.

She makes a noncommittal noise in the back of her throat, thinking of Blythe, of mothers without children, of her friend drunk in the dim morning. She is unaware that Francis stiffens beside the window. She plays another winning card, and Henry curses again, his face cracking into a smile.

'You're getting good.'

'Getting?'

Henry makes a face.

'Who's Annabel?' Francis asks.

The laughter subsides. 'A friend of Edmund's.' She has learnt to say his name as though he is only a story. It isn't true, of course.

She has dreams about her husband. Last night she had a nightmare that he died again, and she hadn't been able to get to him, and awoke wishing he was beside her, gold hair tickling her cheek.

'You play cards with her?' Francis's question isn't really a question.

'Nothing much else to do,' Henry jibes, eyes bright, 'gentlewoman.'

Francis walks to the mantle, where, since Thomas's death, Ma has propped Eliza's self-portrait. His shirt is dirtier than usual; he must have come straight from the forge. He stands in front of her portrait which stares back into the room. Two Elizas, observing the scene from different vantages. She wishes she had the portrait's perspective, so she could see Francis's expression.

'You painted this?' he asks.

'Yes.'

'Easy life. Gambling, cards and painting.' A haunt of bitterness. He turns away from the mantle dismissively.

How eager she'd been to show Edmund her portrait, to gain his approval; how willingly and generously he'd given it, an unassuming smile pushing at the corners of his mouth as he ran his forefinger over the paint. She realises she neither desires nor needs Francis's approval of her work.

'I've always drawn,' she says, trying not to sound defensive.

'Not painting.'

'I never had the tools.'

'How did you get them?'

Henry flips a card between his fingers, frowning slightly.

'Edmund bought them for me.'

Francis sniffs, tries a laugh that sounds like a cough. 'He must be wealthy.'

Money, that old refrain.

'He thought it would make me happy.'

'And has it?'

'Yes.'

The cards, the coins, lie forgotten on the table. Henry stands, and squeezes her shoulder and mutters, 'Have it out then be done with it.'

He has never told her what to do before, but the look in his eyes is stern and says: stop this now. Go home, to your husband.

'Be done with me?' Francis says, loudly.

Henry looks straight at Francis, the labourer he was once friendly with. 'I owe Edmund a great deal.'

After Henry leaves the hall, Francis says, 'What did he mean? You've hardly told me anything. I don't know about Annabel, or what debt your brother owes to your' – word halting on his tongue – 'husband.' His voice is sharp, harsh, loud, and she realises that the last person who spoke to her in such a way in this hall was her father. 'You've come back a different woman, full of secrets. A goddamned gentlewoman who plays cards and paints! Where is the woman I knew before? You dress differently, you act differently, even your voice is different. Where is the woman who used to tell me everything?'

'I didn't want to hurt you.'

'Too late for that, isn't it?' He holds up his arms, Christ on the cross. 'Look at me. Look what happened to me. Then look at yourself.'

Her softer edges, body filled out. Her nimbler mind. 'I thought you were dead.'

'So did I,' he says, closing his eyes, dropping his hands to his sides, defeated.

She wants to reach for him but can't bear the sharpness of his body or the stink of the sea. 'You know, if I could take it all back, turn back the years, I would.'

He slumps into Henry's vacated chair, runs his blackened fingers over his hair, stares into his lap. 'Thomas did all of this, you know. He was a cruel man.'

She thinks of her own cruelties. The fury she harbours within her. The painting of Edmund, broken apart. Her own infidelity making her a hypocrite. Her reflection in the glass, with the same jut of Thomas's chin.

'Sometimes,' she says, 'I worry I'm becoming him.'

She has never spoken to anyone about this. Only Francis. Francis returned from the dead, Francis slipping back into her life, Francis opening her soul as easily as a hot knife through butter.

He looks up at her, expression almost furious. He reaches across the table, cups her face in his hand, close enough that she can see her own reflection in the orb of his eye. His hand is warm on her face.

'You're nothing like him, you hear me. You deserve only good things.' Then, speaking so softly she almost doesn't hear it. 'Thomas got what he deserved.'

It takes her a moment. 'What do you mean?'

He is blinking very fast, eyelashes fluttering like the wings of a moth.

She recollects the grazes across his knuckles. She pulls away and his hand tightens for a moment about her cheek, fingers grappling at her jaw. For the first time with him, she is afraid. Afraid of what he can do, afraid of what he has done. He drops his hand, and she instinctively rubs her face. She steps backwards until she feels the wall bump against her back, window still ajar, cool breeze stroking her skin.

'I left him alive,' he says.

CHAPTER 43

H E tells her of that night. Picture it: an empty street, the dregs of dusk long past. Thomas, already drunk, made the job easy. It didn't take much to grab him from behind, to throw him against a wall. Even now, with Francis's body wasted, all excess stripped away, it wasn't difficult for him to repeat and repeat this. To beat a man as he had seen officers flog crewmen. To channel every anger into attacking the son-of-a-bitch who writhed on the ground.

It had been an effort for Francis to stop punching the old man. For that is what Thomas had become - a drunk, old man. A final blow to the head with the butt of his knife and then Francis leant against the wall, breath ragged and the taste of metal in his throat. He righted Thomas to his feet, blood already making a dark and sticky bloom across his face. Fuck with me again, Francis told him, and you'll never see another morning.

The old man stumbled off, bloodied and dazed. Maybe it was the ghosts catching up with Thomas that made him mild, that meant he didn't turn back for Francis, or maybe he thought he'd punished Francis enough, or maybe he had a heart after all, dormant deep within, that made him feel guilty. Or maybe he was too damned drunk to think straight. Whatever it was, Francis didn't wait for Thomas to change his mind; he raced away, winding through the streets, circling out and round, the route planned in his head. He always was the fastest of his siblings.

Philip let him in, an alibi, saying nothing as Francis pulled off his shirt which was decorated with blood, half-naked man in the kitchen. But Francis hadn't been worried; he reckoned Thomas's tongue was tied. It would all come out - Thomas's scheming, his injustices, the extent of his violence – Francis would make sure of it, if Thomas opened his mouth to accuse a waif of a man for beating him bloody.

But it was death, in the end, that ensured Thomas's tongue was stilled.

Eliza tries to digest her shock, her hands gripping her throat where her pulse bounds.

The fire has fizzled low, casting Francis's face into malicious shadow. Did he always possess such ugliness? The violence she always detested within her father, within herself, has insidiously crept into the man before her. Like poison in water.

She heaps wood on the fire, needing to occupy herself. She fails to notice a coarse edge of wood before it splinters into her finger. Later, when this is over, she will tease it out with a needle. Later, she will curl up on the floor, hug her knees to her chest.

She closes the window and stays there, looking for the stars and finding them absent. She can't bring herself to look at him now that she has taken her eyes off him. He speaks again, says he will never be sorry for what he did, that Thomas deserved it. After a while she stops listening. She is tired of listening, tired of teasing out the truth as though it is a knotted thread in need of her delicate fingers. A stitch similar to that of Cecil Hall. She holds up a hand and, as though she is a cunning woman with magic in her bones and power over others, he falls silent.

She doesn't mind that Thomas is dead.

In fact, she has almost revelled in it, has tasted the freedom of it.

But it was Francis's hands which, albeit unwittingly, dealt a blow so heavy, so full of vengeance that it dragged the last breath from Thomas. The same hands which have known her body, her face. The same fingerprints, with their whorls and ovals, have rusted with her father's blood. The same blood that flows in blue rivers beneath her skin.

Where is the boy she first met, with his long arms and sweet smile, who took her to his parents' home? The boy who saved a cat, cradled it in his arms? He who danced with her until their skin was as salt-slicked as the sea?

She understands it, she can even forgive it. But she cannot reconcile it. Cannot match the contours, the outline of the lad who left her with the man who returned.

Francis wraps his arms around her, his lean body encasing hers deep into the night. She is both captivated and captive. Part of her wants Francis to stay holding her. Wants it to be the Francis she used to know. The other part wants him to disentangle his arms from around her, this stranger who has returned and tried to claim her.

He takes one of her hands, clasping it, as though willing her to say something. But his hand will do nothing for them now. Another hand has reached down, down, through the depths, to find her and is hauling her back up. Her head breaks through the water, through blur and blindness. To clarity. Her firmness, her strength – the things she learnt growing up in a house that was never safe – are resolute.

They are chasms apart. Changed people. What once was, cannot be resurrected. It took a death, a manslaughtering, for her to realise it.

For how long he holds her, she doesn't know, but eventually she says, 'I need to go home,' and steps out of the circle of his arms. She has survived losing him once; she will survive again.

'You are home,' he says.

She says nothing. He bows his head to look into her face, and she steadily, determinedly, meets his gaze.

He wrenches away to the wall sliced with beams and throws both his fists against it, and a sound that is animal ruptures from his mouth. He swears like a sailor because, she realises, he is. The sea and his journey have become him, made him. The sound brings Ma and Henry's footsteps out, creaking across the ceiling, before they hurry downstairs.

Eliza is body-weary, emptied of feeling by the time he leaves. A cove worn away by a relentless shush of the ocean. A husk. She sinks to the floor in the doorway as she watches him disappear down the lane into the swell of dawn. Watches as he takes the turn and is lost from view.

Once she had thought of them, their love, as a fortress that nothing, not giants nor dragons nor men with fists and minds of gore could tear down. Forever enduring, like ancient forests, like endless fields. She realises now, that their love is malleable, mouldable, breakable. As soft as dreams. Who they once were, what they once had, is consigned to memory, foundering in oceans of the past.

CHAPTER 44

THE years are made up of fragments. Flashes of detail whilst the rest merges and blurs. Memory is a forgetful thing, but some things remain.

She doesn't remember the first night she returned home. The first week. The first words that passed between Edmund and her.

But she remembers how, for a time, she and Edmund did not share a bed. How he presumed it was because she couldn't bear him, and she had let him, when really she couldn't bear herself. Her own duplicity. She slept across the passageway in an empty bedchamber, in cold sheets.

⚬⚭⚬

She remembers Annabel's inability to keep still, the first time she had visited. She fiddled with her rings, her skirts, stood and sat, drank too much, had said that she never wanted to deceive Eliza, that she was sorry, that she feels nothing for Edmund, that she was sorry, that it was before she knew Eliza, that she was sorry, that Eliza had been a comfort when everything else had been so bleak. Eliza, drained, exhausted, had said, 'Please stop Anna. I'm not angry with you.'

⚬⚭⚬

She remembers hunching over the chamber pot at twilight, staring into the gloomy bedchamber, and thinking that her adultery was too big a secret to keep within her. A raven in a cage, waiting to escape.

How had Edmund kept his daughter a secret from her? How had he suffered it?

She had stood, piss swilling in the pot in her hand, and imagined telling Edmund everything. How she first met Francis, how it was his ghost that lay between them in the early days of their marriage bed. Edmund had found her, standing like that, piss still in her hand and presumed her to be in the strange throes of grief after the death of her father, and extended his arm to her, folded her body into his.

And she had known then what her honesty would cost.

❧

She remembers wondering if Francis regretted it, their love. Imagined asking him whether their time together - a shining comet blazing across the skies - was worth his journey to hell and back? Perhaps he regrets it all, now he knows their ending.

At night sometimes to beat herself up while she lay alone, guilt her only friend - guilt for betraying Edmund, guilt for leaving Francis - she wondered if Francis was warmed by someone else. She thought about their inn in the forest, and whether the roof had finally collapsed.

Her thoughts made her bring her knees up to her chest and breathe hard into the gap between her thighs and torso, warm wet breath on skin.

❧

She remembers meeting some of Leonard's acquaintances, who only bothered to take notice of her when Leonard introduced her as an artist. Later, he invited her to paint at his house; he had chambers standing empty. In case - and here he had spoken haltingly - you ever want to escape Cecil Hall, just for a while.

She remembers two things about the first time she went into her painted chamber after returning to Cecil Hall. First, that lumps of ice plummeted from the sky outside, battering the windows. Second, that someone had tidied the chamber; new pigments in jars, mussel shells cleaned, lustrously glinting up at her, floor scrubbed. All evidence of the ripped papers, the destroyed wooden panel, the wreckage of her anger, removed. Anything for you, my love. She picked up a paintbrush and ran its coarse bristles over the back of her palm and felt ashamed.

She'd had a long hiatus from creating. For so long she had little to give, her well run dry. But when she finally sat down, watching the hail outside, she found that she was craving the creativity – the solace and freedom of it. For the first time in weeks she felt a settling calm, like mist over quiet water, and was able to forget everything for a while and just, just paint.

She remembers taking a chicken soup to Nicholas, who had been in his bed most days, his weak, tired body betraying the brightness of his mind. She sat with him, helped him to eat. His conversations had grown increasingly nostalgic, looking backwards more than forward, talking of his late wife, Edmund's mother.

'I miss Rose, of course. There's so much I wished she'd lived to see, but I'm glad she never saw me like this. Samuel should've been here to see this though.' Her father-in-law rubbed his fading blue eyes. 'He will despise me for saying so, but you will look after Edmund for me, won't you?' The old man shifted in the bed, breathing raspy with the effort. 'He has made mistakes, but haven't we all?'

She found herself nodding, tears slicking her cheeks.

A small boy rushed over the moat, jumping the puddles which had frozen in the holes and ruts in the lanes, a letter in hand. Henry wrote that he had sold their father's house and land, for a price better than he expected. The house of memories, the final vestige of Thomas and all he had strived for, gone.

What had it all been for?

Ma had moved to small cottage near the centre of town, with a rose and herb garden, and hired a local girl who came each day to help in the household. Henry wouldn't suffer their mother another marriage. And with all their affairs in Worcestershire bound up, sold up, Henry had returned to London to resume his work with the merchant. Buoyancy in his step, feather in his hat, lover on his mind.

※

The seasons cycle on. The harvest comes and goes, as does Michaelmas and Christmas, Holy Innocents' Day and Twelfth Night. Eliza learns to collect the rents from the tenants when Edmund cannot. There are weekly church visits, which increase with the oncoming of Easter. The gardens are recovered after the frosts, herbs coaxed back to health, apple trees pruned, dead branches coming away. Bulbs of onions and roots of skirret are planted into the earth, or else lured away from frosty hibernation. The fields fill with lambs in the spring. The sheep are sheered, downy fluff clinging to brambles. Carts of wool hitch upon the highways and lanes for trade in neighbouring towns. Eliza draws and paints in the last of the daylight, long evening shadows rippling on the walls.

She and Edmund migrate back to the same bed. Their bodies curl tentatively towards each other in the spring chill. In the dark, Edmund slowly reaches out and tucks a strand of hair behind her ear. 'I didn't know if you'd come back to me.'

She grips her fingers around his wrist, an eternal circle. They are an alliance, dutiful companions. They are what Ma taught her marriage is meant to be. Staunch and enduring.

Eliza will never give him all the truth. There will always be a part of her hidden from him. But she owes it to him and to herself, when says, 'I didn't know if I would.'

It takes them a long time to fall asleep.

Eventually, just as she is falling, he murmurs, 'I'm glad you did.'

꧁

She returns to Cecil Hall, having gone on horseback along spring-wet lanes to the nearest town with Dorothy, filling baskets and linen bags with market day's spoils. Edmund greets them in the entrance hall when they return, his expression grave.

'What is it?' Eliza asks, holding Edmund's arm. Movement sounds above, travelling closer. A person appears in increments on the staircase, first feet then leg then belly then chest, shoulder, face.

The physician. The corners of his mouth pulled down.

'Nicholas?' Dorothy whispers.

Eliza feels Edmund grow unsteady beneath her hand.

CHAPTER 45

EDMUND stands in the stables, his hand resting on the flank of a courser. His gaze unfocused. Eliza stands quietly beside him, the smell of hay and manure warm about them. Lazy hum of bees on the air.

'My father loved this horse,' he says.

Nicholas had ridden this horse after their wedding; she recalls the bob of its sleek black tail ahead of her, leading the way to Cecil Hall and into the unknown. But in the years since, her father-in-law's riding days had reduced, the world constricting about him.

'I'm thinking of selling her.'

Eliza stares. 'Why would you do that?'

'What use has she now?'

Dorothy and Eliza sit at the table in the kitchen and eat together, the only two left, Edmund having retired early to bed. They eat the mutton broth and hunks of bread, chewing slowly. 'He needs distraction,' Dorothy observes, after Eliza told her about the courser, about how they go for walks together, yet he is absent, his mind elsewhere.

'Is that how you cope?'

'This house keeps me busy. And God is with me.' The older woman rips out the soft centre of her bread. 'You should paint him again.'

'It didn't go too well last time.'

'This time will be different. There are no more secrets.'

Eliza stares into the brown swirl of broth, film of fat at the surface and can't quite bring herself to respond.

The light from the two windows converge upon his body. Edmund squints.

Eliza sketches his features, as he sits for her, again. It is easier, quicker, this second time. As though her muscles remember the shape of him. She draws his hands, different positions, which she will copy afterwards onto a new panel, once she has finished his face.

The sound of geese flying and honking overhead travels into the room. 'I miss the noise of London,' Edmund says.

'What about it?'

'The thrill of it all. The life there. All those people packed into one space.'

'You could go back,' she says, pressing her chalk to the board, the shape of his jaw revealed beneath her fingers. Into his silence she asks, 'Why wouldn't you?'

'I sent her there.' Her: child made of grief, punished for her illegitimacy. Innocent child. 'Walter writes that she . . .' He falters, pinching the skin of his neck, forgetting that he is supposed to stay still.

'You can tell me,' she says, 'I'd like to hear it.'

'She . . . she walks now and can say a few words. Horse and moon and . . . Papa.' He moves to one of the windows. 'Sometimes I can still feel her delicate head resting on my arm. She was so small.'

'She should be with her family, as should you,' Eliza says. The others, mother, brother, father, are not coming back. She remembers Nicholas' request. *Look after him.* 'She should come here.'

She stands behind him, puts her arms about his middle, rests her chin on his shoulder, and feels the shake and heave of his chest, of a man submerged in grief and regret.

'Why are you so good?' he manages.

Guilt, familiar friend, licks his lips and smiles at her. The devil wants his dance.

'I'm not.'

He is gone for over a fortnight. During his absence, summer arrives in her golden glory. Honeysuckle emerges, sweet scent catching in her hair. The moat is periwinkle blue, reflecting cloud-wisp skies. Clothes dry crisp and quickly after their stint in the washhouse.

Eliza occupies herself, drawing pregnant women and children on thresholds, their coming or going ambiguous. She is used to waiting, sitting with the unease of unknowing, but when she finally hears hooves thudding upon the dry earth in the pulsing summer air, the sound is a symphony. Her chalk falls and cracks in two upon the floorboards, but she doesn't care; she rushes barefoot towards the stables.

Her husband removes the saddle from the horse. The child is asleep upon him, her cherubic cheek squashed against his shoulder. A biggin on her head, tied beneath her chin. The hair that escapes it is as gold as the summer's day. Angelic, God-given. Just like her father's.

Edmund turns at the sound of Eliza's feet in the grass.

He will tell her of the long journey home, the multiple stops on the way, how travelling with a little person took longer than he had ever dreamt, of the strange looks folk gave him, a man riding alone with a tiny child held before him in the saddle. He will tell her of the fracturing of his and Walter's kinship, of the coarse truths that had tripped from his cousin's mouth; that in taking the girl, Edmund would be ripping her from Lettice, the mother who had adopted her. That Walter would never forgive him for it. Behind their joy lies a tragedy. Everyone is scrapping for what they want most.

But all of that he will save for later, when his daughter is asleep inside, when the house is quiet once more, when the two of them break bread and drink beer by candlelight.

He is exhausted now, pouches beneath his eyes, hair stuck up at odd angles, dust from the road caught in the creases on his forehead, dirt on his hands. Yet he looks alive, glorious. A line of pink flushes across his cheeks and his chest, where he opened his collar in the heat, has captured the sun. His smile when he greets his wife - love of his life, encourager of good things, forgiver of his faults, who wraps her arms around him and smells of honey-suckle - is an effortless, gentle curve of the mouth.

She eases the child from his arms. The girl stirs slightly readjusting herself into the crook of Eliza's neck. Into the child's hair she murmurs, 'Welcome home Blythe.'

Later, when Blythe wakes from warm, snuffled sleep in her truckle bed, Eliza is there, anxious to leave the child even for a moment before Annabel can arrive. The little girl stretches and looks about the unfamiliar chamber. Eliza squats low beside the bed, stroking the child's face and ruffled hair as she starts to whimper. 'You've nothing to fear,' she whispers over and over, and Blythe calms, watching her with great, blue eyes.

Annabel falls almost to her knees at the sight of her daughter, who, when they were last together almost two years prior, was only a half-formed thing, made of impulses and instincts and long sleeps and desire for her mama's milk. Blythe now is steady on her feet, fearless, finding and forming new words daily. The pain at the difference in her daughter - the years lost, the realisation that she will need to learn this child anew - is writ across Annabel's face. She scoops Blythe into her arms, and Blythe, clutching a carved wooden horse, stares unashamedly, a stillness coming over her, blinking the dark eyelashes she took from her mama. 'Mama's here, and she promises she won't leave you again,' Annabel whispers, so softly, so heart-wrenchingly, that Eliza slips her arm through Dorothy's, whose eyes are silvering with tears, and together they head downstairs, leaving them alone.

CHAPTER 46

A year passes. Summer returns to make honey of the skies. The household is busy. Blythe settles. Life adopts new rhythms.

Dorothy kneads bread with the child sat on her knee, murmuring tales of two other children who grew up in these halls. Two golden-haired boys, brothers. Eliza and Blythe fill jugs of water for the herb garden, water splashing on their gowns, Blythe living up to her namesake with squeals of delight. Edmund tells his daughter stories before bed, waits whilst she gently falls asleep. They forage for wild garlic in the woodlands, coming home with palms sticky and smelling of tangy sweetness. Annabel stays most nights at Cecil Hall, in her old bedchamber with Blythe sleeping beside her in a truckle bed. Everything comes full circle. They spend a lot of time together, Eliza and Annabel, laughing and swearing and groaning as they work. They learn to recognise what the other is feeling with a look. Their moonblood merges, forms the same monthly pattern.

Folk always have opinions, making comments even when you never invited them. Some local tenants and parochial villagers make snide remarks that Edmund keeps two women. That a child, looking nothing like his wife, appeared, devil-spawned and illegitimate. That Annabel is a doxy, and Eliza a fool for allowing her to stay beneath her roof. But Eliza doesn't care. She has forgiven her husband, empathises with Annabel. And when she cannot sleep, caught in a maze of thoughts, she recognises that her complete acceptance of Blythe, and of what happened between her husband and Annabel, is her way of making amends for her own betrayal. It allows her to rest with her conscience.

There was a time when her infidelity had risen like black bile in her chest. But in the two years since Francis disappeared around the curve in the lane, her guilt has eased. Painting calms her, gives her space to mull over the years – just as drawing always has, from when she was a spit of a girl. With each brushstroke, each whisper of charcoal on paper, it feels manageable. She feels a release, as though she is painting everything, her truth, soul, sins, onto the paper.

She still thinks of him. Wonders what he does now with his time. If his life has resumed a pattern like before he went to sea. She misses him occasionally, would be lying if she denied it – but it is for the man he was, and the woman she was. He doesn't dominate her thoughts or haunt her anymore. *Life moves*, Ma had once told her, and she, ever wise, had been right.

Mostly, Eliza is happy. The happiest she has ever been.

With the house so full and life so busy, she paints in snatches, sometimes by fluttering candlelight whilst the house sleeps. Art in life's margins. Progress on her work is slow; her work on Edmund's portrait has stuttered and faltered. She has completed other, smaller projects – sketched people, their profiles, their hands, their clothes. It's a rare jewel of a day when she can just sit and paint, and an even rarer one when Edmund has time to sit for her. So today ranks amongst the most glorious of rubies: here they both are, sitting in the painted chamber, its pomegranate-lined walls peering down at them. The rest of the household has disbanded, ventured into the village.

'I wonder what he'd say about this house,' he lifts his hand, revolves it vaguely. 'Annabel and Blythe being here.'

She runs the bristles of her paintbrush beneath Edmund's eye on her panel. Smudge of violet at his tear duct. Fine pale lines of eyelash. Repainting him is easier; she has already trialled the shades, the colours, the different strokes of her brushes. Her skill has improved since her first attempt; every artwork a foundation for the next. This second time the portrait larger, more ambitious.

She flicks her gaze to the real man before her. 'I think he'd be pleased. You've stood by your duty to them both.'

'I had a duty to you too.'

'Are you not still my husband?'

'But you didn't ask for this. I wonder what you would've chosen, given the choice.'

'I would choose this,' she says emphatically. It's true, of course. She did.

And Edmund reminds her daily that she made the right decision. In his gentleness, speaking softly to his father's horse which she persuaded him not to sell. In refilling the pigments in her painted chamber without her asking. In his waking up beside her each morning, and asking 'Did you dream?' In respecting her ideas and skills as though she is his equal. In the absence of violence in his character; even after she destroyed the portrait that had been a part of their making, he had unquestioningly kept his hands at his side. He accepts and encourages her in all her guises – yeoman's daughter, gentlewoman, artist. In a way that Francis never could.

'Do you think of what happened to your father?' he asks.

'You mean his death?'

She had told him that much – her father beaten bloody on his drunken stagger home from the inn – in the evenings that unspooled between them in those first weeks after she returned to Cecil Hall. Back when she couldn't venture close to the whole story, for fear it would leak out of her. She has more control of it now. The years a comfort, a barrier. She'll never tell a soul of her mother's part. Ma was a victim for years. Now, finally, she is liberated.

'Yes,' he says.

'I know the man that did it.'

Words on Edmund's lips, which part slightly in surprise. *You never said.* But he, master of avoiding painful truths, can accuse her of nothing.

'He said it was an accident,' she says.

'Do you believe him?'

'I think there was a moment when he wanted to kill him, but he pulled himself away.'

It is a while before her husband asks, 'Who is he?'

She is back in her father's hall at Michaelmas. The two men – one golden haired, the other raven haired – stare at each other across the table, through the fug of the room.

'One of the labourers. There was bad blood between him and my father.'

'Why?'

A breeze from the window gusts into the room, bringing with it the smell of leaf and vegetation and forests. It smells like lands unpeopled, when giants walked the earth. She recalls walking with Francis towards the forgotten inn. Remembers walking with Edmund through the woodland at the back of Cecil Hall, when she had first asked to paint him.

Does she dare say it? She who has never held back.

'He wanted to marry me.' It's so simple, when she says it like this. Really, at the heart, it always was. 'But Father wouldn't allow it.'

Dawning on his face. Slow as sunrise. 'The man across the table at Michaelmas.'

'You remember him?'

'I wouldn't forget the first night we met,' he says, playfulness in his eyes, as though their love was easy, instant, born at first sight.

That's how it was with Francis. When he found her, squatting beside a wall, trying to escape her father. She was too young to know it then. But looking back, she knows that that immediate bond between them as children had only ever been love. A childish love. Not made for the world of men.

'You know, as I was leaving that Michaelmas feast, a tall, dark-haired man bumped against shoulder and gave me a look as though he wanted to do more than just that.'

'I never knew.'

'Why would you?' The question lingers, like smoke. She twists the paintbrush between her fingers.

'So Thomas made sure he wouldn't marry you,' Edmund prompts.

'He sent him away. Cast him out to sea, and when Francis eventually returned, he attacked my father.'

'Francis,' Edmund muses.

She never thought his name would be on his tongue. Two worlds dissolving into one.

He doesn't ask whether she felt the same, whether she had wanted to marry Francis too. Perhaps he doesn't want to know. Or perhaps he knows already. Her shrewd-eyed, gentle husband. But she answers it anyway: 'I'm glad I didn't marry him.' She walks over to stand behind him, draping her arms about his shoulders, bending to rest her cheek against his.

❧

The edge of her hand looks bruised from the colours, the blues, greys, greens. Her sleeves are rolled up, her shoes kicked off, a habit she has adopted whilst painting, her hair loose down her back. But she doesn't stop to check herself as she rushes downstairs, as quietly as she can, not wanting to wake Blythe.

She finds him at his desk, hunched over his ledger, the window behind him a picture of fading light, anticipating a still sapphire night. The fire is blazing, as though he has just added extra kindling. When he sees her expression, a smile slips across his face. That familiar smile, the one she likes best on him. He sets down his quill.

'You've finished,' he says.

She imagined she would want to dance or leap or drink until her head hurts. Instead she experiences a great lull of anti-climax and exhaustion. The portrait finally finished, the last of the oil setting.

She is too caught in the moment to notice that Edmund has spilt his cup, dull glint of pewter lying on the floor in a pool of small beer, as though he stumbled when he coaxed the fire and neglected to clear it up. If she had noticed, she would have thought it unusual; Edmund being so clean, steady on his feet, prideful of his home, the relic of his forefathers.

He takes her hand and twirls her around, slowly, their feet falling in step, her chin on his shoulder.

'Can I see it?' His eyes are feverish bright. The ledger is left open, forgotten.

Upstairs her husband sinks into a chair in the painted chamber and stares at himself. The Edmund of her creation sits in a cathedral of trees, the woodland where his mother took him as a boy, and the places where he frequently rides. There is a shadowy suggestion of Cecil Hall in the background, a smudge of a courser in the stable. She has dressed him in deep green, the colour he wore at their wedding, as though he is part of the forest, edges blurring. Rich fur sculpts his shoulders. The hand in his lap holds a small jar.

'What's that?' he says gesturing, leaning closer.

She is shy then, rush of colour to her cheeks. 'My vanity.'

'It looks like powder.' He pauses in understanding. 'Pigment.'

'So you'll always carry a part of me with you.'

His eyes are shining when he looks back at her.

She finds her way around his body easily; she has spent so long studying it, immortalising it in chalk, charcoal, oil and pigment. Their abandoned clothes are distributed across the furniture. The canopied bed cocoons them. The smell of him, of hay and vellum and sandalwood, is familiar, like coming home. Beneath, so faint she hardly notices, is a familiar, unsettling tang of sweat.

They are slow, as though they have all the time they will ever need. Later, she will realise that he moved little, staying on his back or turning on his side. His tongue touches the thumbprint birthmark on her neck. She presses her mouth to the constellation of beauty spots across his shoulder, feels the rise of his chest beneath her when he sighs.

After, he kisses her forehead, the sort travellers make to their wives before they set off on a long journey. The kind where you wonder if you will ever meet again. This thought, caught in a myriad of others, drifts away from her and is lost.

They hold each other, arms making an infinite ring. She rests her head on his chest, and they laugh at their eagerness, as though they are still young. Rabbits set loose for the first time.

'Rabbits have a lot of children,' she says.

'You and me, ey?' he says, tucking a strand of her hair behind her ear.

⁂

His insists on hosting a feast to unveil her portrait. His behaviour is uncharacteristic – he usually prefers the quiet or the company of close friends, he never was the brother that hankered for large social gatherings. Yet she has seen a gleam, a frenzy almost, in him lately that she hasn't been able to decipher.

Edmund hammers a nail into the wall on the last turn of the staircase for the panel to hang, so the first thing a visitor will experience, stepping inside the entrance hall, is the blue-eyed master appraising them on the threshold. Blythe stands watching him, her own blue eyes transfixed, asking, 'What Papa doing?' with each strike of his hammer upon the nail.

'I'm not sure it's good enough to be hung there,' Eliza says, but Edmund ignores her, adjusting the panel so it hangs straight, before covering it with a coarse linen sheet to shield it from view.

'Not good enough,' repeats Blythe, and Eliza has to smile.

⁂

On the day of the feast – the unveiling as Edmund keeps calling it – you see a small army of women crossing the bridge of the moat, skirts swinging about their ankles. Dorothy called in extra hands from the village, diligent daughters who could be spared, husband-men's wives who jumped at the chance to visit Cecil Hall, to glimpse its great kitchen, to nosy about the chambers under guise of work.

You hear the familiar kitchen song: clang and ring of blades being sharpened; thud of knives slicing through hardy tubers and roots; gasps from some of the younger women as the lids of the cheese vats are removed, the stench throat-gagging, ready to be served with the loaves that rise in Dorothy's prided bread oven; creak of the meal chest's hinges, where steady hands remove salted beef and salted pork – the animals slaughtered before their glassy-black eyes could see another winter – and salted cod – carried from seas unknown on the backs of barnacled ships – and there is so much salt that you would taste it when you lick your fingertips; chorus of women's voices, hierarchies forming, natural matriarchs assuming position.

In the great chamber you find Eliza on her knees, sweeping the grate, stacking the fire, placing sprigs of holly on furniture, tying mistletoe above doorways. Her mouth is clenched, as though she is angry, when really, she is anxious. Her painting is soon to be exposed; something so personal will no longer be her own, belonging instead to others to appraise and interpret.

To be an artist. Isn't this what she always wanted? Back when she was a girl, running her fingers over the whitewash of the church's walls, wondering what beauty lay beneath. But isn't finally getting what you want, and witnessing how it compares to your dreams, the most frightening thing of all?

A few doors along, you see Annabel trying to ready Blythe. You can only just see the little girl's head over the height of the bed, as her mama combs her hair which almost reaches her shoulders in fluttering waves. She will grow up to break hearts, all gold and petite and symmetrical beauty. The child, for the most part, is compliant, apart from a few bouts of wailing when she doesn't want her hair to be pinned under her biggin, contributing her own harmony to the kitchen downstairs.

Below, lads arrive from the village, bringing additional barrels of beer, casks of wine and sack. You spy them loitering in the courtyard, blowing on their hands, hoping that Edmund will reward them by opening a barrel. He does, of course, and the lads thank him, murmuring to each other what a fair landowner he is, which Edmund pretends not to overhear. You realise you have barely seen Edmund. Why would you, with the house so busy? But you look at him now as he sips beer with the lads and see him grimace, clenching his mouth shut. And after the men disperse, you notice how Edmund shakes slightly when he walks, how his hand clutches his abdomen.

When he thinks no one will notice he walks across the moat, where the water is dove-white mirroring the December sky, heading for the stables. You follow him, watching as he brushes the mane of his father's favourite horse before resting his forehead against its neck. He gasps then, face waxy, hand holding his side. *Lord give me strength*, you think he says. The horse whickers, flicking its tail. The mane slips from the man's fingers as he staggers behind the stable, where he doubles over and vomits.

⁂

A band plays in the entrance hall as the guests arrive, the music of a flute, a lute, a viol echoing through the halls, off stone and wainscoted walls.

Edmund catches her during the evening, a faint sheen of sweat across his face, 'This is how I remember it,' he says, his breath tickling her ear, his hand warm upon her back. 'When Mother and Sam were here. I wanted you to see it like this.' His face is radiant, the smile so pure she can see the boy beneath. She doesn't care that people are watching as she kisses him.

Leonard arrives, accompanied by women wearing pearls and whited faces and men in embroidered doublets and flamboyant hats. The feasting is noisy, the women from the village serving food as though it's a tavern. Blythe and a couple of other children run between human and table legs, the adults too drunk or tired or both to reprimand them.

Once the pheasant is eaten to the bone, bellies filled, breeches loosened, Eliza stands to help Dorothy clear away, but Leonard lays a finger on her wrist. 'You're the artist tonight.'

The guests congregate in the entrance hall as Edmund stands on the stairs, looking down at the people who have characterised and coloured his life. The band quiets, the last thrum of the lute gliding on the air like a songbird. He seems to sway as though drunk, but when he speaks his words are clear and sober. Sobering.

'Thank you all for coming to the unveiling of my first, and only, portrait, painted by my wife. Eliza is a true artist.' Annabel, appearing at Eliza's side, squeezes her hand, rings pressing into Eliza's skin. 'She sees inside the souls of men. She saw into mine and has filled the gaps within me.'

Edmund casts around the room and his eyes, shimmering sapphires, find hers. She, the ignorant country girl whose father bartered her away for his own status; a girl who always wanted to draw, but never imagined a life like this. He raises his glass, a toast, to her. The company drinks, a tilt of chins to the ceiling.

He pulls the cloth covering his portrait. It catches slightly on the panel, takes a few tugs before it falls, sheet sliding to the floor, like a curtain revealing another world. He stands before the painting, observing it, blocking it from view, savouring the final moment when it is his and hers alone.

The entrance hall is hushed as he steps back and his likeness stares into the room.

She has painted the man she knows: a man suffering grief and loss, navigating a path he never expected. A flawed man but a good man, husband, father. A gentleman, a gentle man. Beneath it all, is the story of them. The first failed attempt to make the portrait is still there, in the foundations, in the skill it took to create this. Their unravelling, her divided loyalty, is there too, in the shadows of the woodland, in the darkened edges. All their conversations as he sat for her, her muse, are locked within the paint. Their healing is captured within every lick and dab of pigment. The piece is a story of perseverance, of devotion, of a love that now feels like instinct.

There is a solitary sound, of Leonard's palm upon palm. The sound multiplies, filling the room like the rush of the Thames. Like the sea. Annabel releases hold of Eliza's hand and joins in, the whole room applauding.

Edmund finds her and holds her, hand on her neck. Right now there are no words, just paint and feeling. She smiles despite the well opening in her throat. Their foreheads rest together, the world forgotten. This is their union, their holy matrimony. After everything.

She realises slowly at first, and then all at once – he is no longer holding her. She is holding him. He is growing heavy, faltering, causing her to stagger sideways, back straining, his body giving way beneath her, beneath him, his eyes unseeing, his hand grasping his side. There are men stepping forward to help take the weight, and someone shouts for help as they lie him on the ground, where his body balls like a foetus quickening in a womb, guttural groans escaping him, eyes squeezed so tightly shut that the lines of his eyelids and about his cheekbones are deeper than ravines, than oceans, and someone folds a cloak to rest beneath his head and another is shouting about the physician and there is a gust of cool air in the hall and people crouch beside her, their arms extended towards her husband, but she doesn't know who, because all she is doing is saying his name, putting a steadying hand on the curve of his back, coaxing him back to her.

CHAPTER 47

T HE halls are quiet by the time the physician arrives, filled only with the desolate scent of old perfume and petering smoke. Edmund's portrait looks on, indifferent to the living and his likeness who gasps in pain upstairs.

During the commotion, Annabel had placed an arm around Eliza's waist and Leonard a hand on her forearm, steadying her. Blythe started crying. Two men half-carried Edmund upstairs, setting him down on his bed. A private space exposed to people who didn't belong in that room, their tread clumsy upon the floor.

The physician lifts his battered case, filled with ointments and pewter instruments, onto a chair. His weary eyes, which glance from Edmund in bed to Eliza standing beside the window, let slip that he has spent his lifetime rushing to sickbeds, trying to maintain life's careful balance on a knife edge. He approaches his familiar patient and there is no joy in their reunion.

Edmund, recovered from his earlier spasm of pain, allows the physician to gently feel his side and lower back. 'Absurd, really. It only aches now.'

The physician raises an eyebrow. 'What colour is your urine?'

'Quite dark,' Edmund speaks quietly, as though hoping Eliza won't overhear, 'and . . .'

'Blood?'

Edmund lowers his chin.

'For how long?'

'A few . . . Some weeks.'

Eliza tightens her grip on the window casement.

'The same as before then,' the physician says.

'As always.' The stones, plaguing him since childhood.

The physician asks more questions, but Edmund shakes his head. Glances at his wife. 'Would you fetch me a drink Liza?'

The cup on the table beside the bed is only half-drunk. She stares at him, ignoring the lick of a smirk on the physician's face. In the passageway outside, she walks the length of it loudly, then removes her pantofles and silently doubles back to the bedchamber door.

'. . . much more painful than before,' Edmund is saying, speaking so low she almost presses her ear to the door.

'How so?'

'Sometimes the pain makes me sick. Sometimes I feel I may go blind with it.'

She catches the physician's arm on his way out. He glances at her, surprised. He's the kind of man who distrusts women. He is defiantly sure of their inferiority, and yet despite this, still sees them as a threat to his livelihood, with their herbs and home remedies and poultices.

'How long will it take for him to recover?'

'Usually a month or two.'

'But it has been that long already.'

'It will depend on the size of the stone. The larger it is the longer it can take. Perhaps a half year.'

'And if it is too big to pass?'

He hesitates, softening slightly. 'He is in God's hands. Goodnight, mistress.'

In bed that night, they lie face to face, his arm across her, the candles blown out. 'I wish you'd told me,' she murmurs.

She senses that his eyes are open. 'I didn't want to worry you.'

'You worried me tonight.'

'I'm sorry.'

'Remember the last time you decided not to tell me something important?'

He hesitates. They rarely discuss it.

'For an intelligent man you can be incredibly foolish,' she says.

'You'd think I'd have learnt by now.'

'Especially under my careful instruction.'

'My clever wife.'

'That's probably how you should address me from now on.'

'Are you mocking me?'

'I'm nothing if not earnest.'

They laugh beneath the coverlet, and it feels a release. It feels for a moment as though this evening, its end, did not happen. As though, after the reveal of her painting, they had danced and kissed and talked to other guests, caught each other's eyes across the room, and later fallen into bed together, warm against each other, with only the weight of pleasant exhaustion pulling at their limbs and hearts.

༺ⷓ༒

Dorothy prepares a caudle for Edmund, splashing ale into a brass pot over the fire, adding eggs, the yolks ridiculing in their daffodil brightness. The feeble light at the window makes her lean low to her task, and Eliza, beside her, realises that soon this woman will need to rest, will need to stop working this house. Everything that once was, will change.

'Perhaps this house is cursed,' Dorothy mutters, more to herself, half stirring, half jabbing the pot in anguish.

'Who said it was?' Eliza asks.

'I did.'

Dorothy has nursed Edmund's mother, brother, father. Eliza gently takes the spoon from her hands and steers her into a chair.

'I've known him since he was a boy,' Dorothy whispers.

'And you will keep on knowing him,' Eliza replies fiercely.

He deteriorates quickly as though pretence had carried him onwards, and now, without it, his sickness rises unbidden, strangling his strength.

As though he knew all along and is finally giving in.

The days take on a slow, poised quality.

By the time his groans of pain won't stop, or he can't seem to get comfortable – every part of him tender and agonising – or else he is so still and quiet, breathing so lightly that Eliza wants to shake him awake, they are already taking it in turns to sit with him throughout all hours. By which time too, Eliza realises her menses have stopped.

The last time it happened, she was only a girl. It was before she'd ever known a man, before she'd known what it was to lose someone. At the time she couldn't understand it, and Ma would give her extra milk and a hunk of bread between meals. But now, when the years between have brought knowledge, she knows it was constant fear and anguish that sapped her body, leaving it with no excess to do what nature willed. It's a relief, always a relief, to remember that Thomas will never torment her again.

Eliza helps Edmund drink his caudles, looking into his face which is slick and tinged yellow by the dancing firelight. She learns which number to count to on her fingers before he will lean over the side of the bed, caudle coming back up to land in the bucket. She helps him to stand as he pisses into a pot, as less and less of the foul, evil liquid dribbles out. She wipes his face with damp cloths as he sinks into broken sleep.

On the first day of snow, Annabel relieves Eliza from her vigil in Edmund's bedchamber, telling her to take some air and rest. The chamber is dense and close, stinking of sweat and urine, but they don't air it. Edmund shivers and shakes so much that they fear the biting winter would shake the soul from him. Eliza has taken to sleeping – or attempting sleep – in another room, fearful of disturbing him in the night.

She is too exhausted to do anything. She rests her forehead against the wooden panelling in the passageway and murmurs prayers to God, who listens, who calms her. She remains there until the freezing dusk collects outside, a swarming darkness.

The snow continues, heavier and heavier. It settles on the ground, cocooning them in the house. The moat freezes. She stays with him throughout the night, keeping the fire high, consumed by a superstitious, invented fear that if she allows the flames to diminish, Edmund will too. She holds his limp hand. His eyelids flutter, the liminal of waking and dreaming. What is he thinking, if he thinks at all? Does he know that she is with him, won't ever leave?

The others have gone to bed. They had come to the bedchamber, kissing Edmund on the forehead. They whispered out of respect, a group collusion, as though fearing they would wake him, even though they knew he couldn't hear them. They asked if there was anything they could do and Eliza had shaken her head. Now the house is still, like the branches of a tree when the last leaf of autumn has been shaken loose. When all that remains is bare, durable bark, ready for wintering.

She doesn't sleep.

In the deepest part of the night Edmund wakes, the fire crackling in the moon of his eyes. She reaches for him, her wedding band glinting in the flickering flames. He isn't surprised to find her there. His skin has a sheen across it, and she brushes a cool hand against his cheek.

'My clever wife.' He tries to smile, but stops with the effort, his muscles slack, his mouth barely moving.

The tears come now, hot, prickling her cold cheeks.

'I've tried to set things right, Liza.'

'You've done everything right, my love. Now I just need you to live.' It takes her everything to say it. She sinks beside the bed, floor digging painfully into her knees, her skirts about her like spilt blood across the floor, so her face is level with his. 'I'm carrying our child.'

She laces her fingers with his.

'Our own family,' he whispers and she sees an echo of that smile on his lips as he closes his eyes.

She jolts herself awake. Their fingers are still interlocked. Did they speak? Or did she only dream? It's almost dawn. He lies on his back, still fighting, feeble rise and fall of his chest. She stands, her legs stiff, the blanket falling to gather on the floor. She leaves the door ajar, lingering on the threshold to glance back at him.

She goes to her bedchamber to piss in her chamber pot, the freezing air biting her. She fetches a fresh cup of small beer from the kitchen, ready for when he wakes.

When she returns, holding the cup tightly, she knows before she steps into the room. Knows that he slipped out whilst she was away. Leaving earthside for somewhere new.

CHAPTER 48

S HE waits for the rise of his chest, knowing it will never come. She wipes her hands, wet from washing him, and touches his face. How, in only a day, it can feel so different. Flesh losing its firmness. She traces the edge of his lips with her fingertip. She bends low and rests her face against his, so they are cheek to cheek, eye to eye, for the last time. When she lifts away it's as though he has been crying. Tears have collected beneath his eye, and she wipes them away before wiping her own.

She sits on the floor in her bedchamber, leaning against the bedpost, facing the window. Green room, arras on the wall. Voices drift along the passageway, the last stragglers of the mourning feast. She had tried to listen to tenant's gripes and lamentations about the harvest, about the hard frost, about a farmer's lad who had got the innkeeper's girl with twins. But she'd felt suffocated, and the pervasive smell of rosemary made her want to gag. The gathering is for the living, and she craves only the company of the dead.

How can life go on?

He is gone. It is an old story, these words like a myth wound up inside her. She used the same words before, for another man. Yet this time there's no question curling about it, no lingering hope. She will never forget the stillness of his body, the emptiness beneath her hands.

He is gone.

And she cannot follow.

Earlier, she watched his coffin descend into a ground so firm and unyielding that she was sure it did not want him. She had felt a rage, so deep and old, that she knew it came from within her blood, from her father and his ancestors. Rage so full and rich, it is horses running wild, frothing at the mouth, it is fields churned to mud beneath a fearsome, bloody sky. She'd wanted to shriek at the frozen earth: *if you don't want him, give him back.* She'd wanted to jump into the grave with him, climb into the coffin, feel his cold body against hers. Have her own body heat them both. Perhaps she gave herself away because a few of the gathering glanced at her, and Leonard laid a steadying hand on her back, which she was grateful for, leaning on it when she thought her knees would buckle.

She hardly notices the sound of the door, the cool movement of air as someone approaches and sits above her on the bed in a billow of skirts. Annabel places her hand upon Eliza's shoulder. Its weight, the grounding, is a comfort. Eliza reaches up and takes her hand, so her arm crosses her body, shielding her heart.

'They've gone now,' Annabel says.

Eliza hadn't noticed that the house had turned silent.

All of the house is hers now. Its chambers, shadows and echoes, cobwebs and stone, hauntings and memories. There are no men left to take it from her. Walter stuck true to his word; he never forgave Edmund for taking Blythe and breaking Lettice's heart. Edmund's letters to his cousin were left unanswered, even in those final weeks, when Edmund knew – knew more than he ever admitted – that he was dying. Some wounds are not meant to heal. And so, the late husband left everything to his widow.

They are quiet, looking out at the sky, white as the snow that still hems the lanes and fields, forms in patches beneath old oaks. They sit like that until the chamber is dark, gloom collecting in the corners, cold creeping into their joints.

'We should light the fires,' Annabel says, stretching.

'How can this feeling ever change?'

'Give yourself time, Liza.'

'Has it for you?'

Annabel pauses. Eliza can make out her friend's outline, the glint of her teeth that bite on her lower lip.

'Sometimes I close my eyes and think, when I open them, Sam will be there. There are so many things I want to tell him, which I have stored them up, waiting for him. I thought I'd never feel anything again, other than his absence. But I have. The pain gets . . . less severe. Mostly, now, it's more a longing rather than . . .'

Rather than howl from your lungs, stab in your heart.

'But it's different for everyone.'

'I'm afraid.'

'Of what?'

Eliza shakes her head, bowing her face to her belly. 'Sorry,' she says.

Annabel takes her hand, helps her to stand, doesn't let go.

She sleeps beside Annabel that night. It's a sad comfort, to know that the woman beside her has experienced this same grief, understands this loss. Has, like so many others, made it through.

In the dark, Eliza props herself on her elbows, and looks down at the soft apricot of Blythe's cheek, bathed by the fire's embers. She whispers, 'You know, this will always be Blythe's home, and yours too. Our circumstances will not change.'

Annabel lies on her back, facing the ceiling. Eliza looks at the gentle slope of her forehead, the silhouetted blink of her eyes.

'If you want, that is,' Eliza murmurs, lying back onto the mattress.

'Of course, I want it. But who will manage his estate?'

'I will. We will. Who is there to stop us?'

Annabel is quiet.

'What is it?'

'I've had my share of bad fortune, but you've always brought the good.'

If Eliza wasn't so drained, so sad, she would have rolled her eyes or nudged her friend on the shoulder or rebutted her with a shrug. But she doesn't. Annabel shifts so their forearms, that kidskin smooth inner part, are touching. A milky tear slides from her eye to the pillow beneath.

※

She doesn't tell anyone about the baby. She wants it to remain a secret between her and Edmund for a little longer. The final one they ever shared.

But Ma arriving with Henry a fortnight after the funeral, in response to Eliza's letter – written when grief was at its rawest, when her hand had scrawled the words that chorused in her head like a dirge, *he is gone* – knows immediately. She observes how her daughter sits when everyone else stands, how she grows pale whilst eating, pushing her plate away, how she retires early to bed. Symptoms which everyone else presumes to be grief.

Eliza retches awake at the first signs of dawn, and Ma rushes in, awoken by instinct, sensing her daughter's pain.

'You were you sick again, dove?' Ma's question isn't a question at all. Eliza doesn't ask how Ma knows that she was sick earlier in the night. Call it intuition, call it witchcraft, Ma can be astonishingly astute. 'You have missed a bleed?'

'Yes, Ma.'

'How many?'

'Three.'

Ma sits on the bed, her woollen nightgown rucked up about her shoulders, and strokes Eliza's arm, as she used to when Eliza was a child.

'Will you stay with me, Mama?' Eliza can't still the quake in her voice. She fears bringing a fatherless child into the world. Fears the birth, the blood, the tales of dead mothers. The loneliness that comes after, if mother and babe do survive. The responsibility that she has been told is her purpose, her reason for gracing His earth – what if she finds she can't do it, wasn't made for motherhood?

Ma pulls Eliza into a hug. 'Always.'

CHAPTER 49

H E travels leagues, feeling the motion of the horse beneath him. He buys an apple from a seller on the highway, having grown tired of scrumping. When it's finished, he launches the core into the air, watching as it arcs and lands out of view in the high grasses. The day is warm and he is sweating, can almost feel the salt leaking from him and is grateful for the cap shading his face.

He'd learnt the news in the town; overheard folk talking with that perverse rush of excitement when gossiping, no matter how sad the story. And Ruth Litton's empty house had confirmed it, locked and shuttered, as though something serious had called her away.

He sent a letter offering his condolences. Felt a sick plummet when the lad departed with the note, knowing the hand that would eventually receive it would be hers. Sometimes he still feels the shape of her hand in his, the lock and tangle of fingers.

It had taken long, long months for him to forgive her for leaving when he needed her most – but you do that, don't you, for the ones you love. He'd missed her, longed for her. Had spent the years hammering metals to shape, working longer hours, trying to clink, beat, fire her from his mind. Had endured circular conversations with his mother and sisters, all of them urging him to find another.

Two months his letter went unanswered. He gave up on receiving a reply, felt a fool, licked his wounds. But eventually a note arrived, written in a hand he knew as though it were his own.

It is good to hear from you. I hope you are well. Eli.

He had tried deciphering it, tried to scrape beneath the words for meaning. He even showed it to Philip, who only shook his head and muttered, 'Women.'

He has gone back and forth on whether he should travel today. But his news drives him on. She needs to hear the words from his mouth. He owes it to them both. So he winds through villages, stops at an inn to piss and ask for directions. The owner, chewing a reed between his teeth, gives precise instructions. People scatter the lanes, preparing for the midsummer celebrations – the longest day of the year, the daylight stretching like a great cloth of gold. He wipes the moisture from his forehead, considering the innkeeper's final words: you can't miss it.

He slows, the horse's hooves growing quieter. He sees it and lets out a laugh under his breath, rubs a hand over his face. 'Lord,' he says.

She hadn't mentioned the moat. Or the great medieval frontage, added to and improved by generations. She hadn't told him much at all. He jumps from his ride, ties him up in the stables.

Takes a breath.

CHAPTER 50

ANNABEL rests a summer crown atop Eliza's head. Nature's circlet of dog roses, fennel, St John's Wort. 'A beauty.'

Eliza shifts the swell of her belly and grimaces, 'I don't feel it.'

She sits on a low stool in the courtyard, her legs forced apart to make room for the baby within her, the sun coaxing out the freckles beneath her eyes. Annabel leans back on her elbows on the soft ground, legs stretched before her, her skirts pulled up in the heat to reveal her legs. The moat is stagnant and midges hover above it, reflections dancing on the water. Eliza weaves a crown for Blythe, using the flowers Annabel collected. Eliza had wanted to search for wildflowers herself, to walk through the fields and forests delighting at the sight of heartsease and columbine, but now, heavy in her state, she is forced to slow, to sit.

'The night of drinking and love-making is finally here again,' Annabel sighs, crowns forgotten on the grass.

'When have you ever needed an excuse to drink? And there'll be no love-making here,' Eliza says, motioning to her stomach. She has no desire to lie with anyone, if it can't be Edmund beneath her hands.

Annabel laughs and flips onto her stomach.

'Has someone caught your eye?' Eliza presses.

'Maybe.'

'Shyness doesn't suit you.'

'Although he would have to be some sort of prince before he could move me.'

They do this, sometimes, pretending as though Annabel would even contemplate another husband. But Eliza knows she wouldn't. Samuel has been gone five years, and still her friend carries his loss like a churchman wears the cross: over her heart, for always.

They play on. 'I've always admired your low expectations,' Eliza says.

'And my determination.'

'That I can't argue with.'

'But lose all this,' Annabel flicks her hand to the courtyard and its ceiling of azurite sky, 'for a husband?'

Eliza smiles. Theirs, a house of women. A house of widows. Four women and a child, crowding about the kitchen table for suppers, surviving the bitter grief of winter and the fickleness of spring. Bound together, carrying each other on their shoulders, making a life for themselves.

She agrees. She can think of none living that would make her relinquish this life.

Only Edmund. But, of course, he is not amongst the living's ranks. She feels the ache of him each day. Ache of absence, ache of longing. Sometimes she spends her days in her bedchamber, not wanting to leave. The ring he gave her hangs about her neck, warmed by her skin, like the whisper of his fingers against her chest.

'You know I first kissed a man on Midsummer's Eve,' Annabel says, then waits, head cocked for a reaction.

Eliza knows the story well. 'Oh, go on.'

But Annabel never starts – hooves sound, slowing on the path at the front of the hall. They glance at each other; they are expecting no one. Annabel heads across the courtyard and disappears beneath the arch of the gatehouse to the front entrance, where the bridge crosses the moat. Eliza hears her friend's greeting, but not the response. Then, silence.

Eliza has set down the crown, has gathered her skirts to follow her friend, when Annabel reappears at a trot. 'Sit,' she rushes.

'Why?'

'There's a man here to see you.'

'A man?' Eliza stares. 'Who is it?'

Annabel smooths the creases in Eliza's sleeves, where the fabric has rumpled and gathered. Eliza catches her friend's wrist, 'Who is it, Anna?'

Her friend presses her lips together.

She'd told Annabel about him. Their plans to run away. The crumbling inn. His silhouette disappearing down the lane. She had told her everything, except that it was he who dealt Thomas a fatal blow. She could not cast Francis as a killer. That part she confessed only to Edmund.

She recalls his letter, received when she had no space within her but for the chasm Edmund had left behind. The letter which she has kept, tucked in the clothes chest in her bedchamber.

But it would be impossible. 'No,' Eliza mutters.

'Yes.'

'Why?'

'Ask him yourself.'

'He can't see me like this.'

Annabel clucks her tongue, glint of mischief in her eyes. 'Well he's here and I've said you will.'

Eliza walks to the moat's edge, her back to the gatehouse. She feels hot and flushed, her dress tight despite Ma's alterations over her stomach. Footsteps come. That rhythm, of shoe on stone, she would know anywhere. Annabel gives her hand a quick squeeze before almost running into the house. Eliza feels a trickle of sweat down the back of her legs. The footsteps stop, and then start again, coming closer. She turns, and for all her self-consciousness, she cannot help but gorge on the man before her.

He is as she remembers, when her mind reaches for him; not the man who the sea spat out, but the other one. The one before. His jerkin fits a body that has filled out, replaced the flesh lost at sea with muscle. He seems taller, stronger. A man who has known what it is to want and hunger and will not venture back to it. Firm calves. Polished boots. His dark hair is long again, how it always was, reaching past his ears. He wears a cap, a brown feather sticking out of it, and she feels a strange desire to reach for it and run its soft down against her palm.

She feels messy, heavy, and wonders what story he sees writ upon her. Yet, despite herself, despite the surprise of his arrival, she can't help but smile, feel joy at the sight of him. That muscle memory of being around him. When they were young.

'I didn't expect to see you.'

He returns her smile, seeming relieved, and says, 'I wanted to see you.' His eyes fall to her stomach, before flitting away. 'You are well, I see.'

'As can be.'

'I'm sorry about Edmund.'

She still hasn't found what to say to condolences. I *miss him all the time*. She recalls the look on Edmund's face when he unveiled the painting at the feast, that night when he went limp in her arms and everything changed.

Francis approaches the moat, hands behind his back, looking out over the water to the fields and forest beyond. Turns a full circle to survey the three walls of the house surrounding the courtyard.

'It's beautiful here,' he says.

'It is.'

'I didn't know you were...' He tails off, fiddling with his earlobe.

She pushes her hand to the base of her belly, her skirts pulling tight to reveal the curve beneath the fabric. 'She's due in August.'

'She?'

She shrugs, 'I feel it.' Wings flap behind them. A blackbird dips its beak into the moat before taking flight. 'How have you been?'

'Well. I've bought a house and set up my own workshop, and business is good.'

'No longer under your father's roof,' she smiles.

'That mad house. Although it's different now, much quieter now the children are grown.'

'I loved it there.'

'It was time I moved on.' He holds her gaze.

'I'm pleased for you.' And she is. She is glad his life has evolved, that he prospers. Yet she can't escape the faint creep of melancholy that she'll never be part of it.

Silence lapses, heavy and full. The sweet scent of the roses that cling to the nearest wall drift past, stems and thorns holding the cracks in the stone together, as though mutually reliant on the other. In the quiet, her heart clenches, and the question she most wants to know spills from her mouth as he says –

'Why have you come?'

'I wanted to – '

Their words stumble over each other and are drowned by three voices, their owners entering the courtyard. Dorothy and Ruth walk side by side, Blythe lagging, humming to herself, trailing a stick along the ground. They have returned from the village where they watched folk pile the bonfire high for Midsummer's Eve, readying it to be lit at dusk. The newcomers pause at the sight of the two people standing beside the moat. Eliza falters over how to introduce him to Dorothy – what to call him, what word can encompass all that they have been to each other? – settling on childhood friend, and Dorothy, astute and unbelieving, appraises him, whilst Blythe turns bashful in the visitor's presence, peering out from behind Ruth's skirts.

'How long are you staying?' Ma asks, curtseying, her eyes on Eliza. They say: is this what you want, dove? You can have what you want now.

'I don't want to overstay my – '

'You could come to the bonfire with us tonight,' Eliza says, 'if you like.'

He shifts his weight from foot to foot, looks at her. She is aware that all the women are watching him watch her. 'I'd like that.'

There is little chance to talk alone after that. The baby kicks. Eliza rests. She lies in her bedchamber, the curtain drawn across the open window, casting a muffled green glow about the room. She imagines Francis downstairs, the questioning looks her women will be sharing, this man the invisible thorn that pierced Eliza's marriage, appearing in their midst. She had once imagined a raven-haired man shadowing the walls of this house, always there, at the corner of her eye. Now, as she slips between the gap of waking and sleeping, she need not imagine it. He walks the boards of her life as flesh and bone and blood, smoothing the feather in his cap between his fingers.

※

The evening tinges pink as the sun sets, casting the ground in a light that looks conjured by angels. The air is sweet. They walk into the village, the two older women ahead, Annabel holding Blythe's hand, the child stomping noisily on the lane. Eliza adjusts her crown of flowers, petals tickling her forehead. She knows most of the villagers, and they greet her, their eyes dropping momentarily to her stomach, or sliding left to the stranger at her side.

As they walk, Francis tells her that Drake, the captain of the fleet, returned home after all. Made it right around the world and earned a knighthood. 'A miracle, really, that he made it home.'

'I could say the same to you.'

Children wheel about, legs streaking through the grasses, chasing each other. In the centre stands the bonfire, piled taller than a person, logs and branches and the bones of small animals balancing atop each other. There are young couples avoiding each other's gaze; there are older men grinning at their wives. There is a stall selling beer; a man heating hazelnuts over an open flame; a local trader shouting about the delights of his apple pie.

Eliza reaches for her purse, but Francis beats her to it. He buys her a slice, handing it to her hastily, awkwardly, so that some of the pastry comes away, and he ducks to catch it but misses, a thick ribbon falling to the ground. She covers the accident in a rush: 'Apples remind me of you.' She is aware that the seller has, temporarily, stopped shouting. She forces a nonchalant shrug of one shoulder, and a grin jerks the corner of Francis's mouth.

'We were always scrumping,' he says.

'We? It was always you.'

'Are you implying I led you astray?' He raises his eyebrows, boyish, rambunctious. 'I think I've finally outgrown it. Scrumping, I mean.' His face is memory. She takes a bite of the pie, sweet and sharp on her tongue.

The dancing starts whilst the light still holds. Morris dancers spin out before them, their bells sounding, two musicians drumming and piping behind them. A crowd forms, clapping along. Blythe turns in circles on the spot, until she leans her head against Eliza's leg, her world apparently spinning off around her, and Eliza cups the child's cheek in her hand. Annabel links Eliza's other arm, and says over the clash of bells and tabor, 'Such a Mama already.'

When the night has fallen to velvet, a wrinkled, sun-browned man parades with a torch – thick branch, flames fighting their way towards the sky. He lights the branches of two other men and the crowd watch as they plunge the flames deep into the heart of the bonfire.

It spreads quickly, the heat a furious dragon bursting forth, and the villagers cheer, eyes reflecting orange, whilst the children who are still awake squeal in awe, as others sleep through it all, heads heavy on their father's shoulders.

Eliza watches the old burning away, going up in flames. Watches as the fire, erratic and careless, destroys and makes way for the new. She can see the new gently tumbling into place. Her baby at Cecil Hall; their home, a stronghold of women.

Ash floats on the air, like dust. Settling.

A great log cracks, and the flames shriek up, sparks flying. She steps back, the heat glaring on her face, and for a moment her body brushes against Francis's. There is a comfort, being near him, an old familiarity. But she steps away. She senses his hand flex open then clench at his side.

⚜

She vomits the morning into focus. It's been weeks since it was this bad, and it makes her tremble, her body covered in gooseflesh. She lies awake for a while, the baby asleep within her, and the bed cold and empty. Mornings are the worst without him. And the evenings. The space beside her, where Edmund's body should have opened for hers, forces her out of bed. She can't lie here, thinking of him, or she might never get up.

At the top of the stairs she sees Francis below, in the crook of the stairs. The dark crown of his head is motionless. He is looking, she realises, at Edmund's portrait.

'What do you think of it?

He glances up sharply, letting out the breath from his cheeks. 'How long have you been standing there?'

She shrugs, 'A moment.'

'You couldn't sleep either?'

She motions to her stomach. 'She wakes me.'

He nods. 'I only saw him once,' he says, turning back to Edmund. 'He looks as I remember him. But it's not how I imagined him to be.'

'How so?'

'He seems kind and sad. Courageous, perhaps.'

'He was.' She takes the stairs carefully to stand beside Francis, and together they stare at her husband.

'You painted this.' It isn't a question. He sighs and it sounds, perhaps, like longing. 'It's good, Eli. Really good.'

'I didn't know you cared for my art.'

'I understand more, now, the need for an escape.'

She thinks of losing herself inside the lines of chalk when she was a girl. Always a release, always a solace. And then she considers drawing and painting Edmund. 'It wasn't an escape, painting Edmund. He encouraged it. It brought us closer.'

If the truth hurts him, Francis doesn't show it. He continues to look at the man before him.

'What are you trying to escape?' she asks.

He pulls his eyes from Edmund's face to hers. 'I have a wife now. We married earlier this month.'

She can blink and see their own story as she'd once imagined it: a quiet life, the two of them, escaping to a middling town or village. Their dark-haired children with his devil-may-care and her eye for beauty, his exuberant gait and her earthen eyes. Falling asleep beside each other each night, the children in truckle beds in the room next door. Arguing, reconciling, enduring, learning, understanding, trusting, falling in love with each other each day, through the perfect mundanity, the trials, the pains, the joys. There was a slither of time when it could all have been theirs. And they both mourn it now; she sees it in his expression, a mirror of her own. A tug of longing, a compression in the stomach, for what was never meant to be.

The space between them has diminished, their bodies grown close as they talk low, glancing between the other and the late husband. She takes an involuntary step back, her heel pushing against the edge of a step. He reaches out and grips her wrist, steadying her.

'That's why you came. Who is she?'

He lets her go. His fingers leave a white mark, which fades instantly.

'Joan. I think you know her.'

Somewhere deep in the recesses and warrens of memory, she remembers a tall serving girl, thin as a maypole, leaning towards Francis. The same girl who accosted Eliza in the street, made snide comments about Eliza's origins and family wealth. Who shared the same opinions, really, as Francis.

'I didn't know you – ' She stops.

It's easy with him, to fall back into speaking as though they are seventeen again, their sexualities and curiosities and jealousies lurking beneath the surface.

'That I liked her?' There is a hint of a smile – and satisfaction – in his voice, but his eyes are serious. 'I've a house, a steady income and my sisters insisted I needed a wife. As you can imagine, my mother wouldn't rest.' They share a look. Joint memory. Old intimacy. 'I knew when you left that you weren't coming back, and I couldn't wait anymore Eli.'

Edmund watches them serenely. She feels the life inside her wake up, move about in her watery cocoon. 'I didn't want you to wait,' she says, gently taking his hand. 'I want you to be happy.'

They stand in the stable, thick with the smell of hay and manure, the horse's breath steaming in the weak sun. His bag hangs over the saddle, the journey home and Joan await him.

She looks at Cecil Hall, then up at him. 'I never thought you'd see this place.'

'Neither did I.'

'I'm glad you came.'

He lowers his eyes to the bloat of her stomach. 'Take care,' he says.

He kisses her forehead, his body resting softly against the dome of her belly. She closes her eyes, feeling the moment leak away like water held in a clasped hand.

CHAPTER 51

THE midwife arrives late with another woman's blood caught beneath her fingernails, bringing with her the stark cold of night. Another woman is giving birth in the village. Eliza watches without seeing as Ruth forces the midwife to wash her hands in a bowl of water beside the bed, the water dissolving to pink.

It's as though Eliza is looking up from the bottom of a stream, water rushing over her, the faces around the bed distorted. There's a moment of delirium, when she tries to stand, saying she doesn't want this anymore, that the birth is over, and small, firm hands guide her back to the pillows. Annabel's hands.

They lie when they say it will be over soon. It is endless, the night infinite. Dorothy comes and goes, bringing cups and fresh linen and respite for the other women. Dawn sneaks in to find Eliza on her knees, the bedsheets bleeding red, clutching her mother's arm as the midwife lifts the labouring woman's nightdress to peer at the life that is squalling into this world. The chamber smells of metal. With a final push, a final groan from deep within her chest, a new life falls into the arms of the midwife.

And it's in that moment, as the babe takes its first breath in the woman's arms, that Eliza sees a figure standing in the corner of the room.

He looks at her, lips steadily curving upwards, eyebrows pulled together in relief. The worst is over. He pushes his hair back from his face, golden strands mingling with the early sunlight, making it impossible to tell where he ends and the light begins. He tilts his head to get a closer look at the babe. Their daughter.

Eliza moves her hand across the sheets towards him, her damp fingers reaching to grasp at the whisper of empty air.

EPILOGUE

FOUR YEARS LATER
1586

T HE girl who sits before her is barely fifteen. She wears an expression of being forced into something that she is adamantly against. Eliza remembers that look, remembers the feel of it about her eyes. But it has been years, now, since she has endured it.

She, mistress of her own time.

The girl's mother had sent her, insistent that her daughter's likeness be captured, so that in years to come they can boast what a beauty their daughter was when she was young, and prove it with a painting. Indeed, the girl is beautiful, the light spilling in through the chamber's great windows upon her unblemished face. Or she would be, if her scowl wasn't so set.

It makes a change, painting someone sullen and silent. Often the women who come – for it is usually woman that request her, wanting their likeness to be captured by someone who sees their desires and ambition, rather than simply their bodies, wombs, duties – cannot help but talk, whispering easily to this intriguing stranger with a brush in her hand. A widow, so they've heard, and mistress of her own hall not far from here.

She listens to their tales, of lies, love, hate, tit for tat, vengeance, schemes, struggles, all the while creating them in pigment and oil, to be displayed amongst the growing art collections in the long galleries that have become essential to all fashionable homes. Yet sometimes, as the women open their souls, she drifts away. To her husband, where it is just the two of them, a great green expanse stretching before them.

And sometimes the women catch her, gone wandering, and ask

abruptly, pray tell, what about you? What of your husband? What of your protector? And she will shake her head and repeat what many have said. Widowhood becomes her.

The girl fidgets impatiently in her seat, fans her face with her hand. Eliza is asking her to move her head slightly when Leonard appears at the doorway. At his insistence she has taken to painting in his house, using a quiet chamber where the sun pokes throughout the day. It is he who has found her clients amongst the throngs of wealthy people who pass through his house as regularly as the bats that flit through the dusk above the fields. He who has set whisperings amongst his circles that a talented artist, yes a woman, can, for a fee, paint portraits.

He rarely disturbs her when she is with a customer. She holds the brush between her teeth as she wipes her hands, yellow pigment staining the cloth, and murmurs, 'A moment, milady,' to the girl, who shows the first hint of interest all afternoon, her eyes darting between Leonard to Eliza.

Out in the passageway, Eliza slides the paintbrush behind her ear and Leonard says, 'A boy has come with a note for you.'

'Here? Not to Cecil Hall?'

'He says he's already been there and will be paid extra for delivering it into your very hand.'

She frowns. 'What could be so important?'

Leonard shakes his head, leading her outside to where the messenger sits on the front step. The boy stands hastily, readjusting his breeches, and it reminds her of the lad in London who brought the news of Blythe's birth. Leonard sniffs.

The boy holds out the letter, and she glimpses the scrawl of writing.

She takes it. Reads it once. Twice. Feels a flapping of wings in her chest.

Both boy and man watch her expectantly.

'Who is it from?' Leonard asks.

She shrugs. 'A man called Francis Marshall,' she replies, as though he is a stranger. The name, she knows, means nothing to Leonard. She doesn't want questions, doesn't want to dredge up old histories.

'What does he want?'

'A portrait of himself to give to his wife. He writes he can pay up front.'

It surprises her. How could he afford it? But then, what does she know? They haven't spoken since that morning when he kissed her forehead and rode away to his wife.

'He told me to bring your reply straight to him, and he said he wouldn't wait months like you made him wait last time,' the boy says, without breath. His note after Edmund died. Her short, delayed response, when had grief sapped all her words.

Leonard raises his eyebrows. 'Last time?'

She might've sent the boy on his way there and then, for exposing her, and to spite Francis for rushing her. But she has been caught off guard, her decisiveness leaked away.

Her mind turns the possibility.

Francis in the lanes, running so fast, soles of his boots kicking up behind him to the lavender sky. His arm about her, her body nestling into his as they walk, side by side. His front teeth biting into an apple. The sound of his voice after a long day. Their childhood together, a strong knot that cannot be disentangled. And after. His gaunt face when he came back to her, a man regurgitated by the sea. The grazes across his knuckles. His anger transforming to violence. And after again. The feather in his hat. Pastry slipping to the ground. The expression on his face, staring at Edmund's portrait. His wife. And now? Perhaps his wife is heavy with child. Perhaps he already has children. Perhaps his business thrives and makes his purse bulge. Perhaps he thinks of her, like sometimes, she thinks of him. Like yearning for a comfort you know no longer exists.

Are they to stand in a chamber together, to pick through the years like scavengers? Are old wounds meant to open, be rubbed with dirt and salt? Is she to revisit his every scar, blemish and shadow, remember it all again, and pour everything she ever knew about him into each caressing brushstroke? Despite all their history, she wonders whether she would find anything to say to him. Everything that was worth saying has been said, and the things unsaid, by now, have lost their meaning.

'I've too many commissions,' she says.

Leonard eyes her shrewdly. Neither of them remark that she has never turned down a commission before, nor that it has been a quiet spring.

'Is that a no, then?' the boy asks, shoulders already slumping, aware that he'll have to deliver the bad news. He grumbles about a long, wasted journey and how he won't be paid the extra coin, and as she makes her way along the passageway, back to the surly girl in the sun-filtered room, she hears Leonard say to the dejected messenger, 'Never mind, boy. Onwards, before nightfall.'

She thinks it over as she paints the girl, who huffs and pouts like the petulant child she is.

Onwards. Moving forward. Not looking back.

The past, its bones, are better left undisturbed.

※

She fills a jug of cold water and takes it to her bedchamber, to wash her face, to scrub at the stains on her fingers, to cleanse herself of the day's strangeness. Cecil Hall, warmed from the heat of the day, cools and creaks gently around her, welcoming her home.

She places the jug on the table beside a half-finished letter to her brother. She worries about him, his inability to settle. He has moved again, is working with a different merchant, has taken different lodgings. His lover grows distant, their relations increasingly fraught; they fear the lover's wife has caught the scent. Eliza prays that the wife never discovers them, never shatters the fragile happiness that Henry had sought for so long. But she knows better than most that some loves aren't meant to last.

Once Henry had promised that he would never control her, and he is a man of his word. He has stood back, allowed her to remain a widow, to run Cecil Hall with her own capable hands, managing the ledgers, hiring men to collect rents. When he visits it is only to get drunk and silly, to play with his nieces, to praise her paintings, to kiss Ruth's cheek, before he is away again, journeying home to London's sprawl. Always too quickly, always with a restlessness in his eyes. She knows he carries a fear that he'll become trapped again beneath the crushing weight of a tyrant. She wipes the back of her neck with a damp linen cloth, remembering a pattern of violet bruises. They are both familiar with that weight.

She looks down from her chamber window. It is a different chamber to the one she and Edmund shared; it had taken her a long time to accept that she couldn't lie with his ghost any longer. She works her cloth into the grooves about her nails and squints into the light. Outside it is golden hour, the warmth like a kiss, the light like a dream. Ruth and Dorothy sit in the courtyard below, peeling vegetables over a big bowl on the ground between them, talking and watching the two girls, whose heads – one gold, one dark – are close together, peering at a chain of daisies in Blythe's hand. The other, younger sister crouches to admire it, knees pressed into her shoulders.

Rose, Eliza had called her, after Edmund's mother. She's all smiles and milk teeth, frothy hair and boundless energy. But sometimes, when Eliza paints in the chamber where pomegranates are limned on the walls, Rose will sit on the floor in spellbound silence and watch. She'll be an artist, they've all said. Chalk and pigment run through her blood.

A soft tread makes her turn back to the room. Rectangle of sun, crisscrossed with diamonds, on the wall. Annabel rests her head against the doorway, twirling a daisy between two fingers. She frowns when she sees Eliza's expression. 'Are you well?' she asks.

Eliza closes her eyes for a moment, thinking of the messenger boy who should have arrived at the blacksmith's door by now.

'Yes.'

A knowing smile kindles Annabel's mouth. 'You'll tell me later.' She nods her head to the window as the girls shriek and giggle below. 'They're asking for you.'

This book has been typeset by
SALT PUBLISHING LIMITED
using Neacademia, a font designed by Sergei Egorov for the
Rosetta Type Foundry in Czechia. It has been manufactured
using Holmen Book Cream 65gsm paper, and printed and
bound by Clays Limited in Bungay, Suffolk, Great Britain.

CROMER
GREAT BRITAIN
MMXXV